DANTE'S JOURNEY

A NOVEL

JC MARINO

ISBN: 978-1-935188-09-4

Library of Congress Control Number: 2010920274

Cover art by Matt Stawicki
Interior design by T.C. McMullen

A Star Publish LLC Publication
www.starpublishllc.com
Published in 2010
Printed in the United States of America

Dedication

To my buddy, friend, long-suffering cohort and just a plain overall great person, Jim Laderoute. If it were not for Jim's great motivational words, this book would never have been written. Jim inspired me to move away from the bustling city of Boston, from the bone chilling weather of winter and the sweat drenching humid days of summer, towards the nice sunny weather in California. It was Jim's haunting words that inspired and motivated me to write *Dante's Journey*. I will never forget his inspiring words when I mentioned that I wanted to write this book, "Nahhh, that's another thing you'll never do!" Thank you Jim, I will cherish those words always.

Acknowledgement

I'd like to thank my editor, Laura Taylor, whose skills and feedback helped me realize my dream of bringing Joe Dante to life (or death—whichever the case may be). I'd also like to thank Roy Phillips, whose wit, humor, wisdom, and uncompromising conviction helped me through an otherwise tedious rewrite process.

TABLE OF CONTENTS

DANTE'S JOURNEY

A NOVEL

SP

A Star Publish Book

PROLOGUE

ॐ॰

Why is it that my love for God, my family, and my job couldn't keep me from wanting to fit Filippo Argenti with a one-size-fits-all toe tag?

Every time I knelt at Kathleen's grave, I felt as though Argenti made his summer home inside my skull. A degenerate like him deserves to buy the farm in the most gruesome way imaginable, and I'm endowed with a particularly gruesome imagination. So says my wife, Beatrice. A drug smuggler and killer, Argenti could fall into a bucket of swill and emerge smelling like a bed of tulips.

This time will be different, Joe. This time, you'll nail him to the cross, and you'll do it strictly by the book.

I suppose you're wondering, *why Argenti?* Why this particular drug smuggler? If you had a daughter in high school, you wouldn't have to ask. You'd want every drug smuggler, distributor, and dealer, for that matter, pitched into the vilest lake of fire in Hell's basement.

This particular smuggler, however, was of special interest to me. You see, my oldest daughter, Kathleen, overdosed on her eighteenth birthday. From that day on, every Sunday after church, I'd visit her grave. *Kathleen Dante, born August 5, 1941, died August 5, 1959.* Instead of thinking of my child, I thought of Argenti, the monster who took her from me. When Kathleen died, I received a calling-card from God Himself for my new mission in life—take down the animal who robbed me of my little girl.

What kind of pervert tries to hook the young and innocent on cocaine, anyway?

It took some doing and no small amount of investigative effort, but I found that sorry waste of space who gave my little girl the coke. He worked

11

for someone, who worked for someone else, and he worked for one *Filippo Argenti.*

I thought it would be a piece of cake to get assigned to the department's undercover drug unit. Hell, with my background and record, I was absolutely positive that, without a cat's whisker of a doubt, they'd jump at the chance to have me on the team?

I failed miserably. So, I did exactly what my Italian heritage had taught me to do in a crisis… I relied on family. Big brother Michael, an undercover detective and higher up in the department's food chain, simply brought me onto *his* team.

You have to understand that in 1961, Boston PD was very much a family affair. If you were Italian or Irish, you were pretty much guaranteed a slot. I was half of each, so I was practically assigned the badge at birth.

The irony—I loved being a beat cop. Beatrice was the ambitious one. *She* wanted me to advance faster in the department than I had in mind. It took an SOB like Argenti to bring me closer to my wife's wishes and our higher income. So, in some twisted way, we could curse Argenti for our family's pain and thank him for our extra comforts.

If it's all the same to everyone involved, I think I'll just hate him.

The name's Joe Dante, Boston PD. This is my journey.

CHAPTER 1
Canto I, II – The Dark Wood – Fear and Despair
≈≈≈

I gave the area the once-over to find myself in dark woods.

Okay, Joe, what's the gag?

I gazed skyward, but the forest's canopy was so thick, I couldn't tell if it was day or night.

It must be daytime, Joe. At least it was when you ran into that weird light. Who brought you here? Argenti's men? Argenti was a pilot, so maybe he had access to some kind of silent aircraft. That's where the light must have come from. So, they came up behind you while your peepers were on the light, cold-cocked you and dumped you here. Makes perfect sense, Joe…yep…perfect sense…if you're applying for a degree in Dipstick University!

A thick mist came up to my knees, flowing around me like cloudy water. It reminded me of my time in England as I waited for D-Day. I felt just about as nervous.

My Italian side took over, prompting me to respond with anger rather than fear. "Argenti?" I yelled. "It's not going to work! I'm going to find you!"

Joe, you marmaluke, why did you drop your damn gun?

I heard a growl. I ducked into a low squat, all of my senses heightened. I saw nothing but the soupy mist floating through the sea of trees.

"Damn," I whispered. When I'd squatted down, I'd noticed footprints through the mist.

One guess, Joe. Whose tootsies are those—Argenti!

The soft ground contained only one set of prints. I felt compelled to follow them.

13

When the growl grew into a chorus of roars, I felt even more compelled to run.

≈୨ଙ

I reached the end of the forest and didn't stop. Instead of the marshy field typical of a foggy wooded area, I reached the top of a giant sand dune. I tried to run, but I tripped and rolled to the bottom, gaining an education on the taste of sand.

I lay there for a while, half expecting the owners of the roars to attack and oddly unsurprised when they didn't. It would have taken something or someone crazed with hunger to chase me down that dune, and if they were crazed, they would have taken me down from the get-go.

Several things registered all at once. I realized that it was, in fact, daytime, which was why I could see the light through the trees. However, I saw no sun and no clouds...only *gray* sky. It was as if one giant rain cloud covered the sky and blotted out the sun.

I got up, gazing from horizon to horizon. I saw nothing but desert— flat, dry, and dusty desert. "Well, isn't this just lovely," I muttered to myself.

Who else was I going to gab to? I was alone, and I felt the resonance of that loneliness.

Then I spotted the footprints again. I thought it strange that footprints would be embedded into the parched earth.

On the ground, next to the footprints, lay my bracelet. It must have dropped from my wrist when I fell. I quickly picked it up. Of everything I processed, the bracelet represented my only link to my family—my Beatrice and Anna. Kathleen had died long before Anna gave me that bracelet, but it also reminded me of her. I put it back on and smiled, forgetting for a moment my current predicament.

Looking back to the footprints brought me back to the fix I found myself in.

They were Argenti's prints. I felt it in my gut. So, it was either climb back up the dune into the forest and face lions, leopards, wolves and God knows what else, or follow these footprints to Argenti.

I'll give you one guess which way I chose.

≈୨ଙ

I followed the prints for hours. I should have been thirsty but I wasn't, which was okay by me since there wasn't any water in sight.

14

The giant dunes were no longer even a speck on the horizon behind me. Just when I began to regret my decision not to go back into the woods and take my chances with the mysterious roaring beasts, I happened upon a strange sight.

Hundreds, maybe even thousands of small wells lined the desert. The wells were too small for a water bucket, but large enough to have an opening. I peered into one of them, not at all surprised by the consuming darkness I encountered.

When I pulled my head out, a woman grabbed me and jerked me down to a squatting position.

"What the... Where did you come from?" I asked.

She didn't answer, not in English anyway. This dame was an odd bird, to say the least. To say the *most*, she was a loon the size of a Buick. I say that, not because of *her*, but rather because of her manner of dress and the way in which she spoke. She wore odd-looking make-up and...ah, the hell with it. The broad was a fruitcake.

I'm not a history buff and rarely read historical novels, but I *did* see *The Ten Commandments*. She wore some kind of ancient Egyptian outfit, and she babbled in a language I'd never heard before.

I knew Italian, and I'd picked up some French and German in the war, but *this* lingo was a whole other ballgame. All I could do was assume it was Egyptian or some African or Middle-Eastern dialect.

"Look, lady, I..."

She put her finger to her lips to shush me. I guess *shushing* is universal because I certainly knew what she meant.

She grabbed my arm and pulled me into a trench, where five or six other people waited. They jerked me down like soldiers pulling me into a foxhole for my own protection.

Everyone spoke at once in different languages.

I decided that I had to take control of the situation. I put my fingers in my mouth and whistled like I was hailing a yellow top. "All right, everybody just simmer down!" I yelled as I pulled out my badge. "I'm Joe Dante, Boston PD." I pointed at my ID. "*Boston!*" I stressed. "I'm looking for Filippo Argenti. He's a fleeing felon. Anyone understand me?"

I noticed that a few of the men wore ancient Roman or Greek garb. The rest, I didn't even want to guess. "I take it that's a *no?*" I continued. Everyone stared at me as if I was the lead banana in a fruit salad play, but

I suppose everyone in a nut house would stare at the only sane man in the same way.

Suddenly, a small flag popped out from one of the wells, floated there for a couple of seconds, and then darted off. It didn't seem that windy, but the flag dashed violently back and forth. The wind must have come from the well itself. Of course, I was just guessing.

Everyone in the trench ducked down. I couldn't tell predator from prey. A second later, all the wells spit out flags as if they were on sale at Gimbles. One of the Roman guys finally stood up, screamed a warrior's cry, and everyone in the trench leapt out as if in battle to chase after them.

As I stood there dumbfounded, the impact of the situation struck me. These weren't just five or six people in one trench. Multitudes of people emerged from a whole slew of hidden foxholes to chase those flags, but their efforts reminded me of trying to pick up sand with chopsticks. There seemed to be thousands of people in pursuit of those flags. I'd never seen so many people focused on one trivial goal.

I continued to watch in amazement as people ran back and forth in this fruitless effort. Several people blew by me, knocking the badge from my hand. "Hey!" I yelled as others crushed my badge into the sand and dirt.

I'd finally had enough. I grabbed a woman whom I thought had the best shot at speaking English. At least, she wore what appeared to be more modern dress. When I say *more modern*, I mean somewhere this side of the Middle Ages. She blankly stared at me.

"Do you speak English?" I said.

She struggled to free herself, obviously desperate to chase those stupid flags.

"Parla Italiano?" I continued in Italian.

If she understood, she didn't care to answer.

"Sprechen sie Deutsch?" I tried again, but this time in German.

I suppose if I knew ancient Chinese, *that* would have been next, but finally, someone spoke to me in English.

"She cannot understand you. She had been long dead before the language of the Brits dominated the land, and those on this level don't attempt to learn from each other," he said in a decidedly British accent.

There were just so many things wrong with what he'd said that I didn't know where to begin. I released the woman, focusing on the man who leaned against the large rock.

CHAPTER 2
Canto III – Vestibule of Hell – The Uncommitted
❧❧

As a cop, I categorized new acquaintances by their potential crimes. It's a flaw, I admit, but when you deal with bad eggs on a daily basis, you see little more of a person beyond what they'd done to attract the intervention of a cop in the first place. Insurance fraud perps, for instance, have a different look than say, murderers.

This character, however, proved difficult to peg. He was young, in his mid twenties, and smart. He looked like he knew something no one else did or had done something no one else knew about. I had to confess, he had a style about him, kind of like a movie star. But he dressed more like a biker, with slick black hair, long black leather coat, and boots—which was also strange because of the heat. Stranger still, he didn't sweat, not even a bead. He had the look of a Nazi, arrogant and of supposed superior stock, yet he spoke with a British accent, more like from the upper crust, classically trained and cultured. This guy was an enigma, to say the least.

"Come now. The way out is down," he said with a scowl.

"I'm Joe Dante."

I instinctively went for my badge but couldn't find it.

"I know who you are," he said.

I should have asked how he knew, but I let it slide. I needed to find my badge. I was still curious enough to ask about this...*situation*. "How come you're not chasing those flags?"

"Banners."

"What?"

"Banners." He pointed to a wisp of a passing flag. "I don't chase them, because I didn't do what these people did."

"What exactly did they do?"

"Their sin is that of opportunism. They had no beliefs in life, you understand."

"No beliefs in *life*?"

"Evolution, abortion, homosexuality, racism—in matters such as these, there are those for and those against, yes?"

"Sure, why not," I said, confused.

"Not so here. When the witch trials scorched Europe as a plague of locusts, some stood for their beliefs, some hid, and some did nothing. Centuries later, armies of evil adorned themselves in swastikas and marched across the face of the planet to find world domination within reach. Some chose a side for the fight, some hid believing courage would best be served another day, and others did nothing. Years later, in *your* country, people falsely accused of Communism faced devastating consequences. Some stepped forward to deny the accusations, some confirmed them, and still...others did nothing. Those you see here are the ones who did nothing. They chose neither good nor evil, but always tried to balance on a wire that didn't exist. So, here they chase banners, believing that capturing one will grant them freedom. Of course, this is an impossible task to accomplish. If this place is nothing else, it *is* ironic."

"Ironic—got it," I said. "Where the devil's my badge?" I expanded my search from my person to the dusty desert around me.

"Your trinket means nothing here. We must leave this place."

"Where exactly is *this place*?"

"Where do you believe you are?" he countered.

"Where do I believe we are? Okay, I'll bite." I looked around. The ugly gray painted the sky to an equally miserable horizon. The earth beneath me was dead with nothing to indicate that any plants or trees could even take root, let alone flourish. One place came to mind. "Jersey?"

He looked away, disgusted with my response, or maybe he was just disgusted with *me*.

"You now reside in the vestibule of Hell. However, this is not your proper place. The light that enveloped you was meant for another. That of opportunism is not your sin. Of the many problems you had in life, Joseph, lack of conviction is not to be counted among them."

I listened to his words and tried not to laugh.

You know exactly where you are now, don't you, Joe? You're in some outdoor nut university having a chat with the head pistachio.

I smiled. "Is that a fact?"

"Virgil DeMini is my name. Remember it. The way out is long for you now, for you chose hate as your path. Come now. We must go."

I half expected him to pull out a pocket watch and, like Alice's rabbit, declare how late he was. He was here, though, whack-job or not, and no one else was going to listen, certainly not the baboons chasing those stupid flags, so I figured I'd see if I could pump him for the skinny on Argenti.

"I'm looking for a man."

"Yes. Filippo Argenti."

"How do you know that?"

"I know all that I need to know about you," he said with obvious disdain.

"Tell me where he is." I demanded.

"He's no longer a concern of yours, I assure you."

"Gee, Virgil, since lack of conviction isn't one of my many problems, why don't I decide what concerns me?"

"Don't you see how lost you are, Joseph? It's guidance I offer you."

"Then take me to Argenti."

"That's not the type of guidance to which I refer."

"You know what? I don't need your help. I know exactly where Argenti is." I was bluffing but, while looking for my badge, I'd just noticed something I'd almost lost track of during all the flag chasing.

"Where is that?" he asked.

I pointed. "Right at the other end of those footprints, so if you'll excuse me, I'll leave you to your…whatever it is you do here with the flag-chasers."

"Banners."

"Whatever." I walked away.

Virgil called out to me. "Don't you understand that you're in the vestibule of Hell itself, where those who made no choices in life are condemned? You may journey a million kilometers in any direction and be no closer to an exit than before you began the journey."

"Kilometers? The metric system, huh… Maybe this *is* Hell after all," I finished with a grin.

❧

I walked. The footprints seemed to go on forever. I felt like Robinson Crusoe searching his desert island right after he found himself marooned.

However, my *island* was surrounded by an *ocean* of even more dry sand and rock.

Those flag-chasing fruitcakes were long gone, not even a dot in my rear view mirror, and I was totally alone. There weren't many rocks large enough to sit on, so when I came to one, I indulged myself. I wasn't really physically tired, which was strange since I walked for hours, but I was sick of hoofing it to nowhere.

That's when I glanced up at the dead sky and spotted a stunningly creepy sight.

CHAPTER 3
Thoughts of Home – Tony
❧

I sat bare-chested in the van as the guys wired me up. The backup team needed to remain inconspicuous, so the van wasn't running. Unfortunately, that meant no heater. January in Boston is a tad, shall we say, *frigid*, so being shirtless during the bugging process was a royal pain in the keister.

Mickey looked more jumpy than me. I could tell because he'd always babble when he was worried. He was a big, hard-boiled hoss, a prerequisite for being a big brother. Every time I looked him in the eye, I'd see that crescent scar across his cheek, and remember how and why he got it, which made me look up to him even more.

When the big lug babbled, you just had to go with it. He normally went on and on about his high school sexual exploits or how the Red Sox would soon break the Bambino curse and take the Series. For some reason, tonight he chose the political arena.

"I'm telling you, thirty nine years and that's it…over and out…end of story…that's all she wrote. The year 2000 is a dead end."

"President Kennedy wouldn't let that happen," I said, trying to reassure him. I knew he really didn't care what might happen nearly forty years into the future.

"What's he got? Eight years, tops. So we have the atomic war in '68 instead of '61."

"In 1968 Bobby takes over, then in '76—Teddy. I'm telling you, this is the start of a golden age. Show a little faith, Mickey."

21

Mick threw me a look. He hated it when I called him *Mickey*. Mickey took after my father's side of the family. He looked very Italian, tough with black hair, and, not that this is strictly Italian, mean. I, on the other hand, looked like I'd been kissed by a leprechaun with a fair complexion and light hair. Stand us side by side, and you'd never even guess we were brothers.

In South Boston and Cambridge, it paid to be Irish and in the North End, you *had* to be Italian, so I told him that if he looked Italian, I'm giving him an Irish sounding name. So, *Michael Angelo Vergilius Dante* became *Mickey*. Unfortunately, all through high school, he got compared to a mouse in the most unflattering ways, hence his *toughness*. Say what you will, but thanks to me, that hairpin knew how to fight.

Mickey checked the transmitter.

"Okay, little brother, put your shirt on. I get the feeling you're getting Tony here all excited."

"That's just *so* funny, you should go on the road with Bing and Bob." Tony laughed sarcastically.

Tony...now there's a good man. There was something about his face that made you trust the guy, which is a great trait to have if you're an undercover cop. Not a bad trait to have if you're a used car salesman, priest, or just about any other career choice, for that matter.

"His nipples are erect, not mine," Tony said, pointing at me.

"You take your shirt off in this igloo and see what happens to *your* nipples!" I shot back.

"Excuse me," the radioman jumped in. "I hate to break into this, whatever it is you're doing here, but I need a sound test."

I moved my chin away from the microphone as I buttoned my shirt.

"Testing...one—two—three—Mickey Dante has a face only a mother could love—and she hates it."

"Check."

"What?" Mickey said none too pleased. "You don't actually *record* the test, do you?"

"Yes, we do." The radioman smirked.

"But, you erase it after the test is done, right?"

"No, we do not."

"But it's not needed," Mickey insisted.

"Sorry, it's policy...*Mickey*," the radioman said with a grin.

Tony and I, on the other hand, slid away as if he'd just yanked the pin from a grenade.

Mickey quietly turned the radioman's face toward him. With thumb and forefinger, he pinched the man's face in the same manner my father did to his boys whenever we got out of line. Mickey gave the radioman the Cyclops with an eye that could stop a bullet in mid-flight.

"Only one man calls me *Mickey,* and guess what?" Mickey said with a confident smile. "You ain't him."

His mouth distorted from being pinched, his response came out as garbled as it was comical. "Yes, sir, Detective Dante…sir," the radioman said.

"Now erase that test," Mickey demanded.

"Yes sir."

From years of practice, I knew just how far I could take it with Mickey. I never went too far, mainly for two reasons—I loved my brother, and I've grown fond of staying vertical.

Mickey turned back to us and buttoned my last button. "You know what to do?" he asked.

"I know what to do," I answered.

"We got every doorway covered."

"I know."

"When you're ready for us to move, you say the phrase *you're under arrest.*"

"I know."

"Remember. *You're under arrest.*"

"I know!"

"I just don't want you to do anything goofy."

"When have I ever done anything goofy?" I said.

"Swimming across the Charles naked leaps to mind."

"That was high school," I said. "And if I remember correctly, *you* dared me."

"Hey! This isn't about *me.* You just stick to the plan."

"Okay—okay—don't worry about a thing," I said. "Oh, by the way… What phrase do I say again?"

Mickey returned my sarcasm with the fish-eye. "Heck, little brother, I'd consider it a personal favor if you just come back alive."

I winked and popped some gum into my yap.

"Now scram out," he said.

I smiled as Tony and I stepped out of the van.

❦

We strolled into the abandoned building with the grace of Cary Grant and David Niven at the Oscars. In this business, arrogance is a first cousin to being believed as the gospel truth.

As always, Argenti's thugs were impeccably dressed and groomed. Half of them looked as if they should be working for IBM. Ironically, the ones who looked most like drug dealers were the two undercover cops.

Argenti's goons brought us to him.

He grinned while two of his men worked over some regular Joe tied to a chair.

Filippo Argenti was a little younger than me, maybe in his late thirties. Some would say he had a charm about him, but I could see through him as if he was made of crystal. The man had the granite stones to wear a crucifix around his neck, as if he knew something about God. Scum like Argenti made me ashamed of my Italian heritage.

The hired muscle was working the guy over pretty good. I wanted to stop them, but didn't know how. I needed Argenti on tape making the sale before I could reveal myself as a lawman. So, I let them beat him. What the hell. He probably had it coming, anyway.

Argenti ignored the beating as he approached us. "You got the dough?" he said. It was always about the money with him.

I snapped my fingers, and Tony handed me the briefcase. I opened it to show Argenti the payment. The scum salivated as if he just took a whiff of a two inch filet mignon. He reached for it, but I slammed the case shut.

"Hey! What's the gag?" Argenti yelled as he yanked his hand back. "I thought we had a relationship."

"What's with the sap?" I pointed to the guy in the chair.

"We found him, chum. He's the heat. Ain't that a kick in the head?" Argenti hauled off and slugged him square in the nose.

I had to hand it to the guy. He didn't cry or plead or say anything that would make me think he was just another bum. He took the beating like a man. In fact, he smiled arrogantly. Hell, for a minute there, even *I* thought he was a cop.

He wore old khaki army pants and a brown t-shirt, though the latter was now stained in blood. I had no idea how anyone could take such a beating. He might have been a war veteran who had been tortured by the Nazis or even the Japs. Even though Argenti's minions were pounding the guy pretty good, he looked as if he was watching a sunset in the mountains. Son of a gun didn't even look like he cared.

But… I guess I cared.

Argenti wound up for another punch, but I grabbed his arm in mid-swing. "Stop hitting him," I demanded.

"You telling me my business?"

"He's not a copper."

"Oh, and are you Boston PD's big daddy?"

I looked at Tony, who couldn't offer much support, other than an innocent, trusting face— not to mention the fact that he was surrounded by four of Argenti's mugs. So, I thought back to what Mickey said—*don't do anything goofy.* I figured something *goofy* might be just the ticket. So, I let stupidity take the wheel.

"Because *I'm* a copper, and he never comes to any of the meetings!" I said.

Time froze. I could just see Mickey back in the van, putting his head in his hands and saying to himself—*that's what I meant by goofy!*

Tony closed his eyes, obviously expecting a hunk of lead to slam into his noodle.

Argenti looked me in the eye, but I stared back without fear. I wasn't afraid of him. If I couldn't get him for drug smuggling, I'd get him for offing a cop. He wasn't going to get away with killing my Kathleen. That's when I realized that I must have had a guardian angel sitting on my shoulder.

Argenti laughed, and then his men busted up. Tony also showed some teeth, more from relief than humor, I'd imagine. I guess Argenti figured that it was such a dumb thing to say, it just *had* to be a joke.

"You're one crazy cat!"

"Where's my snow?" I said, wanting this over with.

Now it was Argenti's turn to snap his fingers. One of his goons opened the case, and I took a taste. Not only was it pure, it was also the good stuff. And uncut.

"Okay, let's do this," I finished.

"Don't be a wet rag. Party ain't over yet," Argenti said.

"What now?" I sounded impatient, which wasn't a good thing for an outgunned undercover detective to be.

Argenti nodded to one of his men, who picked up a gasoline can and poured it over the beaten man. The smell of gasoline fouled the air as Argenti tossed me a lighter.

I'd heard that setting people on fire was Argenti's thing, but I'd never actually seen him do it...thank God.

Anyone else would have been terrified, but this guy acted as solid as a tombstone in December. It was like he didn't even care.

"Light him," Argenti ordered.

"You want to run that by me again," I said.

"You heard me." Argenti paced around the man. "There are two kinds of people in my world—those who are loyal to me and those who are dead." He pointed at the stranger, now doused in gasoline. "This nosebleed is the latter. Which one are you?"

CHAPTER 4
Canto III – The Infinite Desert
ഛൗഌ

I t was hot. No sun and no shade, but the heat persisted no matter where I walked.

Vestibule of Hell, your Auntie Petula. That Virgil character is obviously dipping into the parents' liquor cabinet.

Still, I couldn't deny the fact that I was no longer in Boston.

I was so caught up in trying to find Argenti, questions that should have screamed in my head only amounted to whispers. Questions like *what is this place,* and *how did I get here* became secondary as I trudged across the seemingly endless desert.

All questions, however, melted into one when I first saw *them* flying in the distance.

What the hell...

Three glowing disk-like objects flew off in the distance. Like a scared rabbit, my first instinct was to hide, but, being in the open desert, my choices dwindled down to either doing nothing or flagging them down.

Like planes, they were so high up and out of reach, I doubted that anyone in them would see me, but they were just so beautiful, I wanted to see more. It was almost like *watching* music.

"Hey! Over here!" I waved my arms. I put my fingers in my mouth and whistled like I was at a Red Sox game with the Sox winning twenty to one. "Come on!" I yelled.

"I wouldn't do that," Virgil said, scaring the vinegar out of me.

"What the... Where the devil did you come from?"

"Getting their attention would be akin to setting yourself aflame."

"Come on, nothing *that* pretty can be all bad." I turned back to try again, but the colorful disks of light had gone the way of the dinosaur. "Damn," I muttered.

"Do you have need of food?" Virgil asked.

"What?"

"Food?" he repeated. "Do you desire sustenance?"

"No."

"Do you have thirst, or need of sleep, or use for a privy?"

"What's your point, Virgil?"

"You have no need of these things for you are *dead*, as dead as Julius Ceasar."

"Oh, is *he* here, too?"

"It happens this way sometimes."

"What does?"

"Some believe so strongly that they still possess the breath of life, that the truth eludes them as a bird on a windy day. The truth will strike you, however, Joseph, and of *this* I assure you—you *will* believe."

"You want to know what I believe. I'll tell you what I believe—I'm not dead, this isn't Hell, and you're playing baseball without a bat. So, if you'll excuse me..." I turned my back to walk away.

"So you will continue on this path then? Is that your goal?"

"Yeah, that's the plan," I said with a sneer.

"How long do you believe you've been here, walking this way?"

"You tell me."

"Perhaps hours, days, or even years," he said. "Time is different here, you see."

I took a step and heard a *clink* that sounded more like metal than rock or hard dirt. I picked it up and discovered my badge.

How the hell did it get here when you've been walking for hours in a straight line? Have you actually been walking in circles, Joe? Are you back with those wacky flag people? If so, where did everyone go?

"I lost this way back by those flags."

"Banners."

"Yeah, whatever," I said. That time I actually *did* remember to say *banners*, but I refused to give this Virgil character the satisfaction. "Have I been walking in circles all this time?"

"Perhaps. Perhaps not."

"That's the best you got?"

"Perhaps it's a symbol of your former life, one you are unwilling to release. So it follows you as blindly as you follow your own hate."

"Sheesh, go back to your first answer."

I looked at Virgil's youthfulness. He obviously didn't like me. At least he had an honest face, though I have been tricked by honest faces before. This Virgil guy could have brought my badge and tossed it in the sand behind me before he made himself known. Needless to say, I didn't trust the guy, but I decided to humor him. Maybe he'd give me some dirt I could use.

"Okay, if I've been walking for days, how come night hasn't fallen?" I said.

"Where there's day, there is always day. Where there's night, there is always night. It all depends on the individual's destiny. The punishment, you see, is tailor made."

"Look, I know Hell," I said with conviction.

"Do you now?"

"Yeah."

"Well then, do tell," he said.

"Twelve years of Catholic school taught me well, and the primary asset of Hell is *not* a desert. It's a lake of fire, or boiling sulfur, or even boiling blood."

"I believe Hell is of sufficient size to accommodate all those and perhaps a bit more."

"No place is big enough to keep me from Argenti," I asserted.

"Is it truly your desire to follow phantom footprints for all eternity? Or do you wish my guidance?"

I thought for a moment. One thing was certain... I was going nowhere fast. "Guidance? No, but just for the sake of argument, let's say I believe you."

"Do you?"

"No, but let's say I do. How would you help?"

"This desert stretches on for all time. The only escape is through the river Acheron."

"You know where this river is?"

He looked at me like I was an idiot to even ask a question with such an obvious answer.

I shrugged as if in surrender. "Swell, lead the way."

❧

We walked. Virgil randomly changed direction, so I totally lost my orientation. Even worse, Virgil rarely spoke. When he did, it was only about the business at hand and rather too bluntly for my tastes.

In reaction, I also rarely spoke. I think we had an unspoken competition of stubbornness going and neither one of us wanted to be the first to holler *uncle*.

So, my thoughts went to Bea and my girls. My initial feelings were always of sadness and loss. Oddly enough, initial feelings of happiness and joy would have been worse. Once the realization of my loss hit me, how much greater would have been my fall?

To occupy my mind, I conceded our silent battle and tried to strike up a conversation with my guide—the *nut-job*.

"Not much for idle conversation, are you, Virgil?"

"What do you wish to converse about, Joseph?"

"I don't know...anything. That's why the conversation is called *idle*."

"You believe me to be mad. Why do you desire my thoughts on *any* subject?"

"I'm just talking conversation, Virgil. I'm not asking for the dope on life or anything."

"Pity, for you could use such advice."

"Is that right?"

"There's a ferry on the river. The ferryman's name is *Charon*. When we arrive, it is *I* who must speak, not *you*. Do you understand?"

"Why?"

"Charon is not one for the folly of children."

"What's beyond the river? Wait a minute... Did you just compare me to a child?"

"Virtuous pagans," he said.

"What?"

"Those who reside beyond the river—they lived without the light and knowledge of salvation, yet have chosen the path of righteousness. They are truly the highest advancement humankind can reach without divine intervention."

"Is that where you're taking me?"

"Do you believe yourself someone without the light of salvation?"

"No, of course not."

"Then obviously that is *not* your proper destination."

"You know, we're doing a lot of walking, but I still don't see this river of Acheron."

"I suppose you can always return to following phantom footprints that lead to nowhere."

"Oh, that's funny."

"*You* desired a conversation, did you not, Joseph?"

"Right."

Then a disgusting odor slammed into my senses, and I could actually taste it down to my toes. "What's that stink?" I blurted out, trying not to gag.

"Our objective is at hand."

"Oh God!"

"It's something you will become accustomed to," Virgil said, apparently unaffected by the stench.

"I'll lay you eight to five *that* won't happen!" I choked out.

Virgil was right about one thing—our objective was at hand.

CHAPTER 5
Canto III – The River Acheron
   ↬↭

W̲e waited by the river's edge with many others. Most of *these* people looked like they belonged in Hell, or would have if this was, in fact, Hell—which it wasn't.

Who are you trying to snow, Joe? When was the last time you felt sleepy, or hungry, or needed to shave? You're not dead—you're not dead—you're not dead.

I ignored them all. I was *better* than this.

Although this expanse of liquid filth was supposedly a *river*, I couldn't see the other side. Perhaps, I reasoned, because of the fog, rather than the distance across it.

I choked down the vile stink radiating from the water as the ferry approached.

I don't know why Virgil called it a *ferry*. It looked more like a tall ship with numerous torn sails. To be honest, it soared at us through the fog like a ghost ship.

The plank slammed down and everyone walked across as if they knew what to do.

A crusty old ferry captain, who must have been this Charon goon, stood at the end of the plank with a check list. The schmuck taunted everyone as they climbed on board.

"Welcome aboard, newly damned souls. I'll be your ship's Captain today. My name is *Charon*. Tell your friends." Charon laughed mockingly. "Nice hat, by the way," he added, pointing at one of the wayward characters stepping on board. He repeated it in Spanish.

God, Joe, does this guy like his job or what?

Virgil stood beside me as we moved closer. "Remember, *I* must be the one who speaks, not you."

"You got it," I said unconvincingly.

"I mean it."

"I know you do."

We reached the top, and Charon stopped us. As I studied him, I realized that he wasn't just your everyday, run of the mill skipper. His eyes appeared mutilated in some way. They were as black as an eight-ball without the *eight*.

"Hold it. Who are you?" he demanded in a grumpy voice.

I cut Virgil off before he could respond. "Joe Dante," I said, totally disobeying Virgil's command.

"You're not on the list," he said.

"Since when do you need to be on a list to get on a ferry?"

"You're not on the list. If you're not on the list, you cannot board. Those are the rules."

I pulled out my badge. "Listen, buster, I'm a cop with Boston PD. It's been a real long day. I've been chased by something big and loud, nearly trampled by a thousand crazy people, and wandered in the desert for God knows how long. I'm really not in the mood, so either you let me on board or I swear to God, I'll swim across this river on my own."

Charon looked at Virgil, whose quiet anger for me hadn't yet begun to simmer.

"Fine, swim." Charon smirked.

"Screw it," I said.

What the hell. If I could walk in the desert for as long as I had without fatigue, I could certainly swim across a river.

I reached down from the plank to test the temperature. Excruciating pain prompted me to yank my hand followed by an agonizing yowl, as if it was just dipped in acid.

"What the hell kind of water is this?"

Charon snickered. "It's the kind of water in Hell."

It struck me that Virgil wasn't the only one who thought this place was Hell. "So?" I said, still cradling my hand as I glared at Virgil.

"Yes?" Virgil asked.

"*You* wanted to do the talking."

Virgil rolled his eyes and leaned in close to Charon. "Let us board."

33

"But of course." Charon smiled and stepped aside.

"What are you," I asked as I followed Virgil, "a union boss or something?"

⟨⟩

As the ferry sailed to the other side, I stood at the railing and looked into the water. Despite the murk, I could see people chained below the surface of the water. They kicked and squirmed, trying to get some air but couldn't.

How can they survive under water, Joe? Think! When you touched the water, it seemed electrified. That must be it. These people are long dead, but the electricity in the water makes them look like they're desperately kicking for air. Jesus, where the devil are you?

People cluttered the deck, but I focused on one couple. They seemed to be just about the only people worth the time of day, assuming I knew it.

He wore a tuxedo and she a gown. The looked ready to attend a Hollywood awards ceremony, and they appeared about my and Bea's age. They reminded me of us…but only for about a split second, then I realized they were in a heated argument.

"It wasn't *my* fault!" the man insisted.

"*You* were driving!" the woman replied.

"*You* said it would be okay."

"Fifteen years of marriage and you choose *that* night to listen to me?"

From their beef, I gathered that the man often drove drunk, and his wife was totally fed up with his behavior.

The ferry suddenly jolted to a stop, shifting my attention away from the bickering *love birds*.

⟨⟩

I hoofed it with the crowd from the ferry until I realized Virgil had either ditched me or gotten lost. To be blunt, I felt relieved. My goal had been to get out of the desert. Now that I was, I could go it alone.

As I considered my next move to find Argenti, I felt a hand jerk me out of the crowd.

"What the…" I said. "Oh, it's you." Unfortunately, it was Virgil. He pulled me down, forcing me to squat behind a fine collection of dead and sharp edged shrubs. The crowd moved by.

"Let them pass," Virgil said. "It is other business to which we must attend."

"Where are they headed?"

"That's of no concern to us. A cliff resides this way. It is there we must descend to the next level."

"Level?"

"Hell is divided into nine descending rings, much like a funnel. Each circle is a punishment for a particular category of sin. Through its heart is the way out, so down we must go."

I sat back, staring at him in disbelief. About to confront this delusion of his, I realized I was leaning against something more substantial than brush. A structure…a tall stone wall, to be exact. I shoved the brush aside. "What's this?"

"It doesn't matter."

"What's on the other side of this wall?" I demanded.

"This is of no concern to us, Joseph."

"It's of no concern to us. It's of no concern to us," I mocked. "Is *anything* of concern to us?"

"Yes, the cliff to the next level."

"This is where those pagan guys live, isn't it?"

"Virtuous pagans," Virgil corrected.

Maybe they can help you find Argenti. Hell, Argenti might even be in there somewhere. Any town that included the word virtuous couldn't be all bad. Good thinking, Joe.

I stood prepared to shinny up the wall. The brush and vines that clung all the way to the top made it look easy. Virgil grabbed my arm. "You do not belong there."

"You said that this is the highest humankind can get without God's help. They can help me find Argenti," I said.

The highest humankind can get? Joe, what the devil are you saying? Virgil said the truth would strike you sooner or later. What truth? You're not dead—you're not dead—you're not dead!

"Joseph, if you go in there, I shan't follow you."

"Hot dog! Even more incentive." I left Virgil behind and proceeded to climb the wall.

CHAPTER 6
Canto IV – Circle I – The Unbaptized Infants

I hopped down from the top of the stone wall and landed in a stunningly lush park. Flowers of every color and fragrance flooded my senses. The chirping of birds faded behind the sounds of waterfalls.

If this is Hell, feel free to be damned for all eternity.

My mind drifted back to the strolls I'd taken through the gardens of Boston Commons. I guess seeing green life once again brought me to the realization of just how long I'd wandered in the desert. I needed to cool off and take it all in. I wanted to give my senses a vacation and smell the flowers, but…no rest for the weary. Justice would be served and I needed to find a lead to Argenti.

He was here somewhere, maybe even on this side of the wall.

I noticed a group of kids by a pond fed by the waterfall. Vacation time was over.

They were dressed rather strangely, as if people from medieval times had designed clothing for the 22nd century. Sort of futuristic, but with a hint of the distant past.

"Excuse me," I said.

When they turned, I was immediately struck by their physical beauty. The two girls and boy looked to be in their late teens or early twenties. All three of them looked, to put it bluntly, *perfect*. Even flawless. Not that I'm an expert on perfection or anything. I read somewhere that true beauty wasn't about eye color or the fullness of one's lips, but rather in their symmetry. Then it hit me. Their faces and bodies were elegant, poised and symmetrical.

"Hi, I'm Joe…" I began.

Frightened, the two girls ducked behind the boy.

"No—no!" I said. "I'm not going to hurt you."

They either didn't understand or didn't care, because they ran.

As a policeman, I'd been trained to chase after the strongest first, the theory being to neutralize the greatest threat first. However, *none* of them seemed to be a real threat, but I instinctively went after the boy. I jumped him at the edge of the garden, settling on his chest. He struggled and thrashed, but to be honest, as far as fighting abilities, any Boston youth would eat this kid for breakfast.

"Simmer down," I yelled sternly, as an adult would to a child. He ignored me, so I pinned his arms under my legs.

"You're not going anywhere, kid, so you might as well just relax!"

Finally, he gave up.

"Make my day and tell me you understand English."

He stared blankly at me.

"Great," I said, "another Nimrod."

"You know of Nimrod?" he asked.

"So you *do* understand English."

"I understand your words, but not *English*."

"English is the language we're speaking, kid," I corrected.

"There is only one language, and it is the one we speak. You speak of nations and ethnicities. That is for the outside people. In this place, we all understand each other, without knowledge of language or geography in the place that has life. You bring the stench of *that* life, and the stench of the dead with you."

"First I can't get you to talk, now I can't get you to shut up," I said.

I took a whiff of my shirt to see if I could smell the *stench* he was talking about, but I didn't smell anything. I remembered wanting to heave as we'd gotten near the Acheron River and betting Virgil that I would never get used to it. I guess I lost the bet, because this kid could smell something I no longer could.

"What's your name, kid?" I questioned.

He didn't answer.

"Julius?" I guessed, "Horace? Homer? Come on, pally boy, help me out here."

Still, he didn't answer. He only squirmed like a rabbit trapped by a mangy mutt.

"How about *Luke*? You like *Luke*? I'll call you *Luke*."

I could tell he didn't like me, and why would he? I was someone who stank to the high heaven and was sitting on his chest.

"I'll make a deal with you, Luke. I'll let you up, and you stick around to answer some questions, okay?"

Again, he didn't answer.

"Okay, Luke, makes no never mind to me. I'll just sit here and take in the view. I may even build a house here, right on top of you. You think you'd like that, Lucas boy? Having me around for years to come? Or I could let you up and we could talk. What do you say?"

Luke mulled it over, and then finally nodded.

As I got up, the beauty of the area grazed me like a soft song. We were by the edge of the garden. When I looked up, I saw a great city. It was absolutely dazzling. Huge coliseums sat in the distance. It looked like a European city from the Renaissance. A street edged the park, but there weren't any cars or any other evidence of new technology. Instead, people rode horses.

"Holy God," was all I could muster. I helped Luke to his feet. "What is this place?" I asked.

"This is the place of the virtuous. You cannot be here and must go now."

"Is there a police department around here?" I asked, hoping that there was someone I could relate to.

"Police department?"

"Come on, Luke, work with me here. Police department—badges—guns—cops who catch the bad guys?"

"Nothing like that exists here."

"Who prevents the citizens from committing crimes?"

"Crimes?"

What the hell, Joe? Is this kid thick or just trying to frost your cake?

"Okay, this place is surrounded by a giant wall, right?" I said trying to reason with him.

"Yes."

"Well, who protects you when someone climbs that wall?"

Luke looked past me, prompting me to turn around. I saw the answer to my question.

The two girls had returned with three, for lack of a better term, *creatures*. They were as big as gorillas, but I got the feeling they could move a lot faster.

"What in the name of all that is holy?" I slowly backed away from Luke.

The two girls ran to Luke and hugged him, as if I posed any danger to him.

"What are those things?" I asked amazed.

For the first time since leaving Boston, I saw something that was out of this world. Well, maybe not out of *this* world, but certainly out of *my* world. I'd never seen any animals like these at the Stoneham Zoo and the phrase "*Toto, I have the feeling we're not in Kansas anymore*" slapped me in the face like a bucketful of ice on a hot August afternoon.

Could it be that you're no longer on Earth, Joe? It was that weird light. Virgil said you went through the wrong one. What did he mean by that? Where the hell are you? You know the answer, Joe…say it. No! You're not dead—you're not dead—you're not dead.

"Look, I don't mean anyone any harm," I said, "but I'm looking for someone."

One of the girls glared at me before angrily blurting, "Get him!" She pointed at me.

The three creatures darted toward me like greyhounds out of the chute. I knew immediately that those things weren't in the mood for any kind of conversation, so I ran out of the park and across the street. I ducked into an alley through an open door and into a building. As I raced up the stairs to the roof, I visualized Argenti doing the same thing. I knew what my next move would be.

With all three of them in close pursuit, I leapt to the neighboring rooftop. Unfortunately, the buildings were close together, so the jump proved effortless. These huge goons looked like they could jump a lot farther than me, so I needed a more practical approach to surviving them.

I reached a slanted roof and didn't even hesitate. I slid down into what looked to be a restaurant below. I landed on a customer's table, food flying all around me. As I got to my feet, the people fled in fear. They were all as young and beautiful as the three I'd encountered in the garden.

I looked up. The creatures peered down at me from the roof. I smiled, certain they wouldn't follow my example and slide down the hard way. My pearly whites faded, however, when three more of those knuckle draggers punched in at the far end of the street and dashed my way.

To make matters worse, the big guys on the roof opted to slide down the hard way. Once again, I hotfooted out of Dodge.

I had to even up the odds, because these marmalukes were just too fast. Again, I didn't see a car or plane or anything connected with twentieth century technology, so I either had to grow a couple more legs or find another option.

That's when I noticed several horses tied to a post, their owners no doubt off doing something *perfect*. I clumsily jumped onto one of their backs...the horse, not the owner. I should mention that I was born and raised on the streets of Boston, left for a stay in Europe during the war, then came right back to Boston. Needless to say, I was more adapted for subway travel than horseback. To a city kid, a horse is little more than a big dog. And to a Boston kid, it was something to bet on at Suffolk Downs.

I sat in the saddle, took the reins, and kicked his sides, like the Lone Ranger did in the movies. The damn thing wouldn't budge. "Hey!" I yelled. "Move!" The horse ignored me to the point where I was actually insulted. "Son of a…" I punched the back of his head, but the four legged jerk still wouldn't bolt.

I glanced behind me and saw those goons getting even closer. They meant business. Pulling out my badge, I gave the nag an eyeful. "See this, Mister Ed?" Okay, so I looked like an imbecile talking to an animal.

Turning the badge around, I exposed the pin. "Happy trails, you fleabag!" I stuck the pin deep into the horse's ass.

The horse whinnied and reared onto its hind legs. I would have smiled if I hadn't been hanging on for dear life.

"Holy mol-eeeee!" I screamed as the horse charged down the street, those beast-cops in hot pursuit.

"Faster!" As the distance between me and those big apes grew, I smiled. "Yes!"

I turned back around, and I realized that the horse was charging headlong into a stone building. "No! Left! Turn left!"

In the movies, cowboys used the reins like a steering wheel, so I quickly yanked on them as hard as I could. The son of a gun stopped dead, sending me sailing over his head. I hit the ground, hard.

Staggering to my feet, I was grateful that I, at least, hadn't been hurled through a plate glass window. "You think that was funny?" I glared at my mode of transportation. As he gazed back at me, I'd have sworn that the freakin' fleabag was laughing at me.

Once again, I saw the three goons headed straight for me.

So, once again, I hit the pavement.

CHAPTER 7
Canto IV – Circle I – The Virtuous Pagans
❧❧

I broke into a small cottage-styled home and hid in a closet. Well, to be accurate, I didn't really *break* in. A zero percent crime rate obviously translated to zero percent door locks.

I hoped the creatures would bypass this place, thinking that I might return to the garden.

Hell, for all I knew, they could smell me and, from what Lucas boy told me, *that* wouldn't be a tough trick.

A young woman emerged from the bedroom, and I retreated deeper into the darkness of the closet.

Hey, Joe? She has a bedroom. Where there's a bedroom, there's traditionally a bed. Where there's a bed, there's a need to sleep. Wait… Didn't you see people eating and drinking back at that restaurant? So much for Virgil's 'you're dead' theory. So, Joe, when was the last time you ate or slept? Shut up, Joe! Shut up!

She was dressed for a party or faire.

"Lights," she said. The lights suddenly popped on.

Startled, I peeked through the closet door. The absence of light bulbs or any other signs of electricity definitely got my attention. Still, the place lit up like Bogey's match stick.

She studied her reflection in the mirror as she applied her make-up, but her pace slowed as I snuck up behind her. Sniffing the air, she looked as one does when they smell dog mess on a humid day.

As she turned, I quickly wrapped my hand over her mouth in time to muffle her scream. "Shhhhhhhh. Now you be quiet. Understand?"

She nodded so I loosened my mitts.

"You don't belong here," she said.

"So I've been told."

"You have the—"

"Stench of the dead. Yeah, don't you people ever change the record?"

"Who are you?"

"Joe Dante, and I'm looking for a very evil man."

"Evil?" she said, confused.

"He murdered my family."

She stared blankly at me. "I don't understand," she said.

"You don't understand *evil*, or you don't understand *murder*?"

"I… I don't understand."

"How can you *not* understand?"

"Why would I understand these things?" she asked.

"Look, sweetheart—what's your name?"

"Carmel."

"Carmel. Nice…a very unusual name."

"Is it?"

I nodded. "Look, I'm trying to find someone. Is there someone here I can talk to, someone who knows these things?"

"Carmel!" an old man interrupted.

She looked to him as a child to a parent. The first thing that registered was his age. He was the first older person I'd seen since I hopped from the stone wall. He was a portly gentleman, maybe in his fifties.

"Who are you?" I said.

"I'm also looking for an evil man," he said. "The difference between us, however, is that *I* have found him."

The three knuckle draggers followed him through the door. I slowly backed away when I spotted two more of those things coming through the back door.

"Get him out of here," the man ordered.

Two of those big clods were about to grab me when I found an unlikely ally.

"Stop!" Carmel intervened.

"Carmel…" the man began.

"We must help this man. He's looking for a friend."

"He's not my friend," I quickly said. She obviously just didn't understand what I wanted. "He's thirty miles of bad road, and I'm going to fix him, but good."

"You must help him, Socrates," she insisted.

"But…young Carmel…"

"You must help him. Do you not understand me?" she repeated with more force.

I was surprised that this man of obvious authority seemed to bend so willingly to the resolve of this child.

"Very well," he said. He inspected me, altering his tone to more tolerant anger. "Come with me."

The creatures parted, clearing a path to the old man.

I glanced at Carmel. "Carmel," I said. "It's a very sweet name."

She smiled, but there was a blankness in her face, one I hadn't noticed before. Luke and the girls in the garden had possessed the same look. I just couldn't put my finger on it.

What kind of expression is that, Joe? You should know it.

⋞⋞⋟

As I walked with Socrates, we drew stares from the onlookers. Actually, we drew more than just stares. The locals pinched their noses as if they were going to belly flop into Revere Beach at low tide. Message received— I stank.

"Well, you obviously don't belong here, and the dead don't just stroll on through, so you're something of an enigma," he said.

"I'm not dead," I said.

"You're not dead?"

"No, I'm not."

"Then why do you consort among them, and why do you possess their stench? In fact, you reek of it."

"It's been a long hot day."

"Of course."

"Who are you?" I asked.

"I am one of many guardians of this place, this one island of virtue in an ocean of evil and despair."

"I'm looking for…"

"I don't need to know who you're looking for. There's no one like that here."

"How is it that you know what I'm talking about when Carmel didn't?"

44

"Many who are here never lived a life on Earth. Carmel died at birth and is truly innocent."

That was the look I couldn't place. It was a sort of blankness, or innocence.

"This place is known to some as *Limbo*," Socrates said. "Heaven without God and the dead do not belong here. So, you must leave."

"Limbo? Heaven without God? I don't know anything about that. I only know that I'm not going anywhere until I get what I'm looking for."

"I told you, the man you seek isn't here."

"Then throw me a bone—a lead—anything."

"Look at yourself. You must think you're special. You not only bring that stench, but the hate that comes with it."

"Maybe I'm not special, but I'm certainly higher up on the food chain than the likes of Argenti."

"You think you're a mystery to me, young man? I know everything about you with just a glance."

"Is that a fact?" I mused.

"You have an Italian name, yet your face holds Celtic undertones, so that would make you half Irish. Judging from your accent, you were born and raised in Boston, Massachusetts. So, since the Italians immigrated to the United States after the Irish, the intermarriages began somewhere into the early twentieth century. You sound to be from second generation stock, since you have no Italian or Irish residual accent, which means you were probably born circa 1920. *That* would make you the right age to land you smack dab in the middle of World War II—a war where you people actually showed the good sense to begin a numbering system. So, given the background of a violent war at such a young age, and your ethnicity for the region, when you returned to civilian life, you probably became either a fireman or a policeman, married your high school sweetheart, and thought you'd live happily ever after. Now, however, you're chasing a man whom you believe threatened all that you hold dear. How am I doing?"

"Way off," I said. "I was born in 1921, not '20." What else could I say? That was the only thing the son of a gun missed.

"Right," he said.

"You think you're the only one who can play that game?" I asked. "Mind if I give it a whirl?"

"Do you believe you can?"

"You walk with high shoulders and a straight back, like royalty, but your eyes gaze toward the ground, so there's something humble about you. As a child you were probably raised in the working class, but gained power later in life. My guess would be that your father was some kind of laborer, and your mother, if she didn't die when you were young, she probably kept house, or was in a subordinate or helpful role, possibly a nurse. So, how am *I* doing?"

"Surprisingly well," he said, honestly taken aback.

"You didn't want to be like daddy. You wanted to be a thinker, which is probably why you took the name of a philosopher who died over two thousand years ago."

"I took the name that my parents gave me over two thousand years ago, and I didn't just die. I was murdered."

"Oh, I see," I mused. "So, you're the *real Socrates* now, are you?"

"Corrupting the youth, they said. That was the official charge. The one I'm sure history recorded. I was seventy years old and would have died within five more seasons, but they didn't care. The officials of the government, the ones in power, were far too busy treating the young boys as their personal concubines to worry about one old man *corrupting* the youth. Their concern with me was far more obscure. You see, I taught the young to *think*, and they couldn't have *that*. Old men in authority must always keep the young naïve and powerless over their own fate. So, the guards, the lawmen—men like *you*, forced me to drink hemlock. It was a painful death…slow and paralyzing. I will remember it for all eternity. As one day you will remember your death, I imagine."

"Do I need to say it again?"

"No, young man, you made your point as clear as water. You're not dead. You really can't see it, can you?"

"What?"

"So driven by anger, you see nothing else," he said.

The guy was obviously a few pickles short of a burger, but at least he had class. He spoke English without even a hint of an accent. Despite being delusional, he might help me find Argenti, so I'd happily label him *Socrates*, *Plato*, or *Mae West* for that matter.

We came to a building, and he opened the door. "After you."

"Oh, no, you first, please," I said.

Socrates smiled, aware that I didn't trust him, and went in.

I looked around. "My God, what is this place?"

"What does it look like?"

"Some kind of weapons depot?"

"Then I suppose that's what it must be," he said.

There were weapons of every type—rifles, handguns, bombs, explosives, spears, arrows, and even a few I didn't recognize.

"The people here are beyond this sort of thing," he continued.

"Yet, you still keep these things around."

"As you see, no one's here, but it serves as a lesson to those of us who lived and died on Earth."

"What lesson is that?"

"Small men command the letter of the law," he said. "Great men serve its spirit. For the spirit of the law is justice—and justice is the spirit of God."

He picked up a strange weapon. It was slightly larger than a pistol, but could still be hidden nicely under my belt in the small of my back. It had some sort of weird control panel on the side. I'd never seen such a weapon, but something in me wanted it.

"These are weapons of war…" he began. "If you used a twelve inch ruler to represent the history of mankind, there would be a war somewhere at eleven and three quarter inches of it."

"At least you're not using the metric system," I said.

He handed me the weapon.

"There are horrors and creatures beyond these walls of Limbo which you can't even begin to understand. This may help you, but I can give you nothing that will remove the anger from your heart."

"Is there anyone here who can help me find the man I'm looking for?"

"There is one who knows where everyone in Hell is, and that's because *he* put them there—Minos, the judge of the dead. However, he will not help you."

"We'll see about that."

I took a look at the side panel of the weapon he'd given me. I'm not a rocket scientist, so I took a chance of, once again, looking like an idiot. "How does this thing work?"

"You'll figure it out. Men like you always do," Socrates said.

He didn't bother to try to hide his resentment of me and, frankly, I was filled to my back teeth with his garbage.

"Why do you hate me?"

"You've seen the people here, walking to and fro. I know you've noticed how they look."

"What of it?"

"Some would call it *innocence*, but do you know what it really is?"

"Enlighten me," I said.

"Absence of free will. They walk in the garden and they play at the faire, but they're missing something. Eternity drags on, the guardians guide them and the protectors protect them, but at the end of all eternity, they will still be missing that same thing."

"Yeah, what's that?" I asked.

"God," he said. "The saddest thing of all, they'll never even know. They're nothing more than spirits, amputated from the light of the Most High. You ask why I hate you. I don't. I pity you. *You* had a choice and you chose to walk away from the light. You could have followed God and could have known true joy, but you turned your back on Him when you needed Him most."

"Turned my back on God, huh?" I said. "When I got enough evidence to punish the man who murdered my daughter, the judge let him stroll away with nothing more than a pat on the head. As a reward for my trouble, I got to watch my wife and child get murdered in front of me. Now I ask you, who turned away from whom?"

"You just won't hear my words, but sooner or later, you will. Sooner or later, you'll have no choice."

I didn't care what he thought. I was steamed, so I just tucked the weapon in my belt. "Where's this Minos guy?" I demanded.

CHAPTER 8
Thoughts of Home – Beatrice
❧❧

Y ou want to run that by me again," I said.

"You heard me," Argenti paced around the man. "There are two kinds of people in my world—those who are loyal to me and those who are dead." He pointed at the stranger doused in gasoline. "This nosebleed is the latter. Which are you?"

I popped the lid off the lighter and stared into the man's eyes. I was shocked to discover there was something in me that wanted to do it.

What's he doing here anyway, Joe? He obviously owed Argenti money, or screwed him on an earlier deal. Argenti probably knew that someone was leaking info about him. He's a psychopath, but he's not an idiot. He must have guessed the cops were on to him and probably connected the dots to pin the guy who screwed him over the most as the undercover cop. Only he pinned the tail on the wrong donkey.

Drenched in gasoline and blood, the man stared up at me and smiled with surprising warmth and strength. He seemed oblivious to the stench and his pending death.

"Nothing is ever the way you think it is, buddy boy," he said with shocking casualness. "You just have to answer one question—*who* are you?"

He looked at me as if he could read my mind. Maybe he *wasn't* some drug scum. Maybe he was just some stranger they grabbed to test me.

"What are you waiting for?" Argenti asked. "A Christmas card?"

I lit the lighter up, looked at Argenti's evil grin, then back to the guy in the chair.

I grinned like a Cheshire cat and looked back to Argenti.

"Argenti," I said, *"you're under arrest."*

"That's not funny anymore."

49

"It's not meant to be."

Suddenly, about twenty of my brothers with badges burst in from various doorways. They surrounded everyone, leaving Argenti's men with nowhere to hide. They would either have to fight or surrender. They surrendered—the cowards.

I grabbed Argenti and threw him against the wall.

"I want my mouth piece," he yelled.

"My God, not the lawyers," I quipped. "Now I'm *really* spooked."

You got him, Joe. You got him good!

⤜⤛

The smell of bacon and eggs rolled upstairs to the bedroom as I slowly awakened. Bea rose early on Sunday mornings just to cook a special breakfast. She would crumble the cooked bacon *into* the eggs in such a way, you couldn't eat one without the other.

Being Catholic, Sundays were always a ritual with us.

I loved Sundays with the family, but now we all wore a silent crown of thorns since the loss of Kathleen. I slowly rolled out of bed, looked sadly in the mirror.

As every other Sunday before church since Confirmation, I put my necklace of the crucifix around my neck.

⤜⤛

I kissed Bea and sat at the kitchen table.

As always, Beatrice was beautiful. Unlike me, Bea was first generation Irish, and her accent made her sound as though she were singing rather than talking, at least to *my* ears.

Her family came through Ellis Island when she was fifteen.

I was sixteen when I first saw those big green eyes and heard that voice. When I did, the only thing left was the happy ending. A jet plane could have smashed into a locomotive twenty feet away, and I wouldn't have noticed. Now, *that's* love at first sight.

She had flaming red hair and a temperament to match. In my younger days, we called women like Bea *throwers*, meaning, if you're going to get them mad, don't leave any sharp or heavy objects within arm's reach.

On the bright side, her passion always left me wanting more.

50

Before I could ask Bea about Anna, she walked in and plopped herself down at the table.

Fourteen and as pretty, stubborn, and unpredictable as her mother, Anna terrified me on several levels. The same traits I've valued and even adored in my wife, invited more gray hair at a faster rate when displayed by my daughter.

"*That's* how you walk into a room, young lady? You don't even say good morning?"

"Mornin', Big Daddy," she said.

"What did I tell you about that beatnik talk?"

"Yes, Father," she said with rolling eyes.

"And what sort of get-up is this?" I pointed at her outfit. In 1961, a fourteen year old girl wearing pants, loafers and a beanie cap screamed one word—*non-conformist*. "You're not dressing like *that* for church."

"I'm not going to church."

"What are you talking about? You're in the choir."

"Yeah, I'm quitting that, too."

"Excuse me, young lady!" I said.

If you ever have a daughter, let this be your warning—the difference between birth and twelve years old is insignificant when compared to the difference between twelve and fourteen. At fourteen, something happens to them. It's like they're issued disrespect and willfulness with the birthday cake. Anna had been a different person at twelve, but *when* she was twelve, Kathleen had been her older sister, not just a memory that caused her pain.

I felt bad for Anna. An only child now, she would never know the joy of having a sibling throughout her life. I hadn't seen her smile in months, but I didn't say anything. What was I going to do, bully her into smiling just to keep her old man happy?

I wanted to hug her every time she walked into the room, but something in me made me come down on her even harder.

"You listening to this?" I asked Bea.

She placed the plates of eggs in front of us and sat down. "Do you know the difference between an Irish and Italian temper?" she asked Anna.

"Huh?" Anna responded.

"An Italian will love you even while they're strangling you. But the Irish? They won't kill you. They won't touch you. They won't even talk to you. Understand?"

"No," Anna said.

"I gotta tell you," I said, "I'm a little lost too."

Bea leaned forward and stared Anna down. "You're going to go to Mass, sing in the choir, and thank God for the clothes on your back and the food on your plate. Understand now?"

"Yes ma'am," both Anna and I said.

❧

Sunday morning church in a mainly Irish Catholic town like Boston is like attending a theatrical production with Jesus as the star of the show.

Beatrice and I always chose a pew close to the front, because we knew what would take place after Father Nicholas's sermon.

"Often, people wonder what it takes to have a successful, fulfilling life," Father Nicholas said. "Money? Doubtful. Love? Definitely. But what would love be without forgiveness? *Forgiveness* is the key to any relationship that involves God, and every relationship, in one way or other, will involve God, even if you don't want it to."

The first thing you'd notice about Father Nicholas is his age. He was an old priest, preaching the word even when *I* was a squirt. He kept an eye on Bea when I went off to fight the Germans in the Big One, and he cried when Kathleen died. I think it's fair to say that I loved the man.

He nodded to the choir, and they sang.

"Any news yet?" Bea asked quietly.

"About what?"

"You know very well what I'm referring to, Joseph."

She was right. I knew exactly what she was asking. She wanted to know if I had any news on my promotion. I just couldn't resist toying with her.

"Well, I took the test," I said. "Last week's bust certainly didn't hurt. We should find out later in the week."

"We could use the extra money."

"I know."

"Perhaps we should—"

"Bea, we just have to have a little faith, that's all."

It wasn't what she said, but rather what she didn't say that bothered me. We never talked about Kathleen. Sometimes I wanted to, but for some reason that remained a mystery to me, I equated it with weakness and I needed to be strong for my family's sake.

The choir finished and Anna stepped forward for her solo.

When someone has a great singing voice, they say that *the angels wept*, but Anna's voice was beyond that. When she sang *Ave Maria*, even the *demons* wept. She had more than just a talent—she had a gift.

She surveyed the audience of church goers, finding my approving eyes. She used to smile when she saw us watching her from the pews. Now, she barely acknowledges us with a nod.

She sang and, as always, she didn't disappoint.

❧❧

The station was deserted. I sat at my desk as a cockroach strolled across my paperwork as if he owned the joint. "Holy mackerel!" I screeched.

I quickly rolled up some newspaper, gripping it like Paul Bunyan about to swing his hatchet, but I stopped in mid-swat. The roach looked big enough to apply for a green card. Two inches, it was uglier than Milton Berle in drag. I dropped the paper and pulled off a shoe.

"Get out of here!" I yelled as I swatted the son of a gun with my shoe.

It was getting late and I wanted to get home, but when I lifted my keister, Mickey darted out of his office like a slug from a snub-nose and nabbed me before the seat got cold.

"Where you going?" he said.

"It's late, I'm taking off," I said with a shrug. "What do you think?"

"You can't."

"Why not?"

"Why not? I'll tell you why not," Mickey nervously blurted out between fidgets. "You have to prep the Argenti file for trial, *that's* why not."

"I want to do that tomorrow morning, when I'm fresh. I'm not taking any chances with that scum. What's the matter with you?"

"Me? Nothing… I'll tell you what," he said, "You give it the once-over now. It takes say, what…an hour? I'll drive you home. You won't have to fight the freaks for a subway seat. Deal?"

"Sounds like a deal with the devil if you ask me." I slowly and suspiciously sat back down and pulled out my notes on Argenti. I knew Mickey was up to something, but didn't have the first idea as to what.

❦

True to his word, Mickey dropped me off.

I ran up the stairs to our porch as I looked at my watch. It was late, but not so late as to wake anyone, which is why I wondered why all the lights were out. I cautiously opened the door with one hand and kept my free hand near my back holster.

Argenti was considered a flight risk and was kept without bail, but that didn't mean his goons couldn't find out my real name and get to my family.

I entered the darkened living room, keeping my back pressed to the wall.

CHAPTER 9
Canto V – Circle II – Judgment
❧

I sat atop a steep cliff. I decided on a short rest before my descent, although I didn't think I needed it. I guess I just wanted to think.

I fiddled with the strange popper Socrates had given me. I aimed into the open air, took a shot, but nothing happened. I couldn't make heads or tails of the darned thing.

"Men like me," I muttered as I smirked to myself.

I peered down, but I couldn't see the bottom. I knew that Minos was down there somewhere. At least according to Socrates, he was there, and he'd be hard to miss.

I'd left the virtuous pagans behind and was glad of it. It's bad enough when teens take the father's car without permission or sneak out of the house to go to a party, but when they have absolutely no knowledge of evil, it makes someone who does feel like…a snake. Plus, it didn't help that everyone I'd encountered made it a point to tell me how badly I needed a deep steam cleaning.

I rubbed my bracelet, smiling as thoughts of Anna passed my way. I remembered her birth and her first day of school. My smile faded when I got to the memory of her falling from the roof that last night of her life. The look on her face as she'd fallen would haunt me forever.

I looked down at the impossible descent that awaited me.

"Piece of cake," I said to myself as I ended my rest and started downward.

As I lowered myself to the first granite shelf I could find, I remembered Virgil's comment about Hell being divided into nine levels, each circle assigned to a category of sin.

The climb down wasn't easy. I wasn't raised in Montana, and the only time I even went into the mountains was in the autumn to watch the foliage in Maine, but those were mountains with trails so the day-trippers could watch the colors change and an occasional waterfall. They weren't like this, steep piles of sand and stone where one slip could mean one long fall.

If that Virgil guy wasn't yanking your chain, what category of sin will this next level bring you, Joe?

I thought of the absurdity of my thinking. For a moment there, I thought I actually *was* in Hell, but how could that be when I knew in my heart of hearts I wasn't dead?

Virgil said that, sooner or later, you will believe. Let him play his mind games. He's out of your life now. You're not dead...you're not dead...you're not dead. Maybe you're still on that roof. Maybe you cracked your skull open when you dove for cover, and you're hallucinating this whole thing. That beam of light, or rather those two beams of light, and the one that carried Argenti away. Maybe it really did transport you here, but how? Better yet, why? Oh, Joe, what have you gotten yourself into?

❧

I reached bottom in record time...well, maybe not *record time,* but at least I made it without kissing dirt.

The base of the cliff led to a dirt road, and from there I saw groups of people walking. Some looked like they knew where they were going, while others appeared incapable to say their own names.

"Hey!" I called out to a schmoe in a pin striped suit. "Where are you heading?"

"Just followin' the pack, pally," he said. "Just followin' the pack."

❧

I followed the walking wounded into a large palace. The place had all the trimmings. We're talking *royalty galore.*

The people, however, ran the gamut. Some of them wore suits and party dresses while others looked as if they'd never heard of the word *tie.* One of the latter looked in my direction and smiled as we walked with the large group. He wore a flower-printed shirt, strangely flared legged pants, and had abnormally long hair. He was a young man, probably not even twenty.

"What's happenin'?" he asked with a smile.

"Huh?"

"Que pasa?"

"What the devil are you made up for?" I asked.

"I don't dig, man?" he replied, too casually for my tastes.

"Dig?" I repeated, confused.

"Yeah."

"What's with the shirt and the hair?"

"You mean the threads? The San Fran way, man."

"California, huh? *That* explains a lot," I said.

"This is one far out trip, man," he said.

"That's putting it mildly."

"You the fuzz?"

"What?"

"The fuzz," he repeated, pointing to the shield clipped to my belt. "You just scream *establishment*, man."

"Something wrong with that?"

"Means you're not hip."

"And you are?"

"Why do you think they call us *hippies*? We're the future of mankind. After all, make love, not war." He smiled and flashed the *victory* sign with his two fingers.

"Peace, man," he said.

"Peace, huh?"

"Oh, man…when did you kick the bucket?"

"I'm not dead!"

"Far out! Then you really made a wrong turn."

"You're telling me."

"Silence!" a voice boomed from the front of the large, crowded room where our blind walking had led us. The *hippie* and I ironically had the same response.

"Shit," we both said to ourselves.

Above the crowd on a stage-like setting sat a large throne guarded by several groups of men. Some of the characters wore combat gear and held rifles, while others resembled ancient Greeks or Romans with spears. There were others, French knights with crossbows, Chinese warlords sporting swords, British soldiers from both World Wars working beside Nazis, and American Civil War Yankees standing beside Confederate troops.

The guards, however, didn't disturb me as much as the *guarded*.

Minos sat upon the throne, and he was an imposing figure, to say the least. If he stood, I guessed he'd be about seven feet tall. He looked more beast-like than man, but there was wisdom about him. He seemed as regal as a lion. He was as magnificent a being as he was intimidating.

"Who will be next to stand before Minos?" he bellowed. Hard to believe that anyone with a snout like that could speak *English* so clearly.

If I learned anything in the Army, it was to never volunteer, so I waited to see who would stand before Minos first, just to test the waters. Apparently there were a lot of people who'd done time in the Army, because we all had the same idea. Finally, one of the Nazi guards grabbed a couple and pushed them before Minos. They looked familiar. In fact, they were the drunk drivers I'd seen on Charon's ferry.

"It wasn't *my* fault!" the husband said fearfully.

"I see," Minos replied listening as a shrink listens to a nut job.

"If it were up to me, I would have slept it off."

"So you claim no responsibility for your actions?"

"Absolutely none!" he said with surprising pride before glaring at his wife.

"What?! You're blaming me?" She quickly turned to Minos. "I told him a thousand times, if he's going to drink and drive, don't get caught!"

"*She* got in the car with me," he defended. "I wasn't responsible. *She* should have stopped me."

"You're fat!"

"You're ugly!"

"Enough!" Minos shouted, obviously annoyed by their sniping. Couldn't say I blamed him. The bickering couple froze in horror as Minos's giant tail encircled them both.

Right after the tail wrapped around them, I noticed something strange—*He had a giant tail!*

His tail squeezed the two together until they gasped for air, and then it covered them entirely. When his tail unfurled, they were gone. This was nothing like Houdini or The Great Svengali. They didn't disappear into the next room only to reappear in front of an applauding audience. They were *gone*.

Minos looked over the crowd, bellowing yet again. "Who is next to stand before Minos?"

I'd seen enough. I came here for a reason and figured now was as good a time as any. "I will," I said as I walked past the guards.

A look of shock crossed the guards' faces. Maybe I was the first guy to actually volunteer to talk to this—and I use the term loosely—*guy*.

I must admit I was a little worried about the whole *tail making people disappear* thing, but I had everything under control. I still had an ace in the hole, in the form of the weapon Socrates had given to me. It was safely tucked away behind my back and under my belt. I just wished I'd spent more time fiddling with the blasted thing.

"I'm looking for a man," I said. "Well, you can call him a *man*. He's more of a walking plague that goes by the name of Filippo Argenti. I've been told that you're the guy to talk to about these things."

Minos stared at me without responding.

"Look, I admit there are some strange happenings going on here," I said, glancing at the Civil War guards. "I may not be able to explain a lot of it, but I do know that I don't belong here. I just need some answers."

"Confess to me, and you shall have them," Minos commanded.

"I have nothing to confess," I said. "I've done nothing wrong. I'm a good person."

"There's one thing I've always noticed about humans," he said. "Each of them has *one* sin, one that stands above the rest—the one that haunts them in their sleep and in their private thoughts. In that way, all people are alike. What is your sin, Joseph Dante?"

"How do you know my name?" I said, surprised to hear it slip out of a mouth with six inch fangs.

Minos, however, obviously didn't have the need or desire to explain himself. He opened those powerful jaws and roared in my face.

I closed my eyes, half expecting to have my head bitten off at the neck.

"Do you think you're special?" he said. "Everyone is the same!"

Minos could have ripped out your throat and didn't. Now, it's your turn. Time to squirt lead, Joe!

"You had your chance, buster!" I said.

I grabbed the weapon from behind my back and pulled it out. I knew I had to be fast. Unfortunately, I wasn't fast enough.

Minos's tail wrapped around me and squeezed hard. Like a boa constrictor, it circled my waist and neck. The tip clenched around my wrist, forcing me to hold my gun in the air.

"Confess to me and behold your judgment!" Minos yelled.

Suddenly a voice called out from the distance, and I was surprised at how welcome it was to hear.

"Stop!" Virgil shouted as he approached.

"Why do you intervene?" Minos raged.

"This man doesn't belong here," Virgil said.

All eyes turned to watch as Virgil, strangely fearless, climbed the stairs to the stage where Minos sat.

"I am Minos, guardian to the entrance of Hell. He belongs where I put him."

Minos's tail wrapped tighter around me, and Virgil did the unimaginable. He grabbed Minos's arm.

Instantly, I could tell that was an unhealthy move. To begin with, Virgil was no larger than me, so the sight of an average sized man grabbing the arm of a beast who looked like he could dine on us for lunch and pick his teeth with our bones was not what I would call *savvy*.

Second, every guard in the joint pointed the weapon of his day in our direction.

Minos stood, his anger apparent. I was wrong about his height. He wasn't anywhere near seven feet. Unfortunately, he looked to be more like eight.

"You forget your place," Minos accused, looking as though he was locking his temper in a cage of straw.

Virgil fearlessly looked him in the eye. "I know my place." He spoke through gritted teeth. "Do *not* forget yours." To punctuate his point, Virgil poked Minos in the chest.

He reminded me of a school boy standing up to a bully. It was almost comical, as if I was to poke the chest of a grizzly bear, expecting him to back down.

"You will not deter me from my task," Virgil convicted.

Everyone and everything froze. Maybe it was my fear of disappearing to God only knew where, but time really seemed to slow to a crawl. I looked at the guards and saw fear in their eyes…fear of Minos? The only one in the whole place that didn't seem afraid was Virgil, which begged the question…why?

Slowly and surprisingly, I felt Minos's tail loosen and uncurl from around me.

"The man you seek is on the fifth ring," Minos admitted, "that of the wrathful."

"Wrathful?" I said, confused. "That means *bullies*, doesn't it? There must be some mistake."

"Minos is never mistaken," he roared, clearly insulted.

"He's a drug smuggler and a murderer. If this is really Hell, there must be a lake of fire around here somewhere. Argenti should be in it up to his eyeballs!"

I didn't know if this was really Hell or what, but any place that would pile Argenti in with bullies and *not* with the murderers, is quite frankly, one hundred percent, grade A, uncontested, *screwed up.*

"The man you seek is on the fifth ring," Minos repeated. "Now, leave this place!"

Virgil put his hand on my shoulder. "We must go now, Joseph."

Virgil and I walked across the hot sand.

I didn't like the guy at first, but I had to admit, he *did* save my skin. Maybe he wasn't such a nut-ball after all. I mean, let's face it. We certainly weren't in Kansas any more. So, I could see why someone could *think* we were in Hell.

"Listen, I want to thank you for getting me out of that jam back there. I don't know how you did it, but…"

My voice trailed off, and my thoughts became unsettled.

How the heck did he do it, Joe? A creature of that size looms over us, backed up by a couple of dozen armed guards, and all this Virgil character does is yell, let him go? This wasn't Charon. Minos wasn't some old man with black eyes, but a beast of grizzly proportions.

"Come to think of it, how *did* you do it?" I asked.

"If you are to leave this place, you must follow me and ask no more foolish questions."

Again he sidestepped my question. Just like that, I was back to not liking him.

"Now, just hang on a minute," I said. "Thanks for the help and all, but I'm not going anywhere until I find Argenti."

"Why must you find this man? Tell me."

"I'm particular, see. When somebody murders my wife and children, I take it personally. Call it a quirk."

"I assure you, Joseph, his punishment accommodates his sin."

"Yeah, with the *wrathful*. Oooo, I'm impressed."

Virgil stood in my path.

"So inflexible are you that you're willing to sacrifice your very soul?" He stopped and took a breath. "Very well, I will strike a deal with you, Joseph."

"I'm listening."

"Together we will find Filippo Argenti, and once you see his punishment, you must come with me."

"If I'm satisfied with what I see," I added.

"Agreed."

"Why are you helping me?"

"I'll take you to Argenti, but you must trust me. I'll ask nothing of you that's beyond your ability, but what I ask, you *must* do. This is the only way. Do you understand?"

"If you take me to my family's killer, you got yourself a deal." I had no idea why he was helping me, and despite what he wanted, I *didn't* trust him…but what's the old saying—*any port in a storm*? "Swell, lead the way," I said.

CHAPTER 10
Canto V – Circle II – The Lustful
∽✧∽

W e walked until the hard desert ground became grubby and the hot still air turned stormy.

"We now walk the second circle of Hell, that of the carnal," Virgil offered.

"Carnal?"

"Those controlled by physical lust."

"Thanks a million, but I know what *carnal* means," I said, insulted. I decided to listen until he started sounding wacko again.

"Hell contains nine circles. The journey ahead is long, so we must be aware of demons."

"Hold the phone!" I guess I didn't have to wait long to hear something *wacko*. "Demons?"

"What would Hell be without demons, Joseph?"

"Oh, I don't know. This place is pretty horrendous as is."

"As with the circles of Hell, demons can also be divided into nine classes, three sets of three—reptilian, insect, and mechanical, each for land, sea and air."

"Right."

"Heed my words, Joseph. You'll need them!" he said in anger.

"Swell, I'm all ears."

"Insect demons detect their prey by heat, reptilian by light, and mechanical by motion. This means *any* motion to include blinking, breathing, and eye movement. Do you understand?"

"I'm sorry, did you say something?"

63

Virgil shook his head in disgust. "Do you still not believe, Joseph?"

"Believe what?"

"That this is Hell."

"I know I'm not in Hell, but looking around, I can see how *you* might think so."

"So you believe me mad or a prevaricator."

"Huh?"

"How do you then explain what lies before your eyes, Minos, and perhaps what you might have seen beyond the walls of the virtuous?"

I didn't answer.

"Did you not hear me, Joseph?"

"I'm just trying to figure out what *prevaricator* means.

"One who speaks in falsehoods."

"Ahhhh…you see, we in the colonies call that *scamming*, and no, I don't think you're lying. It's just that…"

"Yes?"

"Well, I'm what you'd call a *good egg*. I go to church every Sunday, and I go to Confession twice a month."

"Do you believe that Hell is only for the murderers and rapists?"

"Isn't it?"

"Hell is also for the *good eggs* that go to church every Sunday, and to Confession twice a month," Virgil said.

"How is that, huh?"

Virgil put his hand on my shoulder and said something slightly unexpected. "Joseph, get on your belly and crawl."

"You want to run that by me again?"

"Do you not hear the storms?"

He was right. I heard a distant howling from the winds that seemed to get stronger. Virgil nodded to the ground. I looked at the mud. How ironic that it was *then* we had to hit the ground and not when we wandered in the nice dry desert.

"Must I remind you of our agreement?" he continued.

"Swell!" I said. "If it will get me to Argenti, why the devil not?"

We crawled through the mud.

As the winds grew stronger there was something else, another sound filled the already turbulent air. There was an eerie wailing under the wind, a sound that could only come from people in pain.

"Well, *this* brings back memories." I raised my voice slightly to be heard over the wind.

Virgil didn't answer, but I felt compelled to speak my mind just the same.

"Normandy. Of course, there were German slugs whizzing over our heads for incentive to eat the French mud."

"If you desire incentive, Joseph, there it is," Virgil said as he pointed.

I peered up to see the source of both the wind's howl and the mysterious wailing. A giant tornado swirled toward us, but this tornado didn't just contain the dust and debris that you'd see when you watch the weatherman on the six o'clock news. This massive spiral of wind also included people—hundreds, maybe thousands of people.

In the distance, other storms and tornados swirled. Some were so big, they sparked with electricity from the sky.

"What kind of place is this?" I yelled.

Joe…maybe you're in Hell after all, but you're definitely not dead. Could you be the only living man in Hell? What are you, a marmaluke, Joe? When was the last time you ate, or slept, or even needed the can? You're dead! Say it! No! You're not dead— you're not dead. You just have to find Argenti. Everything will be swell once you find Argenti.

"Quickly!" Virgil shouted.

I could feel the wind yanking at me. I tried to cling to something, but there was nothing to hold on to, only mud. I suddenly found myself very fond of the sticky mud as I attempted to dig myself in.

I screamed as I felt my feet being pulled off the ground and into the winds, but Virgil suddenly grabbed me by the shirt, and we rolled down into a pit of filth and muck.

"Where the hell are you taking me?" I yelled, as I tried to wipe off some of the mud. In vain, I might add.

"The mechanics of Hell prevent us from avoiding the storms on this level."

"Isn't there any other way out of here?"

"Perhaps, but…"

"But what?"

"You would be required to abandon the notion of finding Filippo Argenti."

"Never mind. This way's swell!" I quickly replied.

"Then we must cross this trench to the other side. The cliff to the next level awaits us at the other end. Come."

"What?" I said.

"We must cross—"

"Not you." I heard something in the mud. Between the darkness of the storm and the mud all over him, I didn't see him at first.

A young man sat in the mud with his face in his hands. He wept like a child.

I immediately felt compassion for him, probably because I couldn't remember the last time I'd seen a grown man cry. "Are you okay?" I said.

He babbled something in gibberish of the French variety.

"Hey," I tried to interrupt, but he just kept jabbering. "Hey! Speakity English? Parle vu Englise?"

"Oui."

"Yes?"

"Yes," he finally said.

"Okay, now simmer down and tell me what's going on."

"I will never find her," he said in a thick French accent.

"Who?"

"My Francesca! Swept up by the storms… I swore never to leave her side." He raised himself to his knees to peek over the trench at the passing tornado. "She is out there somewhere," he said. "I must find her."

"Look, Frenchy, you're not going to find, locate, or stumble on anyone out there," I said. "Why don't you just come with us for a while?"

"I can never leave my Francesca. How we loved together to read the stories of Camelot. They used to speak of us, that Paolo and Francesca were the reincarnate souls of Lancelot and Guinevere."

"Paolo? Is that your name?" I said.

"There are many feelings we are cursed with," he said, "but none as grand as the touch of a lover."

"I know what it's like to lose a wife," I said trying, to commiserate. It wasn't until his reply that I realized I couldn't *commiserate* with him at all.

"She was not my wife, but my brother's," Paolo said.

I never understood why a man would go after another man's wife. I always went for the *if you love somebody, go after them* philosophy, but there were limits. I tried to imagine how I would have felt if Mickey had made a play for Beatrice. How would I have reacted when I found out? Who would I have blamed?

Making a play for another man's wife is bad enough, but the wife of his brother? If this was Hell, this mutt deserved what he got. "I guess I don't have to ask why you're here," I said.

"It was not like that!" Paolo snapped. "They were married for political gains. She really loved me, but we could never be together. We were murdered by my brother while we slept in each other's arms. Now, never to touch again." He stood, a dangerous move given the strength of the winds.

"What are you doing, Frenchy?" I yelled. "Get the hell down!"

When he planted his feet, I realized that he wore nothing more than a muddy bed sheet, which he'd wrapped around himself like a Roman toga. "Another storm comes," he said. "Maybe this be the one."

I looked to see yet another circular wind spiraling toward us. The people looked like rag dolls, with no control over where they were or where they were going.

Paolo tried to climb out of the trench, but I stood to grab him. Virgil, on the other hand, stood to grab me.

"What are you, a screwball?" I screamed. "Get down!"

"I must find her!" he yelled over the howling winds.

When I grabbed him, I realized just how big and muscular this guy was. He was well over six feet with biceps like coconuts, which probably helped keep him earthbound despite the power of those winds. "You're not going to find anyone in this," I yelled.

"What else must I do?" he said.

The tears streamed from his eyes, but I tried not to feel pity for him. The man betrayed his own brother, after all.

"They say that this circle is for those who have forsaken all reason to satisfy their own carnal appetites," Paolo said. "Perhaps that is true. I could not be a slave to reason, nor morality, nothing that would keep me from my Francesca."

Then, he said something I'll never forget.

"I am trapped by the circumstances of love."

I saw something in Paolo's tears. Was it guilt, or maybe shame? I didn't want to feel anything close to compassion for the man, but I did.

Paolo brought me back to reality when he broke free and climbed from the trench toward the coming storm. "Francesca!" he yelled in a vain attempt to locate her among the thousands or even tens of thousands of people caught in the maelstrom.

"Hey!" I grabbed for his legs.

God Almighty, Joe, this is one strong son of a gun!

I looked to Virgil for support. "Help me!" I yelled, but Virgil did nothing. "What the hell are you waiting for, a bus pass? Help me!"

Again, Virgil didn't even raise a hand to help.

Paolo finally broke free and I instinctively climbed the trench to chase him, but Virgil grabbed me.

"Let me go!" I screamed at Virgil.

"To what end?"

He was right. There was nothing I could do now. In an instant, Paolo disappeared into the murkiness of the debris.

❧❧

The winds finally died down after we crawled for what seemed like hours. It felt good to stand again, but I was still hacked off at Virgil.

"We must cross the open field quickly," he said. "If we falter, the winds will return and take us. Beyond this field is a cliff leading to the next level."

"Why did you let the tornado take that guy?" I asked. "You just let him blow away."

"He wasn't ready."

"Ready?"

"He didn't wish my help, nor did he desire yours."

"That doesn't matter. I just can't stand by and watch another man die."

"Pity that wasn't your philosophy when Argenti clung to the edge of that roof," Virgil remarked.

That came out of nowhere.

Who the hell is this guy, Marty the mind reader?

"How did you know about that?" I tried to sound more angry than hypocritical.

"You still don't understand? While you ran for the door on the rooftop, you heard a gunshot, did you not?"

"What of it?"

"The bullet went through your head. You died on the roof that day, Joseph. You are as dead as Paolo."

68

"I'm not dead!" I shouted, trying not to consider the alternative.

"Then what explanation comforts you for this?" Virgil swung his arm to showcase the dead horizon that lay before us.

"I know exactly where I am! I'm in a hospital bed at Boston General, in a coma, and the only way out is if you help me find Argenti!"

"Hate is your guide, Joseph, not I… And hate is your master. Let it go, and see the truth before you."

"Now you listen to me. I'm not letting anything go until I make damn sure that Argenti gets what's coming to him. Neither you, nor Argenti, nor God in Heaven will stop me, got it?"

Suddenly, I heard a humming sound. This sound struck me as strange. It was the first time since I'd come to this place that I heard something that sounded man-made, rather than a noise produced by nature.

Three huge hovering crafts rose in the distance, beautiful glowing disks the size of small jet planes, but they moved more like humming birds. They resembled the ones I'd seen in the desert when I first got here, but these were closer, close enough to hear.

"Joseph, we must go," Virgil warned.

"Why? What are those things?"

"Nothing you'll wish to see up close. Now come."

"They're beautiful."

"They shan't remain that way," he cautioned.

"You want to know what I think? I think they're my ticket to Argenti." I ran to flag them down. "Hey!" I yelled. "Over here!"

"Joseph!" Virgil barked as he chased me.

I ignored him, whistling loud enough to wake the dead.

"If your goal is to damn your soul for all eternity, you've just succeeded," Virgil said.

The son of a gun was right. As they drew closer, the vehicles changed.

The glow faded and they transformed into giant mechanized insects. Dark and menacing, they looked like something out of *Science Fiction Theater*. Definitely things I didn't want to see up close and personal.

The sound also changed as the soft hum became a high pitched wail.

Just my luck, they started toward us.

CHAPTER 11
Canto VI – Circle III – The Gluttonous
❧❧

W e ran like the wind, but didn't have much of a choice since the wind tossed us around like a flag without a pole. Let's face it, outrunning those mechanical insects was like trying to outrun a shooting star.

Six thick mechanical legs unfolded from under one of the crafts, landing in front of us. It lifted and plunged one of the legs just inches from us, forcing us to roll out of its path.

I'd had enough. If I was going down, I was going down shooting. I pulled out the weapon Socrates had given me and turned to shoot. "Swallow lead!" I shouted as I yanked the trigger. I suppose I would have looked slightly more threatening if the damned thing had actually fired. Instead, all I heard was a malignant *click*.

Virgil ran up to me. "No time to delay!" he said in his all too annoying British accent. "We must flee!"

"*Virtuous* pagans, my Aunt Fanny! If I ever see that old man again, I'll…" My tirade ended with the firing of the cannons on those ships, and *those* weapons didn't misfire. I'd never seen anything like it. This wasn't Army artillery sending off a shell of lead and steel. This was a giant ball of fiery light. When it hit the ground near us, it was like an earthquake and enough to knock me off my feet. "What do we do now?"

"Do you really not know?" Virgil replied as I struggled to my feet.

Okay, it was a stupid question with an obvious answer.

I didn't have to run far before I discovered what Virgil had in mind. We paused at the top edge of a cliff. This was nothing like the one that brought me down to Minos. Where the first cliff was mounds and mounds of sand and rock, this one was like hard dirt that had been rounded by centuries of wind.

I peered down…*way* down.

Virgil and I glanced back at the insect-like ships as they made a strafing run toward us.

"We must jump," Virgil said.

"Down there!" I pointed. "I can't even see the bottom!"

"No need to worry, Joseph. The bottom is there, I assure you."

"What the—is that supposed to be funny?" I said amazed. "You choose *now* to tell your first joke?"

So, I could either leap into a bottomless pit, or stay and face three flying ships that looked like something out of *War of the Worlds*, complete with lightning ball cannons. I thought of the absurdity of my choices.

Not sure which decision was the least crazy, I looked down again. "You first!" I yelled.

Virgil threw me a look of impatience and jumped.

"Son of a bitch jumped!" I said to myself, astonished. I had to admit, the guy had stones the size of Mount Rushmore.

The ships got into position and fired again.

As a light ball flew in my direction, I closed my eyes and jumped.

❧❧

I landed in a soft sea of papers and rotting food, rolled over, and swiped a chunk of stale bread from my sleeve. This sea of trash appeared more like an ocean. It was, in fact, a garbage dump, as far as the eye could see…and nose could smell for that matter. The flies and insects ranked about as high on the *annoy-o-meter* as the stench. Virgil had told me that I'd get used to the smell of the Acheron River, but this was a whole new ball of wax.

"Oh God, I really *am* in Jersey," I said.

Virgil walked over to me. Well, I guess you could call it *walking*. It was more of a saunter. We both struggled to maintain balance on this pile of crap.

"The third circle of Hell awaits us, Joseph," he said.

"Lovely. Oh, hey, here's a quick question," I said with casual sarcasm. "What the hell were those things shooting at us?!"

"What do you think they were?"

"Well, they looked like gigantic insects and were mechanical, *and* they flew. So, could they be—oh I don't know—demons?"

"Perhaps," he said, "but those who reside inside are an even greater horror."

"Dare I ask?"

"Geryon and his minions—for we are now fugitives."

"Geryon?"

"Yes."

"Okay, I'll bite. Who the devil is Geryon?"

"Once a great light in Heaven, now damned by his own making, he is the personification of fraud. Now he finds the faithless that refuse their destined circle, and puts them in their proper place."

"Proper place?" I gulped, trying to conceal the willies that crept in.

"After a suitable dismembering, of course."

"Oh, of course. What good would relocation be without a suitable dismembering?"

Virgil looked up the hard cliff. "They're not pursuing us for the moment, but I assure you, they shall return. There are many such demon patrols. Geryon's is but one."

"Swell. That's just swell, Virgil, and these goons are after us?"

"Not *us*, Joseph… Just you."

"You know what I think? I think those things are after *you*."

"Believe this, it's not I they pursue. If that were the case, they would have no ability to discover my whereabouts."

"Oh and why is that, exactly?"

"Faith, Joseph."

"What about it?"

"I possess it."

"Oh, and I don't?"

"You said it, not I."

"Oh really?" I snapped.

"We must leave this place," he said.

I didn't want to let it go just yet. I grabbed his arm and started to confront him. "Not so fast!"

I slipped as if the soles of my shoes were coated with grease. Virgil tried to steady me but all he could do was join me in my tumble. We both rolled down the long hill of garbage.

"Crap!" I screamed on the way down.

I opened my eyes at the bottom of *garbage hill*. Several large men and women looked down at us. Behind them were other large people, some obscenely large, and all engaged in eating. They were actually *eating* the rotting, disgusting garbage.

As Virgil and I got to our feet, I noticed that many other landfills painted the horizon beneath the dead gray sky.

These people ate as if desperate to consume anything and they weren't just eating the food. They ate discarded papers and even dirty diapers.

I wanted to upchuck.

They were too big for normal clothes, so they wore huge moo-moos. Thank God...the thought of seeing one of them naked... Did I mention that I wanted to upchuck?

"Fresh meat!" one of them yelled, pointing at us.

The way he said it, I thought for a moment that he was going to try and eat *us*. Instead he handed me a slice of rotting pizza with a topping people rarely order—maggots.

Disgusted, I immediately dropped the slice.

"What are you doing?" he asked, incensed. "Hurry. Eat!"

"No thanks. I'm trying to cut down on my...maggots."

He backed up, amazed that I refused.

"Can't you tell they don't belong here?" one of them called out. "They're skinny!"

"We all started out skinny," another one chimed in.

Virgil leaned toward me. "The gluttonous reside in this place," he said.

"Gluttons, huh, well that makes sense," I said. It actually *did* make sense. All these men and women were beyond fat, and they kept eating.

"You there!" one of them called out, trying his best to maneuver toward us.

I say *maneuver* because some of these people were so buried in their own body fat, I could barely see their limbs. It was almost like a cartoon, where the artist drew a character as one lump of flesh, with only head, hands and feet as slight protrusions.

"Did Minos send you?" he continued. "I knew it! There's been a mistake. I don't belong here!"

"Minos didn't send us," Virgil said.

Another glutton waddled closer with obvious desperation.

"Please take me with you."

Virgil eyed him with a coldness that would chill a polar bear. "You are *not* ready," he said.

I had trouble imagining this guy traveling to the next landfill that sat a couple hundred feet away, let alone with us to where we were going.

Then it hit me. Behind all that fat, there was something in his face that actually looked familiar.

"Where are you going?" he asked.

"The fifth circle," I answered.

He laughed and the other gluttons quickly joined in. I was a little surprised that someone would laugh about where we were going when where we *were* was little more than a garbage dump. I didn't want to be here either, but at least I had a mission. What was their mission? Eating dirty diapers?

Still this guy looked familiar. I just couldn't peg the man.

"Down?" he said. "Do you think I was sent here for being a simpleton? Nobody goes lower."

"Excuse me?" I finally said. "Do I know you?"

"No." He looked away, shamefaced.

I felt certain I knew him. Not like a friend or relative. Perhaps someone famous. Someone I'd seen on the television.

That's it, Joe! The television.

"Senator Ciacco?" I asked.

He turned to face me. "Yes," he said, grief-stricken. "I was a senator, once upon a time."

"You're part of Jack Kennedy's staff. I saw you on the television."

"That was a long time ago."

"What are you talking about? I saw you not two weeks ago."

He looked at me as if I'd just been released from the state laughing academy. "I left politics after Jack was assassinated."

"Assassinated?" I said, amazed.

Nothing here rang true. But this? JFK assassinated? Impossible. He was one of the few presidents everyone loved. Hell, he was one of the few that *I* loved, and I hated them all.

"They shot him in the head on a lazy November day," he said, his voice filled with sorrow and pain.

"How? Why?" I said, still amazed at even the thought.

"After him, they killed Bobby. Then they killed Martin Luther King… and they elected Nixon. With him, Watergate, CIA hit squads, Kent State, the gas shortage, and a hundred other things that led our country down the dark gray path of compromise. The world was changing for the worse. Why should I try to make it better? So, I gave up. Nothing I could do would change anything. So, I decided to grab my piece of the pie," he confessed with quiet anger. "At least we made it to the moon. We made it to the moon for Jack, and a fat lot of good it did."

"A little too much wine and women, eh, Senator?" a maggot immersed glutton asked as he laughed.

Senator Ciacco ignored him and continued. "I used to think that gluttons were just obese blobs with no purpose in life," the senator said. "Before Minos put me here, he told me that gluttony had nothing to do with one's weight. Gluttony is the sin of taking from the earth and not giving back. Gluttons turn the earth into their own personal trash heap. Now, in this place, we can never stop eating the garbage we created."

"If you do?" I asked.

Suddenly, I heard barking and howling echo down the trash-decorated path.

"You're about to find out," he said.

"This way." Virgil grabbed my arm.

"But…"

"Now!"

We ran up a small trash heap as dog-like beasts ran toward the gluttons. Larger than dogs, maybe the size of hefty Great Danes, they all had one distinguishable difference—they each had three heads.

They attacked the gluttons like a pack of wild mutts pouncing on a rack of raw meat.

Some gluttons frantically grabbed the rotten food from the heap of crap and ate it desperately.

"See! I'm eating. I'm eating!" he said as a dog furiously growled at him.

The senator was a different matter. Two dogs stood on top of him, tearing into his flesh. The man screamed his agony.

"Do something!" I pleaded with Virgil.

"What would you have me do, Joseph?"

"I thought you said that demons were only reptiles, insects, or machines! What the hell are those things?"

"They're not demons but only the mechanics of Hell."

"What's the difference?"

"Do you not know what a demon is, Joseph?" Virgil asked.

Demons used to be angels. Catholic school served me well. These things? These *dogs* didn't possess angelic origins. Though, I suppose the difference was merely academic to the gluttons.

I didn't know what Virgil could or would do to help these people, but *I* had to do something. I pulled out the weapon Socrates had given to me. It hadn't worked against those mechanical ships—maybe it would work there.

I aimed and quickly fired. Yet again, I was only greeted by a feeble *click*.

"Son of a bitch!" I yelled.

I couldn't stomach their tortuous screams. I looked around and found a hunk of rotting meat. I quickly picked it up, hoping to bribe the beasts away from the gluttons.

"Hey!" I yelled as I held out the decomposed beef. "Over here!"

They ignored my summons and the meat. They obviously preferred human flesh.

I hoped the horrid screams would eventually end, but they never did. These poor people didn't die.

"Virgil, God damn it! Do something!"

Virgil did nothing, however.

I couldn't believe the coldness of this son of a bitch. Frantic, I threw the meat at one of the dogs attacking the senator. Pausing, the brute looked up at me. The other dogs followed suit. They all stared up at me and it became obvious that I'd maybe bitten off more than I could chew. While I wanted them to stop attacking those poor people, I didn't want to offer up myself in trade.

I thought they would make a play for us, or climb up the trash even a little, but they didn't. They didn't bark or howl or even growl. They just stared at me. I finally realized that they weren't staring at me at all. They were staring at Virgil.

Virgil coldly stared back.

The dogs slowly backed away and fled.

It was my turn to stare at Virgil. When I asked for his help, I thought we could come up with some plan to divert the dogs. I didn't expect him to scare the hell out of them with a single glance.

Who the devil is this guy, Joe? The Lord of the land?

I ran down to the senator, thinking he must be dead.

"You all right? Are you going to live?"

"Live?" he cried through blood stained teeth. "We have little choice." He rolled over, grabbed a handful of garbage, and shoveled it into his mouth. "We must eat or they will return," Senator Ciacco said in pathetic desperation.

"Come with us," I said. I didn't care how big he was anymore. He was a senator and a good man. He deserved better than this.

"What? Down?" he said. "As bad as this is, it can be much worse. The lower you go, the worse it gets. Everyone knows that."

"Senator, I need to ask you something," I said. "It's not a little thing, it's a big thing."

"Yes, young man."

I didn't really believe he was dead, but I needed to appease his pain, even for a moment. "When did you die?"

"In '74. Why?"

"When you died, how were the Red Sox doing?"

"We took the Penant in '67." He flashed a bloodstained smile. "We made it to the Series against St. Louis, but we blew it... Damn those Cardinals."

"Still the greatest team in all history," I said, trying to keep him focused on something other than his pain.

"Damn right," the senator said.

CHAPTER 12
Canto VI – Circle III – The Garbage Dumps
༒

T he gluttons far behind us, Virgil and I walked. The trash heaps and landfills grew smaller. There were no more people to be seen. They remained concentrated where the garbage was piled high. The farther we walked, the darker it got, until it seemed like dusk, even though there was no sun to set.

Other flying disks sped off in the distance.

"Come!" Virgil warned.

We hid beneath more trash.

These vehicles were different. They glowed a different color, and when they drew close enough to pass overhead, they looked more like airborne tall ships than the insect-like craft that Geryon's crew piloted.

"How could this happen?" I asked.

"As I said, demon patrols are frequent in upper Hell."

"I'm talking about Senator Ciacco. He's a good man, and how could he look like that?"

"You'll discover that you'll see people at different stages of life, the way you need to see them, and the way they need to be seen."

"Yeah, but…"

"The patrol has left. It's time we go." Virgil stood.

I could have asked Virgil a number of things. *Is it true that the lower you go, the worse it gets? How could a man take such an attack from those dogs and still live? Why the hell were those dogs afraid of the very sight of him?* Instead, I decided to sound like a broken record and ask what was mostly on my mind. "How long before we reach Argenti?"

"Remain silent." Virgil pointed.

Distracted, he climbed up a small mound of trash and peered over the edge. I followed, spotting those three large, demonic vehicles in the distance.

Unlike the *tall ships* in the distant gray sky, these were the mechanical insects. Once again, we were in range and in sight of Geryon's brood.

The ships sat on the ground, and some kind of—for lack of a better word—*beings* knelt by the trail and pointed, like trackers pointing to footprints. They were big, and not creatures to be toyed with.

"What are they doing?" I whispered.

"They're looking for you."

"There are rocks over there. We can walk on them."

"For what purpose?"

"So they can't find our footprints. No harm in trying to be a smart fugitive."

"It's not footprints they need to find us," Virgil said.

"Then how are they tracking us?"

"We shall find Filippo Argenti soon enough, but you may not like what you find," Virgil said, ignoring my question by answering a previous one.

"What's that supposed to mean?"

"How can you look yet still be blind to the truth?"

"What truth is that?"

"Do you still believe you're not dead?"

"Yes, I do." I spoke confidently, even though I believed it less and less.

"Why?"

"Because."

"Why, Joseph?"

"God would never leave me here!" I said in anger.

"Did *you* not reject *God?* Did you not hurl your own crucifix into the earth?"

"I'm not dead!" I said. I didn't even care how he knew about the crucifix.

"Joseph, you must face the truth and surrender your hate of Argenti."

"I'm not dead!" I shouted.

"Silence!"

Suddenly, we heard the whine of those flying machines.

Virgil and I looked at each other in anticipation and ran. The ships rose up behind us.

One shot a ball of light at us. The others followed suit. The balls exploded, knocking me off my feet.

Virgil quickly grabbed me. "Rise, Joseph!"

We made a beeline for the cliff that led to the next circle.

This cliff was different than the previous ones. No soft hill of sand or hard dirt, this one was composed of sheer walls of jagged rock. It was an incredibly intimidating sight. I felt like I stood on the top peak of the highest of all the Alps and Rocky Mountains combined.

Virgil didn't even hesitate. He immediately began his descent. "Hurry!"

I stood there, feeling defeated.

"We'll never make it."

"We have little choice. Now descend."

He was right, but I felt so tired. The ships flew over us, spinning around to face the walls of the cliff.

I climbed into the rocks and we tried to take cover.

The ships fired on us again and again.

The deafening barrage brought back terrifying memories of Normandy, where there'd been nowhere to hide. The noise hammered so loudly, it knocked the wind from my lungs.

I finally lost my footing. With my feet dangling, I clung to a small crevice between the rocks.

"Keep a strong grasp, Joseph!"

"I can't!"

I tried to regain my balance, but another barrage from those ships loosened my hold. Hell, it even loosened my teeth!

My grip weakened. I closed my eyes and felt the inevitable approach. As if he could predict my fate, Virgil grabbed my wrist the instant my hand slipped. He held my entire body weight with one hand while he clung to the rocks with the other. He was a lot stronger than he looked. Not that he looked weak, but holding a hundred and seventy pounds of *dead* weight was no easy task.

"As I swing you to the right, you must gain your footing!" he yelled over the explosions.

"Do it!" I yelled.

Virgil braced himself as best he could. Before he could swing me, one of the giant ships descended to our level. Like a giant face peering into a fish tank, it stared at us. Virgil and I looked at each other, knowing what was next.

A lightning ball exploded next to Virgil and he lost his grip, falling beneath me. I managed to grab onto a small ledge of rock. I gripped Virgil by his wrist. It turned out I was right. Holding a hundred and seventy pounds of dead weight proved to be one tough gig.

"Jesus Christ!" I yelled as I tried to hang onto Virgil.

Another barrage shot out in our direction, and this time, we lacked any cover. Several balls of light struck the rocks above us, and the entire wall gave way.

We tumbled down the side of the cliff to about halfway. This time, no soft pile of garbage broke our fall. I slammed against the rocks and a sharp pain exploded through my arm and shoulder. Screaming from the agony, I saw a bone protruding from my forearm, followed by an endless stream of blood. I waited to pass out, but it never happened.

Virgil quickly ran to me and clasped a hand over my mouth.

"Swallow the pain, Joseph!"

I screamed from the kind of agony I'd never before experienced.

"You will heal," he said. "Now, remain silent lest they find us again."

"Knock me out!" I cried. "Do something!" Anything would have been preferable to *that* anguish.

"There is no unconsciousness here," Virgil said. "There's no sleep, only torment."

I peered at Virgil through tear-filled eyes, realizing that he seemed to be the exception to the rule he preached.

"Not for you," I said. "There's not a scratch on you."

"I have faith, Joseph, and only faith will make you whole."

"I want to die!"

"Do you now understand Hell? It never ends."

How could the human body endure such pain without falling into unconsciousness, or going into shock? It simply couldn't. It was time for me to admit what, deep down inside, I'd known all along. I could no longer deny the undeniable.

Say it, Joe. Say it you unbelievably stubborn bastard.

"Oh God," I screamed. "I'm dead. I'm really dead!"

CHAPTER 13
Thoughts of Home – McMontey

❧❧

I entered the darkened room and cautiously pressed my back to the wall.

Suddenly, the lights snapped on.

"Surprise!" everyone yelled.

I lowered my hand with a silent sigh of relief—thankful that I hadn't *surprised* them with a concert of hot lead. "What the heck is going on here?" I said.

Mickey ran in behind me and picked me up.

"You got it, little brother," he said. "You got the promotion!"

"I got it?"

"You got it." Bea flashed her pearly whites.

I looked at the guests, understanding now why the station house had been deserted. Everyone was *here*.

Tony raised his glass.

"To Detective *First Class* Dante…one swell guy."

Everyone drank.

❧❧

Anna sat on the stairs, avoiding the festivities.

There's nothing sadder than a young girl who feels alone. Her grief radiated from across the room, so I sat beside her on the stairs, away from the guests.

"Do you know what's worse than someone with a great smile who doesn't use it?" I asked.

Anna didn't answer.

"Nothing," I continued. "Especially when your old man shells out nearly five C-notes for braces."

She smiled sadly. "Nobody says her name anymore," she said. "It's like Mom doesn't even remember her."

"That's not true, Sweetheart. We're just all dealing with it the best way we can."

"Nobody should be happy."

"When you get older, you'll realize that we don't have all the answers. We're just faking our way through this grief thing. I'm sorry you had to find out so young."

"I got something for you."

"What?"

"I got something for you," she repeated. "It's not much. I saw it and thought you'd flip for it. Got it with money from babysitting."

She handed me a small box and hugged me.

"I love you, Big Daddy." She let go of me, all too soon, and ran upstairs.

"And enough with the beatnik talk!" I called after her.

I opened the box to find a bracelet. It was plain with links and not much to look at, but to me, it might well have been platinum encrusted with diamonds.

I put it on, vowing silently to never remove it.

"I love you too, kiddo," I said quietly to myself.

With everyone long gone and Anna asleep, I watched from the kitchen doorway as Bea washed the dishes. God, I loved watching her body move. The only thing I liked better than watching her was touching her.

So, when the radio played *I Love How You Love Me* by the Paris Sisters, I refused to let the moment pass unnoticed. I took Bea by the hand and pulled her away from the sink full of plates.

"What are you doing?" she said.

"Dance with me."

"Joseph, I can't."

"Come here." I pulled her to me.

"You'll get wet."

"I'll risk it."

"The food will stick," she said as she pulled away.

"Let it."

"But Joseph…"

"Bea. There's only one person in the world more stubborn than you… and that's why you married him," I said with a grin. "Now, dance with me."

She finally gave in and put her head on my shoulder.

Whenever she saw me looking at her, she would always smile, but I knew when I couldn't see her face, her sunbeam faded. I knew because when she looked away from me, I would stop smiling, too. We both thought about Kathleen, more than we wanted to, but less than we probably should have.

"Bea?"

"Yes Joseph," she answered, still facing away from me.

"Do you believe in happy endings?"

She stayed quiet for a long time, but then finally answered. "No," she said. "I believe in happy journeys."

"Will you be there, Bea? For me in my journey?"

"Joseph?" She said raising her head from my shoulder to face me. "Wherever thou goest, I go, my love." She kissed me.

ॐॐ

It was a green Boston day in spring when Argenti got the upper hand.

I sat in the hot seat while the Assistant DA spoke a lingo that only lawyers and snakes could fathom. We called it the *hot seat* because anyone being questioned by some of these defense attorneys would, very often, break into a hot sweat.

The Assistant DA was on my side, though I personally think all lawyers have their own agenda. I knew what was coming from the defense once the ADA was through with me.

I eyed Argenti, and he fearlessly stared back. He sat there with his evil counselor, defense attorney *McMontey*. While Argenti made me ashamed of my Italian side, McMontey made me want to blood let this Englishman and replace it with something less cold blooded, like an iguana.

So caught up was I with staring at these wicked men and day-dreaming of bringing back the days of the guillotine, if the ADA hadn't said my name at the end of his sentence, I would have forgotten he was talking to me.

"Detective Dante?"

"I'm sorry. What?"

"Could you explain the events that transpired on the fifth of January, as you recall them?"

"Yes, of course, after seven months of undercover work, my partner and I were able to secure a deal with Mr. Argenti for five hundred thousand dollars worth of pure cocaine with an estimated street value of three million. After we made the deal, I informed Mr. Argenti that he and his men were under arrest. Our backup arrived and we placed everyone under arrest."

"No further questions, Your Honor."

I'd practiced that answer a hundred times in front of the mirror. The only thing I'd forced myself to change was saying *Mr.* Argenti, rather than *that scum sucking piece of dung, son of a bitch murderer* Argenti. However, we were instructed to address the defense with courtesy and respect, so as to show the judge and jury that our testimony isn't personal, even though we all know it really is.

Then it was McMontey's turn, but I wasn't afraid. The fat cat got up and buttoned the jacket of yet another expensive suit. I think the world would be far better off if everyone in an expensive suit would just spontaneously combust.

He was about sixty, but looked younger. His charm was enhanced by a thick British accent. "Detective Dante, could you please identify this for the court?" he said, pointing to the contents of the briefcase.

"Yes, that's the cocaine we purchased from Mr. Argenti."

"You're certain?"

"I tested it myself."

"How did you test it, mate?"

Where's he was going with this, Joe? He's got to be setting up some sort of ambush. It's always a chess game with these guys. It's never about what's right or wrong...only the kill.

"I tasted it," I said.

"Maybe you'd like to taste it again, just to be sure."

85

The ADA jumped up, obviously as in the dark as I was. "Objection, Your Honor. Detective Dante's skills are not in question here."

"Your Honor, those skills are very much in question," McMontey said. "Detective Dante is stating that his skill in tasting what he believes is cocaine is enough to convict my client. In my client's best interest, I'd like to put those skills to the test."

"Overruled," the judge said with the tone of a preacher.

In my client's best interest. I'm of the opinion that every despicable thing that every defense attorney has ever done stems from the phrase, *in my client's best interest.*

The son of a pig handed me a sample of the coke.

"Now, Detective Dante, test this substance in the same way you tested it on the night you arrested my client, please."

Here's something that most decent people don't know. Cocaine has *no* taste to it. When testing by taste, the only flavor it would have would be that of its cutting agent, like flour, sugar or cornstarch. Uncut snowcaine like this, however, meant that the *taste test* was misleading. Like the related drugs novocaine, benzocaine, and lidocaine, cocaine is an anesthetic, so it will actually numb the tongue. *That* proves the soundness of whether it's cocaine.

This however? This didn't numb my tongue at all. This was bland...like...flour! I quickly concluded that McMontey was obviously trying to trick me—the English louse.

"Well mate?" He smirked.

"This is flour, and don't call me *mate.*"

"Did you not just identify this as the case you purchased from Mr. Argenti on the night in question?"

"You obviously switched the samples to test me," I said with confidence.

"No, I surely did not—mate."

"What? But..." I trailed off, drawing a blank. "I don't understand."

"I'm sure you don't," McMontey said, sounding both sarcastic and triumphant.

I glanced at Argenti. He smirked like a genie, whose master had just granted him his wish for freedom.

CHAPTER 14
Canto VII – Circle IV – The Cave

☙❧

I was in too much pain to even move my arm, let alone seek cover. Virgil looked up to see the three demonic vehicles darting toward us like sharks to a blood feast.

Hooking his arms around me, he dragged me into a nearby crevice in the rock which led to a cave. I don't want to sound like a softy, but I screamed the whole way.

The ships fired over and over again, but the explosions sounded more and more distant.

"I should think that they won't find us here," Virgil said.

"Gee, that makes me feel so much better," I yelled.

"Remain quiet. I'll see where this cave leads."

"What? But…"

"Quiet. I shall return, Joseph."

With that, he departed.

☙❧

Angry, I lay alone in the depths of the cave, awaiting Virgil's return.

It felt like days had passed since I'd seen him last, but it was more likely only hours. I didn't know which ticked me off the most—the bone sticking out of my arm, the non-stop gushing of blood, or the nail-biting agony I felt.

When I saw the ships searching in the distance, I realized why I was so mad. I was dead and in Hell! *That* was more than enough to steam Saint Peter himself. Was Virgil right? Had that last bullet gone through my noggin?

87

On the force, we often heard stories of fellow cops who'd been shot in the line of duty, rushed to the hospital, died on the operating table, and brought back to life. They would speak of a tunnel of light, but little else since they'd been revived so quickly.

Was that second beam of light meant to transport me to *my* afterlife? Had I, in fact, escaped it when I ran into the one that whisked off Argenti? Was I in Argenti's afterlife? Could the inner workings of fate be so blindly haphazard and mechanical?

These things were beyond me and all I felt was an all-consuming rage. I wanted to get into a brawl and beat the crap out of someone, but those demon ships were my only company. I watched them from the cave opening, scurrying around like bees in a field of flowers, desperately searching for me as if it meant their very survival.

I swallowed my pain as I rolled over onto my stomach. From the back of my belt, I pulled out the popper that Socrates had given me. I'd tried to use it several times before and failed miserably. With any luck, this time would be the charm.

I was in so much pain, I dropped the stupid thing. Finally, I realized why it hadn't worked for me. When I picked it up, I saw that a small flap had opened to reveal a hidden compartment. I studied the small side panel with two dials and sliders on it, along with what looked like a safety switch. What was it that Socrates said? *You'll figure it out. Men like you always do.* Well, finally, it was time for a man like *me* to figure it out.

Virgil had told me that time was different here. That kid, who'd called himself a *hippie* at Minos's palace, hadn't looked to be from any time I knew. If he was from the future, then maybe this weapon was too.

How are you going to figure out this gadget? Do you see any instruction manual around here, Joe? There's only one way to do this, pal, trial and error. First things first.

I switched off the safety, aimed, and pulled the trigger. Nothing happened. Maybe it was the fact that I was just so steamed, but I decided to go for broke. "Screw it," I said.

I turned up one of the dials a notch and one of the sliders all the way to the top. I heard the weapon begin to hum. I guess I was getting used to the pain, because I found it in me to actually smile. That is, until the hum turned into a high pitched wail.

I quickly pointed the gun out toward the cave's opening and gave the trigger a yank. A ball of light, similar to those that came from the ships, but smaller, bolted from the barrel. The damned recoil pushed me half-way across the cave. I picked myself up and ran to the cave opening, and when I say *ran*, of course, I really mean…*weakly staggered.*

It's a ray gun. Socrates gave you a ray gun, Joe! Hmmm… Socrates gave you a ray gun? Did you ever think you'd be stringing those words together?

The ray gun started to hum again and I instinctively knew that if I didn't turn the safety back on, the cycle would repeat and begin to whine again.

Unfortunately, the ships saw the burst of light come from the cave and flew up for a closer investigation. With the sliders all the way forward, I clicked the dial up another notch. I quickly aimed the gun, braced myself, and fired at the largest of the three ships.

As the ball of light left the barrel, a larger ball of light left one of Geryon's ships. The two bursts of energy collided, exploding in mid-air.

The explosion occurred so close to the ships, it knocked all three off balance.

Oh Joe, if you could only see the look on Geryon's face. Actually, don't you wish you knew what he looked like so you could see the look on his face?

"That's it!" I shouted.

I'd finally discovered how to use the weapon. As for the safety switch, I had a hunch that there would be another selection beyond switching the safety on and I was right. I adjusted the safety to the third selection as the gun began to hum again, and my suspicion proved correct. It was an automatic.

The demon crafts regained their balance, heading for the mouth of the cave, and *me*. The ships, themselves, were pretty much the same as before, but from my perspective, they *looked* decidedly meaner.

I braced myself and aimed again. This time, when I pulled the trigger, it reacted like a Tommy gun with a burst of five to seven balls of light.

I didn't know any weak points or strengths or the layout of the ships, plus I was in too much pain to effectively aim the thing anyway, so I basically just shot at what I could see.

I was just so happy to no longer be a victim to these demonic goons.

"I got you, you bastards!" I yelled, but I quickly followed it with "Uh oh," when the ships came in closer to the mouth of the cave.

They shot at the cave opening and the walls shook so hard that some rocks fell from the ceiling.

"Damn!" I screamed as I crawled as far away from the cave's mouth as I could.

"Joseph!"

I turned to see Virgil.

"Do you call this *remaining quiet?*" he said.

"Well, yeah, during a Red Sox game," I said.

"Come with me," he ordered.

I raised my hand so he could help me up. He didn't. So I sucked it up and pulled myself to my feet. We disappeared into the darkness of the cave's inner belly.

❦

I sat in the darkness of the cave, watching as Virgil tended the fire. I knew what was coming since the bleeding wouldn't stop.

"You said that there are three types of demons—insect, mechanical, and reptilian. Which is Geryon?" I asked, trying to focus on something other than the river of blood flowing from my arm.

"You no longer believe you possess the breath of life, Joseph?"

I didn't answer. I don't know why I didn't trust Virgil. I knew he was hiding something, but still, he'd helped me on several occasions. I guess I just didn't want to give him the satisfaction.

Yet, there was something in me that wanted to trust the guy. Under his leather coat and joyless face, I sensed goodness in him. His eyes telegraphed his concern, but I just didn't know if I trusted my own instincts anymore.

"Refutation is a terrible thing," he said, "is it not?"

"Fine. I'm dead. I'm in Hell. Happy?"

"No Joseph, I'm not happy. However, I do have my faith."

"Ready," I said, remembering what Virgil once said.

"What?"

"You said that Senator Ciacco wasn't *ready*... Ready for what?"

"What do you think?"

"What makes me ready and him not?"

"Never once did I say that you were ready, Joseph."

"Then why are you helping me?"

"Everyone has a journey. Some long, some short, but all leading to the same place. In this way, everyone is the same. So, I must help you reach your destination."

"To Argenti?"

"Is that truly your destination?"

"Where else?"

"There are two roads within you, Joseph—one of hate and anger, and the other... The other is not of wisdom nor strength nor courage, but of faith. On *that* road, you have most certainly lost your way."

"I don't think so."

"Was there ever a time in your life where you had, in fact, known that God was there for you?"

I ignored the question.

"God knows all, does He not?" Virgil said.

Virgil rolled a red-hot piece of deadwood from the fire and looked at me. I knew what he had in mind and, as much as I agreed with him that it had to be done, I still hated him for doing it. "This will hurt," he cautioned.

"Let it," I said through gritted teeth.

He took my wrist and yanked it, so the protruding bone retracted back into my forearm and I shrieked as if my arm was being amputated.

He pressed the white hot wood against my open wound, searing it. Just when I thought I couldn't feel more pain, more came and I screamed in agony.

I couldn't *just* scream, however. I needed to scream words, focused words on who had become a symbol for my rage. If I could just reach my destination, just maybe, the pain would somehow be worth it. So I screamed.

"I'm going to kill you, Argenti!"

CHAPTER 15
Canto VII – Circle IV – The Hoarders and Wasters
∾

I wore a make-shift splint on my forearm as we left the caves and the sheer walls of the cliff far behind. We seemed to have lost our demon bounty hunter *companions*, at least for now.

The pain in my arm remained intense, but compared to when I was first injured, this was a Christmas sleigh ride.

This level of Hell was engulfed in darkness, and a heavy mist covered the rocky ground like syrup over pancakes.

Pancakes… God, don't you wish you could be hungry again!

When I checked the splint on my arm, I noticed the bracelet on my wrist, which only served to remind me of my losses. I wanted my body to crave sex with my wife, but it no longer craved food, water, sex, or any other desire of the flesh.

I guess it was an advantage to have no physical requirements in Hell. Still…I missed things.

I should have been depressed, but I wasn't. I was *angry*—steamed beyond the boiling point—ready for a ground level, grade A, number one conniption fit. Hell, I was totally frosted.

As always, Virgil kept our conversation to a minimum. He knew that I was only using him to find Argenti, and I knew he wasn't being up front with me about why he was helping me, so we kept our discussions to the exchange of information only—what kind of demons there were, how to avoid them, etc.

Bea called *me* stubborn. True, but I had nothing on this guy. I wanted to ask him how he'd died, but thought he would just dodge the question anyway, so I figured I'd ask in a round-about way to see what I could get out of him.

Hell, I *was* a cop after all. I knew how to interview suspects, even when they were unaware of the fact that they were being interviewed.

"Virgil?"

"Yes."

"I was wondering… Here's the thing… Well…" I began.

Virgil stared at me as I stammered, probably not knowing what the devil was wrong with my tongue.

"Ah, the hell with it… How did you die?" I asked, taking the direct approach.

"Is that the question you wish to ask me, Joseph, or perhaps another?"

I thought about it and maybe he was right. You didn't ask an inmate what he'd done on the outside. You asked him how he landed in the slammer. We were, in actuality, all students in one hell of a crossbar college, so I asked a different question. "Okay, how did you end up here?"

"So, you wish to know my sin, Joseph?"

"Sure, why not?"

Before Virgil could answer, a voice called out from the distant fog. "Look! Newbies!"

I wish I knew the words to describe him. If I had a gun to my head, I guess I'd say he looked like a scary, face painted, transvestite clown. He wore skin-tight clothing with high platform shoes, which seemed designed for a man. His face was covered in white make-up with black lipstick and long *poofy* hair. About six foot three and fairly muscular, he wasn't even trying to pass for a woman.

"We got a boulder with your name it," he announced.

"Boulder?" I repeated.

"Yeah, come on—and hurry. It's almost time for another go."

I had no idea what this schlep was talking about, but I just had to ask. "Excuse me, but what kind of twisted party are you made up for?"

"What? Aren't you getting any flashbacks on my face, dude?" He looked sincerely offended.

"Sorry."

"I'm Plutus Kisma… Of *The Poisonous Vixens!*" he continued as if I'd be crazy not to know him.

"You lost me."

"The heavy metal band… *The Poisonous Vixens*. Come on! I died on stage and everything. We were totally stellar."

"Heavy metal?" I blankly repeated.

"Yeah, hard rock—*rock and roll*."

"What the devil are you talking about?"

"Sure, like, you know," some girl wearing an amazingly short and even more astoundingly tight snakeskin skirt said. "I want to rock and roll all night…and party every day…" she sang.

"I keep telling you—*that* wasn't me," Plutus said, irritated.

"Like *yeah*, it was." She tilted her head, announcing how dumb Plutus was to even consider disagreeing with her.

"No, that was *Kiss*!"

"Oh, right," the girl conceded. "Those guys were totally awesome!"

"So, you sing… Like Buddy Holly," I said, finally realizing what this guy did, although the reason for wearing four inch heels escaped me.

"Buddy Holly? When the hell did you give up the ghost?" Plutus said.

"1961," I said, only half believing my own voice.

"Oh my God, so you weren't around for the robot wars in '93 and the destruction of San Fran in '99!"

"What?"

"I'm just scamming you, dude… If you died before I was the bomb, then you're way behind the learning curve. Now, shoulders to the boulders…and you, too." He pointed to Virgil. "Cool jacket by the way."

"We are non-participants," Virgil said.

"Non-participants? Go back to the first level, biker-boy! *Here* we fight!"

The fog began to lift and an endless row of giant boulders lined our side of the hill—and I mean *giant*. These babies must have been about sixteen feet in diameter. Behind each stone stood groups of people. Some of the women wore about as much make-up as Plutus.

I must still be a beat cop at heart, because the first word that screamed in my head was *prostitute*.

There were pirates, cowboys and ancient Greeks, to name only a few. If my life depended on it, I couldn't even guess what they all had in common.

"Hey dude, if they don't want to fight, they shouldn't have to," a young man in a Roman toga spoke up.

94

"You speak excellent English," I said.

"Why wouldn't I? I'm from Florida."

"Yeah, but the..." I pointed to his toga.

"This? Dude—I drowned at a frat party in '83." He laughed to himself. "Now, I have to go through eternity looking like this. Go figure. I just wish I'd died drunk."

"The young buck's right," added an elderly cowboy. "If they don't want to duke it out, they don't have to. Now let's bushwhack them hoarders real good!"

"Excuse me!" the heavy metal guy screamed. "I'm the alpha dog here and when people don't fight, demons come, and let me tell you, they're not exactly keen on conscientious objectors. So, you fight!"

"They're getting ready, I can smell it," a pirate scowled.

"Come! We go now!" a southeast Asian prostitute nervously interrupted. "Bay gio!"

"Will everyone just chill out! We're the lead boulder," the big rock and roller from the future said. "Nobody will budge until we do."

"What if they do?" asked the kid in the toga. "Remember last time?"

"Shit! You're right," Plutus said, obviously not happy. "Okay, time to fly." He leaned up against a boulder next to the prostitute. "Ready people?" he yelled. "Heave-ho!"

They pushed and the boulder slowly moved. It picked up momentum as it rolled down the gentle slope. Hundreds of boulders followed suit, each with people shoving from behind. They pushed as if they were in some kind of ancient battle. Then I realized *that* was exactly what they were in.

"Faster! Push!" one of them yelled.

On the other side of the far hill, hundreds of giant rocks also began to move, both opposing sides heading for each other where both slopes met at the bottom of the two hills.

"Hoarders and wasters," Virgil said. "They allowed the money, or lack of it, to control their lives. Now, they must try to crush each other with the weight of the money they created."

The side we were on obviously held the *wasters* of money. *That* was what they all had in common. Pirates, cowboys, prostitutes, and ancient Romans...they were all notorious for just taking what they wanted and tossing it away, because they assumed there would always be more. These heavy metal guys must have been the same.

"Nothing symbolic about that, huh?" I said sarcastically.

"*Everything* in Hell is symbolic, Joseph."

As they got closer, each side began to yell at the other. "Cheap bastards!" a pirate yelled. "We'll crush your scurvy hides!"

"It's you who will be crushed. You and your kind, spendthrifts!" came the reply from a money hoarder who wore an old Pilgrim suit. If he was in modern times, then he might have been Pennsylvania Amish.

The two sides smashed into each other in violent disarray. Men and women were thrown in all directions, like flies being scratched from the back of a mangy mutt. But it didn't end there. Without the boulders or any other weapons, they began to fight hand and tooth. They fought as if they were alive and their lives depended on it.

If they didn't, I suppose that demons would come and make things even worse for them. They fought with such passion, I felt the hate and disdain they had for each other. It was as heat from a steam radiator.

"Let's leave this place," Virgil said.

"That's it? Just go?"

"Is it your wish to see them push the boulders back in place so that they may begin again?"

"They just stay here and do this over and over again?"

"This is their penance, Joseph."

"There's nothing else for them?"

"They're not ready for anything else."

"Who are *you* to say that?"

"Do you believe the truth would sway them from their goals and desires?"

"Why wouldn't it?"

"Has it swayed you?"

"We're not talking about me," I said.

"Aren't we?"

"There's got to be something more than this," I said, angry from his last remark.

I looked down the slopes to the fighting masses. It looked like some twisted out-take from the movie *Spartacus* and I felt nothing but sorrow for them all.

"Fine... Swell," I said. "Let's get the devil out of here."

"Wait," Virgil said in a surprising turn. "Get their attention."

"What?"

"You know what I'm asking Joseph. Do you not?"

I thought for a moment, and then I realized what Virgil wanted me to do. So, I reached behind my belt and pulled out the weapon I'd used against Geryon. Now I knew how to use it—well, sort of—and it would certainly get their attention.

I shot a fireball in the air and the explosion lightened the murky, sinister sky like a flare at midnight. It looked spectacular, and it shut every yap in the joint—including mine, since the recoil nearly dislocated my shoulder.

"Now, behold the truth," Virgil said with conviction.

He climbed upon a rock and looked down on the crowd. His voice boomed down the sloping valley as though he stood in an auditorium made for such an event.

"Gather around, all those who wish to hear the truth," he began.

Confused, everyone looked at each other. This was obviously something that hadn't happened here too often.

Some hesitantly approached us.

"Yes, assemble," Virgil continued. "Hoarders as well as wasters."

Both hoarders and wasters walked to Virgil, either from need of something different or from sheer curiosity.

"Listen to me, all you who are willing to hear the truth," Virgil shouted.

Through the fog, Virgil presented an eerie sight as he preached to the growing crowd. With his leather jacket and slicked back hair, I couldn't tell if he looked more evil or good, anymore than I could discern the nature of his message.

"All you hoarders and wasters, miserly and prodigal… You reside here merely because you accept it. If you have faith and if that faith is strong, forgiveness is yours. Then, you will discover the way out."

I watched the crowd as Virgil delivered his message in a warped version of Jesus' *sermon on the mount*. People from 1920's Chicago stood shoulder-to-shoulder with Muslims. Pirates clustered with pilgrims. Heavy metal rock stars leaned next to... Well, more heavy metal rock stars. Those who'd lived life too much gathered beside those who hadn't lived enough.

"Any one of you may walk out of here at any time, but you must accept the truth. You must know the truth about God, about yourself, and about your faith. For that, you must begin by answering one question— *who are you?*" Virgil continued.

The crowd remained silent for a moment, and finally, someone laughed. Another joined in and soon, everyone was laughing.

The only ones who didn't laugh were Virgil and me.

"There is no way out. This is Hell!" a waster yelled out. "Our fate is to be tortured for all eternity!"

"It's not *torture* that is your fate, but *torment*," Virgil said.

"What be the difference?" a Pilgrim hoarder hollered.

"In life, you each created your path, one that led directly to where you stand now," Virgil lectured.

"In life, our greatest sin was trying to have a good time," a waster called back. "Don't you want us to have fun?"

"I want you to experience *joy*," Virgil answered, "and true joy begins in knowing who you are."

"Damn Sam, you are one crazy dude!" another waster yelled out.

"It's never too late to repent," Virgil said.

"Repentance for what," the Pilgrim shouted back, "saving thy monies for a rainy day? If anyone needs forgiveness, it be them." He pointed to yet another heavy metal rocker.

"Why? Because we knew how to have a blast of a time? Party down, dude!"

"You be an abomination unto God," the Pilgrim said.

"You... Republican!" the rocker said, as if he was calling the Pilgrim gentleman a rapist murderer.

Plutus picked up a large stone and whipped it toward Virgil. I thought for sure it would hit him in the face, but Virgil plucked it from its path like Tye Cobb. It would be like someone nabbing a line drive bare-handed. It would have broken *my* hand, assuming my arm wasn't already in splints, but Virgil remained unharmed.

Shocked, the heavy metal guy backed up in fear as Virgil stepped down from the rock.

"Don't you understand?" Virgil said. "I speak the truth."

The pilgrim guy stepped back, accidentally bumping into a cowboy. The cowboy responded by shoving the pilgrim, and a group of pirates jumped on the pilgrims.

That was all she wrote. The fragile truce between the hoarders and wasters concluded and the fight re-commenced.

Suddenly, a horn sounded so loud that it would have restored hearing to the deaf, and then rendered them deaf again.

I looked up to see numerous horns positioned on tall poles. Each horn rotated atop its pole. I had no idea how or why.

What sort of joint is this, Joe? Whatever it is...could there be electricity?

The horns howled as if to announce, *time's up*.

"Hurry!" an Amish hoarder yelled. "Get back to thy places or the demons will come!"

Everyone desperately ran back to their boulders, pushing them into position for yet another round in their endless battle from a long ancient war.

঩ঌ

We walked in the opposite direction, abandoning the hoarders and wasters of money.

"Do you now see, Joseph?" Virgil said. "The truth means nothing to those who will *not* hear it."

"So, is it true?"

"What?"

"The only way out of Hell is to simply say who you are?"

"It's only the beginning."

"The beginning of what?"

"The one true path begins and ends by admitting what your heart already knows. So I ask you, Joseph. *Who* are you?"

"I don't understand."

"Who are you?" he repeated.

"I'm a cop."

"This is nothing more than a profession in life and one of days long past. You carry that trinket with you." He gestured at my badge. "For what purpose?"

"It's my badge."

"It means nothing here."

"It means something to me."

"So I ask again. *Who* are you?"

"I'm a good man," I said with conviction.

"Do you truly believe this?"

"Excuse me, man," a young fellow with long hair interrupted. Apparently, he'd followed us from the hoarders and wasters of money.

99

"Can I trouble you for—I mean to say…" He stumbled over his words, obviously nervous and afraid. "This is a bad trip, man," he said.

Virgil didn't answer.

"Dig?" the young man with long hair continued.

"You look familiar," I said.

Beneath the soil, I saw flowers printed on his shirt. That's when I recognized him. He was the *hippie* I'd encountered at Minos's palace, and I realized that he *wasn't* nervous or afraid. He was broken of spirit.

"San Francisco, right?" I asked.

He smiled sadly.

"Do you think it's possible—I mean, you see, man…" His chin began to quiver. "I don't want to be here. I just…need to hang somewhere else," he said as tears filled his eyes.

"Hey, kid," I said, "don't worry about a thing. You can come with us. Okay?"

The hippie weakly nodded. "Groovy," he said.

"Right, groovy," I said. "Whatever *that* means." I looked to a stone-faced Virgil. "Well, I guess somebody listened after all." I couldn't help myself from rubbing it in.

Virgil looked the hippie up and down. "He's not ready for the path ahead," he said.

"Well, ready or not, he's coming with us," I said, even surprising myself with my insistence.

CHAPTER 16
Canto VII – Circle IV – The Muddy Slope
❧❧

T he climb down this cliff was different. No more sheer cliffs or sandy hills. This one boasted a long, muddy slope. Not as hard to descend, but our trek seemed endless as we made our way down the gradual slope covered in dead plants and tree stumps.

Come to think of it, Joe, other than the land of the virtuous pagans, have you ever seen any living plants at all in this place?

As in the other levels, everything here was dead, but here, the tropical-type plants *looked* as if they had been alive at one time.

At least it was light again. If I'd seen a sun through the ever-present gray overcast, I'd have said it was bright enough to be high noon.

The sad hippie followed us down. His loneliness helped me overcome my initial dislike for him, so, as Virgil took the point, I slowed my pace to keep him company.

"I'm Joe Dante."

"Liberty. Liberty Sky," he said eagerly.

"Liberty Sky? Your parents named you *Liberty*, did they?"

"No man, I gave myself the handle. My parents named me *Hector*."

"What's wrong with *Hector*?"

"What's wrong with *Liberty Sky*?

"Well, I gotta tell you, I'm a little bit uncomfortable calling you *Liberty*, so how about I stick with *Hector*?" I said with a smile.

"Rad," he said.

"Rad?"

"Radical—cool. Dig, man?"

"Sorry."

101

"Understand?"

"Well, I understand *cool*, so that's something."

"Far out!" He smiled.

I could tell he was the type of kid who liked to laugh. When you're with someone like that, you can't help but smile back. Come to think of it, that was the first time I smiled out of genuine joy since I got here. "How did you die, Hector?" I asked.

"I burnt my card at a demonstration."

"Card?"

"Sure man, my draft card. I didn't want to fight for *the man*. Dig?"

"Well, sometimes we have to fight, don't you think?"

"That's cool. I'm no smack. I just want to believe in what I'm fighting for."

"Not to worry Hector, we saved Europe without you."

"Europe?"

"Yeah—the Germans, remember?"

"I'm talking about Vietnam, man."

Of course, this kid's from the future. What are you thinking, Joe? He's talking about a totally different war, some future war.

"Never heard of it," I admitted.

"You're lucky."

"Look, kid, you don't get to pick your war, but when you're called for duty, you step up to the plate."

"Fighting is all your generation knew, man. Mine wanted peace."

"My generation stood for something. What did yours stand for? Pacifism?"

"You don't know anything about me, man."

"I know you're a coward." I felt regret the moment the words came out, but the kid got me steamed.

My generation also had bleeding heart peace lovers. I'm all for peace, but you have to draw the line somewhere. If my generation felt the way he did, we'd all be speaking German, now. Hell, for all I knew, everyone in America now *was* speaking German.

"Don't you know that there's nothing finer than the American soldier," I said.

He looked at me as if I'd just graduated with an advanced degree from the laughing academy.

"What?" I asked.

"American soldiers were the ones who murdered me."

"That's got to be a mistake."

"It was the song that made me want to hang in San Francisco," he said. "To get there, I had to drive my van through Texas on the I-40—bad trip man. A couple of soldiers on leave saw my long hair and bell-bottoms, and took them as a personal invite to hassle me. I told them there was no way I was going to fight in a war where the soldiers burned babies, so they grabbed me in the night, and drove me to a field…where they hung me."

"I'm sorry, Hector. I don't know what to say."

"My father called me a coward, too. You remind me of him. He wasn't hip, either. I just wanted to live, dig, man? When I got here, I guess Minos thought that I wasted the chances I had in life, so he confined me to the fourth circle of Hell for all eternity."

"Minos is a schmuck," I said.

"I sure did dig that song," he said. "Are you going to San Francisco…" he sang. "Be sure to wear some flowers in your hair…if you're going to San Francisco…you're going to meet some gentle people there."

Hector slipped but I grabbed him before he fell into the mud.

"Whoa, I got you," I said. "You slip here and you'll be sliding down for a month." I smiled, trying to make up for my Italian/Irish temper.

The look on his face reminded me of my partner, Tony—young, innocent, and someone you could trust, but remembering Tony only served as a reminder that I *couldn't* trust anyone simply because they looked the part.

I didn't want to like the kid. I could read between the lines of his story. He was a peace-loving draft dodger who probably only thought of himself, at least in life. My smile faded. I guess Hector sensed my distrust, because he smiled back at me.

"What happened to your arm, man?" he said motioning to my splint. "Bad trip?"

"Oh this, well, I…" I stopped in mid-sentence, realizing I no longer felt any pain. "Huh, isn't that a screwball thing." I pulled off the splint to discover that my arm had completely healed. "Son of a gun," I said. "Not even a scar."

Not only that, but my sleeve was no longer ripped. Come to think of it, you might expect that swirling around in a giant tornado or pushing huge boulders up and down a hill would result in, at least, one torn pants. Yet, I saw none here.

Not only that, but I could see the flowers on Hector's shirt more clearly. The dirt was gone. He hadn't brushed it off, and safe to say, Hector didn't sneak off to a twenty-four hour laundry mat. The dirt, as a tear on clothing, had simply vanished.

I didn't realize that Virgil had stopped. Suddenly, we stood beside him and he was prone on the ground. His hand came up and yanked me down next to him. Hector looked around in confusion to spot what we would need to hide from, but Virgil's hand came up a second time to pull Hector down as well.

We slid into a small pit resembling a foxhole. There seemed to be a lot of those here.

"Silence." Virgil pointed beyond the edge of the mud.

I looked up to see a demon patrol in flight. High up and far away, they didn't look like Geryon's gang. These ships looked more like giant sleds.

"Not them," Virgil continued. "*Them*," he said, pointing to a muddy field at ground level.

I peeked over the edge to see a group of... I don't know what you'd call them. Then I thought about it and I knew exactly what they were. "Demons, right?" I whispered.

"Insect-caste." Virgil nodded.

They reminded me of giant cockroaches, but stood upright like men. The largest one looked to be over seven feet tall, not exactly something I could crush under my heel.

"The Malebranche," Virgil said, to educate us.

"What are they?"

"A group of demons who patrol the Malebolge in the eighth circle."

"Aren't we in the fourth circle?"

"We are."

"So why are they so far from home?"

"The one with the tail," Virgil began as he pointed, "Malacoda, the leader. A paralyzing stinger resides at the tip. Avoid it...and him."

Hector and I glanced at each other.

"No problem," we chorused.

"They don't belong here," Virgil continued.

"Looks like they're building something," Hector added.

He was right. They were sharpening sticks and placing them in a wooden box so that the sharp ends pointed to the center. It reminded me of a crude medieval wooden form of an *iron* maiden.

"For transport," Virgil said.

"Transporting what?" I asked.

Virgil didn't answer. So, I guessed.

"What? Me? What the devil did I do to them?"

"The Malebranche would only leave Malebolge for one reason. To find a fugitive."

"I liked this place so much more when I thought I wasn't dead," I said.

The Malebranche didn't move like men. They actually *did* move like insects by darting from one point to the next. It was pretty damned amazing to watch. One of them ripped a branch from a dead tree. Less than a second later, he was twenty feet away, positioning it so another of his crew could sharpen it. It was almost like he disappeared between point *A* and point *B*. The way they moved together brought one word to mind—*teamwork*.

"We'll have to take the long way around," I said.

"Four," Virgil said.

"What?"

"There's only four of them."

"So?"

"The Malebranche travel in groups of eleven. The others are here somewhere, patrolling the area. There is no *long way around*."

"You don't know that. The rest might be on vacation or something."

"They exist as a group, Joseph."

"Okay, so what do we do?"

"We wait," Virgil said.

"How long?"

"As long as they stay before us."

"That's your master plan?"

"Yes."

"Well, not for me."

"Don't you know who they were? God's elect. They're smart, fast, and have the patience of angels. So, we must have more."

"I'm not waiting around forever."

"You think as a living man, Joseph, not as an immortal."

"Immortal?"

I thought about that. I guess that's what I was. That's what we all were now. I finally understood what Virgil meant by time being *different* here. We were no longer ruled by the next meal, or when to sleep, or hitting the head, or having sex. We were ruled by our own stubbornness and impatience.

"Maybe," I said. "Maybe they'll give up and leave in an hour, or maybe they'll be there for the next hundred years, just waiting, assuming that we're the ones they're after."

"It doesn't matter who they're after," Virgil said. "If they see us, it is *us* they will pursue."

"*See* us?"

"Yes."

"Didn't you say that demons sense the world differently? What was it? Mechanical demons can only sense movement. Reptilian, light. And insect demons? Heat."

"This is pointless, Joseph."

"Is it?"

I looked around to see a group of dead trees in the distance.

"If I lit that forest on fire, you think they'd go for it?"

"Perhaps." Virgil looked toward the horizon. "But it's foolish to try."

"Maybe." I pulled out my trusty fireball gun and started to crawl out of the muddy foxhole.

"What are you planning?" Virgil demanded, annoyed.

"I'm going to low crawl up a bit and see if I can get a clear shot at those trees. If I can set them on fire, the heat will attract them and we can get the hell out of here," I said.

"This is foolhardy," he said.

"Hey, *foolhardy* is my middle name!" I looked at Hector. "Keep your head down," I said. "I wouldn't want you to lose your pacifist standing." I focused on Virgil's disapproving gaze. "Let's just hope that those things are dumber than I am."

As I crawled away from the hole, I heard Virgil's last comment.

"Unlikely," he said.

I kept my face in the muck as I crawled my way toward a small peak of mud. Again, I was reminded of the war. I'd spent the better part of two years with my face in that filth. We often say that war is Hell, but never in my wildest dreams did I think that *Hell* would remind me of the war.

I got into position and aimed my weapon. It powered up with a high pitched squeal. "Damn it!"

I'd forgotten about the sound the weapon made. I glanced over the

Malebranche, hoping that they were as deaf as real insects. My hopes were dashed, however, when they all paused to look in my direction.

They suddenly vanished, and then reappeared even closer to me. Instead of firing at the trees, I quickly devised a *plan B* and shot at them instead. I missed, not because of my aim, but because they darted away so fast, the fireball was no competition.

I raced back down the slope as the fireball exploded into the trees behind them. Virgil and Hector hopped out of the foxhole as I approached.

"Did the plan work, Joseph?" Virgil said sarcastically.

Three of the Malebranche darted our way and I fired again. This time, I blasted into the ground as near to them as I could. The subsequent explosion knocked the demons off their feet. Unfortunately, it knocked us down as well. The impact hit us with such force, we slid down the muddy hill with the speed of a roller coaster.

Six or eight more demons darted our way. I wasn't in any position to count exact numbers, but there were more than four, which meant that Virgil was right and all eleven of the Malebranche were there—damn, I hated the guy.

They were fast, but not fast enough to catch us as we continued to slide down the long muddy hill. I thought we might lose them, but their backs opened up and their wings emerged.

Of course, Joe, they're freakin' insects. What insect would be complete without the standard issued set of wings?

I lost sight of Virgil, and could barely see Hector rolling through the brush with two more demons pursuing him. I wanted to help, but didn't know what to do.

Still sliding, I rolled over onto my stomach and faced my pursuers. I put my shooter on automatic and shot up the entire area behind me. I thought if I could fill the air with enough fireballs, at least one of them would hit the bull's eye. Plus, the recoil acted like jet propulsion, making me slide through the slick mud even faster.

I was right. I hit two or three demons.

Malecoda reared his tail to come at me with his stinger. I knew that if he stabbed me with it, I'd be paralyzed. I just didn't know for how long. When I thought things couldn't get any worse, I looked behind me to see a wall of dead and leafless trees blocking my path and coming up fast.

I moved like a speeding car into a dead end. "Damn!" I rolled over onto my back, sat up, and blasted at the trees.

An explosion later and a path made itself clear. When I reached it, my feet hit the stumps and I flew into the air like a pop-up fly ball in Fenway Park. I landed on my gut, now facing away from Malecoda.

Malecoda closed in on me, and I spotted another demon carrying Hector away.

"Hector!" I shouted.

That demon's backside faced me, so I figured I could shoot and he wouldn't see it coming. I shot again on automatic, nailing him. He dropped Hector and I didn't know if I had done the right thing when he fell hundreds of feet below.

Finally, Malecoda caught up to me and I rolled just in time to dodge his tail. Malecoda whipped his tail around like a scorpion and I ducked it again. I shot at him, only to have him dodge the fireball.

I knew he'd keep swinging his tail over and over until he stung me, just as I knew I couldn't evade the giant bug forever.

A screwball thought entered my brain. So outlandish, it had to make sense somewhere. I just didn't know where.

As I expected, his tail came down again. This time, I grabbed it. My thought was to have him pull me up to him. The closer I was to him, the harder it would be for him to strike me, but instead of me going up to Malecoda, he came down to me.

I clutched his tail with one hand and tried to aim the weapon with the other, but Malecoda grabbed it. We wrestled in the mud as we slid headlong down to the next level. Malecoda forced my hand away from him, so every time I shot a fireball, it went everywhere except where I wanted.

If you only had another weapon, you could surprise him with it. Come on, Joe. Think! You big goof! The answer's in your other hand—use the tail.

Malecoda opened his powerful jaws that resembled those of—what else—an insect.

There's something primal about fearing insects, no matter how small. In human perception, there's no such thing as a *pretty* insect. Even butterflies, without their appealing and colorful wings, are pretty damn *ugly*.

I jammed Malecoda's stinger into his own neck.

I don't know if insects on Earth have the capacity to show *surprise*, but this one sure did. His grip on me loosened. I let him go, aware of his paralysis.

Just when I thought I could relax, I reached the conclusion of the roller coaster ride.

The muddy slope ended. I came to a sheer drop, which obviously led to the next level.

My initial belief that the slope was the path to the next level was obviously full of beans.

It came upon me so fast that I had little time to slow myself down, so I grabbed a vine and prayed it was well rooted enough to hold my weight. At least this way, it would keep me from falling like the dead weight I became with the last two cliffs.

I clung to the vine about twenty feet below the cliff's edge when I realized every cop's nightmare. I'd dropped my freakin' gun!

I saw it in a crevice by the overhang, where the muddy slope met the sheer drop. Even worse—it was close to the *temporarily* paralyzed Malecoda.

I slowly climbed the vine, hoping it wouldn't uproot at the worst possible moment, although that seemed to be the way things worked around here.

As I pulled myself closer, I heard Malecoda thrashing around, trying to regain power over his body. I could relate since my own body was failing me. Exhausted and beaten, I needed time to rest. I suppose even immortals experience physical limits.

I reached up to grab the ray gun, but couldn't stretch far enough.

Malecoda screeched in anger. He was probably frustrated that he couldn't move so easily, but the fact he could bellow such an unearthly sound meant the poison from his stinger was wearing off.

I saw, in the distance, several other Malebranche approaching. I realized then that Malecoda hadn't shrieked out of frustration, but had summoned reinforcements.

Desperate to get the ray gun, I pulled myself closer to the ledge. My fingertips barely brushed the edge of it. "Come on, come on!" I said, urging myself closer.

Malecoda suddenly sat up, startling the vinegar out of me. He wobbled, still affected by the poison. He lunged toward me like a drunken sailor looking for a brawl on a Saturday night shore leave.

I slipped from the vine, tumbling down the cliff and leaving the ray gun behind. Unfortunately, I didn't leave the Malebranche behind. They followed me down.

CHAPTER 17
Canto VII – Circle V – The Wrathful
❧❧

I lay sprawled on my back in the mud. The fall knocked the breath out of me, but I was amazed that *this* fall felt like a warm day at the beach compared to the last one. That is, until I saw the Malebranche fly down from above.

I staggered to my feet and ran. Correction! I stumbled like a one legged frog. I repeatedly fell, but kept dragging myself through the mud and unintentionally tumbled into a massive muddy ditch. I tried to get up again, but a hand covered my mouth and restrained me.

"Say nothing," Virgil ordered. "Don't move."

One of the Malebranche landed in the ditch, and scanned the area. When he looked in our direction, I thought for sure the jig was up. Instead of making a move, he screeched that God-awful sound, calling for his backup. My soul shuddered from that inhuman shriek.

The others arrived and Malecoda was thirsty for blood. It must have been a blow to his pride to have a mere human kick the snot out of him. Okay, so maybe I just got lucky.

I tried not to make any sudden movements and just kept my head down. Virgil was just as covered in mud as yours truly. The hot mud masked our body heat and the Malebranche couldn't attack what they couldn't see. To them, we were just a couple of piles of mud. They dashed about, obviously searching for us. They came up dry, which was the only thing in this place that *was* dry.

For the first time, I could see them up close without repercussion. They wouldn't win any beauty contests—that was for damn sure.

One of them resembled the offspring of a dog and a cockroach, if that sort of union were even possible. Another looked more like a ravenous boar, if a boar had been magically transformed halfway into a water bug. Still another resembled a dragonfly. One even boasted a curly beard where his chin would have been, if he had one. It wasn't made of hair, but more like the hard shell-like substance that crunches when you crush a roach under your heel.

All were ugly, but something about them was *elegant*. They moved with amazing swiftness and a singularity of purpose. Each acted more like a *part* rather than the *whole*. They were, as Virgil said, a choreographed *group*.

Their solidarity only seemed to be surpassed by their fierceness, the most ferocious being Malecoda himself. At long last, they flew away. I couldn't help but sigh with relief.

How did that joke go? I met a man in a bar who continually smashed his hand with a hammer. When I asked him why, he said *because it feels so good when I stop*. That was how I felt. I shouldn't feel this good, but the hammer was gone, at least for now, and I felt relieved.

I sat up as Virgil got to his feet. "Thanks," was all I could muster.

Virgil answered with a firm look.

I was stunned to see Hector sit up next to me, but more so, I was surprised to be happy to see him. "Are you okay?" I asked.

"Yeah man." He winced. "Guns are a bad trip, but groovy shot."

The ground was level, so it was easier to walk in a group than when we'd tried to traverse the slope. It was still muddy, but at least the sky was bright. Flies and insects infested the mud, but luckily, *these* were Earth-size insects. A stink rose up from the sticky mud as if the humidity had been this thick and unceasing for a thousand years.

"The wrathful and the sullen reside in this circle. All are brooding and angry bullies," Virgil said. "If you forget everything else, remember this— *always* remain on the path."

"Why?"

"Believe what I tell you, Joseph, for there are dangers off the path that you surely do not wish to confront."

"Oh really?" I said, amused.

I moved off the path, ready to stick a toe in the soft mud, but stopped short. The mud began to shift and move, taking on a life of its own as air bubbles pulsed to the surface. I pulled back my foot and back-peddled onto the path once again. "Okay, no problem," I said.

"Perhaps next time, you'll more readily believe."

"Yeah, next time."

This is it, Joe. Finally! This is the circle where Argenti is condemned. You're almost there, buddy boy. Hang on.

"Where's Argenti?" I knew I sounded like a broken record, but I didn't care.

"All we must do is follow the path. The River Styx flows on one side, the wrathful on the other," Virgil said. "We have done well, for if we came upon the far side of the river, we would be in need of the boatman, Phleygas, and he is *not* one you want to need."

We've done well? Yeah, Joe, you must have the luck of the Irish.

❧

We walked for a long time—me, the draft dodging hippie, and my mysterious guide.

Far off in the distance, I saw the River Styx, but it didn't concern me.

The path we walked was decorated with giant cages. They reminded me of bird cages, each suspended anywhere from eight to twenty feet above us. Each cage enclosed a person, and each cage was too short for its occupant to fully stand, yet too narrow to sit down.

Atop each cell was a pivot, which allowed them to slowly and relentlessly spin. It actually looked like a miracle of architecture.

Walking the path reminded me of walking down a prison hallway. The wrathful looked at us with anger and, well, *wrath*. Some screamed obscenities. I expected some to throw toilet paper or even their own feces at us, as in an Earthly prison, but there was no toilet paper, no feces, and no toilet. There was just one person per cage and room for little else.

"The wrathful stand above," Virgil said. "Bullies and thugs, in life, they tried to put their victims in a cage of fear and anguish. Now and forever, they will rot in those cages."

In my day, I'd seen a lot of bullies. In many ways, they were worse than murderers. A killer will take your life, but a bully can take just about everything else. They make you ashamed to even look in the mirror. They will humiliate you in front of loved ones, stealing their respect for you as well as the respect you need for yourself.

Loan sharks, leg-breakers, extortionists, and even dirty cops must have been here somewhere. I'm sure if I looked around enough, I'd find a few schmoes I'd arrested.

"If these are the wrathful, where are the sullen?" I asked.

Virgil didn't answer. Instead, he glanced up behind me. Before I turned around, I knew exactly who would be waiting for me.

Argenti! You got him, Joe. You got that son of a bitch!

He squatted in his cage, giving me the once over. He looked exactly as when I'd last seen him, except for one thing—a brand spanking new hunchback.

"Holy Christ!" Argenti said. "Dante?"

"Thought you could get away from me that easy?" I said.

"Why would I think a little thing like death would separate us?"

I stared at him, relishing the moment. He was wedged between an American Army Captain with a green beret and some Middle Eastern thug, complete with robe and head dress.

Something was missing, though. I couldn't put my finger on it.

"Does this quench your thirst for revenge?" Virgil interjected.

That was it. I didn't desire revenge, I wanted justice. How could this be justice?

"This is it?" I said. "This is all he gets? The cages don't even spin fast enough to make them dizzy. This isn't punishment. It's a rest stop!"

"Hell has places of unspeakable torment, places where flesh is torn from the bone because it's simply the job of a demon persecutor. But sometimes Hell is comprised of nothing more than tedium. This is Hell, Joseph—*his* Hell."

"And I'm telling you, it's not enough! He shouldn't be here."

"Where should he be? What could be enough to satisfy the hate in your heart?"

I thought about it for a moment. It was obvious that Minos was soft on criminals. The big creep was probably a Democrat, so I would have to do *his* job for him. The punishment must fit the crime. For someone who liked to set people on fire, *this* sentence fit like a blanket too small to even cover his face.

Think, Joe. What would be poetic justice for this scum? He should burn for all eternity. Burn? That's it! Argenti likes to set people on fire. He should burn!

"You know this place," I said to Virgil. "There's a lake of fire around here somewhere, right?"

Virgil didn't answer.

"Well?" I prodded.

"Yes."

"Then *that's* where he should be."

"Remember our pact, Joseph," Virgil said sternly. "I have brought you to Filippo Argenti. The time has come to follow the path with me."

"You said I'd be satisfied at Argenti's punishment. I most certainly am *not!*"

"No matter," Virgil said. "We are to leave this place *now.*"

"No!" I yelled.

Virgil stared at me in anger but did nothing else, and that's when I realized something I should have known all along. He didn't force me or push me or whisk me off to places unknown. It wasn't because he respected my wishes. It was because he *couldn't.*

"You can't make me," I said. "I've seen you push around creatures twice my size, but not once have I seen you force a regular Joe into anything. You can't, can you? You can't *make* me do anything."

"Hell's forge created these cages," Virgil said, side-stepping my question. "No door to open, and no lock to pick. It is merely one solid piece of metal. Many men of far greater strength than you have tried to escape their cells, but none have succeeded."

I looked up at the cages realizing that Virgil was right. Not only was Argenti's pen about ten feet overhead, but there was absolutely no point of entry. It was like the cage had been forged around him.

The pole that suspended Argenti's cage was made of thick solid metal, not easily dug up or hacked away. Even if I'd been able to chop down the pole, what then? Would I drag his entire cage to the lake of fire, wherever *that* was?

I loved Bea and my girls too much to let Argenti get off scot free, but how could I find true justice for them?

"Dante, you didn't come all this way just to give up, did you?" Argenti mocked.

"Shut your yap!" I yelled.

114

"Or what? You're going to find a step ladder, come up here, and give me a stern talking to?" Argenti laughed as he swung his cage back and forth. "Weeeeeeee…"

"You sorry waste of skin, if I had my gat, I'd shoot you right here."

Shoot? The blaster! You need that darned ray gun you dropped by the cliff. Good thinking, Joe.

I looked at Virgil. "The heater."

"What of it?" Virgil asked.

"I left it on the cliff's edge. If the Malebranche have gone, it should be easy to get… Well, *easier.*"

"And if the demons haven't left?"

"I already know how to evade them. Just cover myself in that hot mud."

"Be heedful Joseph, for the Malebranch are not to be trifled with."

"Hey, I'm thinking like an immortal with nothing but time on my hands. I'll still get Argenti. It will just take some time. You should be proud of me."

"Amazingly, I am not," Virgil said.

"I get it. If I go, I go alone."

"Yes."

"Swell," I said.

"I'll hang with you, man," Hector chimed in. "I want to."

"It's better if you don't." I put my hand on his shoulder. "I can make it there and back much faster without you, but I do thank you, Hector."

I looked up at Argenti and smirked. "And *you* don't go anywhere."

"Oh, that's funny. You're a funny guy," Argenti said as I walked away. "You ought to take it on the road with Hope and Crosby."

"Joseph," Virgil called.

"Yeah?"

"Never forget—always remain on the path."

❧

I didn't actually think it would go faster if I went alone, but I wanted to go by myself just the same.

I needed time to myself.

I knew he was just a kid, but I didn't think much of Hector. He'd been a draft dodger, after all.

When we joined the war against the Germans, none of my buddies needed to be dragged into the service. We were all ready and willing.

Still, Hector *did* offer to help me. I guess that took a certain amount of guts.

And Virgil? What about him? The guy was a hard nut to crack. I'd walked with him for God only knew how long, and I *still* barely knew anything about him.

There were really two questions I needed answered about Virgil— *what had he done to land in Hell,* and *why was he helping me?* I figured with those answers, I could nose out the rest of the puzzle pieces. Unfortunately, there was no way I was going to figure it out on my own. He could have been a petty thief from the 1840s, or a British sovereign from the Middle Ages, assuming that Brit accent was even legit.

So, I let my mind, as well as my body, take a vacation from my traveling companions and allowed my thoughts to slip to Bea and my girls.

I toyed with the bracelet around my wrist and thought back to when Anna had given it to me.

The ever present feeling of loss nagged at me. That night on the roof tore through my very soul.

↬↬

I reached the base of the muddy cliff and looked up. It wasn't logical, but I still hoped it would be a shorter trip *up* than *down*.

I grabbed a fistful of mud and tried to climb, but slid back down. I tried again, this time with a running jump and tried to get some footing, but I got nowhere fast. I hadn't come all this way just to give up, but as I was thinking of possible alternate routes, the strangest thing happened.

A *rope* uncoiled from above. "What the..." I looked up, but saw nothing except the smooth walls of mud. "Hello?" I called out. No one answered.

What the hell is going on, Joe? Did you get lucky, or is someone trying to pull a fast one?

I tugged at my end of the rope to test it. It seemed to have been tied off up at the top of the cliff somewhere. It was strong enough to hold me and the rope was knotted, so the climb up would be a pillow walk now.

116

The phrase *he who hesitates is lost* came to mind, so I latched onto the rope and began to haul myself up.

Yet again, two questions popped into my head—*who threw the rope* and *was it a trap?*

"Who's up there?" I yelled angrily.

Again, no answer. Perhaps the person who tossed me the rope was too far up to hear me.

So, I climbed as if the rope came from an ally, rather than an adversary.

෪ලා

It took a while to reach the top, but I dread to think how long it would have taken without the rope.

I reached up over the lip of the cliff as cautiously as I would have entered a reported B&E location at 2:00 A.M.

I peered over the edge and saw the rope had been secured around the base of a dead tree. Next to it, I saw the ray gun. Definitely not where I had dropped it.

Someone must have found it and placed it there.

I low-crawled to the lifeless tree, feeling a sense of safety when I grabbed the heater from the future. My good feelings quickly diminished when I heard the shriek of one of the Malebranche.

I quickly hid behind the tree, frantically rolling in the mud to mask any body heat they might have sensed.

I got what I came for, so I low-crawled back toward the cliff's edge. But, I stopped dead when I heard the cry of a woman.

Still in the mud, I peeked from behind a tree to see two of the Malebranche manhandling a young woman.

"Please," she cried, but to no avail.

There was something *odd* about her. From my vantage point, she seemed twisted or deformed. I didn't know if she'd thrown me the rope. The *cop* in me not only didn't want to leave her alone, but wanted to investigate the situation.

Maybe my initial problem with the Malebranche was that I thought of them as giant cockroaches. Insect drones doing the bidding of Malecoda, yet another insect. This time, though, I would think of them as a gang from south Boston, harassing a poor innocent woman on her way home from the market.

I knew this woman must have been in Hell for a reason, but thinking of her as a victim somehow made it easier for me not to forsake her.

Three of the Malebranche swooped down with the *wooden* iron-maiden box they had constructed, and I realized that they weren't here because of me at all. They were here because of her.

They opened the box full of sharpened spikes and she screamed in horror at the sight. One Malebranche wrapped himself around her and, with his claws, dragged the box toward them and forced her in.

I needed to act and fast. Once they got her in the box, they would probably fly away with it. I knew that if I powered up the gun, it would wail and alert them to my presence, so I had to think of something.

Covered in mud and hopefully invisible to their eyes, I stood up just as they shoved her into the box and slammed it shut. I powered up the gun and waited. They all looked my way, as I guessed they would.

They knew the sound was coming from the area of the dead tree, so shooting *at* them would only reveal my position.

I blasted a dead tree near me. It burst into flames, producing, thankfully, the heat that seemed to attract the Malebranche. As I hoped, the Malebranche flew by me and surrounded the tree. With their backs to me, I ran to the abandoned *wooden*-maiden. I knew I didn't have much time to execute my plan, so as quickly and quietly as possible, I forced the lid open. It was more than a make-shift iron maiden. It resembled a coffin.

The girl looked up at me, bleeding from wounds made by the sharpened points that kept her in place. "Oh God, please help me!" she cried.

"Shhhh! We don't have much time," I said. "I'll help you, but you have to be quiet, okay?"

She nodded frantically.

She looked familiar, but from where didn't immediately occur to me, plus there was something strange about her body. She was extremely flat-chested, and when I pulled her out, I noticed her arms and legs didn't bend the right way.

I didn't have time to discuss the matter. Instead, I grabbed fistfuls of mud and hurled it into the box. "Help me," I said. I quickly dug up anything I could find and threw it in the coffin. "What are you waiting for?" I whispered. "Help."

She grabbed handfuls of mud and threw it into the box.

I finally realized why she didn't look *right*. Her head was twisted around, back to front. Either that or her body was on backwards. "My God," I said, stunned. "What happened to you?"

My shock dissolved when I saw the Malebranche coming our way. "Get into the mud, quickly!"

"What?"

"Do it!"

As she burrowed into the mud, I closed the lid of the wooden crate and hoped the weight of the mud I'd thrown in was somewhere near that of the girl.

The demons swarmed about us and the box.

We stayed low in the mud, frozen in place like a block of icy steel.

The girl looked terrified, so I wrapped my arm around her and put my finger to my lips to make sure she knew not to make any sounds...not that it needed to be *said*.

Finally, two of the Malebranche picked up the box and flew off, followed by the others.

We sat up from the mud.

"I can't thank you enough," she said in a combination of smiles and tears. "You're like, my very own angel."

I wiped the mud from my face. Before I could say that she looked familiar to me, she beat me to the punch.

"Do I know you?" she asked.

Without a thought, I wiped the mud from her face, knowing it wouldn't be so easy for her, her arms being on backwards and all.

I finally saw her face clearly—clearly enough to know that she was the young beatnik palm reader I'd met that day in Boston Common... the day I tried to...well...the day I thought about eating a bullet. "Tonya Tiresias," I said, "TT for short."

"That's right," she said, trying to place me. She clumsily took my hand, to study my palm. "I remember the life line." She thought for a moment and then met my gaze. "But not your name," she sadly smiled. "I'm sorry."

I understood. My encounter with her obviously had more of an impact on me than her. Plus, in her defense, I don't even remember if I ever told her my name.

"Joe Dante," I said, forcing a smile.

She was older now, maybe in her late-thirties. No longer the young tomboy I'd met so long ago, but now very feminine, with big poofy hair styled as though it was from the 1950s, a very short skirt, and shoes that matched.

To see her body so twisted touched me in a way like nothing else had since I'd landed here. I felt so sorry for her, I was overwhelmed by grief. I held her as she cried.

CHAPTER 18
Canto VII – Circle V – Phleygas and the River Styx
ఌ

Maybe it was because she was the most tragic figure I'd seen here so far, or because she seemed so fragile, but I felt a sort of kindred spirit in Tonya. As we walked toward the wrathful and the sullen, I noticed how gracefully she moved. She really had walking backwards down to an art.

"How do you do that?" I inquired.

"What?"

"Walk backwards with the poise of a ballerina?"

"I've been doing it so long, I barely notice it now. My arms make things rather awkward. Have you ever tried picking something up from behind?"

"How did you die?"

She didn't answer.

"I'm sorry," I said.

"It's okay."

"If it's too personal…"

"It's okay, Joe." She smiled. "I'd just moved to California. I heard of a new business and wanted to get in on the ground floor. It was called *The Psychic Hotline*. Instead of people calling those nine hundred numbers for sex, they called in for a reading. It was really a wonderful concept. I'd be able to use my power to help people on a massive scale. My first night there, I was murdered by my ex-husband. I didn't know he'd moved to LA after our very ugly divorce. Before he killed me, he said that if I was *really* psychic, I should have seen it coming."

I tried not to laugh. At first, I held it in, but like holding sand in the palm of your hand, some grains slipped through.

"What?" she asked.

"Nothing!" I couldn't hold it in anymore and I laughed openly. Maybe I just needed to and she happened to be there at the time, but it came on like gang busters.

"It's not funny!"

"I know!" I stifled my laugh, but again, it burst through.

Tonya snickered. "I guess it's a little funny," she said.

"Yes, it is."

We both laughed.

Our laughter eventually died down. Amusement here would be impossible to maintain longer than a few seconds.

"By the way, what's a nine hundred number?"

"That was in the mid-eighties," she said.

"Mid-eighties? Have I been here *that* long?"

"Longer, since I've been here for longer than I can remember."

"Really? It doesn't seem that long to me."

"To me, it seems like forever," she said.

Maybe that's what Virgil meant by time being different here, Joe. Maybe he meant it was different for each individual.

TT looked to be in her thirties, which made sense if she'd died almost twenty five years after me. As with the dirt from Hector's shirt, the mud had faded from her dress. I quickly noticed that she dressed more like a teenager than an adult…although not a teenager from *my* time.

"Is this the way women dressed in the 1980s?"

"Oh yes," she said. "It's totally awesome."

"Awesome?"

"Teenage '80s slang," she said with a smile. "*Living large, narley, to the max, totally tubular, make me barf.*"

"Let me guess," I said. "This place would *make me barf.*"

"Damn Sam, now you're chillin' with the homeys!" she said mimicking the lingo of her time.

"So, did we win the war?"

"War?"

"Yeah, what was it called? Vietnam?"

"Well, that wasn't really a war, but no. No one won that war."

"Too bad," I said.

"By the time we reached the eighties, a lot of people thought it was a mistake. It got so that we were ashamed to be American. President Reagan changed all that. Within a week of Ronald Reagan's inauguration, the Iranians let all those American hostages go, and with the introduction of aerobics, big hair, Madonna, spandex, Reaganomics and Star Wars, we were proud to be Americans again. And the music? The heavy metal bands of the late '70s became like gods in the '80s!"

"Heavy metal? You mean as in Plutus Kisma?" I asked, recalling the heavy metal rock and roll guy condemned to languish with the hoarders of money.

"Oh my God! I love *The Poisonous Vixens!*" she said. "I want to rock and roll all night…and party every day," she sang.

"That wasn't them."

"No, I'm pretty sure it was."

"Nope…that was *Kiss*," I said, repeating what I'd heard on the fourth circle, but having no direct knowledge, and from what I could gather—thank God!

"Oh yeah…you're right. I love those guys, too," she said. "Anyway… Unfortunately, the eighties also brought AIDS."

"AIDS?"

"A horrible disease. In my time, there was no cure. If you got it, you died, and it looked like millions had it. Some called it the *wrath of God*. I don't know, maybe they were right."

Most of what she said went right over my noodle, but one name did sound familiar.

"Ronald Reagan," I said, "Funny, I seem to remember an actor by that name."

TT stopped in her tracks.

"What's the matter?" I asked.

"I shouldn't be going with you," she said. "I'm a fugitive, you see."

"What? You think I'm afraid of those bugs? Are you kidding? A jar of roach powder and a rolled-up newspaper are all I'll need." I wanted her to feel safe.

"It's not that."

"Then what?"

"Minos condemned me to the eighth circle of Hell, in the fourth bolgia of Malebolge for false prophets, astrologers, and magicians."

"Is that where they did *that* to you?" I asked, referring to her twisted neck.

"Yes, Minos said that, because we pretended to see the future, we would spend eternity unable to even see where we're walking."

"Is that what they call *irony*?"

"In my case, it's called a mistake. I never *pretended* anything. Some people really do have the gift. So, I escaped and the Malebranche have been after me ever since. I mean… Is it a sin if I used the gift that God gave me?"

"Well, your gift certainly helped me. I don't know how you knew I was at the bottom of the hill, but that rope came down at the perfect time."

"Right. The rope."

"Where did you find it, anyway?"

"What?" she said confused.

"The rope. Where did you find a rope that long?" I repeated.

"Well, if you look hard enough, you can find anything here, even a way back to Minos, which is why I'm going up. Once he hears my case again, I know he'll release me." She backed up, but for her, she walked forward. "So, I want to thank you, Joe Dante, but I have to go."

"Wait. Don't go." I took her arm. "Come with me—just for a while. Consider it a vacation from your journey."

"You're going down, Joe. I've been there. Trust me, no matter how bad you think it is, the lower you go, the worse it gets. You don't want to go down there alone."

"I'm not by myself."

"You have friends here?"

"Well, *friends* is a relative term," I said with a smile, "but it beats being alone." I didn't realize it until I said it, but it was true. Maybe I didn't trust Virgil or respect Hector, but at least they were company. "Maybe that's a big part of being in Hell, Tonya—being alone. Come with me. Keep *me* company, just for a while."

Like I said, maybe it was because she was the first good person I'd met here whom I'd actually known in life, but I didn't want to let her go, not yet anyway.

She smiled slowly. "Okay."

We looked across the horizon as we walked along the river's edge. Every hundred feet or so stood a fifteen foot pole, and on top, an unlighted torch.

"Do you know where we are?" TT said.

"Of course I do," I said. "We're totally and absolutely lost."

"I'm going back. I can be lost on a higher circle."

"No, wait." I squatted by the river and tried to look to the other side. About halfway across was a dense fog. There hadn't been any fog when we'd walked on the path of the wrathful, and I realized the problem. "We're on the wrong side," I announced.

"We can't cross the river. The water here is—"

"I know," I quickly responded, remembering the last time I'd stuck my hand in water. I'd have been better off just plugging my finger into a light socket.

"So, what do we do?"

"The boatman!" I said.

"What?"

"Virgil mentioned a boatman who crosses the River Styx. What was his name? *Phleygas!* That's it."

"This *Virgil* is your friend?" TT asked.

"Friend? Sure, why not?"

"What did he say about the boatman? Is he friendly?"

I didn't answer.

"Yeah, I think my *vacation* is over, Joe, so I'll be going now."

"Wait! TT, don't go." I placed my hands on her shoulders. "Look, nobody knows anything, but I really think you'd be better off with us, at least for now."

TT looked down, indecisive.

"Please?" I added.

"Well, how do we get across the river?"

"That's what these poles must be for. I bet if we light one of them, this Phleygas guy will come."

"Do you have a working match, Joe?"

"That's cute—very funny."

I ran my hand up and down one of the poles. Sure enough, I found a switch.

"Well, here goes nothing." I flipped the switch.

Just as I'd hoped, the torch atop of the pole lit up.

"Cool…now what?" TT asked.

"Now, we wait."

❧

Through the fog, the boatman came. Phleygas guided a large flat raft by sticking a long pole in the river, pushing it forward.

Both TT and I watched as he drew closer.

Frightened, TT backed up.

Phleygas, an imposing figure, towered to the height of seven feet tall with torn flesh and exposed bones.

"I'm not sure this is such a good idea, Joe." She shuttered at the distant sight of Phleygas's rotting face.

"So what would a 1980's teenager say right about now?" I said.

"Gag me with a spoon."

"Amen."

"I wonder if I can outrun him, running backwards."

"I've got an idea," I said. "Can you act scared?"

"I don't think that's going to be a problem, Joe," she said.

"I mean scared of *me*."

Phleygas pushed his raft ashore and coldly stared at us, an easy task since he lacked eyelids.

"Well now, I see two souls plum for the plucking," he bellowed in a strong and angry voice.

"Sorry to spoil your day, pal," I said, flashing my badge. "I'm taking this prisoner back to the eighth circle, fifth bolgia."

"Fourth," TT whispered.

"Fourth bolgia. I said *fourth*, damn it!" I added with force.

"I will take pleasure in your pain when I chain both of you to the bottom of my river!" he said.

"Oh yeah? Swell. When Malecoda comes looking for us, be sure to mention that's what you did."

"Malecoda?" he asked, with ever so slight jitters. So I jumped on the opportunity.

"Yeah, you know him, don't you? Big cockroach, six arms, or legs, depending on your point of view. With ten others in his crew. You want to steam *his* potatoes? Good luck to *you*." I yelled.

Phleygas didn't answer.

"Not so tough now, huh?" I said as we stepped onto the raft. "Now take us to the wrathful, dick-weed!"

Without a word, Phleygas pushed off. We drifted toward the far side of the river.

TT didn't say a word. Instead, she hid behind me as I glared at Phleygas.

"It's not fair to get into a staring contest with someone who has eyelids," I said, trying to sound fearless.

"The Malebranche never employ human souls to do their bidding," he said through gritted teeth, though they might have just *seemed* gritted, since he also had no lips.

"Really. I guess they didn't get that memo, since they did, in fact, hire me—Flatulence."

"Phleygas!"

"Whatever you say."

"I don't believe you," he said.

I slowly reach behind me to where my ray gun fit snugly in the waistband of my trousers. "You really want to chance it—Fatgas?" I said with an evil grin.

I purposely kept getting his name wrong. It's an old police tactic. The thought behind it is to keep the suspect too emotionally off balance to do anything against you.

Phleygas didn't answer.

"Get us close to the path," I ordered.

CHAPTER 19
Canto VIII – Circle V – The Sullen
❧

We returned to the wrathful to see that little had changed.

"You're back? Far out!" Hector said.

"Didn't think I'd make it?"

"No way, man. It never crossed my mind that the Malebranche would have had you like a brisket," Hector said with a smile.

I looked at Virgil, who as always threw me a disapproving glance.

"Come on!" I said. "You have to be a little impressed."

"Perhaps," Virgil said.

"What's that?"

"What?"

"Was that a smile?" I said.

"No," Virgil said.

"Are you sure, because I could have sworn I saw a smile."

"I'm merely amazed that you've returned with all of your limbs. However, I suppose someone with lesser intelligence could confuse the two."

Argenti and the other wrathful looked down at us.

"Holy Christmas," Argenti said looking at TT. "What the devil happened to your girlfriend? A train wreck?"

I didn't answer. Instead, I pulled out the weapon I'd gone through great pains to reclaim, and showed it to him. "You know what this is, Argenti?" I turned the blaster's switch selector to *semi*. "A key to a cage with no door."

"This won't work," Virgil interrupted.

128

"How do you know?"

"Believe what I tell you, Joseph. I know this to be true."

"You might have mentioned that *before* I took the long walk back."

"Would you have believed me then?"

"I don't believe you *now*."

"Is that right?"

"Yeah, you don't know everything," I said. "The Malebranche weren't after me at all. They were after her." I pointed at TT, who smiled, apparently embarrassed by the notoriety.

"Then turning that weapon on may alert them to her presence, will it not?" Virgil asked.

Didn't think of that one, did you Joe?

"Not a chance," I said, trying to cover. "They're miles away by now. Probably well beyond the seventh circle."

"Perhaps. And as you Americans say, *for the record*, not once did I indicate that the Malebranche were after you," Virgil said, just having to get in his licks.

He was right, though. He never actually said those demons were after me, and if I powered up the gun again, the loud squeal could actually give us away. They might have stopped their transport to double check on the wooden maiden by now, and discovered nothing but rocks and mud inside. If they were searching anywhere nearby, they'd recognize the sound of the gun powering up.

So, I had a tough choice to make.

I glanced at TT to see her looking back, worried. I didn't want to endanger her and for the first time, I actually considered just walking away.

So what if you leave Argenti here, all hunched over in a cage just small enough to guarantee an eternity of only discomfort? Would the universe explode?

I peered up at his smirking face. All I could do was remember the sight of him in that courtroom, the day he walked free…the smug SOB.

The answer struck me like an electric charge. I didn't want him just *uncomfortable*. I wanted him in pain. *That* was the only way in which justice would be served.

The high pitched squeal whined as I powered up the weapon.

I smiled as Argenti nervously looked around.

"What are you planning to do with that thing?" He squirmed in his suspended cage like an oiled-up worm on a greasy hook.

He looked as worried as the soldier and the Arab squatting on either side of him.

"You just make sure you aim that thing at *him*, son," the American Captain with the green beret said in a southern accent as he pointed to Argenti. "I don't need to be an *accidental casualty*."

Virgil looked at me, and I saw his disappointment. I don't know why, but I felt like I'd let him down. Plus, I felt bad for exposing TT, but I would have felt worse if I'd walked away and left Argenti to gloat for all eternity.

The fireball blasted from the barrel and hit Argenti's spinning cage. Instead of blowing a hole in it, it ricocheted off the bars and burst into a score of smaller fireballs. They went off in a variety of directions and some went through the bars to hit several other wrathful.

Those of us not in cages hit the dirt. Those in the cages screamed.

"What the hell!" a mobster yelled.

A Japanese ninja shouted what I could only guess to be the exact thing the mob guy had yelled, except in Japanese.

I knew there had to be some way to release Argenti. I just had to think of it.

"Christ, Dante!" Argenti screamed. "You're not cashing in your chips already, are you?"

I thought for a moment, and then studied the wall of rock behind and above the cages. "No, I'm not." I switched the weapon to *auto*, allowing it to power up again.

"What are you doing, man?" Hector yelled over the whining weapon.

"I didn't come all this way for peanuts," I shouted back.

I let the weapon squeal, but this time, I waited. The squeal grew louder and louder. It became so loud, my head started to hurt and some of the wrathful covered their ears. "Hector, get Tonya to some cover," I ordered.

"Joe?" TT looked at me with concern.

"It will be okay, just go with him."

Hector took Tonya's arm, but Virgil stopped them.

"No! Stay on the path. Get behind those rocks," Virgil said as he pointed.

I feared I'd bitten off more than I could chew when the gun began to tremble in my hand. The *tremble* became a vibration, then a violent shaking. "You may want to take cover, too," I yelled over the high pitched whine to Virgil.

Virgil remained unaffected by the loud piercing shriek. He didn't budge. Instead, he eyeballed me like a parent would a child who was afraid of the monster in his closet.

I got onto one knee and aimed the weapon as best I could with the violent thrashing. There was nowhere for Argenti to hide as I pointed the gun in his direction. Son of a bitch killed my family, and he was going to pay for it the right way. Justice *would* be served. I finally pulled the trigger and a violent multiple burst of fireballs screamed out of the barrel. The recoil threw me to my backside.

The fireballs went every which way, exploding into the walls of rock behind the cages. Giant rocks rained down on the cages, smashing into a group of cages, just as I'd hoped.

Two cages came crashing down, one of them Argenti's.

The concussion knocked me down, but Virgil, yet again, remained untouched and unaffected.

Argenti dug his way out of the rocks and wreckage of his cage. I was surprised to see him stop to help the occupant of the other fallen cage, the American Army Captain.

As I got to my feet, he stretched as if he hadn't stretched in decades, which he probably hadn't.

Both Argenti and the Captain had hunched postures, from being forced into a cage too short for them.

"Damn, Dante," Argenti said, "you are one crazy cat!" He stretched again and moaned in pleasure. It made me sick to think that anything I'd done would give this mug any pleasure. "Well, I have to thank you for that *crazy* gene you obviously have. Now that I'm free... It's time I take it on the road." He tried to walk away.

"I'm as crazy as you are stupid, if you think I'm letting you go." I grabbed him by the collar. "Amnesty's over, jerk-off. You're taking a little swim into a big lake of fire."

"I'm not going anywhere with you." He shoved my arm away.

"Oh yes you are! You're going to pay for killing my family!"

"You're such a nosebleed, Dante! I didn't kill anyone."

"And I'm the Pope," I said.

"Well, look around, *Your Holiness*. This is the *wrathful*. You think there was a clerical error and I ended up here by accident?"

"Hey! If *I'm* here, mistakes are made," I said.

"I didn't kill your family!" he yelled. "A cop did!"

"What?"

"That's right, a cop on the force," he said. "This is something you don't want to hear, Dante."

"If you're talking about my partner, we got that son of a bitch," I said, still peeved at Tony. "Now, it's your turn."

"I'm not talking about him. I'm talking about the other one, the one with the scar under his eye."

The second he mentioned the scar, my heart sank. How low must this mutt be to implicate my own brother? "Mickey?"

"He's the one who switched the cases that night before the trial. He and your partner betrayed you. They were behind everything—the drugs, the killings, everything! They'd been doing it for years. I was just the front-man."

"That's my brother you're talking about!"

"I know."

"You're lying, you son of a bitch!" I shoved Argenti into the rocks, "I'll kill you. I'll kill you!" I shook him, but Argenti replied with a bitter laugh.

"Kill me? We're in Hell!" he screamed. "Don't you get it? In Hell! I can't die. We're already dead. All of us!"

"Not all of us. Not Mickey."

"You stubborn son of a bitch—you can't even see what's in front of you."

"What's that supposed to mean?"

Argenti focused on the American Captain, who now sat on the pile of rocks from the blast.

"You see him? Captain Jason Richards. He died in a place called Vietnam."

"So?"

"We went to war with a small country in Asia."

"Yeah, I know all about it. So what?"

"Actually, it wasn't a *war*," Captain Richards interrupted as he hopped down from the rocks. "It was more of a police action."

All the wrathful in the area moaned.

"Not again," a mob guy in a pin stripe suit groaned.

"Well, it's a fact! Damn politicians," the Captain said. "Don't know how to fight a war. We would take two weeks to take a hill at the expense of a hundred men, only to surrender it the next day because some politician wanted to look good on the six o'clock news. It wasn't *my* fault! You can't fight a decent war when our politicians are in bed with the enemy!"

"He was shot in the back by his own men," Argenti said. "Ain't that a kick in the head?"

"They call it *fragging*. I call it *cowardliness*. They had no right to shoot me. It wasn't my fault!" Captain Richards repeated in anger.

"Do we have to hear this every bleedin' time you open your mouth, mate?" a red coat yelled from his cage.

"But it wasn't my fault!" Captain Richards repeated, as if he'd said it a thousand times before.

"Excuse me! I still don't see what this has to do with me," I said, bringing the focus back to *my* story.

"He died in 1971, Dante, ten years after us." Argenti said.

I'd already met people from the future. TT and Hector were two of them. So I didn't see Argenti's point.

"Where are you going with this, Argenti?" I asked.

"The point is, you've been in Hell for years. So, either your brother is celebrating a hundred years of being a dink, or he's down here somewhere," Argenti explained. "Unless, of course, he found Jesus."

"Bologna, no way Mickey's down here," I said.

"You're here."

"Yeah, because of you!"

"Now *that's* bologna."

"I've heard enough. You're coming with me."

"I'm not going anywhere with you!"

I grabbed Argenti, and he jumped on me. We rolled into the mud and off the main path that Virgil held so dear.

"Remain on the path!" Virgil commanded.

We kept rolling in the thick mud, trying to overcome one another. With all the yelling and cheering from our captive audience, I felt like a pit bull trying to get the better of his opponent before having his throat ripped out.

"We have to get on the path!" Argenti shouted.

"Kiss off." I nailed him with a right cross.

Captain Richards ran into the mud as well. He'd probably just had enough and wanted to escape our private little *police action*. Argenti and I stopped our brawl when we saw a hundred hands emerge from the mud and pull the Captain down. It looked like quicksand mixed with human beings.

I was on top of Argenti, so he was the first to get the same treatment. Hands popped up from the muck and wrapped around his chest and waist.

"Damn!" I said as I got up to run back to the path, but hands grabbed my legs before I could get very far. They pulled me down waist deep in the mud while I was still within striking distance of Argenti. I struggled and hit those I could see. The problem was I couldn't see anyone's face, only their arms.

Suddenly a long metal bar from one of the freshly demolished cages appeared in front of me. I looked up to see Virgil holding it out to me. I grabbed it and Virgil pulled.

"Wait," I yelled, reaching for Argenti. "Take my hand, you son of a bitch!" He wasn't getting away from me now! Looking back at Argenti, I saw that the hands had pulled him down chest-deep in the filth. He forced one arm out of the mud and reached for me. "Stretch it!" I hollered.

Argenti stretched farther, grabbed my hand.

Both Virgil and Hector pulled. A long arm reached up and hooked itself around my neck, clinging to me and Argenti as if they gave out prizes for those who could hang on the longest.

I bit the weasel's hand. He finally let go, and Virgil and Hector pulled us free of the mud.

Argenti and I fell to our knees and coughed up mud.

"In case you were wondering, *those* are the sullen," Virgil said.

"Beautiful—just beautiful," I gagged out.

I looked up to see dots in the sky. The dots became larger. I didn't have to count them to know that there would be eleven.

Malecoda and the Malebranche had returned.

CHAPTER 20
Canto VIII – Circle V – The Mud
❦

Argenti and I didn't even have enough time to pick the mud from our teeth. Those demons must have heard me squirting out those fireballs from the ray gun. Okay, I admit it, it was my fault.

"The Malebranche has returned," Virgil said. Even when he didn't sound smug, he was.

"Don't you ever get sick of being right?" Before Virgil could reply, a frightened TT reacted.

"No. No!" she screamed.

My concern centered on TT, not Argenti. She was in this situation because of me. I'd asked her to come with me and I'd ignored Virgil's warnings about the possibility of the Malebranche returning.

Last time, we'd escaped these heat seeking demons by covering ourselves in the mud. Now, the mud was infested with multitudes of sullen sinners, just waiting for us to join them…forever. Talk about being trapped between a rock and a soft place.

"Run!" I yelled, speaking primarily to TT.

Argenti and Hector backed up as I pulled out the blaster.

The wrathful quieted, looking down on us as if they were in church. I guess none of them wanted to take a chance on annoying any of the Malebranche, from fear of becoming the focus of a *demon's* wrath.

"You guys are gonna be fried," one of the wrathful muttered.

I powered up the heater and aimed, but Malecoda moved too fast. He knocked the ray gun from my hand and jumped on me. We fell to the ground as the high pitched whine grew louder and louder.

135

Where's Virgil now, Joe? Maybe his authority here only spreads so far.

I couldn't tell where the rest of the demons were, but I suspected they must have been chasing TT.

The weapon's wail became too loud to stomach, but I couldn't block my ears. I was spending all my energy on Malecoda. For all the good my punches did, I might as well have just blocked my ears.

It wasn't until I saw Malecoda's tail that I remembered the stinger meant instant paralysis. He swung it around like the Babe poised for another grand slam, but I grabbed it. In response, Malecoda reached up and plunged one of his razor sharp claws into my shoulder. I screamed, feeling as though I'd been stabbed by a frozen carving knife.

The ray gun remained out of reach and began to vibrate.

Does this thing have a limit before it will overload and explode? Man oh man, that would be one massive explosion. Have to get to the gat, Joe. Have to get it now!

Suddenly, the gun fired, sending forth a multitude of fireballs. I felt the heat as one hit Malecoda head on, knocking him away from me.

I looked up to discover that Hector had picked up the piece. "I thought you were a pacifist," I said.

"No pacifists in Hell, man." He helped me to my feet. Clicking a dial up a notch, he pushed one of the sliders halfway.

"How do you know how to use that?" I asked.

"The dials are for the juice, second dial in powers of ten. The sliders help with the recoil. Doesn't take a genius, man."

"Give me that." I grabbed the gun, somewhat annoyed that a peace-lover could instantly figure out what a trained law enforcer couldn't.

Three of Malecoda's brood flew our way. I turned to see two more coming from the opposite direction, and just to give me extra motivation, Malecoda got back on his feet.

"We have to get out of here!" I yelled.

"Where?"

I looked at the mud then back to Hector, and we both knew the answer. "We're not going to stay on the path, that's for damn sure," I said.

We sprinted for the mud. Almost instantly, we were snatched by the sullen. Hector and I were separated as we sank into the hot pungent mud.

Before I went under, I saw the rest of the Malebranche land on the path…but they had no victims to torment. I couldn't see Virgil, Argenti, or TT as I submerged completely into the filth.

I held my breath as long as I could, but my body demanded that I breathe. I was dead and immortal, but I still needed my lungs to push air in and out. I understood the reason. The body's needs only increased the effect of torture when they were denied.

These people were the *sullen*. Miserable, detestable people in life, they found no joy in how they lived, whether with their families or in their professions. The only time they felt happy was when everyone around them was miserable, and they'd probably done everything in their power to make *that* happen.

They obviously didn't want to be here. It occurred to me that they weren't taking pleasure in pulling me in, but rather desperately clutching at anyone or anything capable of yanking them out.

Finally, I couldn't hold my breath any longer, so I sucked in a lungful of mud. Instantly, I was enveloped by the sensation of overwhelming suffocation. Unfortunately, I couldn't die and I couldn't pass out.

It felt like a pillow was being stuffed down my throat. When I thought things couldn't get any worse, a hand reached up from the muck and mire to pull me down even farther.

CHAPTER 21
Thoughts of Home – The Stranger
෯ඁ෯

I looked at Argenti. He had the smirk of a genie, whose master had just granted him his wish for freedom.

"On the night in question, it was pure cocaine," I said in an attempt to recover.

"Did you or did you not just identify this as Mr. Argenti's case?" McMontey said.

"I did, but—"

"And it contains flour, correct?"

"As I said, *that* night it was pure cocaine."

"Based on your tasting skills?"

"It was tested at the lab that night."

"Approach Your Honor?" McMontey said, breaking away from me.

McMontey and the ADA approached the bench. I tried not to fidget, waiting for the other shoe to drop.

"Your Honor, I have a copy of the lab results. It says that the case in question was filled with cocaine with a street value of three million dollars," McMontey said, as though producing a pawn to put my king in check.

"That's right," the ADA replied, hemorrhaging confidence.

"Yet, Detective Dante has just identified it as flour. If it is, in fact, cocaine, Detective Dante's skills in identifying said drug are not reliable. If it's flour, the lab report is in error."

Block your ears, Joe. This guy has double talk down to a cheap science. If he keeps it up, you're going to have to introduce him to Saint Peter.

"The Boston PD had better produce a case of cocaine and be ready

138

to justify their chain of custody procedures, or explain why their lab has identified a case of flour as cocaine," McMontey continued.

"Your Honor, there obviously has been a small mix-up," the ADA said.

Someone should have told this legal eagle that, if he's going to say things like that, he should at least *act* like he believes it.

"A *small* mix-up? What do you classify as a moderate mishap, Counselor? World War II?" the judge asked, obviously displeased. For the record, I wasn't too happy, either.

"Your Honor, the People stand behind Detective Dante's testimony," the ADA said.

"Are you done with this witness, Counselor McMontey?" the judge asked.

"No, Your Honor."

The ADA slinked back to his table.

McMontey circled me like a shark that smelled blood. I floundered in the witness chair, hoping all he would do was rip off my leg below the knee.

"Detective Dante, do you still insist that the case in question was filled with cocaine that night?" McMontey said in his all too superior British accent.

"Why would I lie?" I said, probably looking about as guilty as Norman Bates.

"Yes, why would you lie? Let's explore that, shall we, mate? How could you possibly benefit from arresting my client, Detective *First Class* Dante? It wasn't always *First Class*, was it?"

"What are you getting at, Counselor?"

"Point of fact, Detective, you received a promotion not one month after arresting my client, did you not?"

"That has nothing to do with this."

"Big raise. I bet the family could use the extra money."

"Is that a question, Counselor?"

"Forgive me, Detective, but your family isn't as large as it used to be, is it?"

"How do you sleep at night?" I demanded through grinding teeth.

"Objection, Your Honor!" The ADA jumped to his feet—finally.

"Goes to Detective Dante's state of mind, Your Honor," McMontey said.

"I'll allow it," the judge said, as anxious to hear the answer as the jury.

"Now, Detective Dante, didn't you lose your eldest daughter?"

"Yes," I said coldly. I wasn't going to show any emotion to this inhuman creature.

"She *overdosed* on cocaine, did she not?"

"Yes."

"When you arrested and questioned the dealer, did he not give you my client's name as his contact in return for a deal that included a lesser sentence?"

"Yes."

"Isn't it true that the Boston PD drug lab took your word for it that the case was filled with cocaine?"

"No! That's not..."

"Isn't your vendetta against my client nothing more than a misguided attempt to avenge your daughter's death?"

"No!"

"And you did it by taking the word of the drug dealer—the same drug dealer who gave your daughter the drugs in the first place?"

"No!" I yelled, losing all composure. I jumped to my feet and pointed a finger at Argenti. "It was him! That son of a bitch is the killer. Him!"

"That's *Mr.* Argenti, isn't it, *Mr.* Dante?" McMontey said.

The ADA put his head down in defeat.

"No further questions," McMontey said.

"The witness may step down," the judge said.

"But Your Honor... I..."

"You may step down, Detective," the judge repeated.

McMontey got you, Joe. He got you good.

❧❧

I didn't blame the judge for declaring a mistrial. I didn't blame him for following the letter of the law. And as odd as it sounds, I didn't even blame him for putting Argenti back on the streets.

My *judgment* on his *Honor* was far less central. I blamed him for a lack of imagination. He forgot what it had been like before he started treating the bench like his own private commode. So caught up was he in following the letter of the law, that he forgot about its spirit. He forgot about *justice*.

I stepped out of the courthouse and onto the front steps to see Argenti and McMontey in the center of a gaggle of reporters.

140

By the time you've lived for forty-one years, you pretty much figure you've felt every feeling there is to feel, but this feeling in my gut was different. I couldn't figure out if it was depression, dejection, blind anger, or the shame of failure. Truth is, I didn't know what or how to feel.

That's when I saw *him*. He was just a face in the sea of people walking by the courthouse. He looked strangely familiar, but at first I couldn't peg him. He wasn't a reporter, but he wasn't a rubberneck jockey either. He just stood there and stared at me from a distance. He smiled sadly at me, as if he shared in my disappointment. When I noticed that he wore army khaki pants, it finally hit me.

He was that guy in the warehouse, back in January. He was the one Argenti wanted me to light up like the fourth of July.

Why is he here, Joe? Maybe he thought you saved his life that night. Maybe you did but it's strange how you forgot all about him. You can't even remember if anyone took his statement or even if anyone untied him. Can you, Joe? Yet, here he is.

I was about to go to him when Mickey and Tony came up behind me.

"How are you holding up, little brother?" Mickey followed his question with a brotherly slap on the back.

I looked at Mickey for a second, then back to the stranger, but he disappeared. I glanced around, but I couldn't spot him.

"That guy," I said.

"What guy?" Tony asked.

"The one that night… When we arrested Argenti. He was here."

"Who?"

"The guy. The guy!" I implored.

"We arrested everyone that night, Joe," Mickey said.

"Not them, the one in the chair. The one Argenti wanted me to torch. Remember?"

Mickey and Tony looked blankly at each other as if I just transferred in from the loony tune squad.

"I don't know what you're talking about," Tony said.

"Don't you guys remember him?"

Mickey and Tony gaped at each other like I was ready for a rubber room.

"You cool?" Mickey asked as he put his hand on my shoulder.

"What do you think?" I said.

"I think you're steamed. Hell, I'm steamed, but we just have to move on."

"Right, move on."

"You have to keep it together, little brother. Now you're starting to see phantoms?"

I ignored him. Instead, I watched McMontey preach his false gospel to a gullible media.

"This is obviously a case where one police officer allowed ambition to get the better of his judgment," McMontey lectured.

"Will there be a civil suit filed against Detective Dante?" one of the reporters inquired.

"That's up to my client."

Argenti took the pulpit.

"I'm just an honest businessman. I have no malice or anger toward Detective Dante. I just hope that, in the end, he realizes the error of his ways."

What the devil did he just say? You're not going to take that, are you Joe?

I raced down the stairs of the courthouse, Mickey calling out to me, "Joey—don't do something goofy."

"You jackal!" I shouted at Argenti, but for some reason, my eyes found McMontey. "And you! You piece of filth! *He's* a drug smuggler and murderer, but you're worse! You know what he is and still you fought to free him."

"If I were you, mate, I'd worry about Internal Affairs," McMontey said scornfully. With that limey grin in place, he returned his attention to the reporters. "This interview is over," McMontey said.

I wish I could say that the reporters dispersed, but they didn't. Who would? A defendant's attorney arguing with the chief witness against his client must have been fodder for anyone with a microphone.

McMontey turned back to me.

"Oh, and to answer your question, Detective, I sleep quite well." He took Argenti's arm. "Let's go."

Argenti wasn't going though, not without getting some licks in first.

"Look, Detective," he started in an innocent sounding tone, obviously not wanting to reveal to the viewing media his true nature, "maybe you can get beyond this and focus on the living, like your pretty wife and young daughter. What's her name? Anna?"

"You son of a…"

I wound up to hand that scum a knuckle sandwich with mustard but Mickey grabbed me. He pulled me away from the anxious reporters itching for the chance at a page one story—KEY WITNESS ATTACKS DEFENDANT ON COURTHOUSE STEPS.

"For the record brother, *that's* what I meant by *goofy*."

"You heard what he said," I said.

"Yeah, I heard a victim of the court system show concern for the pig who tried to frame him, because he blamed him for his daughter's death."

"You forgot I was doing it for a promotion, too," I added.

"Yeah, well, the reporters won't, so keep a lid on it," Mickey said.

"So that's it? He just gets away with threatening—" I stopped in mid-sentence.

"What?"

Up until that moment, I hadn't believed that Beatrice and Anna were in any jeopardy. If I had been any more naïve, I could have starred in my own Disney movie.

"Mickey, Bea should be picking up Anna at school. Get to a phone and get a black and white down to the Immaculate Conception."

"Why?"

"Just do it!"

I ran for the subway. I didn't know if they were in any immediate danger, but I wasn't about to roll the dice.

◦◦

I always loved walking through Boston Commons with Bea, especially in spring. As far back as high school, I can't remember a time not loving her, and not holding her hand for an afternoon stroll through the park… But this time was different. This time, instead of talking about our future or family, we talked about hiding in fear.

"You think he'll hurt us?" she asked.

"No, I doubt it," I lied. Of course, she saw right through it.

"You doubt he'll hurt us, yet you believe Anna and I should run away to Cape Cod to stay with my parents?"

"It's not *running away*. Think of it as a *precaution*."

"I'm just trying to figure out which lie you expect me to believe," she said in her lyrical accent.

She'd never accused me of lying to her in the past, but then again, I'd never actually lied to her before.

"Okay. What do you want me to say, Bea?"

"Tell me it's possible. Tell me that this man is a stone cold killer and would take great pleasure in seeing us buried in the earth. Tell me the truth. Don't shut me out, Joseph."

"It's possible, Bea."

"When should we leave?"

"As soon as you get packed, I'll drive you both down tonight."

"You know what's funny?" she asked. "For a stone cold second, it almost sounded as if you weren't going with us."

"I can't run, sweetheart, you know that."

"What happened to *this isn't running away, think of it as a precaution?*"

"I thought we agreed that I was lying."

"What's this about, Joseph? Saving your family or vengeance?"

"You come first, but…"

"But?"

"Don't you understand, Bea? If I run, he wins, and he gets away with it."

"With what?" she said.

I didn't answer. Instead, I looked away.

Bea grabbed my chin and forced me to face her.

"Speak…with killing Kathleen?" she said.

I didn't want to say it, but she was right. I was afraid to even utter the words, but that's what I thought.

"Joseph! She was my daughter, too. *My* child!"

"How do you do it, Bea? How do you survive the days?"

"By remembering that I have another daughter who needs me even more now, and that I have a husband I love with all my heart."

"Then how do *we* do it, Bea? How do we get beyond it?"

"You have to remember that you have a family who needs *you*, too."

"I'm taking you and Anna to the Cape tonight," I said. "I can't stay with you. I'm sorry, but things *will* get better. I swear to God, and you know I *never* swear to God."

"Joseph," she said, "You are the most stubborn man that walks the earth."

"That's what you love about me, isn't it?" I asked with a grin.

Good thinking, Joe. You'll take them to a safe place tonight, and tomorrow, you'll reassemble the puzzle that had become your case against Argenti…and you know just where to start. Don't you, Joe?

CHAPTER 22
Thoughts of Home – Father Nicolas
❧❧

I strolled through the station house as if it were just another day. Today was different, however. Today I looked at everyone through different eyes. Every cop I saw could have been the *one*. Every detective I greeted with a nod might have been the double-crosser in the mist. Any one of them might have been the one who switched a case full of cocaine with one full of flour.

I didn't know Eddie that well. He was a large unmade bed of a man, but he pretty much seemed to be a stand up guy. You have to be when you're in charge of evidence lockup.

Be careful, Joe. Don't appear to be too accusatory.

"Bright day, aye Joe?" he said. "What can I do you for?"

"Let me see the duty roster for the fifth of January, would you?" I said, trying to appear casual.

"I was on duty that night. You know that. I worked through the holidays."

"Let me see it anyway, and the claims' report, too."

"Why?"

"I want to know everybody who touched that case."

"What case are we talking about?"

Is this clown a dim-witted lug or is he just trying to steam your potatoes? Keep your cool, Joe.

"The case of cocaine? The evidence against Argenti? We had a trial and everything. Maybe you read about it in the papers," I said, wearing sarcasm like a tux.

So much for being casual, Joe.

"Wait a minute…" Eddie returned. I could see exactly when the bulb snapped on and lightened up his otherwise dim noodle. "Are we having a conversation or an *interview?*"

"That case goes in full of cocaine and comes out full of flour? Did you think *that* would slip by me unnoticed?"

And so much for not being accusatory.

"Stop right there. Don't go where I think you're going."

"Let me see the duty roster," I repeated.

"Oh, you want to see it?"

"I want to see it!" I yelled.

Eddie looked over my shoulder, forcing me to turn around to gaze upon a sea of faces.

Tony, Greg, Paul—they all stopped what they were doing to see the ruckus I'd started. It almost looked like the night of my promotion party. They all looked at me as if they were waiting for me to say something. Far be it for me to disappoint.

"Unless we had an angel with a fondness for pillars of flour instead of salt on the premises the night of the fifth, somebody had to switch that case."

I scanned their faces, all like family. All cops just like me, but one of them *wasn't* like me. One of them was a rat the size of a rhino, so I continued my sermon only to him.

"You listen to me, whoever you are. I'm on to you, and I'm not stopping until I find you, or until I'm dead, and when I find you, expect no mercy. I'll see you rot in prison!" I kicked over a trash can for flavor.

I admit it was probably a dumb thing to do, and I probably would have said something even dumber if Mickey hadn't interrupted.

"Joe! In my office. Now!" he yelled.

He was furious, but so was I. "Mickey, I—"

"Get in my office now!" he said again, this time through gritted teeth. We went into his office, and he punctuated his anger by slamming the door behind him. "Go home!"

"Mickey, somebody out there's a stinkin' squealer!"

"Scram out. Take a shower. Have Beatrice make you a hot meal."

"She's not there."

"What?"

"I sent her and Anna to the Cape."

"What the devil's at the Cape?"

"Her parents."

"Why did you do that?"

"You know why."

"Do you actually think Argenti's sappy enough to try anything *now*?"

"Sappy? No, he's not sappy," I said, "but I still think he'll try something."

Mickey sat down and thought for a moment. "Maybe you're right, but that doesn't excuse whatever it was you'd call what you did out there."

"I call it a quest for the truth."

"Let IA handle this. Now, go home and maybe, just maybe, if you're really lucky, you'll still have some buddies here when you come back to work tomorrow."

I left.

∾♡∾

I didn't go home, not at first. Instead, I went to church. It was too early for evening Mass, so the place was as empty as Revere Beach on a Christmas Day. I wasn't much for lighting candles, so I just sat in the pew and gazed on the large crucifix behind the altar.

It reminded me of the cross I'd worn when we'd gone to church on Sundays. Unfortunately, it also reminded me of the cross Argenti wore when he handed off coke to his minions for distribution to children.

Father Nicholas walked out of a confessional and, surprised to see me, sat down.

"Joseph? Is it Sunday already?"

I smiled. Father Nicholas was a good man. He was good friends with my father and, I suppose, knew me about as well. He certainly knew my sins, every other Wednesday at Confession.

"I just felt like dropping by, I guess."

"It's hard," he said. "I know what happened in court yesterday, but you can never give up. Never give up the fight, because what you fight for is good and pure."

"It's not easy, Father."

"We don't do something because it's *easy*, young man. We do it because it's *right*."

"Yes sir."

He got up to leave and pointed at me. "Kiss that wife of yours tonight and thank God for what you do have...not curse Him for what you don't."

I nodded as he left.

I looked at the bracelet on my wrist, a gift of love from Anna on my promotion. It's ironic that I would get a gift from my family on some supposed success in my life, when my family *was* the only real success in my life.

I looked up at the crucifix and into the face of Christ. "Protect them... please," I said quietly, but not so quiet that God couldn't hear.

∽∾

I finally made it home. I wasn't looking forward to a lonely evening watching *The Honeymooners* and choking down a Birdseye frozen dinner. However, I looked forward to talking with Bea and Anna.

I knew Bea was still mad at me for not staying with them down at the Cape. I wanted to square it with her and remind her that I loved her, so I decided to have dessert first and get them on the horn.

Bea's mother picked up.

"Hi, Ma, it's Joe."

"Joseph! My God, my God! We've been trying to find you for the last two hours," she frantically said in her heavy Irish accent.

"Wait—calm down—what's going on?"

"Joseph, someone took them!"

"Someone? Who?"

"Two men in ski masks. Joe—"

"Hello?"

A man got on the line.

"Hello?"

"Yes, who's this?" Fear swelled in my gut.

"Officer Stanton, Hyannis PD. Is this Detective Dante?"

"Yes."

"Sir, I'm sorry, but it seems that your wife and daughter have been abducted."

CHAPTER 23
Canto VIII – Circle V – The Dark Pit

I lay submerged in the mud, unable to even take a breath. How long had I been here? I lost count of the hours…days…months. Where was Argenti now? And Virgil? Was he searching for me?

I was ready to toss in the towel.

I tried to force my eyes open although I knew I didn't have a prayer of seeing anything through the mud. Instinct urged me to keep them closed. I sank deeper and deeper, aware that if I could see, my view would be the feet of the sullen. Perhaps not even that.

I reached up to grab a foot, but it slipped away as I sank even lower into the muck and mire.

So, this is eternity for the sullen, to choke forever in the swill of Hell. What kind of God would do this, Joe? Is this the God you've been worshipping for your entire life?

I've heard it said that, in Hell, one abandons all hope, but it seems to me that faith, not hope, is ripped away from unwilling souls, forever lost to an angry God.

A strange feeling washed over me. I don't know how long I sucked mud with the sullen, but I no longer felt angry. These things were beyond my control. If I ever got out of this, I vowed that everything would be different.

I didn't believe what Argenti had said about Mickey, but if I managed to dig my way out, I'd give him a fair chance to prove it. That is, if I ever

JC MARINO

found him again. I hated Argenti for making me think this way. I also hated God for putting me in this place, but still, if I got out of this, things would be different.

I realized that this was a near impossible bargain to negotiate. I must have been twenty or thirty feet under the surface, if not hundreds, and probably continually sinking lower. I tried to kick my way up to the surface like a swimmer, but something tugged on my ankle. Yet another hand pulled me lower. How could this be? How low could I sink?

◈◈

I fell from a ceiling into a deep cavern.

Mud remained in my eyes and filled my lungs. I vomited, puking until I thought my head would explode and my spine would slice through my skin. Finally, the majority of the mud left my body. I looked up, realizing that I could, in fact, see again.

How can you see in a cavern this deep without any light, Joe? You know what? Who cares? You can breathe again!

Yet, although the cave was dark, I *could* see. I spotted Virgil. *He* was the one who'd yanked me from the vile mire.

"I guess *thank you* doesn't exactly cover it," I coughed out.

"Perhaps next time, you'll listen to the voice from my mouth, rather than the one from your angry heart."

"Gee, I missed you too," I said. "How long has it been?"

"What are you talking about, man?" Hector said. "No more than a New York minute."

"How can that be?" I said. "Look at me."

Hector stared at me as confused as an infant staring at a Chinese dictionary.

"My shoulder," I continued. "When I went into that mud bath, it was torn to shreds by that Malecoda character. Now, it's fine."

We both turned to Virgil, since I now joined the ranks of the Chinese dictionary reading infants.

"As I once told you, *not* so long ago," Virgil said. "Time is different here."

"Well, I knew you said different. I just didn't think you meant *different*," I said.

150

I got to my feet and looked around. TT sat in the corner, and Argenti lounged on a rock near the side wall. All of us had the same look, as if we'd choked out an ocean of mud. All of us except, of course, Virgil.

"Where does this cavern lead?" I asked.

"This path leads back to the hoarders and wasters..." Virgil pointed. "...and this way takes us to Hell's next level."

"Let me guess, smokers and drinkers."

"Heretics," Virgil replied.

I staggered over to Argenti. He got to his feet, as dizzy and disoriented as I was. He obviously expected a fight, and I certainly wanted to give him one.

Argenti straightened up as best he could with the hunchbacked posture of an old man who'd never heard the word *calcium*. As I closed in on him, I noticed Virgil. He was looking my way to see what I would do next. I remembered the bargain I made with myself while sucking down sludge like a chocolate malt. I fully intended to start the conversation with a right hook to his kisser. Instead, I surprised myself.

"I want you to know that I don't believe what you said about Mickey..." I began. I looked around and saw that Hector and TT expected me to continue our brawl. To their obvious surprise and my own, I didn't. "But I'm willing to give you the chance to prove it," I said.

"How am I supposed to do that?" Argenti asked.

"I don't know, but you'd better think of something fast."

"I went from the North End of Boston, to Minos's palace, and into a freakin' cage. How the hell am I going to prove anything down here?"

"That's not my problem, is it, Quasimodo?" I said.

"Hey! You stand hunched in a cage for Christ knows how long, and you see how good *your* posture is!"

"There is a way," Virgil broke in.

"There is?" both Argenti and I said. I admit I was a little thrown.

"I will strike a deal with you, Joseph," Virgil said. "I will take you to a place where you will find your answers. However, you must swear to me that once answered, you will have no more questions, and you will end this foolishness and come with me."

"Fine," I agreed. "How do we verify his story?"

"In the city of Dis."

"A city in Hell?"

"As much as a city can be a city in Hell."

"Swell, lead the way."

"We must go lower still," Virgil said.

"I'm not going," TT spoke up.

"What?" I said.

"I can't go, Joe. Please don't make me."

"TT, listen—"

"Nobody's called me that since I was a teenager. It seems so long ago."

"Tonya—" I started.

"No! I've been in lower Hell," TT said. "It only gets worse. I can't go."

"I'm not leaving you here alone," I said.

"I never threw you any rope!" she blurted out.

"What? I don't understand."

"When you saved me from the Malebranche, you asked me about throwing you a rope. I let you think I had because I wanted you to believe I was psychic. I wanted *everyone* to believe I was psychic."

"What are you talking about?" I said. "On Earth, you knew so much, and you knew just what to say."

"That's the con, Joe. I convinced people I knew something about them, asked for money to light a candle, read their palm, give a tarot reading, or some equally absurd thing. Sometimes, I'd pretend something bad was about to happen to them, and I'd even walk away without asking for money. *That's* when they'd give it to me."

I felt like a fool. That's exactly what she'd done to me, but I didn't want anyone to know, so I swallowed my feelings.

"Minos was right about me," she cried. "I must have devastated so many lives by pretending to help people with false predictions. I don't want to talk to Minos. I just want the pain to end. I'm so sorry."

"It's all right, TT." I tried to console her.

"I didn't throw you any rope, Joe. I don't even remember you from life. I was just so lonely, so desperate for company. I didn't know what else to do."

"It's all right," I repeated. Even after what she'd confessed, I still felt bad for her. A thought struck me, and I couldn't help but snicker.

"What's so funny?" she asked.

"If you had told me this back on Earth," I admitted, "I would have told you to go to Hell."

She laughed through her tears, as did Hector and Argenti. I'm not sure, but I think Virgil cracked a smile, too.

"There's a favor I need to ask you, Joe," she said.

"Okay."

"Feel my face."

I felt her cheek and forehead. "It's cold," I said, but her skin was more than just cold. It was like ice.

"The Malebranche don't see the same way we do. They see us by our body heat. They recognize astrologers by the lack of body heat above the neck. To them, I'm headless. It's part of the symbolism, I guess."

"I don't understand what you're trying to tell me."

"I think it's because my head is twisted around. The blood doesn't flow the right way. My face feels like I'm back in Boston and it's twenty below zero, so I need you to do something for me."

"I'm not going to do that," I said, realizing what she wanted from me.

"Please."

"I can't!"

"It's the only way for me to escape the Malebranche."

"She speaks the truth, Joseph," Virgil added.

"You think she's right—then *you* do it."

"She didn't ask me, but you, and it was *you* she asked for a reason."

"Hell, I'll do it." Argenti made a move toward her.

I jumped in his path and stared him in the eye. "I'll do it," I said. The thought of that monster even touching her was enough to make me do the unthinkable.

I slowly hugged Tonya pressing my face to hers. Her face reminded of ice from the Frigidaire. I felt for the base of her neck, trying to figure out which way to wrench it. One wrong twist and her head would be 360 degrees out of whack instead of 180.

The poor kid trembled with fear. Not surprising. This would be painful. "I'm sorry," I whispered in her ear.

"Thank you, Joe," she whispered back.

I jerked her head around to align it with her body, and she screamed in blood searing agony. Her head didn't go all the way around, so I had to wrench it further. Again, she screamed.

She slumped against me. Suddenly *I* was holding her upright. I lowered her limp body to the ground. She screamed in pain...a kind of pain I couldn't even imagine.

Hector gathered up some rocks as a brace for her neck.

Virgil, Argenti, and I looked down on her like three specialists peering at a patient who'd been just diagnosed as terminal.

"Quiet now." Virgil knelt beside her.

He put his hand on her forehead and she stopped screaming, as though just injected full of morphine.

"Your neck has been fractured once more," Virgil said. "Time must pass before you will heal. This time, however, it will heal as should be."

"How long will it take?" I asked.

"Perhaps months or years, perhaps even decades…the answer lies within her."

"We can't just leave her here," I said.

"I'll hang," Hector offered.

I didn't acknowledge his remark. "We can carry her," I continued.

"She has no desire to join us, Joseph," Virgil said.

"I'll stay," Hector said more forcefully.

"You?"

"Sure man, why not? I'll hang as long as it takes. Then, I'll go up with her. I don't want to go down. It sounds like a bad trip either way."

Hector had saved me from Malecoda, betraying his own beliefs in the bargain. Maybe he hadn't *betrayed* his beliefs. Maybe he just outgrew them in a place where they no longer possessed value.

It's funny…I finally found some respect for him, and now we would go our separate ways.

"There's a place on the top level," I said. "If you can make it, you may be happy, at least for a while. It's on the other side of a big stone wall, where the virtuous live, but stay away from the people…either that or take one hell of a bath."

Hector grinned.

"May I speak with TT alone?" I continued. "Just for a minute."

Everyone moved off to give us some privacy and I knelt by her. "How do you feel?"

"I can't feel anything below my neck and if I move my head, it's like the devil's kiss, but my face is starting to feel warm again. It was the right thing to do, Joe. Thank you."

"Now, it's my turn to ask *you* something. It's not a little thing either, but a big thing."

"Okay."

I wanted to say that I would miss her and that I forgave her for lying to me in life. I wanted to wish her well and tell her she'd gotten a raw deal, but I didn't.

"You said you died in the eighties?"

She nodded. "1985."

"Tell me…how were the Red Sox doing?"

She smiled playfully. "They made the playoffs in 1978…but they blew it. Damn Bucky Dent."

I leaned down and kissed her warming forehead. "A Bostonian to the end," I said with a smile. "Okay," I called out to the rest. "Let's hit the bricks."

Virgil and the others returned and we prepared to leave Hector and TT to what might become several decades of healing.

"Wait," I said. I went back and slipped the ray gun to Hector.

"I can't take this," he said.

"Sure you can," I said. "You're a natural gladiator, kid. I see that now."

"But…"

"No pacifists in Hell," I repeated the words he'd said when he'd saved my skin from Malecoda. I wanted him to protect TT. Plus I needed to feel better about how I'd treated him. I put my hand on his shoulder and looked him in the eye. "Your father was dead wrong about you. You're no coward, kid," I said, meaning every word.

"Thanks."

"If you make it to the virtuous, tell Socrates…tell him…a man like me *figured it out*."

"Solid, man," Hector said.

"Good luck, *Liberty Sky*," I said calling him by the name *he'd* chosen rather than the one *I* wanted. Hell, what's in a name, anyway?

He took the blaster. "Peace, man," he said with a smile.

Nothing more needed to be said.

I walked up to Argenti as he grinned.

"Didn't think you had it in you, Dante," Argenti said, "but now that you don't have a gat, how do you figure on keeping me in line?"

"Oh, I'll think of something." I slugged him with a right cross. Argenti hit the ground in short order. I put my knee in his back and tied his hands with my belt.

"There's no reason for this," Virgil said.

"It's all right. Let him," Argenti said before I could answer. "He'll look all the more sappy when he digs up the truth."

I jerked him to his feet, gripping his shoulder as we left.

As we walked away, a strange question dripped into my muddy noggin.

Excuse me, Joe, but if TT didn't throw you the rope, who did?

CHAPTER 24
Canto IX – Circle VI – The Heretics

❧❧

Still in the underground cave, we made our way down a slight incline and deeper into the belly of Hell. The muddy cavern soon turned into a rocky tunnel.

Argenti remained uncharacteristically quiet. I admit that I was surprised Argenti allowed me to tie his hands without a fight, and even more so when he didn't complain during our descent.

This time, at least, we bypassed the ever present cliff to the next level.

What would become of TT and the draft dodging hippie? That's not fair. I know I shouldn't refer to him that way. His name was Hector. No, *Liberty Sky* was his name. I knew I wasn't square with him and hoped that giving him the ray gun had evened things between us. Now, at least, he could protect TT if the need arose.

As we reached the end of the long tunnel, I finally saw illumination. Unfortunately, it was through a wall of smoke.

We emerged from the cavern and into an ugly, desolate cemetery. In *this* graveyard, none of the coffins were actually buried. They sat lined up in rows of wood or steel, each positioned before a head stone. Just for atmosphere, the coffins all blazed. The wooden ones burned bright, but were never consumed in the fire. They burned incessantly. The metal ones glowed red hot.

"Behold the city of Dis," Virgil said.

"Looks more like a boneyard to me," Argenti replied.

"Did you expect Disneyland?" I didn't want to admit it, but Argenti was right. *City* of Dis? That was using the term with a wide amount of latitude.

Giant, half demolished buildings in the distance burned so brightly, all the firehouses in New England couldn't have dowsed them. The intense heat, which undulated like waves, washed over us like the Pacific Ocean crushing a crippled surfer.

"In each tomb lays a heretic," Virgil said. "Those who perverted the word of God are punished in graves of God's wrath for all eternity."

"Perverted how, exactly?" I asked.

"They denied the truth of God's word by substituting their own."

Growing up in Catholic school, I recalled the nuns warning us against listening to false prophets and cult leaders. Of course, when a nun warned us of anything, the caution often came with a swinging yard stick.

I supposed that cult leaders came in many flavors, all of them capable of twisting the word of God in order to confound the innocent and uninformed. Millions who didn't know their own faith could be easily manipulated.

Like the cages in the circle of the wrathful, these coffins of searing heat were of the sinner's own making.

"Here I can prove my story?" Argenti said. "I can show this misguided flatfoot that I'm no killer?"

"That way," Virgil said as he pointed. "At the end of the road is a mausoleum. The answers you seek lie ahead," he told Argenti. To me, he said, "and the evidence you desire, Joseph." He encompassed us with his gaze. "A warning to you both—take nothing, disturb *nothing*."

"What kind of evidence are we talking about?" Argenti asked.

"You will discover that when you reach the mausoleum."

"Let's get this over with," I said.

I knew in my gut that Argenti had lied to me. When he couldn't prove his story, I'd have him, and then Argenti would burn.

Argenti and I started down the road, and I realized that Virgil wasn't following. "Aren't you coming?" I asked.

"I will see you again...*after*," Virgil said.

Is it me, Joe, or does Virgil look a little worried?

Flaming coffins lined our path, like trees on either side of a highway. Only this *highway* was a miserable, dusty, desert road.

I walked behind Argenti, whose hands remained tied with my belt. I trusted him about as much as I would have trusted Phleygas with my soul.

"Your time is growing slim, Argenti, almost as small as the corner you've painted yourself into."

"Dante, what are you going to do once you see the light?"

"You made a mistake. You should have fingered some other cop, but you picked my brother. Bad move, buddy."

"I only told it like it was."

"Yeah, like you were a fighter pilot in the big one."

"I was," Argenti said defensively, "and I lied to get there."

"Oh really?" I laughed.

"I was only sixteen, Dante."

"Even back then you were just itching to off someone, huh?"

"Everybody killed someone in that war, Dante." He turned to look at me. "My country called, and I answered."

"You know for a moment there, you sounded honest... But the moment's fading."

We reached the end of the path. It was just as Virgil had said—a great mausoleum. "Locked," I said, trying the door.

"I can open it," Argenti said, moving his hands around for me to untie him.

I ignored him, trying the door again. It was solid metal, locked up as tight as a sardine can. I didn't want to untie him, so I tried the obvious. I smashed my shoulder against the metal and covered my wince.

"God, Dante, that looked painful. Was it?" Argenti asked with a snicker.

I turned Argenti around to untie him. "You try anything, and I'll—"

"Throw me in a lake of fire," he finished for me. "Yeah, I know." After I unwrapped the belt from his wrists, Argenti put his hand out to take the belt, which I gave him.

"What do you plan on doing with that?" I asked.

He knelt by the door and began picking the lock with my belt buckle. It looked like an attempt at futility, but I thought I'd give him his shot. "So," Argenti said, "if you find your brother down here, what do you plan to say to him?"

"Since my brother's *not* down here, I haven't really thought about it."

"You know what I think? I think you've done nothing *but* think about it. Do you really believe you can dish out a harsher brand of justice than Hell itself?"

"Save the social commentary."

"You know your problem, Dante? You think everybody's worthy of your judgment, and you honor us with your hatred. Hell, if you ever get to heaven, they're going to have to change all the rules just for you."

"I hope you can pick locks better than you can read minds."

"You're no better than anyone else here."

"Oh yes I am!" I said impatiently.

Argenti had used up his chance at the lock. Now it was my turn. I looked around for something that would help me with the door.

Each tomb included a headstone and some of the headstones were larger and topped with statues. One boasted a jeweled blade, like a trophy of some kind.

Behind it stood several giant metal statues. They were hard to describe. They looked like giant two-legged tanks. Some had arms, but they weren't like human arms with hands and fingers, just long, thick cylinders. Some were about seven feet tall, while others seemed well over nine.

I reached for the blade, even though I thought it might be hot. I just didn't realize how hot. I immediately yanked my hand back.

"What are you doing?" Argenti asked.

"What's it look like?" I picked up a stone and smashed it against the metal headstone. I hit it again, and the blade fell off.

"Don't do that!" Argenti yelled.

"Tie it in a knot, Argenti." I used my shirt to pick up the blade and it cooled quickly once separated from the metal.

"Virgil told us not to take anything," Argenti said.

I'd forgotten about that, but didn't want Argenti to know. "Think for yourself, will you?"

Instead of trying to pick the lock with the blade, I used it to pry out the hinges. The first one came out with surprising ease.

"Put that back," Argenti demanded.

"Don't talk to me like that, you son of a bitch!"

"You think you're special? You think you're above the rules? So, your brother killed your family. Welcome to the real world!"

Argenti grabbed for the blade, but I shoved him against the door. I put the blade to his throat, almost choking on my own bitter rage.

"What are you gonna do? Huh? Kill me? Do it! Please!"

"He's my brother!" I screamed. "My brother!"

"I'm sorry," Argenti said.

160

"Trash the phony sympathy. I know Mickey's innocent, and once I prove it, you're going to burn."

"What…"

"I said to trash the phony sympathy…"

"Not you! Didn't you hear that?" Argenti asked.

"I didn't hear anything." I returned to the task at hand and easily removed the second hinge.

"Uhm, Dante?"

"What now?" I said as I dug the blade under the third hinge.

"Hurry up."

"You've changed your tune awfully—" I stopped short when I saw why Argenti decided to come over to my side.

One of the *statues* had moved.

It made a sound - a *squeaking*, like two pieces of metal rubbing against each other.

"Tell me that thing didn't just move," Argenti begged.

Unfortunately, it *did* move. It moved again, faster this time.

"Damn." I quickly focused again on the last hinge. Of course, *this* hinge gave me the most trouble.

"Hurry up!" Argenti yelled.

"I'm trying!"

"Try faster!"

I looked up to see the other statues move, huge ancient toys finally resurrected by fresh batteries.

The blade I took must have kept them frozen in place somehow, like a pin in a grenade.

I finally dug out the last hinge. Argenti and I grabbed hold and pulled.

One metal statue pulled away from its platform, ripping a huge hole in it and releasing a hundred metal spider-like creatures from underneath.

"Faster," I sang out.

"I am," Argenti sang back.

"Pull!"

"What? Are you pulling?"

"Yeah."

"I was pushing."

We stared at each other for a moment, not knowing which one of us was the idiot. We both pulled at the door.

The big biped tank charged us, followed by a multitude of smaller creatures.

We finally got the big metal door open, just slightly, but enough to squeeze through.

"Move," I shouted.

I instinctively let Argenti go through first, but if I'd thought about it, I probably would have just shoved him aside. I followed him through and we ran through a second doorway, and then another. The metal beast burst through the first door like it was made of tissue paper, then the next one.

Finally, Argenti and I made it to a huge metal sliding door. We quickly slid the door shut and leaned against it, out of breath and desperate.

With a squeal that seemed to always accompany jammed gears, the big steel goon slammed against the door with such force that, even though we were on the other side, we were still knocked from our feet. To our good luck, the door remained intact. To our bad luck, however, the many little spider-like things crawled under the door.

Suddenly, the sound of gunshots banged loudly from the other side. Between the stress of the pounding and the gunshots, the heavy metal door finally cracked. The big metal beast kicked in the door. We watched, mouths agape, as several of those huge statues walked in. We also spotted the source of the gunshots. The long thick cylinders I'd mistaken for arms snapped opened to reveal huge machine guns.

Argenti and I separated, running down different hallways.

Just my luck, the biggest metal lug decided to bird dog me.

I ran through a door and into a long hallway of columns.

The metal grindings of that demonic machine snapped at my heels every step of the way.

I couldn't run forever, so I needed to come up with something, but quick.

Think Joe...think! This thing is metal. A metal demon? Maybe it was a mechanical demon. What did Virgil tell you about them? They only sense motion. If you stop running and remain motionless, maybe it will just pass you by.

I turned a corner, briefly left its line of sight, and stopped dead in my tracks. The demon took the corner like an Olympic track star and then skidded to a halt.

I stood in plain sight, but didn't move. The metal beast looked directly at me, but didn't do anything. Without realizing it, I instinctively blinked.

The goon immediately lifted its large cylinder-like arm and backhanded me into the columns.

I staggered to my feet, but lost my balance and fell again. As I gasped for breath, the demon aimed at me with both arms and fired. I dove out of the way as hot lead came at me like a supersonic swarm of locusts. Spotting a door on the other side of the hall, I ran for it. Before I could open it, someone kicked it open from the other side.

I slid to a halt when a stranger walked in. He was dressed like a soldier, complete with flack vest and Tommy gun, the latter of which he pointed at me. I thought I was a goner until he slightly lowered his weapon.

"You may want to duck about now," he said.

Realizing that he was more ally than foe, I dove out of his way.

He quickly aimed his Tommy gun and fired.

The bullets bounced off the robot demon with sparks like they would from a tank. At least he managed to get the beast away from me. It charged at him, ramming him into the wall. The soldier got to his feet, less affected than I would have been, and hit the metal demon square in its block-like featureless face.

The demon hit him again, knocking him against the columns, closer to me.

"Turn to stone," he said.

"What?"

"Don't move! Not one toe!"

The beast surveyed the area, as if someone had just flipped off the lights. He leaned close to the soldier, but the man didn't move. He didn't breathe or even blink. The son of a gun looked like a statue himself.

I also stayed as still as possible. I held my breath as long as I could, but had to take a breath. I raised my chest, ever so slightly, just to secretly steal a breath. That was enough for the metal schmuck to zero in on me.

That thing made a move toward me, but the soldier pulled out some kind of mini flame thrower from his backpack and fired again. The stream of flame burst toward the metal creature as if it came from a dragon's gullet. The blast knocked the metal brute back.

"Get down!" he yelled to me as he pulled out some hand grenades.

Like a seasoned veteran, he yanked out the pin and hurled a grenade at the monster, then another. Finally, the demon retreated. The soldier pulled out the flame thrower again and kept the stream of flame alive until the demon was long gone. Finally, he killed the flame thrower and glared down at me.

"If you're going to stop moving when one of those things comes after you, you can't breathe, blink, or even sweat," he said. "Otherwise, you might as well just do an Irish jig in front of him."

"Who the hell are you?" I asked amazed.

"The name's Virgil—Virgil DeMini." He wiped some blood from his lip.

I was speechless. He actually had the same name as Virgil, my mysterious guide.

"What? But…" I managed to sputter.

"*He* said his name was Virgil, too. Am I right or am I right?"

I nodded. "Yeah."

"Well, ain't that a kick in the pants?" He reached down to help me to my feet.

CHAPTER 25
Canto X, XI – Circle VI – The City of Dis
~༄྄~

You're in lower Hell now, pally-boy. It's a whole different ballgame," the soldier said.

"I don't understand," I said. To put it bluntly, I felt as lost as a five year old in the New York subway system.

"Well, to begin with, pulling the blade from the headstone released the demons from their prison," the soldier said. He lit a cigar with his now somewhat dimmed flame thrower. "And, I gotta tell you, out of the three of them, the robot demons are the most irritating, probably because they're the most pissed off. Can't say I blame them, being forced into those tin cans and all. The problem is—they know you're there. But they can't lay a finger on you until you move. It's in their programming. Well…maybe not *finger*," he laughed. "You see, it's funny because they have no fingers."

"That's not what I'm talking about!" I said. "Why is your name the same as Virgil's?"

"Hello! *His* name is the same as *mine*!" He removed his helmet.

With his helmet gone, I saw his face clearly. He actually looked familiar.

"I know you," I said.

"You should."

"The warehouse! Argenti wanted me to set you on fire. You were fearless."

"Yeah, thanks," he said with a smile.

"You were at the courthouse…and again in the subway. You followed me, and now you're here. How? Why?"

"Do you believe in angels, buddy boy?"

165

"In this place? I'd call it a toss-up."

"Well, you're looking at one, and that's a fact," he said with a grin.

I scanned him up and down. Clad in combat gear and armed to the teeth, he looked like he just staggered through the Hurtgen Forest. "You don't look like an angel to me."

"How many angels have you seen in Hell, Joe?"

"Okay, good point. So, what are you supposed to be? My guardian angel?"

"Uhmmm...not exactly."

"Okay, then who are you?"

"Just the messenger."

"What's the message?" I asked.

"Whoa, whoa, whoa...slow down, cowboy. All in good time."

I noticed his hand was bloody from hitting the demon. At first, I thought nothing of it. I mean, you slug a hunk of metal with a right cross, and you're bound to have an injury. Then it hit me. "Your hand is bleeding."

"Yeah, don't worry. I'm fine," he said dismissively.

"That's not what I mean. Virgil told me..."

"Yo, *I'm* Virgil!" he said impatiently.

"The *other* Virgil told me that those who have faith are never hurt in Hell."

"Is that how it worked on Earth? Is that how it was with Job or Moses? Or even Jesus?"

"Well, I guess not..."

"What do you think faith is, a *get out of jail free* card? You want to take a stroll through Hell, you better have faith, and what good is faith if it's not tested?"

I had to admit, the angel made sense.

"Okay, so why are you here?" I asked again. "To take me to heaven?"

"Yeah, right." He laughed openly.

When he realized that he was laughing alone, and I had no immediate plans to join his humor fest, he stifled himself. "Oh, you were serious," he said. "Look, I can't take you anywhere, let alone to your proper place, until you do something."

"What's that?"

"You know who Cain was, don't you?"

"What is this, a Bible lesson?"

"Do you want to hear this or not?"

"Sorry," I said.

"Because I can leave right now."

"I said I'm sorry."

"Okay, let's try it again. Do you know who Cain was?"

"Yeah, he killed his brother, Abel."

"That wasn't Cain's sin," this new Virgil said. "Here's something most people don't appreciate. Up until the time of Cain and Abel, nobody had ever cashed in his chips. Cain wouldn't even have known the concept of murder let alone death. Cain's sin wasn't murder at all. His sin was that of betrayal. He betrayed his brother. The ninth circle of Hell has three rings— Ptolemea is for traitors to guests, Antenora is reserved for traitors to country, and the first ring is Caina. Caina, named for the infamous Cain, is for those who betrayed their families."

"Why are you telling me this?" I said, terrified of the answer.

"Michael Angelo Dante, born 1916, died 2010, Boston, Mass. He now resides in the ice plain of traitors." He placed a comforting hand on my shoulder. "And among his victims were Beatrice and Anna Dante."

"I don't believe you!" I shoved his hand away.

"Yeah you do, just a little."

"He wouldn't do that!"

"I think you know better than that, Joe."

"But… Why?" Tears puddled in my eyes. "Why would he do something like that?"

"It was his choice, Joe."

"You call that an answer?"

"Look, I know it sucks…" he began.

"You don't know anything!"

"Okay, then let's talk about what I do know. You got a job to do."

"What do you mean?" I said.

"You have to find your brother, and then you need to do what needs to be done."

"What's that?"

"I think you already know the answer to that one."

I wanted to get out of this place. I hated it. I hated everything.

This is the feeling, Joe. This is what it feels like to be totally and utterly betrayed. You're a sucker, Joe—an all day sucker the size of Ohio.

I hoped this guy was a real angel, because he seemed to be the only one in this place who agreed with me. I'd have to find Mickey. I'd have to find him and get justice. Only then would this angel be able to take me to heaven to be with Bea and my girls. "Take me to him," I said through mashing teeth.

"I can't do that."

"Take me to my brother!" I shouted.

"I can't do that!" he shot back.

"Why not?"

"Like I said, I'm just the messenger," he said. "You want me to get you out of this pickle? You do what needs to be done."

"Who sent you?" I said.

"You're kidding, right?"

"No."

"You really need me to say it?"

"Yeah, I need to hear it."

"You were murdered on Earth, chased by demons, have seen and experienced things that no living man can comprehend, and all you want to know is who sent me?"

He pulled out his handgun and jumped toward me. At first, I thought he was going to attack, but instead, he shoved me out of the way.

He fired behind me and shot a group of those smaller mechanical spiders sneaking up on us.

Metal parts flew in every direction.

"*God* sent me," he finished.

I didn't know what to say.

He smiled and settled his helmet back on his supposedly angelic noggin. "Okay, gotta go," he said. "Oh, and by the way, the other guy who took my name…he's in league with Geryon and Malecoda and all those other demonic schmucks."

"What?" I said in amazement.

"He's bad news. Don't trust him."

"What makes you think I trust *you*?"

He scratched his chin covered in two days of growth, geared up, and headed for the door that he had kicked open. Before he went through it, he stopped and turned to face me one more time. "Remember when you climbed up the side of the cliff from the angry to the greedy?"

"How could I forget it?" I said.

"Who do you think threw you the rope?" he said as he left the way he came.

I felt as if I'd just been strapped to the electric chair and pumped full of juice. I backed against the wall sliding down until my keister hit the floor. I had to think, and I wanted to be alone.

Was that soldier an angel? Was he just waiting here for me? Questions beyond questions popped into my head as I tried not to cry. Why would demons be imprisoned here? I'd assumed they ran the place. Was Virgil really in league with Geryon and Malecoda?

Joe, if that angel really threw you the rope that helped you back up to the hoarders and the wasters, he must have been following you all this time. If he's really an angel, why doesn't he just help you? Why didn't he just give you the ray gun back then? Because he's just the messenger, Joe. Maybe he's just helping you as best as he can, or maybe he's just lying through his government issued teeth.

The angel had been right about one thing. I *did* believe him about Mickey, *just a little*. I don't know why, but I'd started to believe it was possible. I'd always known that Mickey had a dark side, but there was no way that he would do *this*. And certainly not to his own brother.

I felt totally and absolutely lost.

❧

I left the mausoleum and walked back down the path to a waiting Virgil. He leaned against a half crumbled statue of a gargoyle, his arms folded across his chest.

I didn't see Argenti. For the first time, I wasn't sure if I wanted to. Had he killed my family? I wasn't sure anymore. I wanted to see my brother. I needed to face Mickey.

"Were the answers forthcoming, Joseph?" Virgil said.

"Yes," I said, "but it's funny."

"Is it?"

"You brought me here to get the answer I was looking for."

"Yes, of course."

"It's not *that* I found the answer, but *how* I found the answer that's strange."

"Was the angel not awaiting your arrival?" Virgil said.

"You know about him?" I said, surprised by his casual tone.

"Why else would I accompany you to this place?"

"He told me not to trust you."

"Do you?"

I hesitated. "No," I finally answered.

"Yet you still desire my knowledge."

"Aren't you going to tell me not to believe him or not to trust him or that he's not an angel or *anything?*"

"How could I say that, when an angel is exactly what he is?"

"By chance, he just happens to have the same name as you."

"What do you think?"

"I think I have to find my brother."

"You wish me to take you."

"Will you?"

"I have fulfilled my end of the bargain, Joseph. I said I would take you to Filippo Argenti. Now, it's time for you to come with me."

"Actually, you said that you'd take me to my family's killer."

"So, you now believe your brother to be a murderer, then?"

"What do *you* think?" I said.

From the far end of the road, I saw Argenti running toward us. "So, what did I miss?" he asked.

CHAPTER 26
Canto XII – Circle VII – Round I – The Violent Against Mankind
❧❧

We descended the cliff to the next level. This *cliff* wasn't a cliff at all, but rather a jumbled mess of rocks and boulders We stepped across the large loose stones only to slip on other smaller wobbly rocks.

I had a lot to think about and didn't intend to confide in Virgil, nor was I thrilled about playing nice with Argenti, so I kept my mouth shut on the way down.

"So, Virg," Argenti started, "you don't think I'm *ready*, aye? Tell me, ready for what?"

Virgil didn't answer.

Like it or not, Argenti took Virgil's silence as an invitation to keep the yap machine at full power. "Hell is a contradiction in and of itself anyway," Argenti continued.

"Do tell," Virgil said with an ever so slight smirk.

"Unless I miss my guess, Minos judges everyone based on their conscience. If he can look into our eyes and see our guilt, what happens to all those crazy wackos out there with no conscience or guilt or shame? What happens to all those nut-jobs who go on a killing spree with the nearest Tommy gun, then sleep like a baby at night? I'll tell you what. Nothing. That's what. Minos can't touch them, because they don't think they've done anything wrong. So, I ask you, *Mr. Leather Jacket*, why is that?"

"If you were *ready*, you would know the answer," Virgil said.

I had to admit, it was sort of refreshing to watch Virgil scramble someone else's eggs for a change.

"Oh, that's funny, real funny," Argenti said. "You ought to take it on the road with Bing and Bob."

"On the road is where you made your mistakes, Filippo, where you lost one so dear that it shook your soul to the very core," Virgil said.

A double whammy washed over Argenti's kisser. "How do you know about that?"

I didn't know what Virgil was talking about, but Argenti seemed honestly hurt. Don't ask me why I came to his defense because I still don't know. I just knew I wanted to break the tension.

"What the devil happened here anyway? An atomic war?" I said, referring to the endless rubble that might have once been a steep wall of rock.

"Something happened here, very long ago," Virgil said, "something that threatened the very existence of Hell itself."

"No foolin'? What?" I asked.

Virgil didn't answer. Instead, he stared at both of us. A sad look filled his face as he squatted to pick up a small rock. It was the first time I'd ever seen him sad. It was the same look on my own face when I thought of Bea and my girls—one of loss.

"Sacrifice," he said softly as he tossed the stone away. "Come now, this way to your brother."

♫♪

Slowly, Virgil, Argenti and I peeked over the rocks to the ocean below. I could barely remember what beaches on Earth looked like, but I remembered enough to know that this scene was a sad caricature of what a real seashore should look like.

There were no roller coasters, arcades, pizza joints, or suntan lotion. This *ocean* was filled with bubbling, steaming reddish water. Thousands of men and women stood at various depths of the water in absolute agony as the boiling liquid consumed them.

"The seventh circle lies ahead," Virgil said, "that of the violent. This first round is fated for those who were violent against their neighbor, the second for violence against themselves, and the third, violence against art and God."

"Dear God in Heaven," Argenti said.

"These are the warmongers, gangsters, tyrants, and highwaymen," Virgil explained. "They are the bloodthirsty, and their torment is to reside in the boiling blood of their victims for all eternity."

"You mean that ocean is an *ocean* of blood?" I said, amazed at even the idea of it.

"Jesus freakin' Christ, that's a lot of victims," Argenti said.

"The level in which they stand depends on their level of violence in life," Virgil said.

"I don't get it, why are they just standing there in agony?" I said. "Why don't they just pack it up and get out of Dodge?"

"So, there's a way around this, right?" Argenti asked, terrified of the answer.

I also waited for an answer, but Virgil didn't offer one.

"An underground passage? A land bridge? A ferry? Something?" Argenti continued.

Again, Virgil didn't answer.

Suddenly, a scream from the ocean captured our attention.

"I can't take it anymore!" a Ku Klux Klan member screamed.

He wore a white sheet, now drenched in blood, and ran for the shoreline. That's when I found out why all of those people willingly stayed in an ocean of boiling blood. Large mechanical tank-like guns sprang up from the sand and immediately shot the Klansman with a burst of fire. He stood still for a moment, and then burst into flames. He screamed like a banshee and ran in a frenzy back to the blood in order to extinguish the flames.

"The time is now, Joseph," Virgil said.

"Huh?" was all I could squeeze out of my dumbfounded kisser.

"If you truly desire to reach the ninth circle, you must pass the seventh. Three rounds occupy this circle. Six thousand kilometers await us in this round."

"I don't know how far that is, but it doesn't sound good," I said.

"Remain here. Stay low so as to not be seen," Virgil said as he got up and ran down to the shore, behind the giant tanks.

Argenti and I looked at each other. Like children instructed to stay away from the cookie jar, we both disobeyed Virgil and peeked over the rocks.

Virgil climbed up onto one of the tanks and opened a panel. I was surprised at how familiar he seemed with the equipment.

"There's no way I'm going into *that*," Argenti said.

"You're not out of this yet, Argenti," I said.

"You don't still think I killed your family, do you?"

I didn't answer.

You know Mickey could have done it, Joe. That could be why they were all wearing ski masks that night…the night he killed Bea. Your brother killed Bea? No, Joe, how can you think such a thing about your own brother?

"Dante?"

"Not until I hear it from my brother's own mouth!" I said.

"Come on, Dante, you can't tell me that you're going to willingly wade through thirty six hundred miles in boiling blood."

"Thirty six hundred miles?"

"Yeah, that's six thousand kilometers."

"You know the metric system?"

"Sure, everyone does."

"I hate you, Argenti."

He was right, however. There had to be some other way around this. There was no way I was going into an ocean of boiling blood, at least not without an extensive discussion and an incredible amount of whiskey.

"Maybe we can build a boat," Argenti said, casting about for a solution.

"With what?" I challenged. "Do you see any wood? Or tools? Or anything that wouldn't burst into flames the second we tossed it in there?"

Before he could answer, a voice from behind startled us.

"Yo, listen up—stragglers," one of them said.

We turned to see four American soldiers pointing their rifles at us. All but one was enlisted, but the uniforms weren't from my time even though they looked familiar. When I noticed the green berets, I remembered the Captain I'd encountered in the circle of the wrathful.

All military men have one thing in common. I don't care if they served in Caesar's Roman Legions or General Patton's Third Army; all military men instinctively look at two things when another military man enters—rank and name. You look at rank to know if you should respect his position, and you look at his name in case he doesn't show your position its due respect.

"Stragglers?" I asked. "Lieutenant Alexander," I said, reading his name tag.

"It wasn't easy but we got out of that bubbling ooze. How the hell did *you?*"

"We didn't *get out*," Argenti fumbled. "We're…"

"We're thinking about going in," I finished.

"Actually, *he's* thinking of going in," Argenti said, pointing at me. "I'm not."

"No one in his right mind would willingly step into an ocean of boiling blood," Alexander said.

"See," Argenti bragged, glaring at me.

"Yeah, look who you have on your side," I said, "four murderers."

They aimed their rifles and handguns at us.

"What are you doing? You can't kill us," I said.

"Doesn't mean we can't have a little fun."

"Your uniform!" Argenti blurted out.

"What of it?"

"You fought in the Vietnam War," Argenti said, drawing the same conclusion I had.

"It wasn't a war. It was really more of a police action," one of the soldiers said, repeating what Captain Richards said earlier, as if all the participants were conditioned not to recognize what a *war* was.

"I knew a Captain Jason Richards from the Vietnam War," Argenti said, trying to relate to them.

"That's an incredible coincidence," Alexander said.

"Yeah, I know."

"You don't understand. I shot Captain Jason Richards in the back."

"You did," Argenti said, his hope of making friends with these guys going down in flames.

"Yeah, they called it *fragging*, but I considered it *justice*. That son of a bitch was a bully like you wouldn't believe," he laughed. "You want to know the crazy thing? I killed him because that asshole wanted to recon north. I told him the gooks were north. We have to go south, but he *had* to insist. Damn Captains. They always *have* to be right. So we fragged his ass and went south. Son of a bitch was right. Three clicks later, we walked into a VC ambush. We were all killed that night. Crazy shit, huh?"

"Well, we weren't friends or anything, more like cell mates," Argenti said. "Actually, I didn't like the guy at all."

"Smooth," I added.

"Ah, the memories. Well, time's a-wastin'," Alexander said as he and his men aimed at us again.

Argenti and I glanced at each other. We jumped the soldiers and struggled for the weapons.

There were four of them, so we moved fast. Argenti kicked one of them into two others. I had to admit, Argenti knew how to fight, even with the hunchback. I hated to even think it, but I was actually glad to have him there to watch my back. I hit Alexander and grabbed his handgun. As I straightened, another soldier hit me across the chin with the butt of his rifle.

"Moron!" Alexander yelled. "Use the other end!"

He pointed his rifle at me, but I threw sand in his face.

"Damn it!" he screamed.

I stood up. Alexander grabbed the rifle and put the barrel to my head. Luckily, I still had his handgun, so I pointed it at *his* head.

"Drop it, or I'll blow your brains out!" Alexander said.

"Do it and I'll blow yours out," I returned.

I couldn't see Argenti or the other soldiers. I was too busy staring into Alexander's eyes, trying to find something in him that was still humane. At any moment, he could have pulled the trigger, sending a hot chunk of lead soaring through my skull, and he knew at any moment, I could have done the same. We both could have done it and neither would have died. We wouldn't even be inflicting permanent damage. Just pain for God only knew how long.

Laws mean nothing here, Joe. There's no such thing as murder or death. So, too, is morality just as deficient. There simply isn't a need for it, because, in the end, nothing will have changed. Shoot, damn it, shoot!

Was that what Lieutenant Alexander knew? Was that why his eyes looked as cold as the metal of his rifle?

I looked into his eyes and knew within a split second, he would have committed himself to pulling the trigger.

So, I pulled mine first.

Alexander fell back. His head half gone, he screamed in agony. "You shot me in the head!" he bellowed. "I hate that!"

His men picked him up as Argenti grabbed a rifle and aimed. "If you don't want the same, get the devil out of here!" he hollered.

The soldiers ran away.

Argenti turned to point his gun at me. I quickly did the same to him.

"What are you doing?" Argenti said.

"Don't point that thing at me!" I yelled.

"Don't point yours at me!"

"Put it down!"

"You put it down!"

"I already shot one schmoe in the head today, and it's been one hell of a long day!"

"Not long enough," Argenti said.

"Put the damn gun down, Argenti, or I swear to Christ, I'll empty this clip into your chest!"

Argenti stared at me, and a strange look washed over his face. It was a combination of fear and recognition. He lowered his weapon, but I knew it wasn't because of anything I'd said. He looked behind me, so I turned to see three softly glowing and beautiful disks that I instantly knew to be Geryon's ships.

"Not again," I said.

With a soft hum, they rose above the hill behind us and I knew that within seconds, they would turn into those ugly mechanical spider-like airships.

I quickly picked up whatever weapons the soldiers had abandoned and shouted to a dumbfounded Argenti. "You want to stay? Stay!" I said. "I'll take my chances in the bubbling blood."

"I know them," Argenti said softly.

"What?"

"I know them!" he now yelled.

"Well, they're demons and this is Hell, so, lucky you."

"Not here...on *Earth*. I saw them in life."

"What the hell are you talking about?"

"I know you!" Argenti ignored me and screamed at the demon ships. "I remember you, you sons of bitches! You're beautiful, but you do evil things. Show yourselves!" he shouted. "Show your true faces!"

Just as Argenti demanded, the ships once again changed from beautiful glowing disks of light to those ugly demon ships that were accompanied by a piercing whine.

How had he known?

Argenti looked at me with horror. He fled the approaching ships, heading for Virgil and the shoreline. Quickly following, I felt static electricity as one of the ships fired a ball of light at us.

A second blast knocked us off our feet.

An endless array of explosions followed with the ships firing non-stop. I looked up from the sand to see Virgil atop one of the tank weapons. He poked at the controls until the top cannon spun around from the condemned violent. He sighted down on Geryon's ships and gave us cover.

Visions of Normandy struck me. The ocean of blood suddenly looked very familiar to me, like the day the Germans had turned the Atlantic shoreline red with American and British blood. The Allied strategy was simple—throw more Allied bodies at the French coastline than German slugs.

The memories still tormented me.

I heard voices in my head from that day—*hit it! Joey, help me! look out!* And *medic!*

The last voice I heard, however, hadn't been a soldier on the Normandy beach. The last voice belonged to a little girl who'd needed my help—*Daddy! Help me!* I heard Anna as clear as day, and the memory of it drove a spike headlong into my heart. I'd failed my baby girl.

Argenti, about twenty feet in front of me, was pinned down, too. I peeked up from the sand and exploding fireballs to see other tanks slowly swinging around to aim at Virgil.

"Virgil," I yelled, "the other tanks!"

I couldn't tell at first if he heard me, but he seemed to get the message just the same.

Virgil redirected the tank's cannon to the other tanks and fired again.

He disabled one after another.

Other tanks quickly turned to return fire, but Virgil obviously knew what he was doing.

I kept my head down, shocked when Argenti came back for me.

"It's now or never, Dante, move!" he yelled as he pulled me to my feet.

With some of the tanks disabled, hundreds, perhaps thousands, of people frantically ran from the ocean in a panicked state of unexpected liberation. They scattered across the beach.

Virgil ran for us. "Our chance is now! Geryon and his minions must return the dead to their proper place before they continue their pursuit."

"The rifle!" I yelled. "I have to go back and get it!"

"Forget it. Move!" Argenti yelled.

I got to my feet and we ran for the ocean. We were indistinguishable from the crowd of killers, except that we were running *toward* the shore rather than away from it.

Virgil waded into the blood like it was a warm July day at Revere Beach.

Argenti and I stopped at the shore.

"Now is our only chance," Virgil prodded.

Argenti wasn't looking forward to this anymore than I was.

I stuck my foot into the bubbling blood and let out a shrill scream.

CHAPTER 27

Canto XII – Circle VII – Round I – The Ocean of Boiling Blood

~⊱⊰~

Imagine sticking your foot into a tub of scalding hot water and not being able to yank it out. Imagine the water hotter than scalding hot and then being forced in it hip-deep, hour after hour, day after day, unending weeks, months, even centuries. Now, imagine the water being human blood. That had been the fate of the people on this level, until we intervened. Now, it seemed to be our fate.

We walked, stumbled, and waded until the shoreline, the people, and Geryon finally disappeared from sight. The blood stopped bubbling the farther we trudged away from the shoreline. Still it remained hot enough to poach an egg. Argenti and I were in obvious agony while Virgil, as always, strolled untouched by and immune to Hell's scorn.

I kept my anguish to myself as best I could, mainly because I didn't intend to crack before Argenti. I suspected that he felt the same way. We waged our silent war of stubbornness, waiting for the other to give in.

Finally, one of us did.

"I can't take it anymore!" Argenti screamed as he fell to his knees, submerging even more of his body in the steaming blood.

I don't know why, but I grabbed his arm to try to keep him from going down for the count. Maybe I just needed to believe that he would have done the same for me, though I knew *that* to be a fantasy. Then again, he *had* come back for me on the beach, so my feelings about him were at odds. I slung his arm around my neck to help keep him on his feet.

"We must continue on," Virgil demanded.

"We're being boiled alive," I complained.

"Do you wish to scream, Joseph? Do it then, and be done with it. When the sound dies down, we will still be here."

"We're not like you, damn it! Some of us feel pain!"

"Then release the hate and the pain will follow, I assure you."

"You ask too much. No one could do this. No one!" I yelled.

My thoughts shifted to Tonya. If TT's original fate had been on the eighth circle, that meant she had traveled this very same route. With her head twisted around the way it was, she had to have done it backwards. How the hell had she managed it?

Well Joe, now you know what TT meant when she said that she could never go lower into Hell again.

I gained a new found respect for that poor young woman.

"Argenti, talk to me," I said.

"About what?"

"Anything!"

"This hurts!" he said. "It hurts like hell!"

"About something *else*!" I guess I thought if we could talk about something else, anything else, then we could stomach the pain longer.

"About what?"

"Geryon's ships! You said you saw them before. Where?"

"Life," Argenti whispered, as though revealing a secret.

"Louder!"

"In life!" he shouted, still in pain.

"Where?"

"In the war. I saw them in the war. The pilots... We called them something. What was it? I forget."

"Tell me!" I yelled.

"I don't remember!"

"What are you saying? Demons started World War II?"

"No! I don't know. That's not what I meant."

"Then what?"

"I don't want to talk about this, Dante."

"Argenti?"

"What?"

"It doesn't hurt as much," I said. The blood didn't seem as hot. It still hurt, but it wasn't as blistering. Maybe it only boiled near the coast, where the people were, or maybe it was something else. "Does it hurt you?" I asked.

"No, not as much," he conceded.

Amazed, we both smiled.

I noticed something on the horizon - a person standing on the surface of the boiling blood. Had we finally made it to the other side?

"Look," I said.

"What?"

"Someone is standing on the surface of the blood."

"You mean like Jesus?" Argenti said.

"Somehow, I don't think it's *Him*," I said.

"Why are you helping me?"

That's when I realized that his arm was still around my neck. "I don't know." I let go of him. I guess I felt ashamed for helping him. It felt like I was being weak, somehow. "Why are you still with us? You could have run at any time since I untied you at the mausoleum."

"I don't know Dante," he said. "I do not know."

❧❧

It took some time, but we finally made our way to the man who appeared to stand on the surface, untouched by the ocean of blood.

We hadn't made it to the other side, as I'd first thought, and the man wasn't standing on the liquid in some sick imitation of Jesus walking on water.

A black man with torn dungarees worn *way* below the waist and a t-shirt covered by a baggy, unbuttoned shirt, stood atop a single rock. The stone looked big enough to hold only one person. If anyone else had wanted to take a turn, there would have been a major brawl.

"Well, looky here," he said. "Sup nigga's?"

This guy didn't look like the type to go halfsies on anything.

"Don't give me up to the big *G*," he said, "kay?"

"What?" I asked, certain that this guy had to be from the future. And I'd thought *1980's* lingo was confusing.

"I was busted into the bubblin' *b*, must be at least a nickel now. Hear what I'm sayin'? All the nigga's back where the ooze slaps the sand just gave up on bailin' through the tanks. Dumbshit cracker heads. I hung back and bailed away from those hunks of metal, hear what I'm sayin'? But I had to hang and rest my Reebocks. I mean, this place is whack! Hear what I'm sayin' dawgs? Whack!"

182

"Whack?" I said.

"Did this schmuck just call us *dogs*?" Argenti said.

"Shit dawg, where you from? Ozzie-ville?"

"You know, we could use a turn up there," I said pointing to the rock where he stood.

He wasn't about to divvy up his toys, but I still wanted to give him the chance to do the right thing.

"You be trippin' fool, you think you're takin' *my* crib," he said as he pulled out a handgun from his hidden shoulder holster. "Hear what I'm sayin'?"

As I thought, we were going to have to buy a turn on that rock, and it was going to cost us big.

I still had Lieutenant Alexander's handgun in my belt, but I didn't pull it out immediately. I wanted to wait for my opening.

"Who the hell are you?" I said.

"Bugsy Siegel, dawg," he said.

"Uhm, the 1930's Jewish gangster?" I said. I have to admit, I was a little confused.

"Hell nigga, do I look Jewish to you?"

"That's why I asked."

"Bugsy Siegel's the handle. *The* rapper, dawg."

"Rapper dog?"

"You know—it's Hammer time…can't touch this…"

Argenti and I stared blankly.

"Damn dawg, you croak in the middle ages or somethin'?"

"Wait. You're a singer?" I guessed.

"Boom! There it is," Bugsy said.

"Singers carry guns in the future?"

"Bet your ass, nigga."

"The music industry is tough in the future," Argenti said.

"I guess I don't need to know why you're here," I said as I reached behind my belt to pull out my pistol.

"Damn, dawg, I'm here for one reason—my own brother dissed me."

I froze. I decided not to pull the handgun just yet. What he said struck a cord with me.

"What do you mean?" I asked.

"My own blood set me up. That mofo used my handle to get three pounds of pure smack. Least it was the good stuff. Hear what I'm sayin'?

183

The pigs jacked me instead, but I got big bro back," Bugsy said referring to his gat. "I got him back good. I murked the foo. What the hell! The next week, I was gunned down chillin' at the Grammies. I was up for two awards, too. Shit."

That was it. I'd heard enough, and since I understood about a third of what he said, I pulled out my heater and pointed it at him.

"What the hell," Bugsy yelled and pointed his gat at me.

He held his handgun strangely—sideways.

"I don't mean to be a bother, Bugsy, but we're going to want a turn on that stone."

"I don't think so, foo!"

"Didn't your mother ever teach you to share?"

"I capped my own bro. You think family ties mean shit to me?"

I pulled back the hammer on my pistol, and so did he.

"You're goin' to have to buy it, dawg," he said.

I could feel the bloodlust bubbling in my veins. I wanted to pull the trigger and see his head explode. The son of a bitch did *something* to earn his place here.

Do it, Joe… Do it! Do it before he does the same to you.

If I did—if I pulled the trigger, I'd be too far gone to ever be *human* again.

I looked into his eyes and saw nothing but sadness and desperation. He was as frantic to keep that small flat rock as he was terrified to lose it…and for what? A small rock to balance on, to stay untouched by the scalding hot blood?

When Lieutenant Alexander and I played our version of *chicken*, I felt my morality slipping away. With Alexander, I pulled the trigger far too casually.

I knew, in the end, that he wouldn't have died. God knows how much pain I'd caused him, but I didn't care. Maybe that was part of what Hell was about, not just the loss of one's family or love or what might have been, but the loss of one's own conscience, our moral compass, and in the end, our very *soul*.

Both Bugsy and Argenti waited for me to make my move, and I knew that Virgil was watching too.

I was sick at the thought of what I was becoming and I desperately needed to keep my moral center, as desperately as Bugsy needed that flat rock.

Time to rejoin the human race, Joe. Time to rejoin the human race.

"It's not worth it," I said as I put the gun down. "It's just not worth it...not for a damned rock."

"Better blow my crib before I cap your ass, dawg," Bugsy said.

We walked away. Actually, Virgil walked. Argenti and I staggered.

"If you see the big *G*, don't squeal me out!" Bugsy yelled. "Yeah! Who's da man? Who's da man? This is *my* house!"

❧❧

After what had to have been months of walking, we finally reached the other side.

Argenti and I ran for the shore, immediately falling to our knees. The buoyancy of the blood had held us up so the muscles didn't have to hold as much weight. That wouldn't have been so bad, but the blood ocean had cooked our muscles so that they'd actually tightened around the bone.

Virgil followed us out, paused, and looked around.

"How can you stand when I can't even budge?" Argenti said.

"Rest here," Virgil said, ignoring his question. "I'll look ahead."

Virgil left me alone with Argenti. He rolled onto his back to ease the pain of all the blisters he now owned.

"How are you feeling?" he asked.

"Like a big bag of deep fried clams. What do you think?"

"Well, on the bright side, my posture's improving."

"A perk," I said.

"Fried clams," Argent reminisced.

"What?"

"Remember how they tasted? And Bill Ash's pizza?"

"The heck with that—Mama Lisa's pizza."

"Joe Nemo hot dogs."

"On the beach," I finished.

"Revere Beach."

"Hampton."

"And the foliage in Maine."

"You got that right."

Argenti laughed. Maybe it was that, for the first time in a very long time, I no longer felt like I was being boiled alive in a witch's cauldron, but I joined him in a small chuckle.

185

Slowly, our laughter died down to painful winces.

"I spent a long time in that cage, Dante," Argenti said. "A man spends that much time locked up, he begins to think of the things he's done...of the way he was. At first, I hated you for what happened, but now I understand. You know what I stumbled on in that cage? I beat up a lot of people. I humiliated and intimidated them. Now, here's the kicker Dante. When you do things like that, in the end, you mainly do it to yourself. I deserved to be in that cage. I swore if I ever got out, things would be different."

I didn't say anything. I felt a wave of guilt for being casual with the likes of him. I also felt bad for feeling guilty. All that went away, however, when Argenti opened his yap again.

"I forgive you, Dante."

"*You* forgive *me*?" I felt my anger spike.

"Yeah, I forgive you."

"You listen to me, you son of a bitch," I said. "You're not fooling me. Cross me just once, and I'll dump you into the nearest cesspool so fast, it will make your mouth water—and not in a good way."

It hurt like hell, but I forced myself to my feet. I staggered into the brush, in search of Virgil. I saw him through the dead wood, and was stunned to find him on his knees. He had his head down and was actually *praying*. Shocked, I had no idea what to do, so I just watched him from behind.

That angel in the mausoleum hadn't thought too highly of Virgil, and it seemed that Virgil hadn't cared for him, either. One of them had to be right, which meant one had to be wrong. Of course, the wrong one would also be the evil one.

I waited in silence to see if, at the end of his quiet prayer, Virgil would perform the sign of the cross. That would mean that he was praying in the Christian sense. He slowly raised his head without crossing himself. Even though he was facing away from me, he knew I was watching him.

"There's something you wish to say, Joseph?" Virgil slowly stood and faced me.

I figured if I opened up a little to Virgil, he'd open up to me. "The days my daughters were born," I said.

"Pardon?"

"You asked me a long time ago if there was ever a time that I knew for a fact that God was with me… The days my daughters were born. God was with me then, I think."

"Thy word is a lamp unto my feet and a guide unto my path," Virgil said.

"I don't understand."

"Perhaps when things are at their worst, you can remember those times you hold so dear," he said.

"Why was Minos afraid of you," I asked, "and those three-headed dogs with the gluttons? How did you know how to control those tanks?"

"Why are you here, Joseph?"

"To find my brother," I answered.

"*One* sin keeps each sinner in Hell. What is *your* sin?"

"I don't know what you mean."

"*Who* are you, Joseph?" Virgil asked.

The question immediately reminded me of his *sermon* on the mount in the circle of the hoarders and wasters of money. He'd said answering that question would be the first step to salvation.

What are you waiting for, Joe? Answer the man.

"I'm a family man," I said with a conviction as solid as an oak in winter.

"Is that a fact?"

"Yes."

"Did you put your family first when they needed you the most?"

"What's that supposed to mean?"

"I believe you know what it means," Virgil said.

"Okay, well, if you're so smart, how did *you* end up in Hell?"

"You wish to know *my* sin, then?"

"Yes," I said.

"My sin was one of pride…and betrayal. I was a slave, you see, who desired freedom from my master's voice."

"That doesn't sound so bad to me. What did you do? Off the big boss or something?"

"No," he said. "But in the remains of the day, he knew he was in for a battle."

For the first time, Virgil didn't seem like a riddle. He didn't seem powerful or in control. For the first time, Virgil was *vulnerable*. I saw guilt and shame very clearly in his eyes.

"Did you get it? Freedom, I mean?" I asked, truly interested in the answer.

"Oh yes…and more."

"Who are *you*, Virgil?"

"If I were to tell you that I was God's own saint, sent down to walk you through the heart of Hell and deliver you into paradise, would you trust me?"

"Probably not."

"If I said that I was a minion of Satan himself, sent to provide him your corrupted soul, would you believe me then?"

"I don't know," I said. "Maybe."

"Why would I answer such a question when it has no chance of being believed one way or the other?"

"I don't belong in Hell, you know!" I said, convinced of *that* truth.

"Then let us find your brother."

CHAPTER 28
Canto XIII – Circle VII – Round II – The Violent Against One's Self
⤲⤳

T he brush was thick and trees loomed overhead. It was hard to see the big gray lid that shrouded Hell. I didn't need to see it to know that it was as gloomy as on every other level. Night or day, it didn't really matter.

As always, Virgil led the way, but this time I was a little more worried than usual. So far in my travels, I'd mostly encountered long deserts or oceans that stretched from horizon to horizon. Even within fog-covered hills or cliffs, I'd been able see farther than my own nose.

We hoofed through a long valley which was dense with thick brush and trees. For the first time since the virtuous pagans, the plants were *alive*. In fact, the whole valley thrived with lush green plant life. It should have been a sight for sore and weepy eyes, but it wasn't. To quote TT, *gag me with a spoon*. Perhaps it was the absence of flowers, or maybe it was because I'd been in Hell for so long…but I felt as if I no longer possessed the ability to recognize beauty.

Argenti tripped over a vine, falling into me.

"Hey, you want to watch it?" I sniped, worried that he might push me into a demon concealed by a bush or tree.

"You could move a little faster," he replied.

"Yeah, it's been working great for you," I said.

"What we really need is a machete, or even an axe."

Suddenly, a sword fell through the vines and stuck in the ground, barely missing Argenti and me. Shocked, we stared at it for a moment.

"Or a sword," Argenti added.

Slowly, we both looked up to see hundreds of people, silently hanging from the tree branches like horrific humanized fruit. Men and women of all nationalities had luscious green vines wrapped around their throats. Their faces were tinted green and their bodies were as limp as rag dolls.

"I got a bad feeling about this," Argenti said.

"I thought you told us nobody dies here," I said to Virgil.

"They're not dead, or even unconscious," Virgil said. "Above you swing the violent against themselves—suicides."

The sword had fallen from one of the suicides, maybe a knight, who'd undoubtedly used it to off himself.

"I don't get it," Argenti said. "They're not moving or struggling, not even trying to free themselves."

"Their necks are broken," I answered, realizing the truth as I spoke the words.

"They discarded the bodies God gave them by murdering themselves," Virgil explained. "There are those who die by their own hand or their own action, but who didn't commit suicide. Those are selfless acts committed by people who didn't want to die. This round is reserved for those who didn't want to live."

I began to understand the inner mechanics of Hell's irony. In the circle of the carnal, they'd used their bodies for they're own pleasure, and forever they would drift in the winds never to touch another's body again. In life, the gluttons had pillaged the earth, leaving only trash in their wake. Now, and for all time, they could no longer partake of the fruit, but only the garbage that remained.

The suicides? In life, they'd rejected their bodies. It didn't matter why. Killing yourself is still murder. So, in death, they had been denied their bodies in the only place in Hell that had living plants and trees.

"If Hell is nothing else, it's ironic," I said, looking at Virgil.

"Yes," he said.

I noticed sadness in his eyes. Maybe it had been there the whole time, and I'd just never realized it. For all his authority and strength, he seemed powerless to help those who *would not* be helped.

Would this have been my fate if I'd been successful in my suicide attempt? When I held the gun in my mouth, I had been but a click away from death with less than two pounds of pressure. If that doorbell hadn't rung, I knew in my heart I would have done it. Was it fate that the person on the other side of that doorbell had been my own brother, the sole purpose for my presence here? It would seem that life was just as ironic as death.

"What the devil!" Argenti yelled. A vine wrapped itself around his ankles and yanked him off his feet. "Help!"

I ran for Argenti, but two vines grabbed me. As one of the vines wrapped around me, another circled Argenti's throat, hauling him up into the trees.

Like a giant invisible spider, the vines trapped him in a web of suffocating pressure. Yet another vine dropped down to subdue me. Virgil grabbed at the one wrapped around my throat, which felt like a giant boa constrictor that intended to squeeze the life out of me.

"Can't breathe," I gasped as I felt myself being lifted off my feet. Three other vines grabbed Virgil.

I kicked in desperation. Virgil grabbed the sword stuck in the ground, swinging it at two of the vines and severing them from his neck. But, instead of cutting the third vine, he let it wrap around his wrist. When the vine pulled him up, *he* remained in control.

Argenti was higher up than me. I didn't have to *imagine* what he was feeling, since I was going through the very same thing. As in the circle of the sullen and wrathful, I was being smothered, but this time with the added *joy* of having my Adam's apple crushed against my windpipe.

The vine jerked me up and down in an attempt to break my neck. I clutched at the plant, trying to buy some time. I feared that it wouldn't be long before it turned me into yet another limp puppet hanging from a tree branch.

When Virgil's vine positioned him close to me, he swung his sword over my head, cutting the twining plant away. I hit the deck, rolling beneath some bushes to escape any other determined vines. I gasped for air as other vines dropped down in search of me. Virgil cut the one circling his wrist, fell, and landed next to me.

"So, what do we do now?" I called out to Virgil.

"We go."

"What... But what about Argenti?"

"He's not ready," Virgil said.

"I'm not leaving him!" I yelled. I'm not sure if I said that because I still thought he'd killed my family or if I just felt *wrong* about leaving him behind. "I got an idea."

I pulled out the pistol I got from Lieutenant Alexander.

"Do you think that you can pierce that vine from this distance, Joseph?" Virgil asked, disbelieving.

"I'm a crack shot!" I aimed, fired and missed. "Well, what do you want?" I said. "It's been a long time since I was at the range. I'll have to calibrate. I may have to shoot him in the head just to get my bearings. That's okay, right?"

I aimed once again. I knew I would have to be fast. Right after I shot Argenti down, we'd have to run, or the vines would pursue us again. I fired two quick shots, but I hit the wrong vine. A young girl dropped to the ground as limp as a wet noodle. I shot again, hitting Argenti's noose-like plant. He spun around but it didn't snap. I fired a second time, and Argenti tumbled to the ground.

Argenti scrambled to his feet and ran, his neck not yet cleanly broken.

"Argenti, run!" I shouted. I stopped dead in my tracks when I saw the girl.

"Hurry Joseph!" Virgil said.

"Go on. I'll catch up," I said.

Unlike Argenti's, the girl's neck was broken through and through.

She took a deep breath, and responded as if taking a drag from a cigarette after breaking the habit five years before.

"Sweet Jesus, I can breathe," she said in a thick Irish accent.

"We have to go," I said noticing vines gathering for another attack.

"My neck is broken. I cannot move!" she said louder than before, but still within the ranks of a whisper.

I stared at her for a moment. She was no older than eighteen, about as young as Kathleen when she'd died. Her face displayed a greenish yellow tint from decades of suffocation, but I could tell she'd once been pretty. I knew I'd never seen her before, but I couldn't shake the feeling of familiarity.

"Why do you look at me this way?" she asked, jarring me back to reality.

The vines snapped toward us. I quickly picked up her limp, frail body and ran, following Virgil and Argenti.

❧❧

We crossed a clearing and then ran into a small cavern.

"The path here is safe. For now," Virgil offered.

"It sure is grand to breathe again," the girl said. "My name is Mary Devlan. I thank you for saving my life. Well, perhaps not my *life,* but you understand my meaning?"

Argenti and I smiled. As always, Virgil didn't even crack a grin. Mary looked like a zombie on smack, but somehow, beneath it all, she was still as cute as could be... Well—for a zombie on smack. I couldn't help but like her.

She wore clothing from an earlier time, maybe the 1930s. Her white cotton blouse was buttoned to the top, with a plaid skirt and knee high stockings.

"I don't expect you to wait for me to heal," she said. "It may take years, and I cannot ask anything more of you, so I thank you for taking the time to help me."

"You sound like you think we're going to leave you here," I said.

"Are you not?"

"Nonsense. You're coming with us, even if I have to carry you the whole way," I said.

"Where is the *whole way,*" she asked, "to the gates of Saint Peter, himself?"

☙❧

I knew neither Virgil nor Argenti would hurt Mary, but I wanted to be the one to carry her. She weighed next to nothing and it took little energy, though that wasn't the reason.

She reminded me of my daughters, but that really wasn't the reason either.

I began to realize that the quest of a knight means nothing unless he has something to protect. What was nobility without someone for whom to be noble?

I wanted to be there for Mary. I *needed* to protect her.

I knew Argenti considered me a steamed hothead, and to him, I more than likely was.

Down here, I'd behaved like a jerk most of the time, but for Mary, I felt I could be a good man again. I was grateful to her for the chance.

Out of the valley now, the vines were history. As I carried her through the once-again-dead brush, I could feel her eyes on me. "You have something to say to me, Mary?" I asked with a smile.

"Your accent."

"I'm from Boston."

"I always wanted to see Boston, Massachusetts."

"It's a beautiful town," I said. "At least it was when I saw it last."

I wanted to ask her why she'd killed herself, but didn't want to push it. In prison, you're not supposed to ask what someone *had done* to land in the big house, just how he'd gotten pinched. Hell operated the same way. I figured she would tell me when she trusted me enough.

I was just happy to be there for someone, and glad to *want* to be there for someone.

"Tell me how Boston was when you were there," she said.

"Well, the first thing you should know is that Boston is the home of the greatest baseball team in the history of sports."

"Yes, the Red Sox," she said.

"Good girl."

"I would follow Boston sports when I could."

"Really? Why Boston?"

She didn't answer. I sensed that the answer was a sore spot for her so I changed the subject.

"Of course," I continued, "the second thing to remember is that you absolutely *must* get up two hours before you have to be at work, to dig out the snow pile that *used to* be your car."

Mary smiled.

"Then there's the music in Cambridge," I said. "I love Irish music."

"I don't think I'll ever heal," she said sadly.

"You'll heal."

"If I don't? What's to become of me then, Joseph?"

"Well, you'll just have to get used to seeing this kisser, because it's going to be carrying you for a very long time."

"Come here," she said.

"What?"

"Lean closer."

I thought she intended to whisper something in my ear, so I lowered my head to her. She kissed me on the cheek. I couldn't have asked for anything more.

CHAPTER 29
Canto XIII – Circle VII – Round II – The Tangled Woods
ళఖ

I cradled Mary like a baby through the last of the thick brush. I planted my feet on the path to discover it was *paved*.

"Is it me, or is this the first time I've actually seen a *street* in Hell?" I said.

"It's not you, Dante," Argenti agreed.

Suddenly, a small group of twenty hysterical people ran our way.

"What are you doing?" one of the men yelled at us. "You stand in one place for long, and you'll end up road kill!"

"Why?" Argenti asked.

They ignored him. Everyone, except for one mug, ran off.

In his tux, he plopped himself down in the middle of the street, obviously exhausted. It didn't take a degree in psychology to know that he was more emotionally beaten down than physically.

"This place sucks wind," he said. "If we run into the woods, then the vines will string us up like a lynch mob out for blood, and if we stay here, we..." he trailed off.

"What?" I began, but stopped short. He looked familiar. "Do I know you?"

Utterly defeated, he looked up at me.

"Sure," I said, "I remember you. You're that drunk driver I saw at Minos's palace. Is everyone here drunk drivers?"

"No! And I wasn't drunk!" he yelled in a defensive tone so loud, it could have only come from a guilty man. "Those people came out of nowhere. It wasn't my fault! I could have been as sober as a priest, and she would still be just as dead. Do you hear me? Just as dead!"

"I hear you," I said.

"We all hear you," Argenti surprisingly added his words to mine. Oddly enough, Argenti seemed even more disgusted with this guy than I was.

The drunk driver's wife, still in her gown, ran down the road. "You left me behind, you son of a bitch!" she nagged. "I hope they get you next!"

The drunk driver just sat in the middle of the road, no longer the flippant man I'd watched try to squirm his way out of judgment with Minos.

"My ball and chain, ladies and gentlemen," he said, "the original good time girl. *Let's make love on the beach, no one will see; call in sick tomorrow, no one will know; have one more drink, honey, no one will care.* Well, guess what? Somebody saw. Somebody knew. *Somebody* cared."

"It wasn't my fault! *You* were driving!" she shrieked.

"If it wasn't *your* fault and it wasn't *my* fault, why are we in Hell?"

"Everybody drinks on the fourth, it's an American tradition," she said.

Argenti took notice at her last remark and confronted the man. "Fourth? Fourth of July? What year were you driving drunk?"

"I wasn't driving drunk..." the man started.

"What year!?" Argenti hollered.

"Uhm..." the man stammered. "'56... 1956."

Argenti gripped the drunk's collar in anger. "Where?! Tell me where!"

"Hoboken! Hoboken, Jersey! Why?"

"Was it a woman and a little girl?" Argenti yelled.

"I don't see what this has..." the man tried to say.

Argenti was uncontrollable. "Was it a woman and a little girl?" He yelled as he shook the man.

"Argenti?" I tried to interrupt, but Argenti ignored me.

"Leave him be," Virgil said.

"Tell me!" Argenti shouted.

Suddenly, we heard a screeching sound from just over a small hill.

"They're coming again," the drunk's wife said. "I'm catching up with the crowd. At least, I'll have a chance with them. You want to stay here? Be my guest. Till death us do part, and death has parted us, deary." She raced off, leaving the pathetic drunk driver behind.

"We have to get going, now!" I said, mainly to Argenti. He ignored me and stared at the drunk with a look of hate that reminded me...well—of *me*. "Argenti?"

"What?"

"Let him go," I said as I put my hand on his arm.

Finally, Argenti released the man.

"Holy Mother of God," Mary exclaimed, catching sight of the source behind the screeching sounds.

We saw them where the paved road met the horizon—some kind of demonic vehicles. They looked almost like cars, but were larger, wider, and sat closer to the ground. They resembled giant wood chippers with wheels.

If they were mechanical demons that could only detect their prey by motion, even standing still would mean nothing. These things weren't going to stop and search for anyone. They were just going to mow down anything in their path.

"Come quickly," Virgil said.

Argenti didn't need any added incentive. He ran. I didn't want to leave the drunk driver behind. Maybe he deserved his fate, but it wasn't my call. I felt strange about abandoning him.

"Get up," I said. "Let's go!"

"Go where?" he asked, defeated. "There's never any escape from them. Unless you want to run back into the brush and swing from a branch, unable to breathe for the rest of eternity."

He studied Mary's green tinted face and frail body, atrophied by decades of non-use, and deduced the obvious. "Would you want that, young lady?" he said. "Isn't *that* the fate you're trying to avoid again?"

The drunk driver, tears in his eyes, planted his feet and gazed upon the advancing demonic vehicles. "I want to die," he whimpered. "Please God. This time, let me die."

"Aren't you going to do something?" I said, almost pleading, to Virgil.

"He has no desire for my assistance," Virgil said with a coldness I'd grown used to.

There was nothing more to be said. Staying any longer would put Mary in danger, and I wouldn't have that. Still carrying Mary, I jogged to catch up with Argenti.

The large, wide vehicles sped in our direction with relentlessness, as if they never had stopped and never would.

We caught up to Argenti, who had stopped dead in his tracks.

"What are you waiting for?" I started, but I stopped dead, as well.

My blood ran cold as I saw Geryon's ships speeding toward us from the opposite direction.

Behind us were the speeding cars looking to grind us into hamburger, in front were Geryon's spider-like ships ready to incinerate us with a bolt of light, and on either side of us, brush of living vines seeking new necks to stretch.

"How do they keep finding us?" I demanded.

Virgil ignored me.

"Damn it!" I yelled. "You tell me now. How do they keep finding us?"

"You wish to know how they can locate us, Joseph?" Virgil yelled, obviously disgusted with me. "Your lack of faith is like a beacon in the night to them. The reason is *you*. Now step back and behold the power of true faith."

Argenti, Mary, and I backed up. Virgil stood alone in the middle of the road.

Geryon's ships flew toward us at a low altitude. One lowered its legs and slammed them into the ground. Making the pavement shudder, it lumbered toward us like a dinosaur.

Virgil didn't even flinch. He stood solid and unafraid. Arms extended, he looked ready to embrace our demon adversaries. I glanced behind us, noting the demon cars plowing closer from the opposite side of the road. The drunk driver stood, imitating Virgil's stance as he faced the oncoming slaughter. The cars mowed him down in short order. The drunk didn't make a sound, not a single scream or cry of protest.

Is that what it's like to accept one's fate, Joe? If it is, you better hope you never do.

His bones crushed, he popped back up, only to be run down by the second row of cars.

I looked back at Virgil to see Geryon's ships getting closer. I heard that high pitched sound that always preceded one of their strafing runs.

"Jesus, Mary and Joseph!" Mary screamed, horrified.

A giant ball of light dashed Virgil's way, but he raised his arm and deflected it. The ball of energy flew beyond us and into the demonic cars. Metal flew everywhere when the ball exploded.

Geryon wasn't done with Virgil, however. Or was it Virgil who hadn't finished with Geryon?

All three ships powered up with a high squeal, and a multitude of energy balls came our way.

Every single ball hit Virgil. He glowed bright and, for the first time, I saw him weakened, but he never made a peep—not from pain or anger.

"Virgil!" I yelled out of genuine concern.

Suddenly, a stream of light blasted from Virgil back to the ships, and Geryon was buried in a barrage of light.

I watched in amazement. Hell, we all watched in amazement at Virgil's display of power.

Geryon's ships wavered. Clearly weakened, they flew off.

Unable to concentrate on much other than what I'd just seen, I put Mary down. "How did you do that?" I asked dumbfounded.

"We must leave," Virgil said, his exhaustion apparent.

"We're not going anywhere. You need to rest," I said.

"We must leave *now!*" Virgil insisted.

"Could you have done that at any time?" I asked.

"Virgil…" Mary tried to interrupt.

"Geryon's ships will return," Virgil said. "Their power has been drained, but only momentarily. They shall return when they replenish, and they shall not be so easily dissuaded the next time, I assure you."

A light finally blinked on in my weary head. "Replenish—you mean *refuel?*"

"Yes."

"How, exactly, would they do that?"

"Virgil!" Mary spoke up again.

"Yes, Mary?" I answered, but it wasn't me she wanted to talk to.

"Virgil, can you…" she stammered, trying not to cry, "that is to say…what you did…"

"Speak child," Virgil said as he knelt by her.

"Can you fix me?" She swallowed in anticipation of an answer.

Argenti and I looked at Virgil, both curious for the answer as well. I knew he had powers or connections or whatever you want to call it, but I'd never even thought to ask if he could help Mary.

Virgil held her frail hand. I'd traveled with Virgil all this way, and never once had I seen compassion for another cross his face…until now. He touched Mary's cheek and then her forehead.

Then, Virgil said something I'd never heard him say before. "Mary Kathleen Devlan, you *are* ready."

A glow radiated from his hand, changing the greenish tint on Mary's face into a healthy warm tone. Her body shook as her muscles began their rebirth. Mary drew in her first deep breath, in perhaps decades, as the glow enveloped her. Slowly, the glow faded and Virgil helped Mary to her feet.

She looked around, like a newborn seeing the world for the first time, then she began to cry. "Thank you!" she choked out through her tears. "Thank you."

I gazed at Mary in amazement. She was as beautiful on the outside as I knew she was on the inside. With freckles and bright red hair, she looked like she could have been Anna's sister. There was something more about her, though. I had this nagging feeling that I just couldn't shake.

Is it me, Joe, or do you know her? Why do you think you've seen her face before?

I looked at Virgil, feeling conflicted. He could have healed Mary at any time, but hadn't.

"You wish to ask me something, Joseph," Virgil said knowingly.

"When I lay there with my arm broken, and all those other times, you could have healed me with the wave of a hand, but you didn't."

"You didn't ask. Young Mary did."

"That's your answer?"

"It is."

"Okay, so now I'm asking, where are those demon vehicles being refueled?"

"Why do you wish to know?"

I smiled as a plan began to take form.

CHAPTER 30
Thoughts of Home – Anna

ᴥᴥ

O fficer Stanton, Hyannis PD. Is this Detective Dante?"

"Yes," I answered, terrified of why Hyannis PD would be at my in-laws.

"Sir, I'm sorry, but it seems that your wife and daughter have been abducted."

"I'm on my way."

I hung up the phone and ran for the door, but the phone rang almost immediately. I quickly picked it up, thinking that the Hyannis PD needed some info.

"I'm here!" I said.

"If you want to see your wife and daughter again, go to the abandoned warehouse on Main."

"Argenti!" I immediately recognized his voice. "I know it's you."

"You know which warehouse I'm talking about, don't you?"

"Yeah, the one where I busted your sorry waste of flesh."

"Good, then you don't need a road map," he said.

"If you hurt them, I swear to Christ, you will never be dead enough."

Argenti hung up.

ᴥᴥ

Argenti didn't have to tell me to show up alone. I knew him too well. If I didn't arrive at the warehouse alone, Bea and Anna would be killed.

However, Argenti knew *me* well enough to realize I'd come armed, regardless of his demands. I drew my .38 as I entered the warehouse, with my backup snub-nose strapped to my ankle.

I didn't want anyone to know that I'd arrived yet, so I crawled above them on the catwalk.

Two men in black ski masks tied Bea to a chair while a third held Anna. One of them might have been Argenti, but I didn't want to jump to any conclusions. As far as I knew, Argenti could have been in another part of the warehouse with five other knuckle draggers.

Don't you think it's odd, Joe, that they would wear ski masks? They know you know who they are. No time to think about that. No time, Joe.

I didn't have time to ponder the question as all other thoughts left my mind when I heard Anna's voice.

"Mom!" she cried out.

"Shut her up," one of the men said to Bea. He obviously expected her to follow orders. Heck, she never obeyed *me*, so why would she abide by some jerk in a ski mask?

"Kiss the devil." Bea ended her sentence with a kick to his crotch.

He went down like a darted bear, but one of the other thugs smacked her square in the nose.

Well, Joe, now you know which one you're shooting first.

"Tie her damn ankles, too!" the big one ordered as he tried to shake off the pain.

As they secured her feet, I aimed my .38 at the jackass who'd punched Bea, but I needed to be careful. They were moving around a lot, and the guy holding Anna might get some bright ideas after the first shot rang out. I silently prayed for God to guide my bullets, as a surgeon would pray for Him to guide his scalpel.

I pulled back the hammer, but hesitated when Bea said something that, frankly, had me stumped.

"I know who you are, and I know why you've brought us here," she said to the big mug. "I know because *he* told me. I didn't believe him at first, but it's true! That's why you're wearing masks, isn't it?"

I didn't understand what she meant, but something was obviously going on. I intended to find out what.

"Once your husband gets here, it won't matter to you what's true or not," the big guy said.

"It won't work. Joseph is far too smart for you."

"He may be smart, but love makes people dopey," he said in a gruff voice as he turned to one of the other thugs. "Get the gasoline."

This is it, Joe. Here's your opening. Don't screw it up!

I left the catwalk to greet the goon sent for the gasoline with a gun butt to the skull.

I snuck up behind him as he tried to steady the fifty gallon drum of gasoline. I didn't want the guys in the next room to hear me. I was about to hit him when a rat darted across the floor behind me. The guy in the ski mask turned and saw me.

Ironic that it took one rodent to warn the other.

I nailed him in the kisser with the butt of my .38. Surprisingly, he didn't go down. He grabbed me, and we both fell into the barrel, spilling gasoline everywhere. I rolled on top of him and shoved my gun under his chin.

"Surprised to see me?" I said.

When I pulled off his ski mask, *I* was the one to be surprised. *Tony.* My partner was the rat! "Tony?"

He didn't answer me. Instead, he called out.

"He's over here!" he yelled.

I brained him with my gat and the next second, he was out cold.

The gasoline puddle had spread into the next room and it was now obvious that they knew I was there. I let my .38 lead the way as I made my way into the warehouse's main floor. I peered from behind the corner wall to see one of the thugs holding Anna. The other one hid behind Bea with a gun to her side.

"Come out, come out, wherever you are," he sang out in a scratchy voice.

I stepped into view, my gun trained on his head. "Let them go," I said with as much calm as I could muster.

"Not a chance in Hell," he said.

Bea tried to say something, but he had her mouth covered. "Lower the piece, now!" he threatened.

"I think my wife wants to tell me something," I said.

"Maybe sweet nothings," the big one said.

"Why don't you let her talk?"

He answered by pulling the hammer back on his pistol and moving the piece from her side to her head.

"Okay!" I put my .38 on the floor. "Okay, it's down. You got me cold. Now let them go."

Bea tried to scream something to me but his hand covered half of her face, muffling her words. With her hands tied, she could do little else.

What's Bea trying to tell you, Joe? Something's up and it's not the price of gasoline.

The big guy looked at his comrade. "Shoot him," he said.

He pointed his gun at me. I squatted, grabbing my backup from my ankle holster. "Anna, run!" I screamed.

She broke free and ran, giving me the opening I needed. I rolled onto the floor and shot him.

The big guy aimed at me, but Bea swung her body into his arm. When he pulled the trigger, the round went wide. Unfortunately, the hot slug hit a light bulb, and sparks fell like snow, lighting the gasoline puddle to flames.

"You bitch!" he yelled and did the unimaginable. He shot Bea.

"No!" I screamed. I shot wildly at the son of a bitch.

He ran. I wanted to chase him, but I ran to Bea instead.

"Don't talk!" I screamed. I knew she wanted to tell me something, but I needed her to save her strength. The wound was bad. He'd shot her in the back, with the bullet coming out of her chest. And as if things weren't bad enough, the flames started to climb the walls.

"I'm getting you out of here." I put my arms around her to pick her up. Instead of holding onto me, she grabbed the back of my neck. "Bea, what are you doing?"

She pulled me down to her and kissed me. It wasn't soft and gentle, but deep and hard, like when we'd made love. I knew this was her way of saying goodbye in the toughest way possible. She always knew I loved it when she acted tough.

"Wherever thou goest, I go...my love," she said, as she had many times before, but this time, I knew in my gut, it would be the last.

"Now go save our baby," she whispered her last words.

Hang onto the anger, Joe. Use it. No time to cry. Someone needs you. Your daughter needs you. Find her, Joe. Find her.

I ran to the stairwell, yelling for Anna. The thick smoke and the fire forced me to go up, rather than out. I wound up on the roof, and found Anna, who'd obviously taken the same route for the same reason. She was at the far end of the roof when she saw me. I started to run to her, but part of the roof collapsed between us.

"Daddy!" she cried out.

"It's all right, baby, just stay there." I looked around and saw the fire escape. It was on my side of the gap, and the only way for her to reach it was to jump to me. "Honey, listen to me," I yelled. "You have to jump to me."

"No way. You jump to me!"

"I can't baby. The roof won't hold me and the fire escape is on this side."

"I can't!"

"Anna, listen to me. If you jump, I'll catch you. You'll be all right. I swear to God, and you know I never swear to God unless it's true."

"Where's Mom?" she said through her tears as the black smoke billowed between us.

I reached out, over the flames. "Jump!" I hollered, ignoring her question.

There wasn't a lot of time or room to run, so she held her breath and jumped.

I barely got a piece of her hand, and desperately held onto her as she slowly slipped lower.

She stared up into my eyes with a look of terror that branded into my soul.

"Daddy, don't let go!"

CHAPTER 31
Canto XIV – Circle VII – Round III – The Fueling Depot
ڡ‬⁓

The third round of the seventh circle, soaked in daylight, was perhaps the brightest of places I'd seen in Hell, which was appropriate since what I had planned was a type of *High Noon*.

From a distance, I peeked over a large dune to see the three demon ships parked at a desolate fueling depot. It was actually a comical sight. Three flying ships, so advanced they resembled something you'd see on a sinister version of *Buck Rogers*, sat in front of fuel pumps at a gas station that could have come right out of a Nevada desert city with a population of twelve.

Behind the pumps sat an ugly black box of a building the size of a large theater. For all I knew, it was some demonic bathroom or rest area that included arcade games and a hot dog stand. Each pump had a small mechanism on top that spun slowly and relentlessly. The same was true for the horns that had topped the long poles in the circle of hoarders and wasters, as well as the cages that had encased the wrathful.

What made these things spin with the timing of a Swiss watch? What was their purpose? How many other small mechanisms of Hell had I missed, and what did they all mean?

"This is an exercise in lunacy," Virgil said.

"Why? Why is this wrong?" I said. "I want a straight answer, this time."

"Hell has no shortcuts, Joseph. You know this, so don't deny it."

"You know how far we can get in one of those things?"

"Do you?"

"No, I don't," I said. "So, let's talk about what I do know. You could have crippled those ships at any time, but you let them chase us. Why?"

"That one, you'll have to answer on your own."

I was about to lean into Virgil when I heard something so beautiful, it could only remind me of Anna's singing every Sunday morning. Off in the distance, Mary gazed over to the horizon and sang softly.

I don't know what possessed her, nor do I know the reason why she chose the same hymn that Anna sang in church the last time I'd ever heard her sing. She sounded hauntingly like my daughter. I didn't want her to stop, despite the risk of the demons hearing her.

Argenti spied the demon ships, while I slowly walked up to Mary.

She stopped singing and smiled at me. "I'm sorry," she said. "It's been quite a long time since I could breathe, and I so loved to sing."

"How are you feeling?"

"I can feel everything again. Sometimes, it's better not to feel at all. Hanging from that tree was a horrible thing, but to be absolutely numb can sometimes be a comfort."

"Why would you think that?" I asked.

"Because it's easier not to face the truth."

"What truth?"

"I was born in the south of Cork, just before the turn of the century of 1900. There was a young English man that I came to fancy, and I knew he fancied me. My family was Catholic and very strict, so when I found myself in the *family way* outside of wedlock, I certainly couldn't confess to them. I told my baby's father but marriage between a Catholic and a Protestant would ruin his family. He left for America, you see, to Boston. So I let him go, and when I couldn't hide my pregnancy any longer, the town shunned me... But I didn't care. I was going to have a baby, my lover's baby. I wanted a little girl so badly I'd even chosen her name— *Carmel.*"

"Carmel? That's a very unusual—" I stopped in mid-sentence. It had been so long since I'd been in the circle of the virtuous, I'd nearly forgotten. *That's* why Mary looked oddly familiar to me. She resembled that young girl who'd saved me from the virtuous so long ago...a *family* resemblance.

Socrates had told me that the place for the virtuous was sometimes known as Limbo and that many who resided there had died at birth. Never in my wildest dreams could I have imagined meeting the parent of one.

"That's a very unusual name." I smiled sadly.

"But it wasn't to be." Tears came to her eyes. "She..."

"Died at birth," I continued for her.

"How did you know?"

"I'm a detective." I wiped away her tears. "I know these things."

"I killed myself right after, with this." She pulled out a small handgun.

I looked at the chamber. "There's one bullet left," I said.

"There's *always* one bullet left," she said.

"Well, I'll let you in on a little secret, Mary. I don't think you'll need it, not here anyway." I winked at her.

She smiled. "The truth is... I deserved to be where I was. It was just easier to pretend to be a victim. God gave me the gift of life, and I foolishly rejected it. In doing so, I rejected *God.*"

In reality, Mary was about twenty years older than me, but she looked so young and fragile, all I wanted to do was take her pain away.

I felt like a father again. Unfortunately, I also felt about as helpless as a father could be with the realization that he *couldn't* take away his daughter's pain. What kind of God would give this beautiful young creature such a painful life, only to give her an eternity of misery? I grew fearful of the answer.

"It's now or never, Dante," Argenti said from the dune, bringing me back to reality, back to the third round of the seventh circle of Hell.

"I'll be right back," I said as I smiled at Mary.

"Are you sure this is the right thing to do, Joseph?" she asked.

"I've never been more sure of anything in my life."

I walked past Virgil, aware that he disapproved of my decision. "You could help, you know," I said, trying not to sound like I was asking for a favor.

"No, I cannot," he said.

I scurried up the dune to Argenti.

Seeing Argenti's emotional meltdown with the drunk driver made me feel somewhat closer to him. But don't ask me why.

"I didn't know you had such a hard spot for drunk drivers," I said.

"Drop it, Dante. Drop it, but good."

"Fine," I said.

Intellectually, I knew I needed Argenti's help. I'd seen him fly in life, and if he'd really been a pilot in the Army Air Corps, he was probably as cocky a pilot as he was a drug dealer. Yes, I needed him, but my emotions remained at the helm. "I can do this alone," I said.

"I'm in this, too, like it or not," Argenti said.

"I don't need you."

"Do I need to show you my resume, Dante? I was a pilot, remember? There's not a plane on God's green earth that I can't figure out."

"Do I need to remind you, Argenti? We're not on God's green earth."

"I'm going with you, Dante," Argenti said through gritted teeth.

"Swell, but if anything happens, don't think I'm going to save your skin. You got that?"

"Like a bad cold."

I peered over the dune to see a large tail slide into the doorway of the whopping big black building, leaving the three vehicles unattended.

"Now!" I said, and we ran for the closest demon ship.

Argenti and I made our way up the hatch as quickly and as quietly as possible. The inside of the ship was dark and dingy, as bad as the exterior. The seats and controls had been designed for larger demonic bodies, but not so large that we couldn't function.

I hadn't seen Geryon or his cohorts, and judging from the tail I'd just watched slither into the building, it was an encounter I could do without. "Well?" I prodded.

"Give me a minute!" Argenti tried to make sense of the controls.

"We haven't got a minute."

"How do you know that? For all we know, they could be in that building for the next decade."

"Look, you said you could fly this thing," I said.

"I can!"

"You said you saw these things in the war."

"Yeah—but not from the inside."

"But you think you have some special insight about them?"

"Yes."

"Why?" I said.

"Because they saved my life!"

"What?" I asked, shocked at Argenti's response.

"These things—we'd call them something. *Foo fighters*, that's it. They were always out there, just beyond reach and sight, but we all knew they were out there, watching. Back in the war, there was mysticism in the air. There was a bond between a man and his plane. I saw pilots do things with their machines that the engineers and designers would claim impossible. Likewise were the things I saw while in flight... The government said they didn't exist, but we knew different. It was 1943, and we were in the fight of our lives. There were five of us. You think getting ambushed as a foot soldier is bad? Let me tell you, when those big guns on the ground open up and shells are bursting all around you, the big blue yonder gets small and tight awfully quick."

"So, why didn't you just turn tail?"

"Why? You think because I died a drug dealer, I was always this way? I was young and patriotic, and I believed in the fight."

"You?"

"Yeah, me… Dopey, huh?"

"So, what happened?"

"What do you think? I got hit and went down like a lead brick, but the strangest thing happened. I didn't spin out of control. I went down fast and hard. As I was getting ready to bail out over German territory and probably slip right into a German casket, I saw lights in the distance. Lights that became beautiful glowing disks. I never knew what they were. I certainly didn't know that they were these demonic *things.*"

"What happened?" I asked, as interested as a kid listening to a bedtime story.

"I blacked out and woke up in a field hospital three days later. I thought angels had saved me for some heavenly purpose. Then I was told that everyone else in my squadron had been killed that day. It's a terrible thing to be a sole survivor. Back then, I believed in God. I believed that Jesus was the son of God, and that there was a reason for my surviving—a purpose for my life. But time wore on and no answers came—until now. Do you know why they saved me way back then, Dante?"

"Why?" I gulped, truly interested in his thoughts.

"Because they knew—they knew that if I died on that hot muggy day in 1943, I would be in paradise with my God. So they saved me, knowing that when the answers didn't come to my questions, I would slowly slip and fall into wickedness. I would become an evil man."

I'd always thought of Argenti as an evil man, but I'd never realized that he considered himself one, too.

I didn't know what to say to him. What do you tell a man who has just realized that he was manipulated and seduced into evil by the one life-changing event that he thought was an angelic encounter?

There were no words to take away his pain, and no actions that would alter anything. Argenti had been right about one thing—we were in this thing together.

"Argenti? Look, I…" I stammered.

Ready to continue, a sound from the outside changed everything—the bang of the black building's door slamming open.

CHAPTER 32
Canto XIV – Circle VII – Round III – The Chase
❧❧

W e looked out the portal to see nine large reptilian demons walking toward the vehicles—and us!

We sat in the large seats, frozen with fear.

"Well, *pilot*, what do we do?" I asked.

"Get the devil out of here," Argenti replied with equal astonishment. "*Now* would be nice!"

"The hatch is still open!"

"I got it!" I ran for the hatch.

I grabbed the hatch door, but froze at the sight of demons that appeared to be nearly nine feet tall. Yes, they were evil personified, but there was something else about them. They were oddly elegant, perhaps even graceful.

They hadn't spotted me yet. This was the first time I'd seen Geryon and his minions, so the sight had me somewhat mesmerized.

One demon was decidedly larger than the rest. He also looked to be the strongest and the one in charge of the whole she-bang. Obviously, this had to be Geryon.

He walked with majesty, like a lion born to a bloodline of monarchs. I had expected these demons to be bloodthirsty and thug-like, but they weren't. They possessed ferocious bodies of fierce sternness complete with tiger-like clawed hands and shark-like jaws, yet they seemed tempered with wisdom. Geryon, more so than the rest.

Suddenly, I heard the sound of one of the demon ships powering up and I was smacked with the realization that it was *my* ship.

Argenti had figured it out. Glancing at the cockpit, I saw Argenti picking buttons to push as if he was playing *Three Card Monty*.

"Close the hatch!" he shouted as he looked out the side hatch window.

I peered out the hatch door and saw the demons rushing towards us.

"Damn!" I slammed the hatch shut, then raced to the cockpit, settled into the seat next to Argenti, and felt like a six year old sitting in his daddy's chair after he'd left the room. "Well?"

"Give me a minute!" he said.

"We haven't got a minute. *This time,* I know that for a fact."

A large demonic hand slammed against the window next to Argenti. He yelped with surprise.

I don't know how he did it, but the vehicle started moving.

The ship lifted a leg and plunged it back down in a gawky mechanical walk. The ship we were in had six legs, similar to an insect. As it moved across the ground, I felt as if we were on the back of a Brontosaurus.

"Holy cow, Argenti, we're moving. We're actually moving."

"Was there ever a doubt?"

"That's exactly what we need now, Argenti, a cocky pilot."

The demons ran for the other vehicles.

The ship jolted for a moment, as if we'd run over something. But we hadn't run over anything. A queasiness that accompanies the realization, like when someone suddenly remembers the basics of fueling your car at a gas station, hit my stomach.

"Did you remove that fueling nozzle from the tank?" I asked, certain I already knew the answer.

"I thought you did."

"Now how could I have, when you saw me run up the ramp first?"

"I don't know...kismet?"

"Wait a minute. If this is like fuel on Earth..."

"What?"

"Just keep driving this thing, I have an idea."

I pulled out the handgun I'd taken from one of those Vietnam soldiers. I went back to the hatch and opened it for a look-see. I was right. One of the fueling pumps was gushing fuel and the dismembered nozzle was hanging from our tank.

I shot at the fuel pumps, and they exploded just as the other two demonic vehicles began to move away.

I covered my ears as a series of explosions enveloped the turf behind us. I hadn't expected the explosions to be so powerful. Still thinking like a living man, I felt concern for Mary. But, I also felt certain that Virgil would protect her. I knew she couldn't die, but also hoped Virgil would keep her from roasting like a marshmallow over a campfire.

As bad as the bursts of fire and rock were, it didn't stop or even slow the two demon ships that pursued us.

Our ship thankfully walked faster and faster but our pursuers took flight.

"I don't want to nag, but these things *do* fly, right?" I asked.

"We have to pick up enough speed."

"The ones behind us didn't have to."

"I thought you didn't want to nag," he said.

"Oh, I'm sorry, you want to hear nagging? If those things get any closer, they're going to start—" Bursts of energy from above hit the ground near us. "Shooting!"

"We have to go faster!" Argenti said as we picked up even more speed.

"Argenti, you're thinking about this the wrong way."

"What do you mean?"

"The planes you flew in the war and the ones I saw you fly, they had propellers, right?"

"Yeah, of course."

"Well? Don't these things have jets or something?"

"You're right. I don't think jets are juicing these things. There has to be something else here."

More blasts pounded near us as Argenti tried to make sense of the control panel. I looked out the dashboard window to see that we were fast approaching the end of the road.

"Hurry!"

"I'm looking!"

"Look faster!" I yelled and we both saw that we were about to plummet into a gorge the size of the Grand Canyon.

Argenti reached over and slid a shoulder strap across his chest and waist.

"What are you doing?" I said.

"What's it look like?"

As we closed in on the gorge, I figured it would be prudent to follow Argenti's example. I buckled up as well.

Argenti desperately pulled a lever, and we slowed down.

"What are you doing?"

"Stopping."

"We can't stop!" I yelled as I pushed the lever back up.

"What the hell!"

We both screamed. We dropped into the canyon like a brick tossed into the ocean, both of us mashing buttons with the urgency of a mother about to give birth.

Suddenly, we heard that familiar whine of something powering up. It was the jet engine, or whatever it was that made these things fly.

"Yes!" I yelled.

Argenti pulled back on the wheel, and we pulled out of a dive that surely would have crushed us both. "Who's the pilot, huh!" Argenti yelled in excitement.

"We're not out of this yet," I said. Our pursuers took in residence behind us and shot fireballs that threatened to pulverize us like a mallet would a crab.

We were tossed around like a bean bag at a beach party. Argenti struggled to maintain control. "We have to do something!" he yelled.

"I agree," I managed to squeak.

"Wait! Those things fly, we fly. Those things can shoot…"

"We shoot!" I finished.

How could we not see it? If Argenti's seat was for the flyer, then mine had to be for the shooter.

I searched through my half of the control panel for something with a trigger, or targeting device, *anything* to do with weaponry.

"Well?"

"Nothing! Damn it. That ticks me off!" I hit the control panel, subsequently popping open a compartment with some sort of radar and tracking device.

What looked to be a kind of throttle with a trigger rose up before me. I grabbed it with both hands. When I moved it, crosshairs on the radar also moved. The crosshairs had company however. Three dots—one green and two red behind the green.

Okay, it didn't take Robby the Robot to figure this one out.

"Anytime would be just peachy, Dante."

"Just a minute."

"We don't have a minute," Argenti sang out, mockingly quoting what I had earlier said to him.

"You may be a good pilot, but I'm a crack shot." I took aim and pulled the trigger. Nothing happened.

"Way to go, *crack shot!*"

"Wait a minute! If this is similar to that weapon I got in the circle of the virtuous, there must be something here to build up the energy needed for those fireballs."

I saw a dial next to the radar screen and quickly clicked it up a notch.

We heard another familiar sound, similar to the wail made by the weapon that Socrates had given to me.

I took aim again.

"Wait!" Argenti shouted.

"What?"

"You know about the 3-D coordinate system, right?"

"The what?"

"You can't just shoot. You have to know distance, bearing, and elevation…the X, Y, and Z coordinates. Those ships are above us, on the Y axis."

"I have absolutely no idea what all that means."

"Aim high!" Argenti summarized.

I looked through the windshield to see that we were fast approaching a gargantuan network of rock-like bridges that linked both sides of the canyon. It was a sort of natural honeycomb of rocks.

"I got a better idea. Fly under that bridge and into those rocks."

I swung the throttle so the crosshairs on the radar screen moved to the front of us and away from the red dots.

"Get as close as you can," I said and took aim. "Swing under it."

"*Under* it? What are you doing? Making this up as you go along?"

"Just do it!"

"It's not going to give us a lot of room."

"Don't worry. It won't be there much longer," I said.

"I don't like the sound of that."

"Slow down. Draw them in closer."

"Amazingly, I like the sound of *that* even less."

Argenti slowed down, and the explosions crashed closer, more destructive, as Geryon and his ships closed in for the kill.

"Do something!" Argenti yelled.

Argenti approached the bridge-like configuration of rocks and I fired for all it was worth. We flew under the bridge just as it exploded into hundreds of large chunks.

Boulders rained down all around.

Argenti pulled up and away. The rocks brought down one of their ships, which crashed in a flurry of flames and disintegrating metal.

"Son of a gun, it worked!" Argenti said.

"One down, one to go." I said.

To escape the last demon ship, we practically went vertical. Did Hell have a ceiling? We were about to find out.

⁂

"Go faster," I yelled when the pounding on the hull got louder.

"Christ, Dante, if we go any faster, we'll go back in time!"

I felt as if I was in an elevator rising to the thousandth floor in sixty seconds. I fought the urge to vomit, and grabbed the throttle again.

I swung the crosshairs to our rear in an attempt to aim at the final ship. I was about to shoot, but the radar screen went black.

"What the hell?"

Oddly enough, the pounding on the hull and explosions abruptly ended, too.

"That's it?" Argenti asked, noticing the absence of demonic fire.

"I don't know," I said. "Level this thing off."

"What are you going to do?"

"Unless you have a rear view mirror handy, I'm going to take a gander the hard way." I stumbled to the hatch and unlocked it. It was more like a submarine hatch than an aircraft door.

"What the hell are you doing?" Argenti yelled.

"You just keep this rig straight!"

I didn't want to unlock the damned hatch, let alone open it. We were going at a pretty fair clip and sticking my head out to look behind us was a display of lunacy equal to that of building a ship with no conduit for viewing its rear.

There has to be some other way, Joe. Do you really think it's wise to randomly push any more buttons or levers in hopes of finding a rear view? You've been pretty lucky up until now, and it would be nice to actually do something smart for once, wouldn't it? Do you know what the smart move is, though? Do you, Joe?

I braced myself to swing open the hatch. Winds that made a New England hurricane seem like a beach breeze smacked me in the face. I kept telling myself that no matter what happened—I was immortal now. If the winds popped out an eye or debris crushed my skull, I would eventually heal.

I stuck my head out to look and could barely hear Argenti through the whipping winds and whistle of the engines.

"See anything?" he shouted.

Before I could answer, two strong scaly arms reached down and yanked me out of the ship. When I landed topside, I was amazed to see two reptilian demons, each about eight feet tall. Neither of them as hefty as Geryon, but they were formidable just the same. They must have been hanging onto the hull the whole time, which explained why our pursuers never fired directly at us. They'd been trying to force us to land.

I looked behind one of them to see an open panel and broken wires, and I understood why the radar screen went out so conveniently and at the wrong time. Despite the force of the wind, one demon held me, his ape-like feet firmly clasping the metal pipes on the hull, as the other minion hopped through the hatch to get at Argenti.

"Argenti! A demon—" I yelled, but the demon punched me square in the face.

He picked me up, gripping me by my throat, and stared me in the eye.

If *that* wasn't enough, the ship chasing us began to shoot once again. As before, it didn't hit us directly, but the concussion nearly blew out my eardrums. I grabbed at the demon's arms to try to stop him from choking me when our ship started to sway.

Obviously, there was no longer anyone at the helm. The demon inside the ship was probably beating the vinegar out of Argenti.

I looked at my demon captor. At first glance, he looked to be smiling, but his jaw jutted out in such a way that he only *looked* that way. He wasn't *smiling* at all. He threw me like a baseball. I rolled across the hull and fell over the edge. I clung to the skid, too terrified to let go and too beaten to pull myself up. Peering down, I expected to see the ground way below but saw none. There was no ground…only the dismal gray sky. If there wasn't gravity pulling at me, I wouldn't have known which way was up. But there *was* gravity, which became more apparent when the ship, once again, went vertical. I could only imagine the pain Argenti was facing as I finally pulled myself up to the top of the hull.

The demon saw me get a leg up and immediately came at me. Though the ship wobbled as it flew upward, he kept amazing balance. There was nothing even remotely human about this creature. He even defied gravity, walking where I couldn't even stand.

I dragged myself onto the hull again, braced myself between two of the ship's fins, and pulled out my handgun. I had no idea how many rounds I had left, or if there was an endless supply. Did the bullets grow back like a dismembered finger? I fired. I couldn't have missed, but it didn't even slow him down. I squirted lead like it was going out of style, but the big reptile goon kept on coming.

How great would it be to have the gun you gave Hector? Bright move, Joe. With that weapon, you could have had a chance in Hell. Even Malecoda and the Malebranche couldn't have held their ground when hit with that kind of muscle. You need that kind of firepower.

As the demon came closer, I glanced behind him to the open panel where he'd callously ripped the wires to blind our radar. Sparks bounced from the wires onto the metal…and where there are sparks, there's *power.* Geryon's crony was upon me before I could shoot again. He knocked the gun from my hand, and just like that, it went spinning into the ugly sky.

I crawled across the hull toward the open panel, but the beast grabbed my leg and pulled me back toward him. He picked me up and pinned me against one of the taller fins. I knew exactly what he had in mind—beat the snot out of me, then take me to his master—Geryon. These demons had been after me for a very long time. He had no intention of throwing me off the ship. He owned me, which meant I was now in Geryon's possession.

Why the hell are they after you, Joe? How did you get such an honor?

If I believed Virgil, they wanted to put me in my *proper place*, or perhaps bring me back to Minos for an apt judgment, but did I believe Virgil?

The demon pulled his fist back to pulverize me when a strange thought washed over me. Why not ask him?

If demons had once been angels, they must have some intelligence left. The insect demons seemed to run on instinct, almost like mindless drones, and the mechanical ones seemed like, well…*mechanical.* The reptilian ones? They seemed to be at the top of the food chain. Hell, they could fly these ships, which made them pretty sharp in my book.

"Wait!" I shouted.

The demon stopped in mid-swing.

"Why are you chasing me?" I hollered. "What do you want from me?"

The way he looked at me made my skin crawl. It was as if he was disgusted by the thought of conversing with the likes of me.

"I know you can understand me," I demanded. "Tell me!"

He didn't answer. Maybe he couldn't. Maybe his tongue and mouth couldn't make the right sounds. He put his face next to mine. For some reason, I expected a roar or even a growl, but all he did was hiss.

He either couldn't or wouldn't talk, and I didn't want to continue being a punching bag, so I did what anybody raised on the streets of Boston would do. I kicked him in the balls, or rather, where I thought his *balls* would be.

Catholic school had taught me enough of the Bible to know that there had been a time when fallen angels had come to know humans, and I mean *know* in the Biblical sense. You don't come to *know* someone without sexual organs.

It was a swell plan. Then again, *every* plan is a swell plan when it works. *This* one, however, didn't. Both the demon and I looked down at his crotch, then back up to each other. Maybe this was a female demon, if there was such a thing. Well, either way, it *didn't* work. He didn't look to be in pain nor was he amused. He seized me and threw me across the hull. I landed right next to the open, sparking panel where I wanted to go in the first place.

I was sort of proud that my plan had worked, even if it didn't go the way I'd thought it would.

I immediately clung onto anything I could, in order to stay on the hull.

"Is that all you got?" I yelled. "You hit like a sissy girl!"

I wanted to enrage him so he wouldn't think about anything other than coming after me. I only hoped that the electricity in these wires was powerful enough to give him one hell of a jolt.

He came at me like a bull.

I tried to remember high school earth science class. I either had to be grounded or not grounded. I tried, but I couldn't remember which, and there wasn't any more time to think.

I braced myself, gripped the loose wires, and shoved them into the demon's leg. We both jolted back and forth from the electric discharge. The first thought that burned through my cooking brain was that I probably *should* have been grounded. I knew I wouldn't die, but neither would he. I waited him out as we both started to smoke from the heat.

The ship did a quick roll and the demon finally fell off the hull and into the void below. It took all my strength to control my body spasms and yank out the wires, disconnecting me from the power source. I felt woozy but back in control of my body.

The ship behind us fired again, the shots closer now. Whoever was shooting was probably really ticked off at what he'd just witnessed.

I crawled along the hull until I reached the side with the open hatch.

I spilled my limp body through the hatch and fell back into the ship, where Argenti and the other demon thug waited.

CHAPTER 33
Canto XV – Circle VII – Round III – On Geryon's Back
❧❧

The combination of my body being weakened from the electric discharge and the systematic shaking apart of the ship kept me off balance.

In the far corner, through the dim, blinking lights, I saw the demon beating the tar out of Argenti. If *this* had been another time, I'd have bought some popcorn, sat back and enjoyed the show. But this wasn't another time.

I gathered what remained of my strength, though don't ask me from where, and I jumped on the demon's back. Believe it or not, of the three of us, *I* was the least surprised.

The demon's tail wrapped around my throat and whipped me back to the control panel at the front of the ship. I rammed into a collection of buttons and levers that caused the ship to climb and accelerate even faster. Everything outside looked like a distorted blur. For all I knew, we approached light-speed.

I don't know what you call it when a pilot is pulled back due to a quick acceleration but I felt my flesh pulling me to the rear of the ship. The demon, like the one topside, seemed less affected by the forces, so I needed to think of something fast.

I clung to the control panel, swinging myself into the pilot's seat. "Argenti! Hang on!" I screamed as I jerked the wheel.

The demon lost balance for a moment, buying me some time, even though it was mere seconds.

"How do I slow this thing down?"

222

Argenti mumbled his response, in too much pain to respond.

I saw the demon regain balance so I swung the wheel again. This time, one of the fireballs from the other ship scored a hit on us. The demon slammed against the side wall.

"Damn it, Argenti! How do I slow this heap down?"

"The lever to your right," Argenti gurgled, "by your feet. Pull it back!"

I reached for the lever. Before I could do anything, the demon grabbed me and yanked me out of the seat. He pinned me to the side wall, pounding the snot out of me with a closed fist. Immediately after the searing pain, I felt several teeth loosen. He clasped his claw-like fingers around my throat.

He must have closed off an artery or something, because along with the closure of my windpipe, I felt a tingling on the left side of my head. I wished I would just black out and escape this horrid place, but I knew it wouldn't happen. When I thought I couldn't take anymore, Argenti jumped on the demon from behind. He grabbed one of the demon's arms as I fell to my knees and gasped for air.

"Dante! Help me!"

The demon moved his free arm to swipe at Argenti, but I jumped up and grabbed it.

With Argenti holding one arm and me holding the other, we kept the demon at bay.

"Push him out the hatch!" I yelled.

We both planted our feet to push.

Unfortunately, the demon had other plans. He flung Argenti across the ship and out the hatch.

"Argenti!" I screamed as he sailed into open air and dropped to Hell below, leaving me alone with the brute.

The demon threw me to the back of the ship. As I lay there imagining how far Argenti would plummet, the reptilian creature jumped into the pilot's seat and pulled back the lever. To his surprise, however, we didn't slow down. The demon clicked buttons and pulled the lever farther back.

The beast then flipped a switch and a second radar screen rose up. The demon finally got the ship under control and it jolted back. It slowed like an elevator that, at long last, reached the top floor.

"Hey genius!" I yelled. "You think I'm going to give up that easy?"

The demon got to his feet and stared at me as if he were a lion eyeing a mountain of raw beef.

He grasped me by the throat, reached up to the ceiling of the craft, and fiddled with some metal buckles until a topside hatch blew open.

He jumped through and, once again, I found myself topside on the hull.

He held me like a piece of luggage and swung his free arm to signal the other ship.

I knew what he had planned and wanted none of it. Once on the other ship, I would be dead meat and at the mercy of Geryon—not to mention his horde.

The ship closed in on us while I searched for some way out.

❧

It's strange, the thoughts that pop into your head when you're being squeezed like a grapefruit on a warm Sunday morning.

For some reason, I remembered a Bugs Bunny cartoon. Bugs was boxing some muscular brute twice his size. He looked over his obvious physical superior and, for no apparent reason, wilted into unconsciousness.

His opponent must have spent all his time in the gym, rather than the library, because he dropped his defenses to view Bugs's horizontal body. Suddenly, Bugs punched the big guy's face with both gloves, sending him sailing through the ceiling.

The other ship drew closer. When no other ideas sprang to mind, I went for the cartoonish escape plan.

I let my body go limp. I stopped struggling, closed my eyes, and even held my breath. I felt the demon's grip loosen. Still, I didn't move. Obviously confused, he shook me, but still, I kept my eyes closed, allowing my body to be moved like a rag doll in the hand of a child. I needed to wait for the exact moment when he would jump to the next ship, in order to make this plan work.

Unfortunately, since my eyes were now closed, I couldn't tell where the other ship was. So, I listened for the approaching ship's whining engine sounds.

I figured I would count to ten, and go for broke.

I counted to myself.

One... Two... Three... The hell with it.

I got to *three* and sprang back to life just as the demon started his run across the hull. I grabbed hold of some metal rods fastened to the ship when the demon jumped to the other craft. Since he'd loosened his grip and hadn't expected me to struggle, all he took with him was the skin under his claws. He leapt onto the hull of the other ship—without yours truly.

I rolled across the hull and poured myself into the top hatch, falling onto the ship's floor. With the ship still speeding and out of control, I crawled across the floor to the side hatch. I reached out to close it, and saw an amazing sight. Argenti was clinging to one of the ship's legs.

"Argenti?" I yelled.

He didn't answer.

"Argenti! Hang on!"

The pounding from our pursuers began again. Rocked by blast after blast, I was amazed at how much this vehicle could endure.

I crawled out on the spider-like leg. "Argenti! Reach!"

Argenti clung to the leg like a babe to his mother.

"Come on, Argenti, reach…" I stopped short when I realized what had him so terrified. Several other ships pursued us now, some tall ships, some sled-like, and another spider-like craft. "Oh my God," I choked out.

I finally got to Argenti's hand and grabbed it. A shot whizzed by us.

"Jesus Christ!" Argenti screamed.

"Argenti! We have to do this together. Got it?"

Below us was desert. I hadn't been able to see the ground before, and all we'd done since then was shoot upward, so we must have flown back up several circles. We crawled back up the leg and both of us tumbled through the hatch and into the ship. Rolling onto our knees, we crawled back to our seats.

"Can you control this heap, or what?" I asked.

"Well, I got good news and bad news. I can still steer."

"So, what's the bad news?"

"We're in Hell!"

We both looked through the front shield and although Argenti was dumbfounded, I knew exactly where we were.

"Holy God Almighty!" Argenti said. "What the devil is that?"

Tornado after tornado whirled out of control, the people within the wind spinning as helplessly as the rest of the debris, kind of like airborne junkyards. We'd found our way back to the second circle—that of the carnal.

Just how fast were you going, Joe? The speed of sound?

"I know where we are," I said.

"Yeah, well, we're not going to be here for long."

"Wait!"

"What?"

"That one over there," I said, pointing to the largest and most violent tornado, "fly into it."

"Run that by me again?"

"They'd be loopy to follow us."

"This thing's falling apart. It won't be able to take something that strong."

Again, we felt the impact a barrage of light balls from the ships behind us.

"We're not going to take much more of *that*, either," I justified.

"Okay…fine…swell…no problem! Better strap in because it's going to be a bumpy ride."

Argenti steered the ship between two large tornados. We had about as much control as a bee in a blender.

❧❧

I had to hand it to Argenti—the man could fly like a…well…fly. He kept us from crashing. It was as if he'd been born with wings.

"Look!" I pointed to the radar screen. Red dot after red dot fell off the screen. Demon ship after demon ship had either surrendered to the winds or turned back.

I heard a thump, then another. It wasn't until one of the *thumps* hit the front windshield that we both realized what was happening. We were hitting people. We hit another and then another. I winced each and every time.

"Look out!" I finally yelled.

"I'm trying."

"Do you have to hit so many?"

"Anytime you want to take over, you just speak up," Argenti said.

Another barrage of light balls hit us from above.

"Jesus Christ!" Argenti yelled as he tried to maintain control of the vehicle.

"They're still chasing us." I looked at the radar screen to discover that only one red dot remained. "Geryon," I muttered to myself.

"I guess that makes him as loopy as us, huh?"

"Dive!" I yelled.

"What?"

"Go down. Straight down, toward the ground!"

"Jesus, Dante! Are you trying to be the first mug to actually *die* in Hell?"

"Do it!"

I was surprised that Argenti complied so quickly and easily. I guess he saw no other option, as well.

We dove toward the dirt, Geryon on our rear bumper the whole way.

"When I tell you to pull up, pull up!" My plan was simple—dive, slow down, bring them in close, and pull up at the last second. "Slow down, bring them in closer," I said.

"We can't."

"What?"

"We can't slow down."

"That demon was able to slow it down," I nagged.

"You want to go get him? I'll wait here!"

"Pull up!" I screamed, seeing the ground come up on us faster than I'd anticipated.

Argenti braced his feet and yanked back on the wheel. We leveled off just in time, but weren't able to climb again. We skidded across the ground and the winds only served to perpetuate the turbulence of our slide.

"Hang on!" Argenti yelled and yanked back on the wheel.

The front of the ship lifted for a moment, and I thought we could even go airborne again.

Instead, we crashed back down, only this time, we rolled. The ship crumbled all around us, Argenti's side ripping open and sucking him out.

"Argenti!" I yelled, but he was gone.

I expected the ship to explode. Instead, it finally skidded to a halt as the sudden realization hit me that I was in pain.

The ship crashed in an area away from the tornados, so I was able to get out without being sucked into a funnel of winds. I dragged myself out of the wreckage, rolling onto the dirt outside. I held my sides as I coughed up blood, certain I'd cracked a rib. Sprawled on my back, I rested for a few moments. I drew in a painful breath and looked up at the sky.

I was still on the second circle, surrounded by muddy, dead brush. It reminded me of the place where I'd first struck that deal with Virgil. He would help me find Argenti, if, when it was over, I would go with him. It now seemed like a lifetime ago. Perhaps it was.

In our struggle with the demon, we must have accidentally triggered a control switch that propelled us into thousands, or even tens of thousands, of miles of flight in mere seconds.

Geryon's ship landed a couple of hundred feet from my wreckage, cutting short my rest and my thoughts. I considered getting to my feet to flee, but the pain was too intense. Besides, where would I go?

I watched the hatch open, and three of them climbed out. Once again, they moved with an odd kind of grace. They were ferocious looking creatures but there was something about them, especially the big one. They looked down upon me with neither hatred nor anger, at least not that I could tell.

"Geryon, I presume," I said to the largest one.

He didn't answer, nor had I expected him to. I'd never heard a demon talk, and didn't know if they couldn't or just didn't want to.

"What do you expect me to do?" I asked. "Cry? Beg?"

Geryon knelt beside to me.

"Kiss my ass," I added for flavor.

I thought all was lost, but then I noticed movement out of the corner of my eye. It was Argenti. The SOB was dragging himself from the brush toward Geryon's ship. With the demons still focused on me, I didn't want to rat him out. Once he reached the ship, he could easily get me out of this jam. Well, maybe not *easily*, but I figured he'd be in a better position to try. He knew how to fly, and he knew those ships could shoot fireballs. So I bought him some time.

"What the hell do you want from me?" I shouted at Geryon. "How did I earn such an honor, anyway? What did I do in life that made me deserve having you chase me for all eternity? You don't have to answer. It's because I'm a nice guy, isn't it? You can't stand nice guys in Hell!"

Geryon's ship suddenly powered up. The demons looked at the ship as it lifted up from the ground. Two of the demons ran for it but Geryon stood fast, gawking at me. I laughed in defiance. Unfortunately, to my surprise, that's where it ended. The ship just flew off the ground and away. I stopped laughing when I realized that Argenti had abandoned me.

"Argenti, you son of a bitch!" I yelled.

Geryon plunged his claws into my shoulder. I screamed in agony.

The other two demons returned, hissing at each other. I knew they were communicating in some fashion, but I didn't have a clue what they were saying or what they planned to do next. They circled me.

"What are you going to do?" I asked.

Geryon grabbed my legs, the other two each seized an arm, and the horrible thought occurred to me that their plan included dismemberment.

"No! Stop!" I hollered.

They all pulled. I screamed in blood bubbling pain as I felt my knees and elbows pop and bleed. I felt like I was tied to three horses, each running in different directions. They jerked again.

I suddenly heard the high pitched whine of the demon ship. Half a second later, it flew low enough to ram the demons, but high enough to miss me. Like I said, Argenti was a damned good pilot.

Geryon and the two demons rolled in different directions. All I managed to do was lay there and pray that they were in as much pain as me.

Argenti landed the ship about fifty feet away and slopped out of the hatch. As he dragged himself in my direction, I saw a bone protruding from his leg.

"Come on, Dante, move!" he screamed.

I rolled over onto my belly, but couldn't do much else. My joints had been torn, and I needed time to heal.

Argenti, dragging his bad leg behind him, limped toward me. "What are you waiting for—a bus pass?"

"I thought you left me," I said with honest relief at seeing him again.

"I did," Argenti answered. "Now get the hell up!"

He pulled me up as best he could. I made the mistake of leaning on him. He instinctively shifted his weight to his broken leg. He screamed, and we both fell to the ground.

"Come on, Argenti!"

"I can't," he said.

We helped each other half way up and both noticed Geryon stepping out of the far off brush. He'd been thrown a couple of hundred feet away from us when Argenti rammed into him. We were only about thirty feet from the ship but it might as well have been on the moon. Geryon charged toward us. The other demons filed in behind him.

"We're not going to make it," Argenti said.

"Keep moving!"

Argenti fell again, screaming from the pain. Suddenly, a large man clad in a bed sheet ran out of the dead brush, seized Argenti, and threw him over his shoulder. He used his free arm to keep me on my feet.

When he turned to me, a look of recognition struck me.

"Paolo?" I said, amazed to see the Frenchman again. We must have hit him with our ship when we'd flown through the tornados. The last I'd seen of him, he'd been running into the winds to find his true love.

"Come," he said as he looped an arm around me.

A hulk of a man, Paolo must have been made of steel. He should have been badly injured, but I suspected that running in the winds had given him the strength of a mammoth.

He stuffed Argenti into the hatch, then me. He hopped in just as Geryon and his minions arrived. Argenti dragged himself to the control panel while Paolo pushed the hatch shut.

"Quickly!" Paolo shouted. Before he could secure the hatch, Geryon reached through the opening.

Geryon shoved the hatch halfway open but Paolo refused to toss in the sponge. Bracing himself, he pushed back. I forced myself up to add my weight to his.

"Argenti," I yelled. "If you're going to do something, do it and I mean pronto!"

Argenti powered up the ship and it started its walk.

Geryon stayed with us as we picked up speed. He forced open the hatch, inserting his shoulder and head into the ship's interior.

"We must strike down the beast!" Paolo said as he strained against the hatch. "Something with great size."

I looked around for something big but there was nothing. At my feet lay my badge. It had probably fallen from my belt when Paolo shoved me through the hatch. I picked it up, an idea forming in my bruised noggin.

"No, not big," I said. "Sharp!"

It had been so long, I'd almost forgotten that I still had my badge. It had gotten me out of the jam back with the virtuous and again with Phleygas, so why not now? I pulled it out of its case, unhooked the pin, and jammed it into Geryon's eyes.

"Try to dismember me, will you!" I shouted as Geryon fell away from the hatch.

We flew away, leaving the demons behind. I'd left my badge sticking in Geryon's eye. Gone now, I felt in my heart that I would never see it again. Virgil had once told me that I still had it because it symbolized a life long gone. Maybe now, I no longer needed it. Or maybe now, I just no longer needed what it represented—life on Earth.

CHAPTER 34
Canto V – Circle II – Return to The Lustful
❧

W e landed somewhere in the second circle, with the lustful and the
winds not far off.

I needed a breather, and Argenti's leg needed mending.

Paolo added up to a mystery to me. Though *that* was nothing new in
this place, I still felt the need to resolve my feelings about him. Although
I shouldn't have, I took it personally that he'd cheated with his brother's
wife.

We stepped outside, Paolo and I, and I watched him as he stretched.
He took a deep breath, as if the air was fresh and clean. To him, it must
have been. How long had he been in those dusty winds and tornados,
searching for his true love? In a way, he reminded me of *my* brother. He
was big and strong and, like Mickey, he had betrayed *his* brother.

He looked my way, smiling sadly. "It happened in the year of our
Lord, 1278," he said in his French accent.

"What did?"

"When I fell in love with my Francesca."

"You've been turning this place inside out, searching for her since the
thirteenth century?"

"In the year of 1275, she and my elder brother Gianciotto married for
political gains. He needed a wife for his government position and her
father wanted Francesca cared for, so the decision was made. Years,
however, have a way of changing things around you and within you. You
understand what I say?"

"Yes."

"Three years had come to pass and she and I fell in love. We had not wished this to be, yet what we know to be right means nothing in matters of the heart. In 1285 of the service of our Lord, he discovered the truth, my brother Gianciotto. The truth, you see, cannot be hidden forever. So, he killed us as we slept in each other's arms. Perhaps I had earned his wrath."

"Nobody deserves to be murdered," I said.

"My brother must be here somewhere, I think…somewhere in Hell."

"As is mine."

"Then we are alike in this way, no?"

"Come with us," I said, half surprising myself.

"I cannot."

"Because of your lover? She might not even be here."

"She was condemned by Minos, as was I," he said stubbornly. "She resides here. I will find her and she will know that my love for her is boundless."

"Look, nothing is worth this."

"Your manner of dress is not from my time," Paolo said. "When you had the breath of life, did you not know the touch of love?"

"Yes, I did," I said, thinking of Bea.

"Would you not do anything to find her again?"

I didn't answer. It was all I could do to muster a simple nod.

I felt like a schmuck. Virgil had offered to take me out of here several times, but I couldn't do it. Like Paolo said, what we know to be right means nothing in matters of the heart. It doesn't matter if the heart feels love, anger, or hate.

"I am trapped by my own heart," Paolo said as he walked away.

"Paolo?" I called out. "Good luck."

He smiled, and headed back to the ferocious winds.

The first time I'd met him, I'd felt nothing but loathing for the man. I remembered thinking how I would feel if Mickey and Beatrice had had an affair behind my back, and what finding out about it would have done to me.

I watched this man walk off to the distant winds—the same man who'd come out of nowhere to save my skin—and a different scenario came to mind.

What if, instead of Mickey and Beatrice running around behind my back, it had been Mickey who'd *married* Beatrice? Could I have remained in the background, loving Bea from a distance? Could I have kept my feelings a secret from Mickey? What if, one day, Bea had told me that she loved me?

What would I have done? Could I have been strong? Where is the true strength? In denying one's love or surrendering to it against all barriers?

I now viewed Paolo in a whole new light, and my loathing for him was now rooted only in myself.

I couldn't help Paolo, but I could help Argenti.

It's strange. A broken shin bone protruding from the skin once merited immediate medical attention. But we'd grown so accustomed to life threatening situations being anything *but* life threatening, that the alleviation of pain became the main goal. Even *that* might have become secondary when the situation presented itself.

My knees and elbows still ached, but I managed to bend them again with minimal discomfort. I didn't know if I was healing faster or if I'd just gotten used to the pain. I really didn't care. I was healing, which was good enough for me.

Argenti needed a splint, so I searched through some dead bushes in hopes of finding a piece of wood strong enough to brace around his leg. If nothing else, it would have surprised the hell out of him that I even gave a rat's ass enough to help him out, let alone actually attempted any first aid.

However, I was the one who was surprised when a hand bolted from the dead brush and grabbed my arm.

If I could still take a leak, I think I would have wet my pants. Lucky for me, all I did was jump.

"So, how have you been?" the angel asked, smiling as he stepped out of the dense brush.

"You?" I said, trying not to sound too startled, but relieved that I didn't scream like a little girl who just saw a rat the size of a German Shepherd.

"The name's *Virgil*, remember?"

"I remember."

He still wore his combat gear and I felt a sort of kinship with him. Maybe it was the fact that being in WWII had been a major event in my life, or because I'd seen him during my time on Earth, or simply because he had sort of an inner strength I admired, but I was glad to see him. Even with the rifle on his shoulder and the grenades clipped on his belt, there was humor about him, something I didn't normally see in the *other* Virgil.

"Have you been following me all this time?" I asked.

"Of course. You think I haven't been watching you? Bravo with that whole Geryon thing, by the way. Not many come up against *that* demon and get to keep their arms and legs, or their skin, for that matter."

"You could have helped."

"What, and spoil the show? Besides, I'm just..."

"The messenger," I said, completing his sentence.

"That's right."

"Then why are you even here?" I said.

"Because I made a promise to someone we both know."

"Yeah? Who? God?" I said sarcastically.

"No, well I mean, of course the big guy, too, but I was referring to Beatrice."

"Beatrice?" I said in shock.

"You remember her, don't you? Yay high—red hair—green eyes—freckles. In case you're wondering, she misses you."

I didn't know how to react. It was stupid, but I needed to *do* something, so I gathered wood for Argenti's splint.

"Hello?" the angel said, confused. "What are you doing?"

"I need wood for a splint."

"That's sweet, but hey—I just told you that your wife misses you. Don't you have anything to say?"

I was punched by an overwhelming sense of loss. Trying to fight off memories of being with her, I continued to gather wood.

This must have been how Paolo always felt. It was an unceasing feeling of loss that remained constant and acute. His Hell *wasn't* in the winds. His Hell was in his loss. Perhaps, that's the real definition of everyone's Hell.

Finally, some concern crept through and I spoke.

"How is she?" I asked, looking away from him.

"She watches over you, Joe, and she's very concerned for your faith."

"My faith?"

"Over your wife's grave, didn't you tell Father Nicholas that you had no faith?"

"That was a long time ago," I said, trying not to show even one tear.

"Yeah, it was, but she doesn't know what I know," the angel said.

"What's that?"

"That there's only one way I can get you out of this pickle, and that's for you to do what needs to be done. You know what that is, don't you Joe?"

"Find justice for my family," I said with conviction.

"That's right."

"You tell Bea not to worry." I felt the rage stir within me. The angel was right. I had to get Mickey back and give him what he deserved.

"Good. Oh, and about that *guide* of yours, he's not who you think he is."

"That seems to be the way of things around here," I said.

"Look, I'm breaking protocol by telling you this, but he's really bad. I mean *really* bad. Really, really—"

"Bad, yeah, I got it."

"No, you don't."

"Okay, I give. What did he do in life that was so horrible?"

"He didn't do anything in *life*, Joe. He's an angel."

"You mean like you?"

"Bite your tongue!"

"Then who?"

"He was God's *first* angel."

Slowly, my Catholic school memories resurrected. I finally understood. "You're telling me that Virgil..."

"I'm Virgil!"

"... is Satan?" I finished.

"Yep."

"Why didn't you tell me this before?" I asked.

"Would you have believed me then?"

"What makes you think I believe you *now*?"

"Because you're a cop. Evidence never lies."

"Why me? Why is he spending all this time with me?"

"Hmmmm... Why would Old Nick spend all this time with the one soul that doesn't belong here? Do you really need an answer to that?" he asked.

The angel made sense. The devil corrupted souls. All the other souls in Hell had already been damned, but not mine.

"It will happen like this," the angel said. "He'll put you in a position where there is no way out. Then, he'll tell you to have *faith*. That's his *thing*; he likes to tell people to have faith. Anyway, *that's* when he'll trap you for all eternity." He placed his hand on my shoulder. "Don't let him."

I nodded.

He removed his hand and walked away. "Okay, then. See you in the funny papers."

"What? Where are you going?" I asked, surprised by his abrupt departure.

"I'll be around. Besides, you've got a job to do. When you're done, I'll take you to your proper place."

With that, he walked away.

❧

I dropped the lengths of wood next to Argenti.

"What's that?"

"I'm going to make a splint for you. Brace yourself. I'm going to shove the bone back into your leg. It's going to hurt like the dickens."

"I bet that just breaks your heart, huh, Dante?"

I didn't answer.

I decided not to tell Argenti what the angel had told me about Virgil. To be honest, I didn't know who to believe. Worse yet, I didn't know who to trust.

Who are you going to trust, Joe? For all you know, the angel soldier could be Satan. Hell, even Mary could be Old Nick. Who can you trust, Joe?

I grabbed Argenti's ankle and yanked on it, using my other hand to jam the bone back inside his shin.

I expected him to scream, but no scream came. He was so used to the pain by now, that even something like this wouldn't force a yelp. Hell, we were boiled alive. Was a broken leg something to cry about? Argenti watched me as I wrapped dead bark around his leg and tied off the wood with some thin dried weeds.

"How's that?"

"Why are you helping me?" he asked.

237

"When those demons were pulling me apart, why did you help me?"

"I left you behind."

"You came back," I said. "A lot of mugs wouldn't have."

"Nothing you wouldn't have done."

"I'm not so sure about that." To my own disdain, I meant it.

"Do you still think I murdered your family?"

"What do you care what I think?"

"I think I know why I've stayed with you all this time, Dante."

"Why?"

"I need you to believe me."

I continued to work on the splint, not answering immediately. Finally, the answer fell from my lips. "I believe you, Argenti."

"I'm sorry, Dante. I'm sorry for what happened to your wife, your family, a lot of things."

"I know."

"There's something I need to say. Something I tried to tell you on the roof that day. I called your wife and told her."

"What?"

"I knew what your brother was planning, and I tried to warn her. I knew you wouldn't have believed me. She didn't either, not until it was too late. I called you the night they took her, remember? I told you to go to the warehouse."

"I remember," I said. "I thought you were setting a trap."

"I was trying to help. I thought if you showed up, they would have turned tail. They wanted to kill your family and frame you. Your digging about who took the case of cocaine made them nervous. Killing you would have only left more questions. But framing you? That would have *answered* all the questions."

I couldn't believe my own brother had been this cold blooded about killing my family and plotting against me.

I tied off the last of the splint and, for some reason, I noticed my bracelet. "My daughter gave me this." I smiled sadly. "It was the first thing she ever gave me...and the last thing."

"I had a daughter once, and a wife," Argenti confessed.

"I didn't know that."

"It was after the war. When I first met her, I thought, *this is it*. This was the reason why I'd been mysteriously saved by those *Foo Fighters*. Do you know what it's like to just look into someone's eyes and realize you're home?"

I nodded.

"For a while, I was happy, truly happy. But the journey never ends, does it? They were killed a long time before we met, before I became the man you knew. They were run down by some drunk on the fourth of July in Hoboken…in 1956."

"God, Argenti, you don't think…that," I stuttered. "That mug we left with the demonic grinders? You don't believe—" But I stopped. The evidence was compelling and Argenti was probably right in his assumption. That drunk driver we came to in the seventh circle was the one who ran down Argenti's family.

Argenti laughed bitterly. "At least I didn't want to drag him to a lake of fire, huh?"

"That's what Virgil meant by your *loss* when we were climbing down that jumbled mass of a cliff?"

"The police never caught him…the drunkard. He just disappeared. I was never the same after that. I justified every evil thing I did by saying that I never really *killed* anyone. Someone else was actually selling the drugs. I never did. I never really set anyone on fire. I just told other people to do it. In the end, I was responsible. I killed your daughters, sure as if I shot them myself."

"I understand," I said.

"Now I know the reason I was saved during the war. It was so I could find my true love… and then lose her. That was what those Foo Fighters— those *demons*—had in store for me the whole time. Did you ever think that you were just a pawn in someone else's game?"

"I don't know, maybe."

"You see, Dante, we *do* have something in common," Argenti said. "We have a nightmare in common."

I didn't know what to tell the guy. The man I'd looked at for so long with anger and hate was just a human being. He wasn't a cold-blooded killing machine, but a man who had experienced his own losses.

I knew it was time for me to admit something. Something I knew deep down inside, but couldn't say. "Argenti, you son of a bitch," I said with half a smile and half a tear. "You were right about me…and I was wrong about you. I'm no better than anyone else here."

I pulled Argenti to his feet, and he moaned from the pain.

"Sorry," I said.

"It's alright. I'm used to the pain."

"Yeah, me too."

CHAPTER 35
Canto XV – Circle VII – Round III – The Hidden Circle

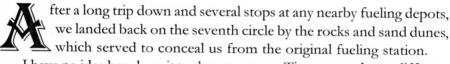

fter a long trip down and several stops at any nearby fueling depots, we landed back on the seventh circle by the rocks and sand dunes, which served to conceal us from the original fueling station.

I have no idea how long it took us to return. Time seemed very different to me now. I worried that Mary hadn't waited for us.

Argenti had an incredible sense of direction. The seventh circle could have been the size of the United States or the whole of Asia. I certainly wouldn't have been able to find them.

If it hadn't been for Mary, I don't know if I would have been so determined to return to this spot, and it troubled me that I might have left Virgil behind.

He had saved me on several occasions, but if I believed the angel, Virgil's motives were questionable. Had his plan always been to entrap me in a coffin of flames, or a lake of fire, or something even worse?

Back with the wrathful, I realized that Virgil hadn't been able to *make* me do anything. He could only advise, and thus, only trick…which was Old Nick's MO.

I felt a sense of familiarity with the angel, but I owed Virgil a debt of gratitude. To be honest, I didn't trust either one of them.

I had trusted my partner, Tony, and my brother on Earth. *Both* had betrayed me.

I helped Argenti from the ship. I looked around, but saw no one.

"Mary?" I shouted. "Mary!"

She stepped out from her hiding place behind some rocks. I can't say I blamed her for hiding. A demon ship comes your way, you'd be dopey *not* to wonder who's behind the wheel.

"Saints preserve us!" She threw her arms around us both. "I am truly amazed, Joseph Dante."

"It's good to see you again," I said.

"And you, as well."

"Where's Virgil?"

"He's in the blackened demon cottage."

"What's he doing in there?"

"This I don't know," she said.

"Okay, hang on, I'll go get him." I turned to the splinted Argenti. "Stay with her."

⚬⚬

I crawled over the rocks to see the fueling depot. Since the explosion, it had become a burnt out shell.

I walked inside, looking around.

I must admit, I was curious about this joint. The demons had refueled their vehicles outside, but why had they come in here?

I walked down the long hallway, which was littered with statues of creatures and humans.

The statues were frozen in poses of agony and terror, with the humans as the terrorized.

I looked at a statue of a man on his knees just inches from a statue of a demon with his huge jaws opened wide, and another statue of an old woman with her arms raised, as if begging to the statue of a demon with an axe.

Each statue contained an inscription on its base. One read *George Erickson: 1792 A.D., for the sin of slave trading*. The statue depicted a chained man being dragged by several demons.

I saw many other statues with inscriptions in other languages.

What the hell are you thinking, Joe? These aren't even statues!

Around the eyes and lips, the stone was as clear as glass. Underneath, the eyes moved.

These were actual *people*. Had their bodies been encased in stone, or had it been their souls? If I could crack through the rock, would there be flesh underneath?

We had to stop several times to refuel and each depot had one of these ugly buildings.

There could have been hundreds of these stations scattered throughout the circles of Hell, and in each, hundreds of statues such as these.

These black box theaters were sort of a hidden tenth circle of Hell.

What of the demons…were they just statues? Or were they also actual demons encased in rock?

Why would a demon be encased in rock? Don't they run this dump?

Back in the city of Dis, the mechanical demons had been trapped under lock and key in the form of a blade. The angel told me that I had released them, but I just didn't get it. Why would demons be trapped here? Were they demons who'd tried to escape from Hell?

The expressions of the demon statues looked familiar to me. I saw no anger or hatred in their faces. They had the same appearance as the demon that had cornered me on the hull of the demon ship…the look of nothing more than just having to get the job done. What would it feel like to be locked in an eternal struggle, poised forever in fear and horror? Not something I wanted to know.

I backed away from the statues and ran to the end of the hallway. I entered a large empty room. For some reason, I immediately thought of an old church, long abandoned and half destroyed by the explosion.

I'd seen holy settings in Hell before, back at the mausoleum and where the heretics were punished. This was different. The circle for the heretics had resembled a caricature of holiness—one of frightening despair. However, *this* place actually looked *hallowed*. Why would a demon need a place of worship?

I made my way to the nearest doorway. I peeked in and spotted Virgil, who knelt by a large altar. If this had been Boston, I would have expected to see a crucifix, but I saw none. If there was any kind of law in Hell, I would assume that a crucifix would be a big no-no. Still, Virgil knelt with his head down in supposed prayer as he had when we'd hobbled ashore from the ocean of boiling blood. I saw him from the side, and with his head down, he didn't seem to notice me.

I didn't disturb him and was actually curious what he would do next. I wanted to know if he would make the sign of the cross when he finished. He hadn't last time, perhaps because he knew I'd been watching.

Quiet, Joe. He's a tricky one with eyes in back of his head.

243

Out of the corner of my eye I noticed a slight movement. I jolted back behind the doorway when I realized the Malebranche had entered the room.

Malecoda and three of the insect demons stood about twenty feet behind Virgil. Malecoda left his cohorts behind to sneak up on Virgil. Before I could get a warning out, Malecoda darted like a winged grasshopper.

Maybe I should have yelled a warning to Virgil, but half of me didn't want to give away my position. The other half wanted to see what Virgil would do.

Virgil lifted his head from prayer, but he hadn't noticed the demon behind him. Malecoda raised his stinger. Virgil actually smiled.

Suddenly, Virgil moved. An instant later, he stood behind Malecoda. He didn't just move quickly. He was a *blur*. He moved exactly like those insect demons! Malecoda whirled to face Virgil. Virgil backhanded him, sending the large demon over the altar like a bowling ball down an alley.

Malecoda leapt to his feet, racing back at Virgil, but Virgil darted again, reappearing behind the demon. Virgil pitched him to the far end of the room, where the other demons waited. All four demons surrounded Virgil, clicking out some God-awful insect sounds.

That's when I got the surprise of my life.

The Malebranche *knelt* before Virgil.

"The one you seek is no longer with us," Virgil started. "She has journeyed upward to the virtuous. Her neck has been repaired, so you must find another way to locate her."

What the hell is he doing? He's ratting out TT. The lousy snake. God damn you, Virgil. Are you nuts, Joe? God already did.

"You must find her and her companion," Virgil continued. "For, if they are successful in reaching the place where no demon can enter, they may never leave and you may never find them."

"Son of a bitch," I breathed. So that's why Virgil hadn't followed me when I'd hopped the wall to the virtuous pagans. No demons allowed, and the rules were probably doubled for Old Nick himself!

Could it be true, Joe? Could Virgil actually be the Prince of Darkness?

He hadn't struck Malecoda in self-defense, but rather to keep him in line. He wasn't praying to God, but rather summoning his minions. It must have taken them this long to get here.

"You will leave the others to me," Virgil finished.

244

I leaned in closer to hear better and slipped on some of the rubble. A *thud* echoed down the hallway. I ducked back behind the wall. I couldn't budge an inch. I didn't want Virgil to know of my presence, and I couldn't look back through the doorway from fear that they were all now looking in my direction.

"Go now," Virgil said. "Take another path. I don't want you to be discovered by the girl."

All I could do was hope that my hiding place wasn't the *other path*. I spotted another door on the far end of the room and I had to get to it as silently as possible. If I ran down the hallway, there's no way Virgil wouldn't hear me. I didn't need the ability to see through walls to know that Virgil was staring at this doorway so I ran into the far room. It led me to another long hallway lined with still more statues. I followed it out of the dark building, holding my breath every step of the way.

☙❧

I raced to warn Mary and Argenti, but I arrived too late. Virgil beat me to them. Why wouldn't he? The man dashed around like a bullet.

"No time to delay, Joseph," Virgil said.

"He went looking for you," Mary said before I could stop her.

"Is that a fact?" Virgil said.

"Yeah, where were you?" I quickly deflected.

"Where did you go to seek me out?" Virgil asked.

"It's a big building. I guess we missed each other."

"Perhaps," he said suspiciously, but then again, every time Virgil opened his mouth, he sounded suspicious.

"Saw a lot of statues, though," I said.

"They weren't statues, Joseph."

"Really?" I already knew but wanted to play dumb.

"They're sinners."

"The statues of demons...are those statues or demons?"

"What do you think?"

"I'm beginning to think they're real demons."

"You'd be correct."

"Why would a demon be encased in stone like that? I thought they were top of the food chain."

245

"Why would you think that?"

"I guess demons are just like everyone else. They have to answer to someone, huh?"

"I am truly impressed," Virgil said, nodding to the demon ship. "Not many escape Geryon with their limbs intact."

"Right."

"Let us leave this horrid place," Mary spoke up.

She helped Argenti to the ship.

I knew that once we got in, there would be no way I'd be able to talk to them away from Virgil. "Wait!" I said with a jolt.

"Yes Joseph?" Mary said.

"What's the matter, Dante?" Argenti added.

"Yes Joseph, speak," Virgil said as he stepped closer to Mary. "If something is wrong, you surely must say."

Virgil sounded like he knew I was hiding his secret. Truth was, I didn't have a clue what he knew, and I didn't want to give anything away. "Nothing," I muttered.

We filed into the demon ship.

CHAPTER 36

Canto XV – Circle VII – Round III – The Violent Against God

ᏀᎧᏀ

W e flew for hours over barren, desolate sand.
Sheesh, Joe, just how much of Hell is nothing more than empty space, anyway?

We were still on the seventh circle, and I began to understand what airline pilots go through each time they make a cross country flight. Each circle must have been thousands of miles long, but this one? I don't know how fast or how far we traveled. For all I knew, we could have gone to the moon and back.

Although, I wasn't yet an expert at landing or taking off, I could steer with no problem.

Argenti, who sat in the back in silent agony, was more than happy to have me in the driver's seat. Mary comforted him by stroking his hair and singing softly.

Unfortunately, Virgil sat in the co-pilot's seat, so I couldn't say anything about what I'd witnessed back at the fueling depot.

"Argenti's in a lot of pain," I observed.

"I know," Virgil said coldly.

"You can heal him."

"Are you asking me to?"

"If I were?"

"Why do you wish me to ease the suffering of one whom you count amongst your enemies?"

"Let's just say I do and leave it at that."

"Let's not."

"Don't you even care? The guy's ready to cut off his own leg."

"Pain is Hell's way, Joseph," Virgil said.

"You helped Mary."

"She was ready. He isn't."

"Heal him anyway."

"Why?"

"Because I'm asking," I said more like a demand.

"Land the craft," he said as he pointed. "There."

"Why?"

"Because *I* ask," Virgil said, also more like a demand.

I let the silence linger for a moment, but finally nodded. "Okay."

❧❧

The legs of the ship unfurled and we landed with a jolt. Like I said, I wasn't an expert in taking off or landing, but I wanted Argenti healed. Don't even ask me why.

Through the windshield, I saw an old man stretched out on the hot sand and tied to stakes among some ancient Roman-looking columns.

"His name is *Capaneus*," Virgil explained. "He was one of seven legendary kings who besieged Thebes, but *this* particular king was different from the rest. He boasted that God Himself couldn't stop him from conquering the world. He was struck by a thunderbolt in retribution. In this place, he is still proud and rebellious against God."

"He doesn't look proud to me," I said, looking at the fragile old man.

Virgil opened the hatch.

Argenti leaned on Mary as we all stepped outside.

Capaneus wore ancient Roman clothing and looked about as ancient as *Old Man Time*. He looked more like a bag of bones wrapped in leather than some historical king. His skin actually appeared as if it had been charred by a trip through the sun.

"Let me untie you, pops" I said.

"English," he smiled. "I know this language, too. You stay in one place long enough and all of Hell passes you by. What class of future world do you hail from?" he asked in a Latin accent.

I knelt to untie his hands.

"What are you doing?" he demanded.

"I'm untying you. What does it look like?"

"Don't do that!" he shouted.

"What? Why not?"

"Because God put me here, and only *He* will release me."

"Wow, you must really have faith in God."

"To Hell with God!" he exploded.

"What?"

"God had the nerve to put me here after all the good works I did—and He wants me to say *I'm sorry*. Well, I won't!" Capaneus shouted. "You hear that God? Give me more, you son of a bitch!"

"Christ," I said as I stood up to join Virgil, "and my wife called *me* stubborn."

"Still believe he's not proud?" Virgil asked.

"Guess not."

"The third round of the seventh circle lies before us, violence against God and nature. Those who reside here would have carnal lusts for anything unnatural—animals, children, the dead."

"Damn you!" Capaneus nodded to Virgil, "and you," to Argenti, "and God too!"

"Blasphemers, as well, dwell in this place," Virgil continued.

"No shit," both Argenti and I said.

Capaneus sniffed in deeply. "Ahhh, smell that?"

"All I smell is ash," I said.

"That's right. Another storm be coming our way. It smells like a big one too," Capaneus said with a snort. "Is this all you got, God!?" he screamed. "Another storm? Let's see what You got You son of a bitch!"

"Okay, this was fun," I said to Virgil. "I did what you wanted. Now, it's your turn."

Virgil stood beside Argenti, looking him square in the eye.

"You have endured much," he said.

"Haven't we all?" Argenti said.

"Do you believe yourself ready, Filippo Argenti?"

"I can't say I know."

Virgil put his hand on Argenti's leg. Nothing happened... No glow—no healing—nothing like when he'd cured Mary.

"You are not ready," Virgil said.

"What are you waiting for?" I said. "Heal him."

Virgil faced Argenti, studying him up and down. "I cannot," Virgil said.

"Why the hell not?"

"You still don't understand, Joseph. The power doesn't lie within me, but him."

"You helped Mary."

"She was ready."

"Ready for what?"

"I think you know the answer to that."

Suddenly, a group of the damned stepped out from behind the giant stone columns.

"We sought out the stones for shelter," one of them said, peering at the demon ship, "but I see something better has arrived."

About a dozen of them surrounded us. Both male and female, different races and sizes, but they all shared one thing in common. They all exhibited third degree burns over the majority of their bodies.

The leader was a big man with dark curly hair—at least, what remained beyond the blisters and scars was dark and curly. There are some types of people who you just know will be criminals from birth. He might have been a businessman or a banker, but you just knew by his looks that he would eventually allow violence to rule his life. *This* was such a man.

I wanted to run for the ship, but I knew Argenti couldn't make it in his present condition. Plus, I categorically refused to leave Mary behind.

"All of you be damned!" Capaneus yelled.

"Shut up, old man!" the leader of the damned shouted, peering at us with the disdain typical of a drill instructor.

"You can't recognize me through these scars, but I used to be pretty famous. My name is Bruno Lantini, and I published my own magazine. Some called it pornography. Hell, what's *pornography*, anyway?" he said, putting quotes around the word *pornography* with his fingers. "In the early 1980s, we went to trial to prove there was no such thing as pornography. Everything is art, and we won." He grinned dryly.

As he spoke, the odor of ash grew stronger in my nostrils and flaming lights began to glow on the horizon.

"I owned the world back then. I could have screwed anyone I wanted, and I did," Lantini continued. "That's why Minos saw fit to condemn me here—unjustly, I might add."

"I thought you were here because of rape?" another of his horde said.

"It wasn't real rape!" Lantini said. "I mean, what is *statutory* rape, anyway," he said, again quoting the word *statutory* with his fingers. "You haven't lived until you've popped a twelve-year-old's cherry; girl or boy doesn't matter." He winked at Mary, who cringed backwards.

The man made me ill.

He shaded his eyes to gaze at the oncoming storm.

We also looked. The term *storm* was a sad understatement. I stared at the giant wave of exploding flames that stretched from horizon to horizon.

In the late fifties, Bea had been so afraid of an atomic war with the Russians, that there was a time when she didn't want to have any more children. That storm looked like a series of exploding hydrogen bombs.

At least in an atomic war, there was always an escape—death.

Here, there was no such luxury.

"Another storm," Lantini said. "Have you ever seen one close up? It really is quite an experience, and judging from your baby soft skin, it will be your first."

The damned surrounded the demonic vehicle.

"You have a demonic craft, but you're not demons. *That's* very interesting," he said.

"You can't all fit in that ship," I said.

"Oh, we'll fit," Lantini said with a grin, "and we'll even have room for one of you." He gawked at Mary and smiled.

"Joseph?" Mary said with fear in her eyes.

I grabbed Mary's hand, but two of the damned pulled me away and Lantini jerked Mary toward him.

"Leave her alone, you son of a bitch!" I yelled.

Some of the damned kicked Argenti to the ground. He wasn't in any condition to muster any resistance.

The damned piled into the vehicle and dragged away a screaming Mary.

"Do something!" I shouted at Virgil as some of the damned restrained me.

"What would you have me do, Joseph?"

"I've seen what you can do!"

"Against demons and the mechanisms of this place, yes. However, I *will not* interfere in the dealings of man."

I slugged one of the damned, and pulled free of the other. "Lantini! You son of a bitch!" I yelled.

He ignored me.

"You're right, Bruno!" I told him. "This *is* a demon ship, and we're *not* demons. The man who can take a ship from a demon should be listened to, don't you think?"

Lantini turned to face me as he held onto Mary like a new toy.

Mary failed to hold back her tears.

"I'm listening," he said.

"I didn't just take that ship from a demon," I said. "I took it from Geryon himself. I wanted it, and he couldn't stop me. I swear to you here and now, if you take her, I will never stop looking for you. I'll never give up, and I'll never deter from my one goal of finding you. And when I do, you're going to wish that firestorm was all you had to worry about," I said with more conviction than I'd ever said anything in my entire life. I meant every word.

Bruno Lantini swallowed from worry, and he wasn't the only one. I think I scared all of them.

"I didn't sign up for this shit. Let the bitch go!" one of the charred damned yelled.

"Release the wench, you fool," another spoke up.

"Let the girl go, or we'll leave *you* behind. I shit you not!" still another piped in.

Lantini looked over his crew, realizing that he didn't have nearly as much clout over them as his sex-ridden brain thought. "Okay!" Lantini said. "Fine, no problem! My bad. Take her." Lantini released his grip on Mary, and she ran into my arms.

"If it's the ship you want, take it and get the hell out of here!" I said.

"I'll keep an eye out for you," Lantini said, really steamed.

"Anytime, buster!" I returned, even more steamed.

I thought about using the same approach to retake the ship, but decided not to risk it. Jeopardizing Mary any further wasn't at the top of my 'to do' list.

The damned squeezed into the craft, and a few even clung to the exterior.

As the ship took off, Mary looked up after having buried her face in my chest. "Thank you, Joseph."

I smiled as I stroked her hair.

Then, I looked at Virgil, and I realized why he'd had us land here.

"You've been planning this since I said I was going to take that ship, haven't you? That's why you had us land here. You were *never* going to heal Argenti!"

"There are no free rides in Hell Joseph," Virgil said.

I let Mary go in order to face him. "Bologna!" I yelled.

"If you trust in your faith, the storm won't hurt you."

"What did you just say?"

That angel had predicted that this would happen, but I hadn't listened. He told me that Virgil would put us in an impossible situation where there would be no escape, and then he would tell us to have faith.

As the storm came closer and grew brighter, we saw people in the flames and more beyond them—hundreds of people running, as they tried unsuccessfully to escape the explosions of blasting fire.

"Faith in what? In who?" I demanded.

"Whom do you imagine?" Virgil said.

"I saw you with the Malebranche!" I shouted, confronting him. "I saw them kneel before you! I watched you betray Hector and Tonya!"

"Not everything is as it appears."

"Sometimes, things are *exactly* as they appear," I said.

"What are you trying to say, Joseph?" Virgil said.

"That angel told me you were Satan!"

A look of surprise struck Virgil's face.

Joe, do you remember ever seeing Virgil surprised about anything? The angel said that he was breaking protocol by telling you Virgil's true identity. What kind of protocol helps the devil keep his secrets?

"How would you have me respond?" Virgil said.

"At least, deny it," I implored.

After a long minute, Virgil finally replied. "I can't do that, Joseph."

I couldn't believe my ears. He didn't even try to refute it. Mary and Argenti also looked on in total horror.

"So, it's true," I said. "You're the devil—the father of lies!"

"Have faith," Virgil said.

"To Hell with faith and, if God left us here, to Hell with Him, too!"

"Now you're talking," Capaneus chimed in.

Mary helped Argenti to his feet. "Dante, we have to get out of here," Argenti said, still fighting off the pain.

"You've never truly had any, did you, Joseph?" Virgil continued.

"What?"

"Faith."

"That's not true," I defended.

"I'm not so sure."

"Now you just hold on a minute," I said, truly insulted. "*That's* not true. I went to church every Sunday and Confession every month. I lit candles for the dead, and I prayed every night."

"Did you mean it, Joseph?" Virgil replied. "Anyone can say the words and perform the acts. Did they have meaning for you?"

"When my family was murdered, when justice wasn't served, when I was shot in the head, where was God then?" I said.

"Precisely where you put Him," Virgil said. "No closer."

"Not close enough!" I said bitterly.

"You still don't know the answer to the question, do you?" Virgil said.

"What question?"

"Who are you?" he said.

Virgil had asked me that on several occasions, and each time I'd had no idea what he meant. Judging from who *he* was, I had no desire to find out. "I'm a *good* man," I said, "and I'm staying that way."

I eased Argenti away from Mary, hooking his arm around my neck.

"Run," I instructed Mary.

"I won't leave you," she said.

"Go, we'll catch up."

"Joseph—" she began.

"Go—*now!*" I yelled, her safety my only concern.

Mary ran.

"Come on! Stay with me," I said to Argenti as Mary raced ahead of us and away from the fireball blizzard.

Argenti put some weight on his leg and yelped in pain.

"I got you!" I said.

"Joseph?" Virgil interrupted.

I gave up precious seconds to hear his last words.

"In every journey comes a moment, one like no other, and in that moment, you must decide between who you are—and who you want to be."

CHAPTER 37
Canto XVI – Circle VII – The Abyss
క్ర౨ఌ

I couldn't see Mary anymore, and I was glad for it. If she had been anywhere near us, she would have felt trapped, and dead center of a five alarm fire.

Argenti tried to help, but I mostly dragged him. We ran as if we were in a three-legged race, and losing badly. The hordes of the damned were still behind us, but they were closing in, just like the waves of searing heat.

Virgil stayed so far behind us, that he'd long been swallowed by the storm. But judging from my past experiences with him, the fire probably affected him about as much as a warm breeze.

Flaming rocks burst out of the storm and crashed near us, knocking us off our feet.

I didn't have time to feel pain. I ran to Argenti and grabbed his arm again.

"We have to get off this level!" I shouted.

"For what? Whatever's on the next level will be even worse!"

Argenti could have been right, but we had no time to debate the issue. I pulled him to his feet, but another rock of flame crashed near us, setting his leg on fire. He screamed as I swatted it out.

"Come on, get up!" I ordered.

Argenti cried in pain, but he also managed an ironic laugh. "This is what you wanted, isn't it? Me in a lake of fire! Well, here comes the first wave! You got your wish, Dante. Now get out of here. You're not responsible for me."

He's right, Joe. This is what you wanted for Argenti way back when you saw his punishment in the cage. He's also right a second time. You're not responsible for him. Leave him, Joe. Get the hell out of Dodge and don't look back.

I stood and ran, leaving Argenti behind. I got about twenty feet, and stopped to watch as the storm closed in on Argenti.

This is it, Joe! It's just how you've dreamt it. Argenti broken and pathetic... begging for God's mercy and getting only the devil's wrath.

It was too late, though. It wasn't what I wanted anymore. I wanted something else. I *needed* something else. Argenti had left me behind once. How I'd hated him when I'd found myself in Geryon's possession as Argenti escaped in the ship. I didn't want Argenti to hate me that way, but it wasn't just that. If I had left Argenti in that fix, *I* would have hated *me* that way. I ran back to Argenti, seizing him by the collar.

"You want to broil?" I yelled. "Get up!"

"I can't!"

"Damn it, Argenti!"

"Just leave me."

"Cadence!" I yelled.

"What?"

"Remember boot camp?"

"Are you running on all cylinders, Dante? What the hell—"

"You pilots, you always had it so easy!" I said. "Pushing buttons from a mile high and never seeing the misery you'd inflicted below! We used to see you guys during boot camp. Every morning we had to run five miles—you mugs never did jack!"

"You don't know what you're talking about, Dante! We did fifty push-ups every morning!"

"It's not the same as cadence!" I yelled.

"We had to do *that*, too!"

"Show me."

"What?" Argenti said, confused.

"*Cadence*, you son of a bitch!" I shook him by the collar. "On your feet!" I pulled him to his feet, and we ran. "Come on—on the left foot—go!"

I dragged him as I ran. "Left—right—left—say it!" I yelled.

"Left," he whimpered.

"Louder!"

Argenti picked up his right foot and hit the sand. "Right!" he yelled.

"Left right left right left..." we yelled as we picked up speed.

We ran, the flames kissing our heels the entire way.

"There it is!" I shouted.

We both saw it. The cliff to the next level looked very different from the rest, like a giant ocean of dark fog.

The firestorm swallowed the people behind us, and we began to smoke from the heat.

"We're going to make it!" I yelled.

We couldn't stop long enough to climb down.

We would have to get to the next circle the hard way.

Together, we jumped into the black abyss. Behind us, the firestorm engulfed the edge of the seventh circle.

We plummeted like skydivers into the dark night. It soon became obvious that this level was going to be perpetual night.

The winds were strong against us. Still we sank like sacks of wet cement.

A gust of wind ripped through us like a blade of ice, separating me from Argenti.

I reached for him, and he for me, but instantly he was out of reach.

I watched him as the wind pulled him away and the darkness swallowed him. We didn't say a word to each other. Not a goodbye or farewell, but I knew we both felt it.

I know it sounds strange, but I felt a chapter come to a close with him.

This man whom I'd hated for so long wasn't an evil man. Neither was he a good man. He was just a man, like me. It occurred to me that *good* and *evil* weren't what we *were*, but rather what we had done. No one truly knows everything that another does, not in action or in thought.

I sank farther into the darkness, plummeting faster and deeper into Hell. The eighth level was somewhere beneath me, but how far? How long would I drop? What would be there when I struck bottom? Mud? Jagged rocks? Pointed stakes? Broken glass? I knew marshmallows or pillows were a long shot. How long would it take before I found out?

I finally hit bottom.

I landed flat on my back. It's funny that I would consider myself fortunate to find rocky mud, rather than dead trees with thorns the size of daggers. The bracelet Anna had given me had been knocked from my wrist. Now, it stuck out of the mud beside me. With only the wind knocked out of me, I considered myself lucky. That is, until I tried to sit up and reach for the bracelet.

I rolled over, immediately feeling pain stab into my neck and down my spine. I howled in agony and fell flat on my back, which intensified the pain even more. Just when I'd thought it couldn't get any worse, my body proved me wrong. From the neck down, I felt a tingling, then total numbness.

"No," I said, aware that I was completely and utterly alone. I tried to roll my body to regain some control or movement, but I could only swivel my neck. "No!" I screamed a final time.

My breathing became so labored, I could only gulp every mouthful of air. It felt like King Kong was tap dancing on my chest. This must have been what quadriplegics felt when they needed an iron lung.

I wanted to move, to scream, to do *anything*, but I couldn't. Instead, I concentrated on drawing in each breath, clinging to the belief that one day I would heal.

I waited for daylight to come but it never did. I was stuck, trapped in my crushed shell of a body in this muddy wasteland, perhaps as demon-bait. I was utterly alone in the perpetual night…not even in a room with a view.

Time passed. I didn't know how slowly or quickly, because it was all the same. I'd always measured time by the events that unfolded around me. Since nothing happened here and nothing changed, I measured the passage of time with only my own thoughts.

CHAPTER 38
Thoughts of Home – Tiresias

᷿

Where's mom?" Anna asked through her tears as the black smoke billowed around and between us.

I reached out, over the flames. "Jump!" I shouted, ignoring her question.

There wasn't a lot of time or room to run, so she held her breath and jumped.

I barely got a piece of her hand, desperately holding on to her with a tenuous grasp. She slowly slipped below.

Struggling to hold on, she looked up into my eyes, with a look that burned into my soul. "Daddy, don't let go!"

"Reach up, baby!"

"Daddy!"

I tried to hang on, but she slipped even lower. "Honey, you have to reach up!"

"I can't!"

"God! Help me!" I yelled.

The roof beneath me gave a jolt, and Anna slipped even farther. I looked into her tearful eyes as her fingers slipped from my grasp.

"Daddy!" she screamed as she fell.

"No!" I screamed as I watched the flames claim my Anna. "God in heaven! No!"

᷿

Alone I watched, despite the crowd of family and friends, as Father Nicholas delivered his sermon over the two coffins.

"When a tragedy such as this occurs, it's only natural to question God's ways. Why would God allow a beautiful and godly woman to die in such a brutal way? Why would He let her daughter die, before her life had really begun? I don't know the answers. Nobody does… But in knowing that there *is* an answer, perhaps there is comfort. Knowing that there *is* an answer is where faith begins."

The undertakers lowered the two coffins into the ground. Next to them sat Kathleen's tombstone, now nearly two years old. I watched as Bea's parents held each other and cried. Even Mickey looked choked up. I wanted to join them. I wanted to cry, to let it all out, but I couldn't. I was drowning in a sea of sad smiles and tears.

Father Nicholas's words echoed in my skull. Why would God allow such a beautiful and godly woman to die in such a brutal way? Why would *He* let Anna die before her life had even begun? Why had *He* permitted Argenti to get his hooks into Kathleen, for that matter? Argenti walks free and everything that gave my life meaning is buried in the dirt.

The crowd thinned out faster than I realized. Either that or time seemed to speed up for me. I waited for someone to call me away from the graves, but no one did, out of fear and respect, I imagined.

Feeling its strangle hold on me, I ripped the crucifix from my throat, and threw it into the loose earth atop Bea's freshly covered grave. Father Nicholas must have been watching, because he came over and immediately picked it up.

"You dropped this, Joe," he said, his voice filled with sadness.

Who is he, Joe? A man of faith? A man of undefeatable strength? Looking at him now, holding your crucifix over the freshly-dug grave of your wife, all you see is an old fool.

"I didn't *drop* anything," I said coldly. I could see the loss and regret in his eyes, but I didn't care.

"Son, if you just try and understand the power of the cross…"

"I know what a cross is, Father. The man who murdered my family wears one." I walked away.

❧❧

I don't know what possessed me to see Tony. He'd been safely locked away to await trial. Other than *burn in Hell*, I really had nothing to say to him.

I shouldn't have been able to see him, since technically, I was a witness against him, but being a cop has certain advantages.

I sat on one side of the wall of thick glass as he was escorted into the cubicle. He sat down on the other side.

I said nothing. If this was a chess game, I wanted him to make the first move.

"Well, well, well, how are you doing—partner?" he asked with surprising smugness.

I didn't answer him. I looked at him with as soulless a look as I could muster, as *soulless* as I now knew him to be.

"Well, *you* called me here. What the devil do you want?" he asked.

Again, all I could do was stare at his face. I peered into his seemingly innocent and trustworthy face, revealing that he was the exact opposite of the image he showed the world. His look of innocence had probably given him a free ride in life, which is why he'd believed that he could do anything.

"You want me to say *I'm sorry?*" he continued.

It's a valid question, Joe. Is that what you want? There's no way you would or could forgive him, but do you want him to feel the slightest remorse?

Again, I didn't answer.

"Look, I needed the money," he said, this time without the smug attitude. "I'm sorry for what happened. Are you happy now? Is that what you wanted to hear?"

It's too late, Joe. Now you know why you're here. It's not to forgive or even to talk. It's to brand his face into your mind. This is the image of betrayal—innocent and honest. This is the face of a man you once counted among your friends. This man who was your partner, worked side by side with you, and never showed you his true self. Did he have a conscience? Or was he just like Argenti, a monster in the skin of a man?

"Look, Joe…what…just tell me why you're here," he stuttered.

He seemed remorseful, but I couldn't trust him, and I no longer cared. As I walked away, I heard him calling out.

"You want me to cry? You want me to beg? What do you want from me?"

※※

I knelt by the freshly buried graves of Bea and Anna, and the not so fresh grave of Kathleen. It was raining, and I should have been cold, but I wasn't. I only felt loss.

261

I thought back to our wedding day. We had danced and the whole world had been at our feet. I hadn't known it then, but I would soon leave for England to fight the Germans. On that night, our first time together, we created Kathleen.

After we'd made love for the first time, Bea had whispered in my ear, *wherever thou goest, I go, my love.*

I decided I should return the sentiment. The three tombstones beckoned me to join them.

The rain stopped as I stood. I decided to do what I'd always thought of as the unthinkable.

❧

I walked through the park on the way home, one last time, to say *goodbye*. I couldn't remember the last time I'd walked through Boston Commons alone and without holding Bea's hand. It could have literally been two decades.

A young boy came up to me, obviously looking for a hand out.

"Tell your fortune for some bread," he said.

"Scram kid."

"Sure thing, big daddy," he said, sounding eerily like Anna.

"What did I tell you about that beatnik—" I stopped short when I realized it wasn't Anna but just some kid, and to my surprise—a *girl.*

She was about fifteen. Her short hair made it easy to mistake her for a young boy. She spoke like one of those beatnik folk singer types, and wore a beret and pants instead of a dress. She probably just needed a few bucks for that coffee house stuff.

"Cool it, mister. Just cruisin'."

I didn't answer. I only stared at this stranger with a familiarity that didn't exist. As she turned to leave, I finally answered. "Okay. Tell my fortune."

"Really? Kookie!"

"I want you to know that I don't believe in this stuff," I continued.

"Don't have to, big daddy, you can't fight fate."

"I already know my fate," I said.

"Just when you think you're hip to your destiny, it throws you a curve," she said with a smile. She put her hand out, as if to shake. "My name is Tonya Tiresias. My jacket calls me *TT.*"

"Jacket?"

"My boyfriend, daddy-o. Aren't you with it?"

"I guess not." I gave her my hand.

She turned it over to read my palm, peering into it with the concentration of a physicist.

"I see loss in your life," she said.

I didn't say anything. I guess I was curious how much she really could see, if she could see anything at all.

"A great loss," she continued.

I was surprised when she let go of my hand and backed away. She was afraid of something. Maybe something she saw in my destiny.

"Keep the bread, big daddy."

"Wait," I said as she turned to leave. "What did you see?"

"Thought you weren't hip to destiny."

"Well, like you said, it really doesn't matter what I'm *hip* to. You can't fight fate."

Unexpectedly, she hugged me. When she let go, I saw genuine sadness in her eyes.

"Be careful, big daddy. Be very careful," she said, on the verge of running away.

"Wait... Here." I pulled out my wallet and gave her everything I found inside.

What does it matter, Joe? You won't need it where you're going.

"Wow, thanks!" she said, taking notice of the saw buck and two fins. She took the dough and hauled off.

❧

I sat in the dark as I loaded my .38. TT's words rang in my head. *Be careful, big daddy.* Had she really seen something? Had she known what I was planning? I put the gun under my chin and pulled the hammer back. Two pounds of pressure stood between me and what was to come.

When you're Catholic, suicide is a one-way ticket to Old Nick's basement, but I didn't even know if I believed in the Father anymore, let alone His Son. I craved the strength for those two pounds. Just as I found the strength and resigned myself to my end, the doorbell rang.

CHAPTER 39
Canto XVII – Circle VIII – Bolgia I – Panderers and Seducers

༄

T ime continued on without me.

I stared at the bracelet, just out of reach, and lost count of how many times I'd thought of Bea and my girls.

Dancing with Beatrice in the living room came to mind at least a thousand times. We danced often after the girls had fallen to sleep.

Where is Bea now, Joe? Is she thinking of you? Does she even remember you?

The night of my promotion to Detective First Class popped into my noggin, and with it, Mickey picking me up in excitement.

I couldn't escape Mickey, even in my memories.

Mickey! Why would he do this to you, Joe—your own brother?

I needed to ask him, but he resided in the ninth circle in a place called *Caina,* and I was trapped at the start of the eighth.

I felt disconnected from the bracelet, and because of its significance, from my family.

Fantasy mixed with reality. I began to doubt my own memories. I was literally locked in a prison of my own lifeless body, without senses or movement. All I saw was my bracelet, but it remained just inches from my paralyzed hand.

As time passed, I began to hear things. The crack of whips, followed by moans and screams echoing in the distance. The sounds came and went. I didn't know if it was because the sounds were actually coming and going, or if my hearing kept going in and out.

Did you go deaf too, Joe? Is your hearing slowly returning? Joe, you poor bastard, how will you get out of this jar of pickles?

Where was that angel-soldier? Was he waiting for me, or had he already left me behind?

Once the spinal cord was severed, a person always took up residence in a wheelchair for life. If he had a thousand years, would he eventually heal? That's what happened with a physical body, however—barring a miracle. My physical body had been long dead and buried for God only knew how long. Healing of the spirit might require less time, or maybe more. I didn't know which.

Once in a while, I'd feel a slight tingling in my fingers and toes. I concentrated with the intensity of a surgeon on moving them, but couldn't. At least, it felt like there wasn't any movement. I couldn't look to be certain. More tingling eventually came for longer times and with greater intensity, but I needed to find a way to help the process along.

Virgil had healed Mary with ease. Virgil claimed he had faith, but how could he if he was, in fact, Satan?

Whose faith had healed Mary? Virgil's or Mary's? Maybe that was why Virgil had never healed me and had refused to help Argenti? Argenti and I hadn't had enough faith for Virgil to leech.

Virgil was *Satan*. How could have I missed that? I was a cop for crying out loud. He'd repeatedly told me to have faith and not to give into hate, but it had all been a trick. How many souls had he corrupted?

At least I had the angel on my side. He knew that the only justice out there was the justice we made for ourselves.

What about Mary? Virgil had said she was ready, but ready for what? Out of all of us, she seemed the most faithful. Faith? How can someone *make* themselves have faith? If there was an answer, I needed to dig it up from my very soul.

I sucked air into my lungs before I attempted to speak. "What do You want from me?" I tried to ask God, less forcefully than I'd wished, and with more arrogance than I'd intended.

Think, Joe. You have nothing but time on a string, so you might as well use your noodle for something other than a paperweight. Why was Virgil praying in the black theater? The Malebranche? Then what was he praying for by the ocean of blood? What would the Prince of Darkness pray for, anyway? New souls? Maybe even your soul, and not in a good way. He was probably praying to corrupt your soul into eternal damnation. Yeah, that's it. Well, I got a question for you, Joe... Exactly to whom did he pray? Maybe, Joe...maybe you should start praying. Lord...hear my prayer... Our Father, who art in heaven, hallowed be Thy name...

❧❧

I said the Our Father so many times, I must have broke the Pope's personal best a thousand times over. Until finally, I listened to my own words—what the words meant to me—what they meant about God. So, I repeated the words in different ways, until I not only knew their meaning—but felt it.

My Father, who waits for me in paradise, thy name is sacred...

So it went, the tingling came and went, as did my prayers. More time passed, and finally, I was able to breathe with less effort.

More sounds of snapping whips and resulting screams filled the night air. Who were the tortured here? What had they done?

My time came eventually. Finally, I was able to sit up. I flopped over in the mud like a beached sea lion, desperately trying to get back to water. I could feel most of my body again, although some parts still felt like stabbing needles.

Mary had once said that, in some ways, being numb from the neck down was welcome. Better to feel *nothing* than the pain. After being numb for so long, though, I actually embraced the pain. Had God healed me? Had my faith in God cured me? Did I even possess faith anymore? What was I supposed to believe?

I reached for my bracelet but out of the darkness, another hand came down and beat me to it. I looked up in terror to see Geryon picking up my bracelet as if it were his. I wanted to run, but I knew I wouldn't get far. It was an incredible coincidence that Geryon had shown up at the same time I'd found the ability and strength to sit up.

"How long have you been standing there?" I asked.

I didn't expect an answer, and Geryon didn't disappoint. I suppose it was possible that Geryon had been searching for me all this time and had just happened upon me at the exact moment when I'd found myself able to move again.

It was equally possible, however, that Geryon had hidden in one of my many blind spots, waiting for me to heal—but for what reason? Had my prayers protected me? Hell, for all I knew, I'd been laying there for a hundred years, and Geryon had been watching me for ninety-nine and a half of them.

Geryon was alone and without his ship. If he hoofed it all the way down from the second ring, it could have taken him decades to find me.

My ears were hungry for any sound, yet I'd heard nothing. If Geryon had been here with me, he'd never made a peep. The entire time I was here, distant sounds of cracking whips and tormented screams had been my only companions.

"I see you're alone," I said. "Where are your pals?"

I weakly stood on wobbly legs to face him.

Who am I kidding? I fully intended to run.

I eyed my bracelet, dangling from Geryon's large reptilian claw-like hands.

"That's mine," I said with surprising anger and defiance. I didn't threaten, and I didn't say it in fear. I said it as if I was stating a fact, and I was.

I couldn't read the emotions of reptiles, let alone reptilian demons, but Geryon's face looked vaguely sad. My initial thoughts about him now seemed accurate. There was wisdom about him. For a moment, I thought he would simply return the bracelet to me. Instead, with a wave of arrogance, he held the bracelet over his mouth and let it fall in, swallowing it.

"You son of a..." I started, but was cut short when Geryon charged toward me.

I turned to run, but it had been so long since I'd used my legs, I immediately fell.

Geryon hauled me up and back handed me.

I fell again, crawling in the mud in a pathetic attempt to escape.

Geryon towered over me, and again, picked me up. This time, however, I threw a fistful of mud into his face.

He dropped me. I got to my feet and headed, as best I could, up a muddy hill.

❧❧

I ran across the flatland, eventually reaching a large muddy crevice.

It was still dark, but either my eyes had gotten used to it, or it was lighter where I was heading because I could see the shimmering water

267

below. A moat that swung from horizon to horizon encompassed the area as far as the eye could see. Still, I could see land on the other side. There would be no crossing over and no going around. The only way to the other side involved swimming.

A stench rose up to greet me—one that reminded me of the Boston subway after hours, when the smells of popcorn and hotdogs had faded, and all that remained were the drunks seeking a place to make their own personal toilet.

I stepped down to make my way into the pit, but Geryon had other plans. He leapt at me from the darkness. I fell and slid down to the bottom, where the shore of the lake awaited. Geryon followed me down with infinitely more grace. I couldn't outrun him, but I hoped I could out-swim him. He was a reptile, after all. Reptiles aren't good swimmers. After I dove in, I remembered that crocodiles were also reptiles.

I also remembered Charon, that old bastard of a sea captain who'd laughed when I'd yanked my hand out of the water after a painful jolt. I could only hope that this particular water was more like actual water than liquid electricity.

As I dove in, I realized both good news and bad news. The good news? No electric water. The bad news? It was about as putrid as a prison sewer—in summer! Being too weak to stay afloat, I sank a few feet below the surface and was somewhat less than happy with my next discovery.

I came face to face with a Chinaman. He jerked back with a start. Dressed as a servant from ancient times, he was held just below the surface. He stared at me, still conscious, though without air for perhaps a thousand years. His arms and legs were bound by chains that were bolted to the moat's floor. They prevented him from reaching for me, but I knew that if he could have, he would.

I kicked away from him promptly and backed into another schmuck. This one wore the spit and polish attire of a butler, though admittedly, in his present condition, he was more spit than polish. Beyond him floated a man in an expensive Italian suit. Hundreds of others, all trussed in chains at different distances from the surface, stared in my direction.

Some struggled as if they had been there only for moments when, in reality, some of them had to have been there for centuries. Others didn't move at all, as if in acceptance of their fate.

I blocked my nose. I felt as if I was swimming in liquid garbage, but the water was clear with yellow lights glowing at the bottom.

What the devil is this place? The lights aren't yellow… The water is. Yellow water? You're in urine, Joe—a lake of piss! Bright move diving in, by the way! Maybe, if you're lucky, you'll get a shit lollipop on the other side.

I started to swim up to take a breath, but as I kicked, I felt a tug at my leg. I looked down to find a hooked chain wrapped around my ankle.

I should have expected this to happen. The vines in the circle of suicides tried the same malarkey.

The chain yanked me down. Other chains rose up from the bottom to pin my arms and I knew I needed to act fast.

On my way down, I'd passed several soldiers. Some looked to be from my time in the Second World War. Others were from other revolutions, conflicts and wars, past and future. From the rank insignia I could recognize, they all seemed to be from the lower ranks. That included the officers.

I spotted a corporal with some type of rifle slung around his neck. If it still worked, it could be my ticket out of here. Ironic that the soldier it belonged to, his arms pinned by the chains, couldn't use it to free himself.

Sinking lower, I grabbed the rifle from the soldier's neck.

I didn't recognize the weapon, and it looked like it could fire more than just hot lead slugs. There were two barrels, one for regular rounds, and a larger one. My guess was that it was some kind of grenade launcher.

I jacked a round into the weapon and said a silent prayer that the thing wouldn't be so *urine* logged as not to work.

The lack of air was getting to me and made me feel like my head was about to explode.

I aimed at the base of the chain pulling me down, but then a new development presented itself. Geryon was swimming toward me.

Jesus, Joe—doesn't this schmoe ever give up?

I had no idea how much ammo this thing had, but I needed to slow down Geryon. I took aim and shot at Geryon instead of the chains.

I expected the automatic rush of a Tommy gun. Instead, the larger barrel spat out a grenade.

It pushed its way to Geryon and exploded near him but didn't deter him from his goal—namely, me.

I intuitively cocked the larger barrel again, like a sawed off shotgun, and fired repeatedly. Explosion after explosion slowed down Geryon enough for me to focus on the chains.

As other chains came up, I turned the rifle to the main culprit, the chain yanking me down.

269

I shot a spray of rounds and snapped several chains. Several people kicked wildly to the surface as other chains scrambled to recapture them.

My chain finally snapped. I frantically kicked free, but unfortunately, right into Geryon's waiting arms.

He grabbed me and bared his teeth. I guess he wanted to do something to scare me since he couldn't hiss underwater, not that he needed to do *anything*.

I thought he was going to bite my head off, but suddenly, this time, it was Geryon who was pulled lower.

Hooked chains had fastened onto *his* leg and pulled *him* down. Geryon, obviously surprised, released me to pull at the chains.

I swam for the surface, then to the far shore of the lake of urine. As I looked back, I saw Geryon unsuccessfully fighting off the chains that surrounded him.

CHAPTER 40
Canto XVIII – Circle VIII – Bolgia II – Flatterers and Gossipers

❧

I dragged myself to shore, spitting the bile from my mouth. I wanted to puke, but didn't have the time, nor the puke for that matter.

I heard a splash of someone popping up behind me and thought it was Geryon—if I had jumped any higher, I would have landed back on the second circle.

I quickly aimed the rifle, but luckily, instead of hearing the sounds of a slithering hiss, I heard the gurgling and coughing of a young woman.

She struggled to the surface, and I mustered what little energy I had left to pick myself up to help her to shore.

About thirty years old, she wore some sort of pants suit. It was obvious that she was from some future time, since the women of my time rarely wore pants, let alone suits. She looked attractive, even with her urine soaked hair.

"Thanks babe," she said as she staggered to shore.

Babe? Oh yeah, Joe, this dame is from the future alright.

"We have to pound leather, and fast," I said.

"Not me, babe, I'm taking a breather."

"You don't understand; there's a demon after me."

"Well, if he's in there, he ain't coming out," she said, pointing into the moat of urine.

"You don't know this demon."

"Honey, you don't know those chains. They don't take *no* for an answer. Hell, if they worked for me back on Earth, I'd be president of both CAA *and* William Morris!"

271

She staggered forward, sat down near a clump of dead brush, and wrung the sleeve of her suit coat jacket dripping of piss.

"You can't rest here," I cautioned.

"Don't be a buzz-kill, babe. If he's in there, he ain't goin' nowhere. Trust me. Besides, judging from those bloodshot baby blues, you can use a time-out yourself."

She had me there, so I conceded the point and sat next to her.

"Thais Angelique, talent agent, New York, bit the big one just after the millennium. You?" She extended her hand for me to shake.

I was confused by her casualness, but shook her hand, anyway. "Joe Dante, Boston PD, passed away in '61."

"Shut up! 1961!" She laughed.

"Did you just tell me to *shut up*?

"1961, now *that's* when TV was a box of gold."

"Where are we?"

"You're in the eighth circle of Hell, babe."

"*That* part, I knew," I said sarcastically.

"All right, all right—don't have a cow. I've been sucking piss for the last few years, so you're going to have to be just a tad more specific if you want to get the straight dope from me," she said.

"Don't have a what?" I asked. "When exactly did people take a baseball bat to the English language?"

"Huh?"

"I just want to know what we just climbed out of."

"This is the second bolgia, second out of ten, that of the flatterers and gossipers."

"Flatterers and gossipers?" I said. "You don't seem the type."

"Hello! If you were a talent agent in my day, your skill set better include both kissing ass *and* shooting shit. If I saw a young Alec Baldwin trying to break into the biz, I'd have to sling the hash better than Polly Holiday."

"Alec who?"

"I think of all the crap that came out of my mouth back then, it's no wonder we're forced to swallow that vile shit for all eternity."

I understood what she meant. I remembered all the garbage and swill that came out of the mouths of suck-ups and brown-nosers in my department. I guess in that giant toilet of a moat, the slime was forced back to its owner.

"So, where did you come from?" she asked. "The first bolgia?"

"First?"

"Duh…were you a dirty cop or something? Panderers and seducers, you know what I mean?"

I gave her a blank look, making it obvious that I didn't have the first damned clue of what she was talking about.

"Pimps and hookers!" she said more definitively.

"Pimps and prostitutes are in the first bolgia?" I said, realizing *that* must have been from where the sounds of cracking whips and agonizing screams had come.

"Yeah, don't you know the eighth circle is that of dupery…the sins of the leopard? All the bolgias here have something to do with fraud, which is really ironic since I represented most of the extras from *The Pretender.*"

"*The Pretender*…right."

"Where are you headed, babe?"

"What makes you think I'm headed anywhere?"

"Doesn't take a brainiac to see that you're a man on a mission."

"The ninth circle," I finally answered.

"Ninth? What! You're going down? Don't you know that the lower you go, the worse it gets?"

"So I've heard, but it's strange, don't you think?"

"What's that?"

"That flattery would be considered worse than murder, and betrayal would be considered worst of all."

"As if!" she said. "You don't get it, do you? You're thinking about man's law. Here, it's all God's rules, babe. Murderers just take your life. Betrayers and the fraudulent take your very soul."

"Maybe," I said, "but how do you know all this?"

"Well, ironically, when I died I was reading a religious novel that included the symbolism of sin. We were going to translate it into a screenplay, but it was just too self-righteous, so we abandoned the idea. Well, I got interested in the damn thing and wanted to finish it. That was September eleventh, 2001."

"You died in 2001?" I said. "I think you're the first person I've met who died in the twenty-first century. In my day, we thought 2000 was going to be the end of the line. We thought we were all going to glow in the atomic aftermath. So, did we ever beat the Russians?"

"Russians? Oh sweetie, *that* country collapsed years before I died."

"Oh," I said, both surprised and relieved.

"It was the Y2K bug that freaked everyone out. We thought *that* was going to throw us back to the Dark Ages, but it turned out to be a big steaming pile of hoo-ha. I guess we had to settle for the tech crash and the terrorist attack on the Towers."

"Terrorist attack?"

"I was in the second tower on the sixty-eighth floor. After the first plane hit, we pretty much knew that it wasn't an accident. We were under a terrorist attack. Sons of bitches flew our own planes into the buildings. Thousands died that day. Too bad, it started out as such a beautiful day, too."

"What?" I asked amazed. "How could that happen?"

"How?" She laughed bitterly to herself. "We were too busy trying to figure out if Angelina's lips were real, who was going into rehab that week, if Ben and Matt were going to make another movie together, or what reality show was coming next. We lost sight of the things that were really important, and the bad guys caught us with our pants down. Do you remember those early sitcoms of the '50s and '60s—*Ozzie and Harriet, Nanny and the Professor, The Ghost and Mrs. Muir*? Those were shows you could hang your hat on. I mean, they really meant something. When I died, we were watching TV episodes showing two women fighting over a condom to figure out which one would sleep with her boyfriend. We called *that* moral because it promoted safe sex. In my time, we actually had bumper stickers urging single mothers *not* to abandon their babies or throw them in dumpsters, and commercials advertising the best medication for herpes. What the hell happened to us?"

"Sounds like a different world than the one I left."

"What about you, Adam-12?" she asked. "What's your sin?"

"My sin?" I smirked to myself. "I used to think I didn't have one."

"And now?"

"Now?" I thought about it, but before I could answer, Thais was yanked away toward the giant moat.

She instinctively grabbed me. We looked down to see a chain hooked around her ankle. It quickly became taut, with the other end submerged under the surface of the putrid lake.

"No!" she screamed.

I grabbed her, but the chain dragged us both toward the shoreline. I don't even think my holding her slowed the chain down.

I pulled her to some brush, and wrapped her hands around a dead root.

"Hang on!" I yelled.

"Don't bail on me, Joe!"

"Just hang on," I repeated.

I needed my hands free so I could try to pull the chain from her. Needless to say, the chain was strong. There was no proverbial weak link. The sharp jagged metal wrapped around her leg like boa constrictor. I tried to find the end of the chain, but when I gripped it, it tightened even further, causing Thais to scream in agony.

"Joe! Please!"

"Hang on!" I yelled as I ran for the rifle I'd dragged ashore.

"Joe! I can't hang on!"

I quickly aimed and pulled the trigger, but was greeted with only a *click.*

"I'm out of ammo? I don't believe it!" I looked skyward to God. "Can't You give me a break?" I yelled. "I thought bullets grew back here!"

"Never mind that, Joe. Help me!"

"How?"

"Hack off my leg!"

"What?" I asked, dumbfounded. Did I just hear what I thought I heard?

"Please!" she screamed. "It will grow back. *Everything* grows back!"

I looked around for something sharp—a jagged rock or sharp-edged hunk of wood, but nothing leaped into view. I quickly swung the rifle's butt end into a boulder, shattering it into a hundred small pieces. The rifle stayed intact, so the butt that remained resembled a broken bottle.

Blood squirted from her leg as the chain tore at the flesh of her leg.

"Hang on." I swung the rifle like an axe, jamming the sharpened butt into her upper leg.

"Oh God!" Thais screamed.

"I'm sorry!" I swung again.

Thais screamed again, letting go of the root.

"Thais!" I yelled and grabbed her.

"Please help me!" she yelled in torment.

I got to my feet and helped her to stand up. By then, our feet were back in the urine-soaked shoreline.

"Please…please…please," she kept repeating in desperation.

A second chain leapt out of the water to wrap around her waist.

We watched helplessly as the chain tightened around her body.

She hugged me and I her.

The chain dragged us deeper, and all I could do was hug her and watch tears puddle in her eyes.

"I'm so sorry for my sins," she choked out. "Please tell God I'm sorry!"

The chains yanked her away and back into the rancid liquid. In less than a second, she'd disappeared into the disgusting moat.

"Thais!" I called, running in deeper to try and find her.

My desperate search for Thais was short-lived. Geryon popped to the surface. He dropped a handful of *dead,* motionless chains that he must have ripped out by the root at the bottom of the moat.

"Damn it!" I shouted and ran back to shore.

⚜

My rest with Thais had done me good. I'd regained some of my strength. At least I had enough energy to run. It was probably not humanly possible to stay ahead of a nine foot charging demon for an extended period of time, so I had to find someplace to hide, and fast.

The area was full of dead brush and mud. I came to a steep hill, remembering that this was a giant pit. I not only had to elude Geryon, but also claw my way out of this mess.

That's when it hit me. Maybe I could do both at the same time. If I could gain some height, maybe I could start a mudslide or something equally catastrophic—certainly a better plan than hiding, because it actually *depended* on that demon following me up the hill.

I reached a spot about fifty feet high when Geryon reached the base of the muddy hill. It figures—now that I had a plan, Geryon couldn't follow me so easily. His sheer weight dragged him back to the base every time he grabbed a handful of mud to try to climb. I got to the top, and was able to see a greater distance than before. This area, lighter than the one I'd left, looked dusky.

Thais had told me that there were ten bolgias, ten pits for degrees and categories of the fraudulent.

I looked down the hill to see Geryon still struggling to claw his way up. There had to be an easier way to get off this level without going in and out of every pit, further exposing myself to the horrors and torment of the damned, and risking the same fate.

I ran along the top of the hill, searching for a different route to the next pit. As with the other levels, this had to be a great ring. If I ran long enough, I would probably end up where I'd started, but this place was so huge I could have been running for months, or even years.

Luckily, I didn't have to run long to find a bridge.

The bridge ran in both directions, which meant that it probably extended the entire length of the eighth circle. But why was it there?

Could it have been created for demonic task masters to supervise the demon underlings in the art of torture? I looked down in both directions, but I saw nothing other than dirt and muck. So, if there were no demon supervisors now, there probably never were, since Hell didn't give me the impression of ever upgrading or changing its policies.

I hopped onto the bridge and got my bearings.

If Thais had been in the second bolgia, then I now stood on the ridge between the second and third, so all I had to do was travel the bridge to the end and, hopefully, to the ninth circle, where my brother awaited.

That sounded easy enough, but only if I didn't factor my best buddy, Geryon, into the mix.

CHAPTER 41
Canto XIX, XX – Circle VII – Bolgia III, IV – False Prophets

I looked over the rotting wooden railing to the third bolgia below, and it wasn't what you would call a *pretty* sight. I inspected the rocky landscape dotted with holes. Each hole was filled with white and red hot coals. Through the coal protruded the legs and feet of the damned, each one aflame. Because they were positioned head-first into the ground, I couldn't identify them or even guess what they'd done to get into such a pickle.

The smell of burning flesh reminded me of the Nazi extermination camps we'd liberated. It literally was the smell of death. I ducked behind the railing when I saw demons carrying in their latest victim—a priest. All the demons were of insect-caste, like the Malebranche, relentlessly unified in task.

"Stop this!" the priest yelled to the uninterested demons. "There must be some mistake. I demand to speak with Minos. I never ever used the church for my own ends. Not once! Not ever!"

From the demons' reactions, he might as well have asked a cockroach to do his taxes.

Other demons flew beneath the bridge, hauling other sinners—some nuns and several more priests.

I thought that this might be the section for those who pretended to be Christian for some personal gain, but I also saw Rabbis and Buddhist monks.

The priest screamed out again as the demons stripped him down.

"Please let me speak with Minos one more time. I was a good priest! I never sold my position for profit!"

Had the church become so corrupt that this bolgia had been created? Had all religions been corrupted in the decades since my death? Or had it always been this way?

Even though I'd left Virgil far behind, I still heard his voice in my head. I could just hear him say, *it's not the church but the people who have become corrupt*. Bottom line, he would have been right.

The demons placed the struggling, naked priest in some kind of Baptistery, and stuffed his legs into the holes where priests normally stood when they're baptized into the priesthood.

The demons picked up the baptismal, twirling it and the priest upside down. They shoved him into the burning coal until only his lower legs and feet were visible.

He screamed in agony as his legs and feet lit up from the sheer heat consuming his upper body.

All those feet sticking out of the coals must also have been through some baptismal ceremony, as well.

The symbolism wasn't lost on me. A literal baptism of fire, a bastardized version of a baptism for those who'd used their positions in the church or faith for personal gain.

I had learned of it in Catholic school—the sin of *simony*.

How many holy men had been corrupted through the centuries? Priests who'd gone bad probably rivaled, or even surpassed, bad cops, lawyers, and politicians. They say power corrupts, and absolute power corrupts absolutely. How much more power had these holy people wielded when dealing with someone's soul rather than their money or standing?

I'd often see Cardinals, Bishops, and even the Pope garnished in chains of gold. Why…when there were so many hungry children?

Now, years after my death, how much more tarnished had the church become?

I moved on.

❧❧

It was between night and day over the fourth bolgia. It looked to me like the moments preceding dawn.

I peered down into the pit and didn't need any further explanation of their sin. Though I didn't recognize the people, I immediately recognized their fate. Every man and woman in the pit had their heads twisted front to back...like TT. These people were false prophets, astrologers, and magicians. Each of them carried a large stone and simply moved it from one point to the next. Simple, that is, unless your body was on backwards.

I felt as bad for them as I had for TT. I didn't want to be so bold as to hope she found happiness wherever she ended up, but I truly hoped that she'd made it to the place of the virtuous, and that she no longer suffered.

From the direction of the third bolgia I heard the rumble of falling rocks. I froze. The moment hung in the balance as I hoped it was something, anything other than what I knew it must be. Out of the distant darkness of the bolgia behind me, Geryon approached. I don't know if he saw me, and I didn't want to wait around to make sure that he did. I couldn't run as this was a straight bridge floor with no turns, and it only got lighter ahead.

I quickly slipped under the railing and shimmied beneath the bridge. I looked up through the cracks of the bridge to see Geryon's approach. He stopped directly above me and looked around.

Virgil had only explained how the reptilian demons saw their prey, but he never mentioned them smelling. Either way, I prayed he wouldn't look down.

Unfortunately, I looked down and saw several insect demons below. If I made the slightest noise, they would look up and probably pitch pennies to see who'd have me for lunch.

The wooden clasp I grasped loosened from my weight. Dust and dirt floated down toward the demons below. I closed my eyes, hoping they wouldn't look up as much as I hoped that Geryon wouldn't look down. The next beam was three feet away. Considering the noise it would take for me to swing to it, it might as well have been on Jupiter.

The beam I clung onto loosened further.

I looked down to see the demons moving away.

I needed to let go and fall into the pit, but I had to wait for the demons to get far enough away so as not to notice me.

I looked up through the cracks of the bridge floor to see Geryon again. That son of a gun wasn't going anywhere.

I let go of the beam and fell.

I tried to land as quietly as possible. When I hit bottom, I immediately rolled under the crevice of some large rocks.

I looked for some mud to cover myself; the insect demons' Achille's heel, so to speak. I found none. If this bolgia was one of the insect demons' domain, it would make sense that there wouldn't be a lot of mud or anything that would help hide the damned. The place was as dry as Minos's wit.

There were no demons where I hit, so I figured I'd wait until Geryon moved on, and try to figure out a way to the next bolgia. Suddenly, a voice from outside my small, self-imposed, rock cocoon found me.

A middle-aged, balding man in a stiff collar and dress coat shuffled backwards toward me. His clothing was from the late 1800s and his shirt was buttoned to the top button. This guy looked so uptight that in life, he'd probably made a list of things to dream about and consulted it while he slept.

"I saw you land," he said in a southern accent. "Did you break anything, good sir?"

"No, I'm fine."

"You seem a bit peevish, perhaps. Shall I help you to your feet, sir?"

"Look! If you don't mind, I'm trying to hide," I said.

"The beasts are no longer present, if that's your concern."

I slowly looked out and then rolled away from the rocks.

I couldn't see if Geryon was still up on the bridge, but I doubted he could see me if he was.

"Dear Lord, sir, your head is back to front," he said, referring to the fact that my head was *not* twisted around. "I mean, well, you understand my meaning."

"I'm not a psychic," I said.

"I see, and have you fallen from the sky for a reason? Or are you one of the good Lord's fallen angels?"

"I'm looking for someone, but I have a demon on my tail."

"Who might you be, good sir?"

"You're the psychic. You tell me."

He thought for a moment, and then a look of realization struck him.

"Could you perhaps be...Joe Dante?"

"What?" I thought for a moment that this guy might actually be a psychic.

"You are, are you not?" he said, "The police constable who searches for his brother."

"How the hell do you know that?"

"She has told us all about you," he said, "and we listened as if fed flapjacks on a Sunday morn."

Other psychics gathered around—medieval sorcerers with black capes, gypsies wearing headbands of gold and long flowing dresses, and soothsayers from ancient Greece.

"You're the fugitive in Hell who stands against the demons," the psychic continued.

"Who told you that?"

"Why, Tonya Tiresias, of course."

"Bologna," I said, astonished. "She blew this joint before she even met me."

"She has returned, my good man."

"What? Where is she?"

"They don't take kindly to people trying to escape their charge, you understand."

"Do I have to ask again?" I said determined.

"Yes, of course. Follow that path, and you'll come to small bungalows. Miss Tonya resides in the first; however, your attempt to rescue her will surely fail."

"Oh yeah—why's that?"

"You have a head, dear sir, at least in the eyes of the beast. You will pop out like a cherry in a bowl of grapes."

When TT's head had been twisted, her face was freezing cold because no blood flowed to it. So, when these heat seeking demons looked at the psychics, they appeared to have no head. I, on the other hand, had one and my noggin would serve as a neon thumb for the Malebranche that I didn't belong.

"I don't suppose you have any ideas short of twisting my head off," I said.

"As a matter of fact, I do." He smiled.

❧

I walked with the southern psychic toward the bungalow, carrying two hot rocks atop my shoulders to conceal the heat that radiated from my brain basket.

For the masquerade to be convincing, though, I walked backwards, which meant I couldn't see anything in front of me.

"You sure this is going to work?" I nervously inquired as we approached a large group of insect demons.

"The stones will cloud the heat from your head," he said. "To them, you will appear as headless as the rest. You must keep the rocks amid you and them."

"Thanks."

"I am Michael Scott," he said. "Have you not heard of me, good sir?"

"Sorry."

"I traveled the south mostly through the 1860s, offering a universal cure of my own recipe."

"I see… You're a snake oil salesman."

"Sir," he said, perturbed. "I've healed many. Of course, on occasion, the town folk needed incentive, so I may have perhaps pretended to see an illness in their future, but in the end, they were the better for knowing me."

"Oh, of course they were."

He looked up to see just how many demons we were approaching. "Dear Lord," he said.

"What?" I asked, not being able to turn around to see for myself.

"This plan is perhaps…imprudent," he replied nervously.

"You thought it was the bee's knees not two minutes ago."

"Pardon me, sir? Bee's what?"

"You thought it was a good idea," I said through gritted teeth.

"That was before I realized that we would be passing such a gathering of beasts."

"What?"

"I shall leave you to your own devices, sir." He walked away.

"Wait," I began, trying not to panic. "I can't see behind me."

"Just continue on your path, good sir. You'll either discover the bungalow or…"

"Or?"

"Or—into the jaws of the beast," he said as he ran back to his version of safety. "I bid you good fortune, sir!"

I continued to walk backwards, trying to pretend that my head was on backwards and that I could see where I was going.

As I passed several large demons, I tried not to gulp. But, I nearly swallowed my own blood pump when I realized one of them was my old buddy, Malecoda.

I bumped into the door hoping to God that none of them would notice when I dropped one of the hot rocks from my shoulder, so I could free a hand to open the door.

❧

When I entered, I looked around. Calling this place a bungalow would be like calling Death Valley a garden spot.

I propped an old wooden bench under the knob.

The place was laid out like a medieval torture chamber.

TT was alone in the middle of the small room, with her arms strung up and tied to a steel rod that ran along the ceiling.

Her head was, once again, twisted around.

"Oh my God," I said as I ran to her.

"Joe, is that you?" She sounded more dejected than in pain.

"What happened?"

"They found us. I don't know how. I was so close."

"What about Hector?"

"I don't know. I think he got over the wall in time."

"Hang on. I'm going to get you out of here," I said. I didn't want to tell her that Virgil had betrayed them. It wasn't out of loyalty. I just didn't see the point.

I started to untie the ropes.

"No," she said.

"What?"

"I'm famous now, you see," she said bitterly. "I escaped for a time. Now the demons make me an example of what *not* to do. They *hurt* me."

"I'm sorry, TT."

"If they catch me again…" she started as she failed to fight her tears. "…they'll hurt me more than ever before."

"They won't find us again."

"How can you say that? How do I warrant anything better in your eyes than the rest who reside here?"

"I can't help *them*," I said.

"You can't help *me*."

"We'll see about that."

"Don't you understand? I *did* those things. I did everything I was accused of. There's no false imprisonment here. Everybody is here for a reason."

"Maybe, but you don't have to accept it." I reached up to untie the ropes that bound her to the steel rod.

"Stop Joe, please." Tears streamed from her eyes.

I ignored her and continued to fumble with the ropes.

"I'm sorry," she continued, rather loudly.

"Keep your voice down."

"I'm sorry, Joe," she continued, even louder.

"Quiet down."

"Help me!" she screamed to the demons outside. "Somebody, help me, please!"

I looked at her, more hurt by her betrayal than from fear of what was to come.

"I'm sorry, Joe. I just can't do it again."

Suddenly, the door shook from the outside, followed by pounding.

I looked around and for the first time, realized that there was only one way in or out of this place—through the door those demons were about to kick in.

"Tonya! The gun? Did they take it when they found you?"

"I'm so sorry, Joe."

"Did they take it?"

"I'm sorry."

"The weapon I gave to Hector!" I repeated as I shook her. "Tonya! Where is it?"

"It's gone!"

I looked around, trying not to panic. I needed a weapon, but could only find rocks that littered the floor. I picked up the two biggest ones I could fit into my hands and watched the door bust open.

They came in like any group of insects. Some crawled on the walls and ceiling, and the largest ones surrounded me. Malecoda led the way.

I put my rock-filled dukes up, ready to fight, but they stopped in their tracks and stared at me.

"Long time no see," I said, staring coldly at Malecoda. "Although I'm sure my face looks like all the others in those compound eyes."

Some of the demons made a move toward me, but surprisingly, Malecoda stopped them.

"If you want me, you're going to have to buy it, *bug face*, because I ain't going softly!"

They didn't move. They just continued to look at me like I'd become Mesmo the hypnotist.

"What are you waiting for?"

I have no idea what Malecoda said to the rest of them in those eerie clicks and screeches they called a language, but they all backed off.

"I see," I said as the answer revealed itself to me. "Maybe you *do* recognize me after all…my voice maybe? Maybe you remember something else. Like a right cross from my old buddy Virgil. What was it he said? You *will* leave me to him."

I smiled as I dropped the rocks.

They weren't going to touch me for fear of the big bad boss, Virgil.

I looked back to TT, who watched helplessly.

"I'm sorry TT. I really am."

"Goodbye, Joe," she said and smiled sadly.

I turned back to the demon gauntlet that awaited me and slowly walked toward the door.

I felt like Daniel in the lion's den, and I wondered if faith alone could carry me through.

Have what it takes, Joe? Do you have any faith left? Did you ever have any?

If Daniel could end up a lion tamer, maybe I could pretend to be an exterminator, at least, for a moment.

I waved my finger in Malecoda's face, half expecting it to be bitten off.

"You will *not* hurt her anymore," I said sternly, referring to TT. "Understand!" I yelled.

Malecoda made a move on me, but he stopped short. Man, oh man, he wanted to twist my head off, but good. It must have eaten him alive to suck it up and let me walk.

I headed for the door.

Outside, I walked the gauntlet as giant insect demons towered over me. I strolled forward with my head on straight, in full view of the demons. They didn't even try to lay a claw on me.

Behind the demons, the psychics watched in bewilderment.

There were wizards in long robes of black, gypsies garnished in rubies and sapphires, and gothic-looking men in black lipstick and heavy mascara.

A young man with long hair looked my way.

"Dude, you rock." He gave me a thumbs-up, such as it was with his body facing the other way.

I smiled as I passed the last of the demons.

It felt good to know that Malecoda and his brood would no longer be a pain in my keister. Unfortunately, Geryon wasn't about to be anywhere near as sweet.

I had six more bolgias to traverse, and only God knew what lay beyond that. I easily could have ended up as a permanent fixture in any one of them if I slipped up but once.

I had to get back on that bridge, and the only way to do that was to draw Geryon down to *me*.

CHAPTER 42
Canto XXI – Circle VIII – Bolgia V – Sowers of Discord

I climbed over the hill to the next bolgia, very careful to keep the bridge at a distance.

The smartest thing Geryon could do was stay on the bridge and look down from above, and he'd been pretty smart up until now. Well, maybe he couldn't give Einstein a run for his money, but he was, at the very least, *relentless*.

I looked down at the next bolgia and saw a large building. As with the moat in the second bolgia, it stretched left to right from horizon to horizon, creating one huge ring. But unlike the bungalows in the last bolgia, this one seemed more modern, at least closer to my time. It almost looked like some kind of government administration building.

Like the other bolgias, the only way to reach the other side was to proceed straight through it.

Once inside, I looked down the long, perfectly waxed hallway floors and couldn't even guess what type of sinner resided here. If I hadn't known any better, I would have sworn that I'd just entered a courthouse or city hall complete with shiny marble floors.

I heard sounds in the distance, like gears grinding and wood chopping. I ducked into one of the countless rooms, surprised to find myself in yet another long hallway, only this one imprisoned men and women who'd been chained to the walls.

As always, there seemed to be no rhyme or reason to the arrangement of the damned. Nazis stood next to American Indian warriors. Beautiful women in clothing from the future had been bound beside Muslim men. The only common denominator was the ghastly scars that covered most of their bodies. They looked as if they were dismembered and reassembled in some hellish version of *Frankenstein's Monster*. For the record—*Yuck*!

Time itself meant nothing in the classification, only the sin, but what was *this* sin?

"Who the devil are you?" a British soldier blurted out.

"Listen, I need some help."

"Do you know who we are?" a Nazi replied. "Or what we did? You seek our advice. Does it change your mind to know that I was the one who wrote the propaganda that made Hitler into a hero?"

"Or that I was a madam to the Hollywood elite who published her book of customers?" a middle aged woman added.

"Or I, who wrote pop culture books, glorifying mob hitmen," a man in a suit continued.

"Writers, advisors, politicians and counselors…" a man in ancient Roman garb said, "we buried the truth with scandal and conspiracies, and crushed it with confusion…creating schisms and factions among those who *should* have been allies. We pretended to tell the truth, but in reality, we strangled it until only the lies remained. We are the sowers of scandal and discord."

My gaze found a Muslim man in his fifties. I don't know why, but I found myself curious about him. "You?" I asked the Muslim man clad in a strange desert camouflaged uniform. I had to resist feeling sorry for him. "What did you do?"

He slowly looked up and spoke low.

"I was a war correspondent in Iraq, and I followed a man who said we were going to fight the mother of all Jihads," he said in his Middle Eastern accent. "I was nothing more than his puppet. I denied the undeniable. When American tanks crashed through our streets, I swore to the public that they never existed. It never happened. Deep down inside, I knew the truth, but I was just too frightened to stand up and say that I wouldn't do it."

"Another war? What year was this?"

"2003," he said.

"So many wars and so many uniforms," I said as I looked around. "It's hard to know who's on whose side. It sounds like my country was at war with yours. Who won?"

"Why does this matter now?" he asked.

"I don't know. It doesn't, I guess."

"Down here, we're all the same," he said.

"I wonder what it is that makes us the same," I preached to them...these *architects of fear.* "Pick any year in history, and it seems someone, somewhere was fighting a war. We're allies one generation and enemies the next. Does that make us human? Does that make us the same? I know we're all different. We're all from different times and countries, but we're all human. We hate, we fight, we forgive, and we rise above. Maybe that's what being human is all about. Maybe *that's* why we're all the same."

I looked around at the array of people before me. I hesitated to ask for help, and had no idea what anyone here could do for me, but the fact of the matter was, I was desperate enough to try.

"I have a demon on my tail, and I need help," I said. "Can someone lend me a hand?" As I expected, no one answered. I turned to leave, but then a strangely familiar voice spoke up.

"I'll help you, mate" McMontey said.

I turned to face him, sucker punched by the shock of seeing him again. I immediately recognized him. I could have been here for a thousand years, but I would always remember that humiliating day in court when that son of a bitch McMontey had accused me of being a dirty cop.

"McMontey," I said, not bothering to hide my disdain. Like the others, deep, long scars painted his body like a road map.

"What's the matter?" he said. "Didn't think I'd end up in Hell?"

"So this is where the lawyers wind up, huh?"

"Only the good ones, mate. Only the good ones."

"Well, like my old man said, never look a gift horse in the mouth," I said. "You want to help? How do I get rid of a demon?"

"Nothing's for nothing, Detective. You get me out of this jam first."

I yanked at the chains, but to no avail.

"Don't you think I tried that?" McMontey said with just a tad too much sarcasm.

"If you've got something better, I'm listening," I said.

"Do you know what they do to us? They come in, chop us up, let us heal, and chop us up all over again. Hell, sometimes, they rip out the lungs from my chest just to see my expression change. Now, get me out of here!"

I heard a noise from the outer hall and ducked by the door so that when it opened, I would be behind it. The sound of whining gears got closer, causing the damned to fidget with fear. Suddenly, the door busted open and giant metal feet slammed against the waxed marble floor. They filed in while I prayed that the door would be left open.

I pressed back against the wall, accidentally making a slight thudding sound. I felt like a marmaluke. The door suddenly slammed closed, revealing me.

I immediately saw that these were metal demons and that they would see me only if I moved. Seeing how hard it was to stand perfectly still the last time I'd crossed paths with a robot, it didn't promise to be an easy task.

I froze as one of the demons stared me in the face.

He, or rather *it*, was big. It looked like something out of *Science Fiction Theater*. The other mechanical demons I'd encountered resembled tanks with legs, loaded with artillery. These demons reminded me of large mechanical men, and they were armed to their metal teeth with swords and axes.

Some had arms made of swords with no hands, while others had hands loaded with razor-like fingers. It was as if they were constructed for the singular purpose of disemboweling human flesh.

I didn't move. I didn't even blink. I held my breath like the air was poison. If I could have stopped my heart, I would have. I remembered how the angel had remained inhumanly still back in the mausoleum, and then clobbered the demon with a right cross. I couldn't do the same. Simply put, there were too many demons, probably one per sinner.

The metal beast didn't move. He continued to stare suspiciously in my direction, coming in for a closer look. The times when I couldn't breathe for unbelievable amounts of minutes while I'd been underwater had trained me well. But, there was a huge difference between not breathing because there wasn't any air to be found and not breathing because you purposely held your breath. This was harder because air was all around, yet even the slightest heave of my chest would be the end of me.

I stared blankly into the demon's eyes. I couldn't even shift my eyes, let alone blink. I'd never realized how hard it was to simply *not* blink. My eyes began to dry up and my lungs demanded that I gasp for air.

My muscles stayed solid, but I knew I couldn't stay this way forever. I wanted to pass out, but even *that* was impossible. My body wasn't physical anymore. I was a soul, but still, I wanted the things my body had desired on Earth, not food or water, but air.

Then, a strange thing happened. A light popped on in my head.

I needed to rise above the physical. There was no *physical* here. *I* was in control. I told myself that I didn't need air. I didn't need to blink. I didn't *have to* move.

The angel in the mausoleum must have known this. That's how he almost literally turned to stone. So too, my skin must turn to plastic, my eyes to wood, and the blood in my veins had to stop in mid-flow.

Stick to it, Joe…you are metal with sawdust in your veins. You are not here. You have no heart to pump, no eyes to blink, no blood to flow. Your corpse is long dead and under six feet of hallowed ground. Your body is dust. You are no one, Joe. You are nothing. You are…immortal.

The robotic demon's eyes lit up, and the light shined in my eyes. The light should have made my pupils shrink, but I wouldn't let them. I told myself, over and over again, that *I* was the one in control. These were *not* physical eyes. Light would *not* affect them.

I supposed I could have stayed this way for hours or even days. There was nothing my body needed to survive, no air or movement, but the denial of these things felt torturous in and of itself.

The demon leaned down, putting his face near mine. He poked me with a needle that extended from his finger, but I didn't flinch.

You're in control, Joe. You're in control…

He slowly raised the needle to my eye.

Could this demon know you're here, Joe? The angel said something about them, didn't he? Maybe mechanical demons can see just like everyone else, but they're not allowed to touch those truly motionless. Could this be some strange law in Hell that metal demons had to obey? It doesn't matter. You're in control, Joe. Your face is plastic. Your skin is rock. You're in control.

When I thought the jig was up and he'd plunge his needle-like finger into my eye, my unlikely ally spoke up.

"Hey!" McMontey yelled to the demon.

The big robot turned away to focus on the lawyer.

"Pucker up those metal lips and kiss my limey ass, you rust bucket," he said.

I had to admit, *that* had taken a lot of stones. Never in a hundred years would I have expected McMontey to come to my rescue, but then again, for all I knew, a hundred years had passed since we'd last met.

The robotic demon abandoned me and took his place before McMontey. I still didn't move. There were a lot of demons in the room and any one of them might have looked my way if I happened to move.

Without any kind of communication among them, all the iron demons started slashing simultaneously. My eyes still forced open, I watched as the sinners were systematically dismembered and disemboweled by the sword and axe-wielding demons.

"Listen to me," a Nazi pleaded. "You never listen to me. I was under orders, you understand. Under orders. Under orders!"

The demon ignored him, plunging his dagger-like fingers into the Nazi's gut. I couldn't move. I couldn't cover my ears to mute the blood curdling screams that followed. Neither could I look away, close my eyes, or even blink.

So, I watched, and tried desperately to not change my expression to fear, pity or sympathy. I tried to disconnect my brain from my body so that not even a single tear would come to my dry and scratchy eyes.

In the hours that followed, I thought about the Nazi words. *Under orders*. Is that ever really an excuse? Maybe Argenti hadn't been responsible for all those deaths. Maybe, just maybe, only those who'd pulled the trigger were culpable. If we were only responsible for our own actions, then maybe Argenti deserved exactly what he'd gotten. Maybe he deserved to be with the wrathful. Maybe there was *justice* in the horrid place after all.

I *did* understand McMontey's plan. He, like most of the others, was cut off at the wrists, and was being cut to shreds. With that, his body would no longer be chained. The robots apparently allowed them to heal, shackled them back up and, hell, even cleaned the gore from the floor, only to repeat the never ending torment. The symbolism here was as sharp as the instruments the demons used to disassemble these human spirits.

In life, these people had created separations, tearing apart countries, generations, and even families with their propaganda. In McMontey's case, he twisted and contorted the truth, dividing those who believed him from those who didn't. So, in death, *they* themselves were torn apart.

In life, I might have smiled at the irony. How ironic that, if I *had* smiled, it would mean *my* end. Being caught would cause me to be dismembered as well, and then chained along with the rest to begin an unending cycle of violence and pain.

Finally, emotion escaped my body, which must have looked more like a statue. A tear puddled up and then dripped from my eye.

I remained frozen, fearing that if anyone looked in my direction, they would see the motion of a single tear. I silently prayed that no demon would glance my way.

❧

In McMontey's blood-soaked suit coat, I dragged his body parts down the hill that led to the next bolgia.

Full light shone on this bolgia, which was a giant desert. As long as it was wide, I couldn't even see the hill at the other end this time.

This bolgia seemed different. Maybe it was of some long forgotten sin or something that stopped being a sin after a certain time, but either way, this place was desolate.

I stopped beside a dead tree and opened the suit coat. McMontey was a mess, but I had to hand it to him. The man hadn't even whimpered.

"Are you all right?" I asked.

"Is that a leading question, Detective?"

I smiled sadly as I lay his half skeleton-exposed body down under the tree.

"I held up my end. Now how do I get rid of that demon?"

"How the devil am I supposed to know, mate?"

"What?"

"I had to get out of there Dante. I'm sorry."

"Jesus Christ!" I said angrily. "You lied to me."

"We're in Hell, Dante. I'm a lawyer. Are you really *that* surprised?"

"Maybe I shouldn't be, but haven't you learned anything?"

"So, tell me, if I told you the truth and just asked for your help, would you have given it?"

"Probably not," I said.

"Haven't *you* learned anything?" he asked as he coughed up blood.

I nodded my head. He was right. "You'll be all right," I said.

"I look at you, and I see years gone past. I lived decades after you passed, Dante. You remind me that there was a time where life imprisonment actually meant *life imprisonment.* At the time I died, do you know that a confessed multiple murderer could get out of prison in less than seven years if he had something of value for the DA. Now, I ask you, mate, is that justice?"

"You're asking the wrong guy, counselor."

His eyes actually puddled up, and it wasn't from the pain.

"When I was a young lad, I abandoned a godly woman who was pregnant with my child. She lost the baby at childbirth, and then killed herself. I let faith and fear separate us. She was Irish Catholic…and I? I was a fool."

"What?" I said, recognizing the story. The last time I'd heard it, it had been from the young woman's point of view.

He was talking about *Mary.* Was McMontey Mary's true love? Was he the Englishman who'd left her to move to Boston? It all fit.

"She committed suicide, because I wasn't there for her when she needed me," he continued. "She was young and she trusted me, but I wanted to be a great lawyer. I ended up defending scum who more than likely ended up down here…and I ended up becoming as much scum as they were. I died nearly seventy years after she did, but whenever I was alone, my thoughts would always drift back to her. That's the reason why Minos condemned me to that cold, awful place, you see. Not because of my choice of careers, but because I ripped out the heart of one I held so dear. I wish I'd had one more chance to talk to her. I don't know why I'm telling you this. I've heard it said that confession is good for the soul. I hope so, because in the end, a soul is all we have."

"When did you die?"

"1994."

Tell him he got what he deserved, Joe. Tell him! What are you waiting for? The old Joe would have taken pleasure in his pain. What's happening to you? Who are you, Joe? Who? Didn't Virgil ask you that question time and time again? What was he trying to say? What was he trying to tell you?

I wanted to tell him about Mary, but what would I say? How would he feel if he was told that she was in Hell, too? I didn't want to pour salt in the poor guy's wounds, so I just sat with him. "Tell me something, when you died, how were the Red Sox doing?"

Slowly, we shared a smile.

"We made the Series in 1986, but blew it. Damn Bill Buckner."

"Are the Sox *ever* going to take the Series?"

"The curse lives, Dante. The curse lives."

"I'd better get going. If Geryon catches us here, there'll be Hell to pay."

"Farewell mate."

I turned to leave, but McMontey called me back.

"To answer your question, Detective, I don't sleep at all," he said, apparently referring to that time so long ago, in court, when I'd asked him how he slept at night.

I left the sad lawyer to heal under the dead desert tree.

CHAPTER 43
Thoughts of Home – Mickey
ೞೞ

I had the gun to my head, and I was ready. Man oh man, and I mean *ready.* Just as I found the strength and resigned myself to my end, the doorbell rang.

I was going to ignore it, and would have, but for some reason, I remembered TT's words... *Just when you think you're hip to destiny, destiny throws you a curve.*

So, I let curiosity get the better of me and decided to see what *curve* destiny had in store for me. I put my piece down, and called out. "Yeah?"

Mickey walked in. "Why are you sitting in the dark?" he asked.

"I got no reason to sit in the light."

"I've seen a lot of things in this world," Mickey said as he sat beside me. "I saw a drowning cop actually saved by the thief he was chasing. I saw a full moon on a bright sunny day. And one time, I even saw a woman in a white cotton dress lift a car off her dying child. But you know what I've never seen before?"

"What?"

"A right thing come out of a wrong."

"I need to be alone," I said.

"What you need is to let this thing go. Listen, Joe, Easter weekend's coming up. Angie and I want you to come over."

I was about to say *no thanks* when my bracelet caught my attention. Could I ever look at it and not think of Anna? Beatrice? My family?

There comes a time in every man's life when he stops looking forward and starts looking back. Sometimes, it sneaks in on him, like when he grows old and memories of children and grandchildren stir nothing but a great amount of joy and fondness. Sometimes, though, it happens quickly, as when all that he loves is butchered like a lamb in a slaughterhouse.

Suddenly, it was as if a light snapped on in a long darkened basement.

If I went ahead with this awful thing I was planning, then *he* would get away with it. I'd been such a fool. TT was right. If I had done this, I never would have fulfilled my true destiny.

"The kids haven't seen their Uncle Joe in a long time and…" Mickey started.

"I'm going to get him," I interrupted, still gazing at my bracelet.

"What?"

"I'm going to get Argenti."

"Joey, remember where I got this?" He pointed to the crescent scar under his eye.

How could I not remember? Every time I saw it, I loved my brother even more for it. "What?" I asked. Granted, it was a strange question given the circumstances.

"Indulge me. Do you remember where I got this scar?"

"Yeah, some chump with a broken bottle came up behind me and you got in his way."

"And?"

"And what?" I said. "You saved my skin that night."

"That's right. Let me save your skin again by giving you some advice. Let the *law* get Argenti."

"The *law* had its chance. Now, it's my turn."

"Joe…"

"Screw the law!" I yelled.

"Jesus Christ!"

"Screw Him too," I said without hesitation.

I saw the shock on Mickey's face. He hadn't expected me to say anything like that but I had no time for the law or for God. I knew what needed to be done. I knew the right thing to do and I was going to do it.

I now had something to look forward to again—finding justice for my family, and getting Argenti without the help or hindrance of either the law or God.

For the first time in my life, I felt liberated from the bonds of both.

I hid in the hangar at the small private airport while Argenti's goons waited for him. I hated them, their limos, and their expensive suits. They were all wise guys and losers. Ironic that most of them went to church more often than me.

I was at a distance and hidden, but not so far away that I couldn't listen to their conversation. I wanted to hear something about Argenti or their next conquest, but surprisingly, they talked about the coming weekend as if it meant something.

"What are you doin'?" one of them grunted.

"Marie's makin' a ham with ravioli. Why, I don't know, but her family's comin' ova so there'll be enough to go round."

"Ham? On Eastah? Aren't we supposed to have fish or somethin'?"

"Don't you even know your own damn religion? Fish is today. You can have anyting you want on Eastah."

Mickey had mentioned Easter coming up this weekend, but it hadn't registered. Then I realized that today wasn't just any Friday, but *Good Friday*.

How could I have forgotten Good Friday? Being Catholic, Easter was a big family event. Bea used to stay on top of me about not eating meat during Lent. She also nagged me into sacrificing something and made sure we ate only fish on Good Friday. I hated fish, but I choked it down because I loved Bea and thought it was respectful to God.

A small twin-prop plane rolled up to them. I expected Argenti to pull up in one of his European cars, or be driven by one of his witless pugs, but he stepped out of the prop job with two of his men. I was surprised to see that he was actually the pilot as well. It had taken me seven months to cozy up to that mutt, and not once had I seen him fly a plane. I hadn't even known he was a pilot.

My instincts told me that, if he climbed back in that plane, I'd never see him again, so if I intended to do something, it had to be *now*.

Argenti opened a case full of coke, and the wise guys responded by opening their case full of loot.

The time was right to make myself known.

I didn't have my gun drawn, nor did I fear that anything would happen to me.

"Hey!" I yelled as I walked over to them.

They pulled out their guns, aiming at me.

"I'm the heat," I said, as foolish as I was fearless.

They were wise guys and cheap hoods, but I knew they wouldn't shoot. In fact, I knew exactly what they were thinking, that there were about twenty other cops hiding in the hangars behind me.

"What the hell's goin' on here?" the obvious leader said.

I didn't stop until I stood close to him, his gun pressing against my chest.

"Want to kill a cop?" I said. "Trust me, not a bright move. I have about two thousand brothers who'd love to take revenge on cop killers. Do you really want that many people with guns after you?"

Argenti remained silent, probably waiting for their next move.

Slowly, they all lowered their weapons.

"I want my mouthpiece," he said.

"Let's get something straight," I said, like a professor to an unwilling class. "I don't give a damn about the law. Everyone except Argenti can leave."

"What the devil?" Argenti finally said.

Dumbfounded, they eyed each other, obviously expecting it to be a trick.

"You wanna run that by me again?" the leader said.

"Get the word out on the streets, Argenti and I are joined at the hip. Wherever he goes, I go," I said, using a bastardize version of the words Bea often said to me. "If you deal with him, the Boston PD will come down on you like a brick falling off the Empire State Building."

Slowly, they backed away.

"What...but...you can't..." Argenti whined.

"Sorry pally, you're poison," the head wise guy said, reaching for the case full of snow.

"Leave the drugs," I ordered.

"We're not goin' to have a problem, are we?" He obviously disliked this latest development.

"You can take the dough, but you're not taking the drugs. You got a problem with that?" I asked, looking him square in the eye.

"Nope. No problem. Nada," he said.

I knew they wouldn't willingly part with *both* the drugs and the cash. I didn't want the coke distributed to any more kids, but I couldn't overplay my hand, so I let them keep the scratch.

As they got in their limos to leave, Argenti tried to back away toward his plane.

"Uh uh." I shook my head *no*. I looked at Argenti's men and enunciated very clearly. "Go away."

They looked at each other, hesitantly, until Argenti finally spoke up.

"What the devil are you waiting for, a bus pass? Ice him!"

I pulled out my gun and smiled. "Well?" I said.

They mulled over their options and then left.

"What the…" Argenti said amazed.

"I ought to bust you wide open," I said once we were alone.

"How did you find me?"

"You're like a cockroach, Argenti. I just have to check the cracks in the darkness and there you are."

I shoved Argenti, turning him around so I could search him, all while keeping my gun at his head. "Where does a piece of crap like you learn to fly?"

"I was a pilot."

"You were in the war?" I said, shocked.

"Yeah, you remember, it was a *world* war after all."

"Which side were you on?" I asked.

"Oh, that's funny. You should take it on the road, you're so funny."

"Shut your yap."

I admit I was shocked to hear that Argenti had fought against the Germans. Then again, with the draft, he'd really had no other choice. I guess both sides had punks and criminals in the ranks, but to become a prop jockey?

I was further surprised when I realized he wasn't carrying a piece. "Where's the gat?" I said.

"I don't carry one."

"Puts wrinkles in your suits?"

"I'm not a killer," he said.

The lie was essentially an insult, which I suppose was the point of saying it, but I wasn't in the mood for insults. "What did you just say to me?"

"You heard me," he said. "Now, are you going to arrest me or what? Because I want my mouthpiece."

"On your knees," I said.

"What?"

"On your knees!" I forced him down with a kick to the back of his knee.

301

His expression changed from arrogance to worry in a flash.

"I want to hear you say it. Say you murdered my family."

"I didn't murder anyone!" Argenti said.

I wanted him dead, but I needed something more. I needed him to confess his crimes. I needed him to admit his *sin*. "Ever play Russian Roulette?" I asked.

"What?"

"Russian Roulette. It's a game. Hear of it?"

He was still on his knees, with my knee in his back, and slammed against his plane. I showed him exactly what I was going to do. I removed five bullets from my .38, left one in, and then spun the chamber.

"Last chance, Argenti."

"You can't do this. You're a cop!"

"I'm the guy with the gun! I can do whatever the devil I please." I put the gun to his head and pulled back the hammer. "Say it. Say you killed them," I demanded.

"Screw you, Dante!"

I pulled the trigger.

CHAPTER 44
Canto XXIII – Circle VIII – Bolgia VI – Hypocrites
⸲ৎৎ৯

I walked across the dead sand in what had now become full daylight. Funny, it reminded me of the beach, although there was no ocean, sun, blue sky, or even shadows. I guess my mind wanted to focus on something pleasant even when pleasantries couldn't be found.

Seeing McMontey again and hearing about his guilt of how he left his true love behind made me wonder about Mary. Where was she now?

What would be the chances of finding Mary here by pure chance and her having this shocking connection to someone I knew in life? The odds were staggering. So maybe it wasn't by chance at all, but by some grand design that I would come to find Mary.

Maybe it was her accent, but when she spoke, it only served to remind me of home and family, and that made me miss her all the more.

I tried not to think about Virgil or Argenti, but the thoughts still came. *Virgil is probably off corrupting another soul. You sure about that, Joe? And Argenti? Where is he now?*

I was in the sixth bolgia. Without the company of sinners or anything that revealed its designation of sin to me, my thoughts, once again, shifted to Bea. How she had loved the beach. Maybe that's why this dead place reminded me of a world full of life.

"Can you hear me, Bea?" I shouted to no one. "Are you there?" I probably would have looked like a fool to the casual observer, if there had been such a person in this place, but I didn't care. "Do you miss me?" I shouted as I opened my arms and peered up at the dead sky.

Far off and high up, I saw the bridge…something I desperately needed to reach to shorten my journey, but as I focused on it, I noticed two things.

First, the bridge ended. I squinted. It didn't just end, it was broken.

It was hard to see the details since the bridge was so far away and high up, but it was as if there had been some great earthquake that had shattered the bridge's path for what could have been miles.

Earthquake? Could it be from that same earthquake that turned the cliff to the seventh circle into a jumbled mish-mash of pebbles and stones? What could have done such a thing?

If I were up there, I wouldn't have been able to jump to the other side. As far as I could see, there was no other side. I would had to have turned around and gone back. Either that or jump down and the distance between this bolgia and the bridge was far greater than that of the psychics.

As it was, I'd have to climb the next hill and hope to pick up the bridge there, if it weren't for Geryon, which brings me to my second and more alarming observation.

Geryon stared down at me.

I could barely see him in the distance, but I knew he spotted me. As I crossed this expanse of barren and motionless sand, I must have stuck out like a flare in the night sky. Plus, it didn't help that I had just been yelling like a marmaluke.

He must have gotten to the end of the shattered bridge and waited. The son of a gun had known that I would try to keep the bridge in sight. It was the only thing that gave me any kind of orientation and prevented me from walking in circles. He leapt off the bridge and hit the desert floor so hard, it felt like a 4.0 quake.

There was still a great distance between us, but that would quickly change if I did nothing. I needed to find cover, but I saw nothing except flat desert in every direction. So, with only one choice, I picked the direction that would longest delay my inevitable confrontation with the demon and ran to it as if it meant salvation.

Geryon pursued me at an alarming pace.

≈≈

I reached a group of dunes, running for it as if God Himself waited on the other side.

When I got to the top, I fell down from exhaustion.

Geryon was closing in on me from one side, but the other side captured my interest.

Hundreds of people dressed in elaborate robes of gold and jewels, each clasping a long lever, walked in unison on a circular path, moving large interconnected gears for some unknown purpose.

It reminded me of the way in which people had once ground the grains for the harvest, or how ancient Egyptian slaves worked in unison to create mud-like cement for the pyramids. At least *that's* how they'd done it in the movie *The Ten Commandments*.

Off in the distance, smoke billowed toward the horizon.

One of the robed strangers noticed me and climbed the dune to lie next to me.

I couldn't see his face. He, like the rest, wore a mask of gold that seemed to be molded to his face.

"What faith were you, young man?" he asked in an American midwestern accent.

"Faith?"

"You don't get here unless you betrayed your own beliefs, you see," he said with an evangelistic tone. "Me? All I did was change a few words. What good is a religion if nobody joins? At the time of my passing, over a million people worshipped the devil. The porn industry netted over sixty billion dollars annually, more than ABC, NBC and CBS combined. And the children? More youngsters under ten years of age knew Ronald McDonald better than Jesus Christ. In the mid '90s, times were changing. People no longer liked words such as *guilt* or *sin*. So, I sweetened the pot, so to speak. I changed the words around. We said *positive thinking* instead of *repent*. Instead of trying to *conquer* evil, we *understand* it. We *tolerate* the sinners...and it worked. Within five years, we cleared over fifty million dollars."

"That's really nice," I said, "but I'm a little busy right now."

"What was my reward?" he asked, ignoring me. "To become one of a thousand small cogs in a giant machine. We are the religious hypocrites, you see. Down that path are those who betrayed the arts...movie producers who knew it was wrong to glorify violence yet did just that for fame and money." He pointed down a different path. "And down that path are the political hypocrites. You'd be amazed at how much of this circle *they* occupy."

"If you don't mind, I need to pound leather," I finally interrupted.

"We all must push the levers that turn the wheels, you see. The wheels must turn, young man."

"I don't care," I said, but then curiosity got the better of me. "Why?"

"Surely you've seen the spinning mechanisms of Hell. Anything that spins starts here."

There were spinning mechanisms on almost every level of Hell. The giant bullhorns that signaled the hoarders and wasters spun on long poles and the lights on top of the fueling pumps where the demons refueled. It all made sense. The second the mechanisms stopped spinning, the demons would be alerted and would know exactly what level and bolgia to come to.

"We pump the fuel to the depots for the demons' vehicles," he continued. "We provide the power in Hell."

"You do all this dressed as royalty?"

"Only half the story, young man," he said as he opened his robes. Underneath all those heavy robes of gold was the even heavier bluish white metal.

"Lead?" I asked.

"Of course."

"That makes sense. Outwardly, you delivered a message of hope and love, but underneath was nothing more than lies and deceit," I said, becoming quite expert in the symbolism of Hell.

"Gosh, I never got that before," he sarcastically lectured. "The symbolism is so clear to me now. It's not like I've had ten or fifteen damned years to think about it!"

"Sorry," I said defensively, "I just got here."

"It's not like I've had any time to think while wearing lead underwear in this sweltering heat! Or that I can take them off, you know. It's like we were dipped in this God-awful metal."

"I said I was sorry."

"By the way, where are your robes?" he asked.

"I don't belong here."

"They all say that. Come now, you must help us or the demons will come."

"One's already here." I pointed.

"What?" He peered over the dune to see Geryon approaching. "Come quickly, we must warn the others to push the gears faster."

"That won't make any difference. This particular demon is tailing *me*," I said.

"Why?"

"It's a long story, but it's time to turn the tables."

"I have no idea which table you wish to turn, but to fight a demon gives new meaning to the word *insanity*."

"Story of my life."

❧❧

I ran down the dune to the religious hypocrites and tried to form a plan. As I neared them, I realized that different robes characterized different people.

Some of them dressed as rabbis, others as Chinese monks. Some women wore the robes that were similar to the habits of nuns, only in gold lace and diamonds.

The clothing they wore was a caricature of what they'd worn in life.

"Hey, listen to me," I yelled to a group of robed sinners at one of the giant gears. "I need a hand."

"They won't listen to you, young man," the preacher said as he caught up to me, gasping for breath. "Damn, this suit gets heavier with each passing day...or year...you know what I mean."

"Hey! Stop!" I yelled, ignoring the preacher's rambling.

Finally, the people pushing one of the wheels stopped.

"There's a demon on its way..." Before I could explain further, they looked at each other and frantically pushed faster.

"No, wait. This demon's after *me*, not you. I need help!"

"What do you expect them to do, young man?" the preacher yelled.

"I don't know. Something. Anything!"

"You have brought a demon with you, and led him straight to us. Do you expect us to stop all the wheels just to help you? And when the hordes of demons arrive to punish us, how do you propose to challenge them when you need help to stop only one?"

"You're holy people," I said under my breath.

"What?"

"I said, you're holy people!" I said for all to hear. "You're priests and rabbis. You're holy people. You're supposed to help those in need!"

"That was another life, young man. Another life! A hundred years ago for some, and a thousand for others. Now leave us be and take that approaching abhorrence of God with you," one of the priests yelled.

"Abhorrence of God," I repeated. "I wonder what affronts God more—the creature that approaches or those who would stand by and do nothing to stop it."

I turned to run, but I stopped when I heard the voice of a young woman.

She left her position on the wheel to approach me.

"Sister, no!" one of the hypocrites called out, but she ignored him.

"You wish to defeat this demon, no?" she said in a French accent.

I couldn't see her face because of the mask, but she sounded young and she wore the glorified robes of a nun. I couldn't tell if she was from my time or centuries past, and I suppose it didn't matter.

"Yes," I replied with absolute commitment.

"We pump the fuel that powers the demons crafts."

"So I've been told."

"The fuel runs deep, beneath us. There are wells that lead to the underground." She pointed to where the smoke billowed, just over a small ridge. "If you could trick this demon of yours and get him into one of the wells, he would fall. The sides are oily and very slick, monsieur. It would take him much time to make his escape. If you could cover the well with boulders before he climbed out, he would be trapped."

"That's enough!" a voice yelled at her. "Now take your rightful place, Sister."

"Thank you," I said as she returned to her place at one of the giant wheels.

Everyone stopped, however, when they saw Geryon standing atop the dune, staring down at us.

"Everyone push!" the preacher yelled and frantically grabbed one of the levers.

Everyone put their heads down and pushed. Geryon ran toward me.

I dodged between the giant gears. Geryon followed me, but I was able to keep a wheel between us. When he shifted direction, I simply ran in the same direction around the wheel.

"What do we do?" one of the sinners cried out.

"Just keep your heads down and push," another answered. "Push!"

Again, Geryon charged around one of the big grinders, and I ran around the wheel away from him. I might have kept it up indefinitely, but Geryon jumped onto one of the turning wheels and then leapt onto me. I jumped to my feet and picked up a rock.

Geryon swung at me. When I ducked, he hit one of the levers, breaking it off. I seized the six foot metal rod with a now sharpened end. I held it up to him like a spear. Geryon didn't even hesitate. He charged at me. We both jumped onto one of the revolving wheels, about the size of a small merry-go-round. As it slowly turned, I held the steel rod defensively, keeping the sharp end pointed at Geryon.

He made a move toward me, but I swung my new spear and slashed his face. He backed up, studying me with greater caution. Geryon slowly leaned down, wrapping his claws around another steel lever. He yanked it up, creating a metal spear of his own, but he didn't stop there. He reached for another, for his other hand.

He pointed both long pieces of sharpened metal my way, striking a pose that included his scorpion-like tail.

"Damn," I muttered. I sprang to another wheel. He followed me, but I jumped back to the first merry-go-round style wheel. He jumped back to the original, and I jumped back to the other. I found it within me to actually snicker. I felt like a kid rattling the lion's cage after all the parents had left the circus grounds.

In anger, Geryon jumped again, swinging the metal rod at me before I could hop to another wheel. I was able to block it, but I couldn't stop everything coming my way. I felt like a swordsman fighting a trio of blade masters, all of which were better than me.

The sinners watched, although they continued to walk their circular path and push the wheels.

I needed to get up that ridge, but once I left the gears, I knew I would be exposed on open ground, and Geryon could easily overtake me. Geryon swung at me, and I saw an incredible opening. The thought came out of nowhere the split second before I did it. I pierced Geryon's foot with my metal rod, impaling him on the wheel. Surprised, he dropped one of his rods, which I immediately grabbed. I darted for the ridge.

∞

I ran down the ridge, following the smoke to an area littered with wells. I assumed they released the pressure built up from the underground fuel.

Peering down one of the wells, I saw the flicker of distant flames in the cavern below. That nun had been right. If I could get him into one of those wells, Geryon would be out of commission for at least a while.

I took a step to strategically place myself between two wells. The ground beneath me gave way. I nearly fell in, but instinctively backed away. Looking into the newly formed pit, I saw more distant flames. The whole area must have had weak points just ready to swallow up the errant passerby. Pity the nun hadn't mentioned *that* little nugget.

Geryon charged down the ridge and I held up the metal rod as if it were a combination sword, shield, and crucifix. He halted a few feet from me, dropping his metal rod. He hissed in anger and struck a pose like a wrestler about to pin his mortal enemy. Had he been toying with me all this time?

I noticed a few faces, or rather golden masks, as people gathered up on the ridge, as if to watch the outcome of this high school wrestling match of the damned.

Geryon stepped closer. I swung the metal rod at him, but he grabbed it and yanked it from my hands. He paused near one of the wells. I went for broke and jumped on him, trying to get him to stumble into one of the pits. Instead, he picked me up and hurled me across several wells.

I slammed into a wall of rock, and quickly got up with a fistful of rocks. "Come on, you son of a bitch!" I yelled as I pitched them at him. "Let's see what you got!"

Geryon leapt across the wells, landed next to me, and greeted me with a closed-fisted right cross. I dropped like a sack of stones and he jumped on top of me. Geryon repeatedly hit me in the face. I coughed up blood, but didn't want Geryon to know how badly he'd hurt me.

Maybe it was just the tension or feeling so much pain, but I was just beyond tears. Instead, I laughed. Geryon stopped hitting me and stared in confusion...not that I blamed him.

I looked over Geryon's shoulder to see more religious hypocrites watching from the ridge, so I laughed even louder. I wanted them to hear as well. I didn't know why, since I didn't think they would offer help, but I just didn't want anyone to know how badly I was losing.

310

"My daughter hits harder than you!" I yelled.

Insulted, Geryon raised his fist to pulverize my face. I grabbed a fistful of sand and threw it in his face, catching him off guard. I squirmed away, crawling toward the metal rods in an effort to draw Geryon back toward the wells. He grabbed my legs and yanked me back.

With insultingly little effort, Geryon put my hand on a flat rock, picked up another rock, and smashed it, shattering every finger and bone. I screamed in agony. Geryon turned me over, straddled me, and raised his fist. About to plunge it into my chest, he stopped when someone jumped onto his back. He stood up to try to flick aside this new annoyance, but she wrapped her arms around his neck and refused to go.

I looked up to see the familiar face of the one person I missed most in this place. "Mary," I whispered, as Geryon violently shook like a wet dog to free himself of her.

CHAPTER 45
Canto XVIII – Circle VIII – Bolgia VI – The Stand
✍

M ary rode Geryon like an inexperienced cowgirl astride her first
bucking bronco.

"Hang on!" I dragged myself toward one of the spears Geryon
had abandoned in the desert sand.

I was amazed at Mary's tenacity.

She looked different somehow, not older but *tougher*.

*How long were you two separated? How long were you paralyzed at the base of
the eighth circle, Joe? How the devil can she hang on in the midst of all that shaking?
Is Mary stronger, or is Geryon weakening? What does she have that you lack?*

Geryon twisted fast and hard, swinging Mary around, making removing
her much easier. When he saw his opening, he grabbed her by the throat.

I picked up the spear with my good hand and, on shaking legs, I charged
for the demon.

I screamed like a Celtic warrior charging into battle against an
overpowering enemy with nothing but a sword, which was dwindling from
its owner's diminishing strength. The only one more amazed than Geryon
when I pierced his thickly plated chest with the steel rod was me.

He dropped Mary, and stared at me with oddly soft and honest eyes.
He looked as if I'd genuinely hurt him, and not just physically. He looked
at me as if I'd somehow *betrayed* him. I kept the spear between us, so he
couldn't reach me. I didn't know what to think as I stared into the beast's
eyes. Fierce and mean and full of hate, he still conveyed a certain intelligence.

"I know that look, Geryon," I said. "How do I know it?"

Mary stayed on the ground, probably afraid to move. The people on
the ridge also watched in silence.

"I know who you are demon," I screamed. "I know who you are! An honest look painted on a face of hate. *You* are the face of betrayal. *You* are fraud. *You* are fraud *personified.*"

That's when it hit me why this creature had been after me for so long. This was the sin that plagued me in my life. I'd been betrayed by my partner Tony and by my own brother Mickey. He probably smelled it, as if draped on me like a cloak. Maybe, he even fed from it. He'd been drawn to me like a moth to a flame. Had he even had a choice?

That was the source of my faltering faith.

Virgil had once told me that Geryon could always find me, because I lacked faith. Now, I understood his meaning.

"You used to be an angel," I said, "but now look at you!"

Geryon's expression slowly changed. This time, he didn't hiss at me. This time, for the first time, he roared his anger. I used the spear as leverage to push Geryon back toward one of the wells. However, he had other plans. I felt like a lion tamer facing an out-of-control cat.

Again, Mary jumped on Geryon's back. I planted my feet, pushing even harder. One of my hands had been smashed and I was in agony, but I somehow felt stronger. Geryon took a swing but he still couldn't reach me. Instead, he focused on Mary, grabbed her from his back, and flung her into a pile of rocks.

"No!" I twisted the sharpened rod deeper into Geryon's chest and nudged him closer to the well. "You son of a bitch!"

What's the gag here, Joe? Isn't Geryon stronger than this? Every time you've crossed his path before, he had the muscle to juggle three Buicks.

Maybe the spear that pierced his chest had weakened him, or perhaps he wasn't weaker at all. Maybe I was stronger. Maybe I possessed Mary's inner strength, after all.

Geryon stepped back, knocking over a loose brick from the well. He glanced behind him at the hole, and I immediately knew that *he* knew what I was planning. He grabbed the rod with both hands, and shoved back.

I held my breath, pushing and shoving for all I was worth. As if from out of nowhere, Mary again jumped on Geryon.

"Mary, no!" I yelled.

I knew she was trying to help, but she didn't know about my plan and I didn't want her to end up at the bottom of the well with Geryon.

The reptilian fiend slipped from the edge. He and Mary went over the well's fringe.

Geryon clung to the rod. What only moments ago had been the source of his frustration had now become his life-line from falling into the pit.

I could have easily let him drop by releasing the spear. But Mary would fall, too.

I used all of my strength to hold the rod.

"Mary, reach up!" I reached for her with my smashed hand.

Geryon responded by taking a swipe at me with his claws extended.

"I can't hold it, Mary. Jump!"

"I can't!"

Geryon tried to dislodge Mary, but continually failed.

My grip grew steadily weaker. If Mary didn't jump soon, I would lose her.

"Mary, please!" I screamed in desperation.

The spear slowly slipped from my hands. Suddenly, a hand grabbed it, and then another. I looked around, shocked to find several religious hypocrites clad in their golden robes gathered around me to offer their assistance.

"We have it!" the French nun yelled.

I let go and reached for Mary.

"Mary, jump!"

She jumped from Geryon's back and I was able to latch onto her sleeve and pull her close to the top of the well's outer boundary.

"Do it!" I yelled to the hypocrites.

They, led by the French nun, yanked the spear from Geryon's chest. He didn't fall, though. Instead, he grabbed Mary's leg, wrenching her deeper into the well.

"No!" I screamed. I was taken by surprise but didn't let go. "Help me!" I shouted to the hypocrites.

They reached for Mary, but no one could reach her. I'm sure being encased in lead underwear hampered their range of motion, but the *reasons* why they couldn't help meant nothing to me. Mary was slipping away, and there was nothing I could do about it.

Geryon climbed up Mary's body, wrapping his large arms around her in a demonic bear hug.

Mary helplessly looked to me for salvation. "Joseph! Don't let go!" It was Mary's voice I'd heard, but someone else's words that came to mind—*Daddy! Don't let go!*

I saw Mary's face, but I thought only of Anna and that night on the collapsing roof, with the flames dancing below.

"I won't!" I tried to reassure her, tears filling my eyes.

Mary tried to reach me with her other hand, but Geryon grabbed it. Bracing his legs on either side of the well's wall, he tugged.

He was no longer trying to escape the well. He intended to take Mary with him. Talk about bad eggs...this lizard was rotten to the nucleus of the core. I reached for Mary with my smashed hand as well. I needed more juice but had none.

Geryon yanked hard and I heard a *pop*. Mary's face changed from fear to utter pain and she screamed in agony.

His weight must have been torturous for her. Her grip on my hand eased, and I knew that her arm had been dislocated at the shoulder. Mary screamed until all the air left her lungs. Then she took a deep breath and screamed yet again.

Tears streamed from her eyes and it killed me inside to know that I was partially causing her agony by not letting her go. If Geryon pulled again, he might rip her body away, leaving me with her disembodied arm.

Hang on, Joe. Hang on! Will her arm grow back or will she spend eternity with one arm missing? It doesn't matter. Don't let her go! Hang on, Joe!

I didn't know and wouldn't find out, because instead of yanking again, Geryon pulled himself higher. He wrapped his huge hand over Mary's face. Geryon looked up at me and I stared down at his razor-tooth kisser. I no longer feared him. I was angry and full of hate. I think he sensed it, and he used Mary to bait me. With a quick thrust, Geryon jerked Mary out of my weakening hand, and they both fell into the pit.

"Anna!" I screamed. It wasn't until after I'd called my daughter's name that I realized the depth of my affection for Mary. I loved Mary like a daughter. I loved Mary like *my* daughter.

Mary screamed as she and Geryon were swallowed by the dark smoke billowing up from the well.

"Where's the steel rod?" I called to the group.

"I have it here," a preacher said.

I grabbed it. Without hesitation, I swung my leg over the well's edge.

"What are you doing?" the French nun asked through her golden mask.

"What does it look like?" I said.

315

"Nay. Nay. Go there not," some medieval priest chimed in. "The beast awaits thee."

"Yeah, and he's got my..." I hesitated. With defiance and confidence, I finished my sentence. "He's got my *daughter!*"

"How will you escape?" the French nun asked in a voice of genuine concern.

"You're going to throw me a rope," I said.

"We have no rope. Do you not understand, monsieur? If you go there, there is no hope of getting out."

"Then, I guess I'm just going to have to have *faith*." I swung my other leg over the edge, took a deep breath and jumped.

"What do we do?" I heard one of the preachers ask as I fell into the smoke.

The last words I heard from the fading voices came from the French nun.

"We find a rope," she said with confidence.

CHAPTER 46
Canto XVIII – Circle VIII – Bolgia VI – The Oily Pit
❧

I hit bottom, with a splash, into a pool of black oil. The smoke, not as dense at the bottom level, made it easier to see, but Mary and Geryon were nowhere to be found.

I pulled myself to my feet. What little pain I'd felt when I'd splashed into the slimy stone ground subsided quickly, although I didn't know why. I walked with deliberate caution through the rocky cavern, holding the metal spear like I'd once held my rifle during the war, when instructed to fix bayonets.

I stopped dead when I heard the distant sound of Mary's whimper and quickly pressed my back to one of the cavern's walls. If I could hear Mary, Geryon was nearby. I didn't want him sneaking up on me. I continued toward the sound, reaching a fork in the cavern.

When I peeked around the corner, I saw Mary. She was stretched out across a pile of rocks like a sacrificial lamb on the altar. I wanted to embrace and comfort her, but I couldn't… I knew Geryon was close by, but where?

This was an obvious trap, with Mary as the bait, but knowing this was little help for whatever plan I could concoct. I remained hidden behind the rock wall waiting for Geryon to show himself. My heart broke as Mary wept, knowing how alone she felt.

"Joseph!" Tears streamed down the sides of her face.

"My neck, my neck," she moaned in pain and frustration.

I realized then that her body wasn't moving at all. Her neck had been broken again, either in the fall, or by Geryon.

Geryon continued to hide. Why wouldn't he? He knew I would come, and he had the patience of an angel.

I positioned my shoes closer to the edge of the cave's entrance, hoping against hope that Mary would see that I was nearby. She couldn't.

However, Geryon noticed. He stepped out from behind a rock-formed column at the far end of the cavern. He charged in my direction, but my shoes didn't move. When he reached my shoes, he discovered them empty.

He squatted down to inspect my shoes, and then he looked up. I stood atop a pile of rocks, poised to jam the spear into the body part of my choice. I quickly leapt down, slicing his arm with the sharpened end.

Geryon jumped to his feet, but I was ready for him. I slammed the spear back into his chest, but this time, *Geryon* was ready for *me*.

He gripped the spear in his chest, shoving me into the rock wall and impaling me through the chest with the dull end of the spear.

I screamed as the metal passed through my chest, which locked me into the rock and to Geryon like a bizarre pair of handcuffs.

Blood spilled from my mouth. Geryon swiped at me, but the spear still wedged into his chest kept him from reaching me.

He pulled himself into the spear, impaling himself further, closing the gap between us.

Mary trembled in the corner.

Wait! How can she tremble, Joe? She has a broken neck…doesn't she?

Geryon paused and followed my gaze to Mary.

When he looked back at me, I could have sworn I saw a grin on his reptilian face.

Hey, Joe… Is this guy a little slice of heaven or what?

I spat blood at him.

He responded by lashing his tongue at me and wrapping it around my throat. His tongue not only strangled me, but pulled me closer to him. I struggled as best as I could, but it was a losing battle.

He brought me in closer as I gasped for air. Shocked, I heard a gunshot.

The bullet sliced through Geryon's tongue, freeing me from his grip. Mary had found the strength to get to her gun. I'd forgotten she still had one, the same one she'd used to kill herself, and with perpetually one slug left. Unfortunately, the round sparked against the rocks, setting the oily walls aflame.

I was glad for that one shot and for her ability to heal quickly enough to save my skin. Renewed strength allowed me to deliver a right cross to Geryon's kisser. The spear at my end pulled free of the rock wall and we both fell to the stony ground. Both Geryon and I freed ourselves from the spear.

I swung the metal rod like a baseball bat across his head, but Geryon backhanded me, sending me back to the ground. I jumped back up and swung the sharp end of the spear, slashing Geryon's face. I dug the metal into his eye and he jerked away. But I wasn't going to let him go. I swung again, piercing his throat.

The fire spread quickly and Mary still couldn't get up. I needed to end this thing with Geryon quickly or she'd roast alive.

I slammed a rock against Geryon's head. He went down in pain. I crushed the rock against his hand, feeling some poetic justice after he'd done the same to me.

Enraged, he seized me by my neck, but again, I used the spear to gut him.

How can you do this, Joe? It's a trick! Is this damned lizard toying with you? Why is your pain subsiding so quickly?

He let me go. I hit him again and again with the rod. I was shocked when I saw him fall to his knees. I didn't let up and knew if I had, he would have chomped my head off.

"Die, damn it! Die!" I screamed out in frustration in a place that had no concept of death.

So, I did the next best thing. I perforated his throat until his head loosened. Finally, I kicked his head away from his body.

Grabbing my shoes, I ran to Mary to drag her away from the all-enveloping fire.

"I knew you'd come for me, Joseph." She managed a faint smile. "I knew always."

As the flames surrounded Geryon, I saw something familiar in the oil. It was the bracelet that Anna had given me so long ago. The last I saw of it, Geryon had swallowed it at the base of the eighth circle. I must have knocked it out of him during our struggle.

I reached for it, but the flames exploded all around us.

I tried again, willing to suffer third degree burns just to get it back, but Geryon suddenly grabbed it. Even with his head cut off, there was no stopping this goon.

"Joseph!" Mary shouted. I realized that she was far more important to me than a piece of metal from a life long gone.

I left the bracelet at the bottom of the pit in the bolgia of hypocrites, but I kept my deep and abiding love for Bea and my girls. Maybe *that's* what I'd been most afraid of losing. I picked up Mary and carried her from the fire to the opening of the well. When we got there, there was no dangling rope, nor a place to climb. Everything was slippery, and the flames were coming up fast.

"Where's that rope?" I shouted out as I looked up through the smoke to the pin hole of light that was the well opening to the surface.

Still, no rope dropped down to us. Instead, the flames licked closer.

"Joseph!" Mary yelled. "We must leave this place!"

"Okay," I said. "Okay…maybe there's some other way out."

I tried to edge us around the flames. But a long stream of cloth suddenly fell to us—one of shimmering silver and gold. It was the long golden-laced robes worn by the religious hypocrites over their lead-encased suits. They'd been tied together to form one long *rope*.

I was thankful that at least one of them had been smart enough to think of it, because I certainly wouldn't have.

For the record, three to one it was the French nun.

"I guess it pays to have faith," I said to a confused Mary as I secured the cloth around her.

I also clung on and gave the cloth a tug.

The sinners pulled us out of the well as the flames swallowed the oil-soaked pit.

CHAPTER 47
Canto XXIII – Circle VIII – Bolgia VI - Reunions
❧❧

They pulled us out of the well and I carefully placed Mary down on the hard rocky ground, wishing it were made of goose-feathered pillows.

The religious hypocrites gathered around us. Clad in only their masks and lead encasements, without the robes, everyone looked the same. I couldn't tell who were priests, rabbis, Muslim holy men, or even Buddhist monks. The masks they wore made them appear emotionless, but I knew they'd obviously retained enough human feeling to take the risk and offer up assistance. Odd, how the ones with humanity enough to remove their robes were now the ones who looked like robotic automatons devoid of all compassion.

"What's wrong with her?" one of the sinners asked.

"I think her neck is broken," I said as I knelt to hold her hand.

Another lead-encased soul knelt beside Mary, peering through the pinholes of his mask to study her. "She looks like your daughter," he said in an oddly familiar voice.

"Do I know you?" I asked.

He stood and removed the fixture that held his mask in place and pulled it off.

"Father Nicholas!" I exclaimed.

"It's been a long time, Joseph."

Some of the others also removed their masks. The petite French nun smiled at me, as did some of the others.

"I don't understand," I said to Father Nicholas. "Why are you here in Hell? You were a good man. You were a very good man."

"We all have our sins, Joseph."

"But you're a priest," I said. "You were *my* priest."

"After you died, I lost my faith. I lost everything, but I kept preaching the word, even though I really didn't believe in it any longer. I was a hypocrite. I did good works in the name of a God I no longer believed existed. Any God, who would allow a man like you to lose his faith and be murdered for his struggle, couldn't be *my* God."

"You're here because of *me?*"

"Don't you see?" he said. "It was my fault. It was all my fault. I should have been able to save your faith."

"No."

"I needed to tell you something the day your wife was buried, but I didn't know what to say. I didn't know the words that would save you."

"It wasn't your fault," I insisted.

"Minos says different."

"Minos only knows what you tell him," I said.

"He knows what's in my heart."

"What's in your heart, Father?"

"The world changed a lot after you passed away, Joseph. I lived a very long time. Long enough to see abortions blessed by the state, men marry men, and the removal of daily prayer from our schools. Even in our own church, allegations of priests and...children. The world you left is gone, Joseph. Gone forever."

What are you going to say to the guy, Joe? What can you say? Maybe you should think about another question to answer...who are you, Joe? Who are you? What did Virgil mean? You know the answer. Don't you?

"It's funny," Father Nicholas said. "Another priest, another man, could have lived my exact same life. He could have made the same decisions in life with the same actions and consequences. But when he died, he would have ended up in paradise with God Himself. Why? Because of faith? His beliefs? Should that make sense? I don't know anymore."

"Faith can be enough, Father, but you have to want it. It's a lesson I've learned the hard way."

"What about you, Joseph?" Father Nicholas said. "Do you have faith enough to leave this place?"

I didn't answer. I didn't *know* the answer.

Maybe God knew what was best, but I just couldn't let go of this need to see Mickey one final time.

At least the angel agreed, and if he'd delivered God's message, wasn't I doing God's work?

I didn't know. All I could do was focus on Mary. The French nun was kneeling and stroking Mary's forehead, trying to ease her pain.

"What about you, Mary?" I asked. "Do you have faith?"

"Yes, I do." She spoke without hesitation and with great conviction. "I think I needed to be here...here in Hell...to find it again... Maybe to even meet you, Joseph."

Virgil healed Mary with but a wave of his hand. How could he do that? He said that she was ready—ready for what? Figure it out, Joe. Figure it out.

"You're ready," I said.

"What?"

"I think I know now," I said with a smile.

I raised my hand, still broken and swollen from my fight with Geryon, and placed it on her chest. Mary closed her eyes, and slowly became shrouded in the glow of a white light. Both of us were bathed in the warm glow and I felt the pain in my hand subside.

"Let it go, baby," I said as tears streamed down the sides of her face.

Her body began to heal, as did mine. Did I heal her, or did she fix me?

The damned watched in amazement as Mary sat up and smiled.

"We can fight the demons," one of the sinners said.

"We can fight them with renewed faith," another added.

I looked up at the ridge, noticing that none of the rotary grinders were moving. So much had happened, I'd totally forgotten the risk these holy people had taken in order to help me.

"If nobody is manning those wheels, won't the demons come?" I asked.

"Let them come," Father Nicholas spoke up. "I, for one, won't be here," he shouted to the others. "I'm a priest! I'll preach the word of God to those who will listen, for I have seen a miracle. God *does* exist here, in the hearts of those who are willing to believe, and I will shout what I've witnessed to each and every sinner in all of Hell."

"As will I," another added.

"And I," the French nun said.

The others stepped forward in this strange birth of a new group of disciples.

"I'll start here," Father Nicolas said, revitalized. "There are many religious hypocrites here who need to know what we've seen. Some won't believe us, but others will, and we will spread out and preach to all, unafraid of what lies ahead."

"But, Father…" I started.

"Yes, Joseph?" he asked.

I'd heard the conviction in his voice, and was reminded of how this tough old guy had been in life. He no longer seemed like the shell of a man I'd encountered only moments ago. Could someone change so much in so short a time? Maybe it was always within him?

"What you're saying…it's not exactly an easy thing to do," I said.

"We don't do things because they're easy." He placed a paternal hand on my shoulder, as he had so many times in life. "We do things because they're right." A smile crept across his face.

જી૭

With one of the metal spears slung over my shoulder, Mary and I walked alone. She didn't know where we were going, but I did, and it was something she needed to see.

"Why are you here, Joseph?"

"To find my brother."

"That's not what I mean. I mean… What sin brought you here?"

"I don't know," I said.

"Yes, you do."

She was right. I just couldn't face it, because I'd needed to convince myself that I really didn't belong here, or that there was some mistake or it was all God's fault… But it wasn't.

I was here for my own sins, the one in particular that Minos had recognized when he'd looked into my eyes. But I couldn't admit it. I just couldn't face it. Not yet.

"I asked for God's help."

"What?"

"The night in the warehouse… That night… I prayed to God for help that night. Still my wife was killed right in front of me. Then, on the roof, as I clung to my Anna's hand, I screamed for God's help… But none came. I tried to blame God the whole time, you see, but that's not the reason. They died because of me. They died because of the life I'd chosen. They died because I didn't have enough faith."

"It wasn't your fault," she said.

"Don't you understand? I couldn't save my wife, or Anna, or even Kathleen. If I'd just prayed a little longer—if I'd gone to Confession more often—if I'd done the right thing more, they wouldn't have died... But I just *had* to get Argenti and damn the rest."

"I think you can always find a reason to blame yourself." She stopped and took my hand. "Joseph, I have had much time to think with a noose around my throat. I've come to know one thing... Even God can't offer up a pardon, until you give yourself one."

"Maybe."

"Come along then, we'll find your brother together."

"No."

"What?"

"We have different journeys, you and I. I have to do this alone."

"And I? What's to become of me then?"

I pointed to a distant dead tree in the middle of a barren desert, and under it was a man slowly healing from being systematically disassembled by mechanical demons.

She looked at the distant tree and saw her true love, McMontey.

"How?" she said as tears pooled in her eyes.

"Call it fate," I said.

"I don't know what—" She stopped short. "What shall I do?"

"You know what to do."

She looked at McMontey for the longest time. I didn't want to prod or force her, though I knew this was something she needed to do. Slowly, she smiled.

"In my time, in Ireland, we would say farewell by wishing them a *safe home*. So I wish for you, Joseph Dante, a good journey, and may the good Lord smile upon your weary soul when you reach your safe home."

She hugged me.

I didn't want to let her go. What do you say to someone whom you know you'll never see again? In life, saying goodbye to someone you've come to love is a simple matter. You may wish them a good life without you, but deep down inside you think that your paths will cross again somehow, or at the very least, that you'll meet again in the afterlife... But in an afterlife such as this?

She let go first, but I held her closer.

325

I was reminded of the last time I'd had Anna in my arms. She'd given me the bracelet and all too quickly raced upstairs. I wouldn't allow *that* to happen this time.

"Not yet. There's something I have to say," I whispered as I held her tight. "Trust me when I tell you this. Your daughter Carmel is happy."

Shocked, she gazed up at me. I kissed her forehead.

"I love you, Joseph Dante."

"I love you too, kiddo."

I let her go, watching as she ran to McMontey.

She stopped a few feet from him and stared for a moment.

Virgil had once told me that I would see people the way I *needed* to see them, and the way in which they *needed* to be seen.

So where I saw an older streetwise lawyer, I knew Mary saw the innocent young Englishman, full of dreams of becoming a great lawyer…someone who would protect the innocent.

From a distance, I watched as she knelt beside him. I couldn't hear their conversation, but I saw that it concluded with a long embrace.

I left them to their destinies.

CHAPTER 48
Canto XXIV, XXX – Circle VIII – Bolgias VII, X – More Fraudulent

~∂ঙ৯~

I made it to the other side of the sixth bolgia and hopped onto the bridge at the top of the hill. The bridge's gap over the religious hypocrites ended and the bridge started again on the hill where the seventh bolgia began.

With Geryon no longer in the picture, I started to relax and rest along the way.

Demon patrols became extremely rare now, probably because most of the sinners would be out of their tree to go into the lower circles. If they did, their punishment would have been greater than the one they left.

The bridge afforded me a bird's eye view of this section of Hell, and even gave me a sense of—and I use the term loosely—*security*.

I stopped somewhere over the seventh bolgia, and looked down into the pit. I saw strange serpents and lizards, chasing people through a maze of rock walls.

The maze seemed to constitute the majority of this bolgia. It certainly extended well beyond as far as I could see. From my skybox of safety, I watched the people dashing about in groups and individually. Cowboys ran with pirates, and a man in a tux teamed up with a woman in shorts and a t-shirt.

A man dressed in black and wearing a ski mask ran for the maze wall, a large lizard hot on his tracks. He yelled in fear as he sprinted, slamming finally into the wall. Jumping up and down in cold desperation, he failed to reach the top. He turned to face the demon, his back pressed to the wall.

"Please, don't!" he pleaded, but the lizard didn't give a squat. "I can't go back again." The slithering beast ignored him and drew in closer, so the schmoe tried a different approach. "Kiss off!" he yelled as he flipped the lizard the bird. He screamed in agony when the creature jumped him and sank sharp jaws into his shoulder.

Is this all there is to this bolgia, demons with sharp teeth taking meaty chunks of flesh from sinners? What the devil is their sin and how the heck is this justice? Is it me, Joe, or is this bolgia just plain boring? Where's the famous symbolism that had become the reasoning of Hell?

The man in the ski mask began to shake and convulse. He dropped to his knees as the demon released his shoulder.

He tried to stand, but his spine curved and he dropped onto all fours.

Surprisingly, the lizard also began to thrash about. The creature rolled over onto its back as its arms and legs grew larger and changed color.

The giant lizard wasn't a demon at all, but another sinner. The lizard sprouted breasts. Its face squeezed and shaped into that of a young woman, fully clothed in a saloon dress from the old west. She screamed as her skull bent and reshaped into that of a human, experiencing as much pain to gain her human form as the man who'd lost his.

The man in the ski mask shrank in size, screaming out his anger and pain as he became a naked lizard. The woman, in desperation, from a need to keep her form, fled from the newly created lizard. The lizard gave chase, but was slower, and so had to depend on cornering his prey.

I heard Virgil in my head, reminding me that the symbolism in Hell was strong and meaningful. I realized then that the sin of this bolgia had to be...thievery.

I could just imagine the man in the ski mask, packing a heater, jumping out of the bushes, and demanding loot, wallets, watches, and other jewelry from his victims. He'd likely been a stereotypical mugger in life that one encountered on a New York Saturday night, and the reason why seasoned New Yorkers never walked less traveled streets and alleyways after the sun had set.

In life, they'd stolen money from people. In death they'd had their very bodies stolen from them. If they wished to retrieve it, they would have to endure the pain of rebirth over and over again. Too late did they realize that when they stole from their unfortunate victims, they were losing bits and pieces of their own humanity. Now, in Hell, it was their humanity that they fought so hard and so desperately to keep, as it was constantly stolen from them.

If I had known any of this during my lifetime, I would have smiled and considered justice served. But, here and now, I just felt pity for them all.

From my *heavenly* path, I departed for the next bolgia.

❧

Over the eighth bolgia, I covered my mouth and nose to protect myself from the rising ash and waves of heat.

I hesitated to look over the edge, but curiosity got the better of me. Once I looked, I wished that for once, *I'd* gotten the better of my *curiosity*.

Cinders as plentiful as fireflies in a warm Nebraska night sky dominated the region. I knew that each cinder was a damned soul.

"My God," I breathed.

I had no idea what sin this bolgia was for but knew, as all the other pits on this circle, it had to do with fraud and deceit.

That was all I needed to know. All I could do was run to escape the heat and painful sounding screams, and be thankful for this bridge. If it wasn't here, the only way to my brother would be *through* this pit of white hot sinners.

I ran through the hot waves, until the heat was behind me, trying not to breathe in the ash too deeply.

❧

I stopped running when I saw the part of the bridge that connected to the top of the ninth ridge. I knew then that the pain of the previous bolgia was behind me. Although I no longer felt smacked by the waves of heat or smelled burning flesh, I was now afflicted with a stench that reminded me of rotting meat.

I looked over the railing. What I saw I could only describe as a leper colony. People frantically scratched sores and scabs only to have them open and bleed, creating an even more intense itch that forced them to further tear into their own skin.

Some of the women wore nurse's uniforms, some of the men, lab coats. I watched sadly, guessing that these were doctors or medicine men that falsely offered cures for diseases, or perhaps used their position of power and influence to gain money by providing a false prognosis to an unsuspecting patient.

❧❧

I didn't have to look over the bridge's railing to see what sin it encompassed when I reached the tenth and final bolgia. Some of the sinners wandered on the bridge. I looked down to see others drifting around the side of the hill and wondered where the demons were. There seemed to be no enforcement in this pit, and no torment.

The young woman on the bridge wore casual attire, but she wasn't dressed from my time. Her hair was unbound and she wore jeans, so I could only guess that she was from some future time.

When she saw me, she ran to me like a child to her father, confused and in need of answers. "Yo... Do you know me?" she asked with a New York accent and a painted on smile.

"No."

"I gotta ask you somethin', pally," she said, sounding decidedly unfeminine.

"What?" I asked.

"Do I look like a *Frank* to you?"

"Excuse me?"

"Frank. Could *Frank* be my name? I know I'm a security guard, but the name escapes me. So, what do ya tink? Could I be *Frank*?"

"Uhm, no?" I answered, now the one confused.

"Why the Hell not?"

"Well, *Frank* is a man's name, and you're a woman. At least, it was a man's name in my time."

"I ain't a man?"

"You don't know if you're a man or a woman?"

"Do you know?"

"Yes. You're a woman."

"Then, *Sara*? Could my name be *Sara*, sugar?" she asked in a now distinctly feminine southern accent.

"Well, I suppose," I said.

"Then, that's my name. Sara, and I'm an artist." She put her hand out to shake mine. "Hello, my name is Sara, and I'm from South Carolina," she said, faking happiness.

"I'm Joe..."

"No! *Sara's* not right. I don't feel like a *Sara*," she said in a British accent. She frantically paced back and forth. She finally stopped in front of me once again, exactly where she'd started. "Thomas! Could I be a *Thomas*, mate, and in real estate?"

"No, *Thomas* is also a man's name."

"I'm not a bloke?"

"No, Miss, you're not."

"You see, it was a pretty sweet scam," she said, sounding like she was from the west coast. "Like, nobody knew who died and who lived, and like, I knew some excellent websites to grab the personal info, so it was easy to take their identities."

"What the devil's a website?"

"Sure, from the internet. Like, once the towers went down, their identities were easy pickin's."

"When what towers went down?" I said.

"At 911, of course... *Bill*!" she said as if a light popped on in her scrambled brain. "Yes, that's my name, and I'm from Indiana, born in 1972. I'm a 3D animator. Does that sound right? Could my name be *Bill*?"

"What's *911*?"

"When the terrorists attacked, of course—the attack on New York. There were thousands of names I could have used. Thousands! When they all died, their identities were free for the taking. I got their names and credit card numbers from the internet and made a ton of money before anyone even knew they were dead. So, is it?"

"What?"

"Is my name *Bill*?

"No."

"Because of the *guy* thing again?"

"911? You mean September eleventh," I said.

"Babe! Could it be *Thais*?" she said in a disturbingly familiar tone. "Thais Angelique? New York talent agent?"

"What?" I said shocked to hear the familiar voice of Thais, the young woman from the second bolgia, that of flatterers and gossipers.

"You going to give me the beef, babe, or are you going to be a buzz-kill? Is my name *Thais* or what?"

Hearing her voice and seeing her mannerisms again only served to remind me of my failure to save that poor girl from those urine-drenched chains.

"You took the identity of those who died in the aftermath of an attack that devastated New York?" I said, trying to piece her story together as anger swelled in my gut.

Thais told me that she died in an attack but she hadn't called it *911*, but how could she have known the name of the event when she'd died before it was even given a name?

"It was a sweet deal, amigo" she said in an Italian accent, smiling deviously.

"So, now you roam in that pit with the memories of all those identities you stole, not knowing which one is really yours."

"So, you think it's *Beth*, then?" She switched to an Aussie accent.

"I don't know," I said, growing impatient and angry.

You know now, don't you Joe? You know where the demons in this bolgia are, don't you? They're inside the sinners, confusing them about who they really are.

Nothing was needed here to force these people in this pit. It didn't matter where they went. They carried their torment *within* them.

In life, they'd stolen the identities of both the living and the dead, robbing them of more than their possessions, but their good names. In death, these deceivers couldn't even stake claim to their own identity.

"You sure it ain't *Frank*?" she said, switching back to the New York accent of the security guard. "Because I really think my name is *Frank*."

"I don't know what your name is," I said in a combination of disgust and pity.

"Because, you see, I think I'm a man," she said with a forced smile and watery eyes. "I really think I'm a man."

A portly fellow in a suit coat climbed over the railing, racing toward me and the young woman.

"Hello there! Do you know me?" he said in a low classically trained voice. He was obviously well polished from his many scams.

"No," I said.

"Well, if I may, do I look like a *James* to you? A Shakespearean actor from Hollywood?"

"Ask *him*." I pointed to the young woman beside me. As I walked away, she put her hand out to shake his.

"Hello. My name is *Bill*," she said with an enthusiastic smile.

The sad thing is, they probably had introduced themselves hundreds of times before, but they'd switched identities so often, that they had no idea who they were or who they were talking to.

The phrase *poetic justice* came to mind. I left the final pit behind me, and I reached the end of the bridge.

CHAPTER 49
Canto XXXI – Circle VIII – Edge of the Pit – The Giants
≈≈

The bridge ended at the final ridge, but this ridge sloped deeper into what was to become the ninth and final circle.

There was no deep cliff here and I could see the next circle from the top of the ridge so I felt I was closing in on the destination of my journey.

Every footstep brought me closer to Mickey. Every step closer got just a little bit darker and colder. The chilly breeze reminded me of the start of a Boston winter, after everything had died in autumn. The ground was nothing but hard rock and frozen dirt, and I felt myself becoming emotionally hard and frozen as well.

What are you going to say to Mickey when you find him, Joe? What are you going to do? You don't know, do you? Where's Virgil, Joe? You don't know that either. The angel…where's he now? Is he waiting for you somewhere at the bottom of Hell? How much time has passed since you last saw him? Who are you, Joe? Who are you? Do you even know?

The horizon was flat and featureless except for one small grouping of towers in the distance. I heard the muffled sound of a horn coming from them. Could there be a city in lower Hell?

I cautiously decided to go in for a closer look.

≈≈

Through the murky air, I stared up in amazement. What looked like towers from the distance were actually giant beings, buried to the hips in the frozen ground. Even half buried, they looked more than forty feet tall, dwarfing even the largest of demons. Though I kept my distance, one of them noticed me. He called out to me in German.

I stepped a little closer, but remained out of reach. I was curious, but not a pinhead, after all. Again he called out for me to come closer, in German.

"No thanks," I replied. "I think I'll try to stay out of arm's length, if you don't mind."

"You speak the language of Britania?" he said, now in a British accent.

"Yes."

"Yet, you understood me when I spoke Germanic?"

"I picked up some phrases in the war."

"Ah yes, the frolics of mankind," the giant remarked.

"Excuse me, but what are you?" I asked.

"Yes! Conversation at last. I will tell you, but you must tell me things. Speak to me of this war."

"I fought in the second world war, the Allies against the Axis. I fought for the Allies...the English. Now, who are you?"

"I am Antaeus. This is Ephialtes and that's Calleus," he pointed as Calleus blew his horn.

"Who's he?" I asked, pointing to a fourth giant.

"He's no one. I'm not talking to him," Antaneus answered, sounding perturbed. "Now, it's my turn. You fought for Britania, yet you have an odd accent. From what kingdom do you hail?"

"I'm not British. I'm American."

"American? I know not of this place."

"It's a new country."

"A *new* country? Nobody tells me anything. The last person through here was Greek, and that was so long ago. He told me of the war in a place called Troy, but much time has passed since then."

Ephialtes yelled at me in yet another language. He sounded Egyptian or maybe even Far Eastern, which made sense because he looked like he could be from Asia...well, if he wasn't forty feet tall, that is.

"What did he just say?" I asked.

"How the bloody Hell should I know? Now, tell me of this American."

"That's *America*. Why can't you understand him?"

"Our curse is to never again understand each other."

"Why not?"

"Now now, this is my turn," he said. "When did you die?"

"1961," I answered.

"This means nothing to me, mate. You must give me more information."

"I don't know what else to say. It was about two thousand years after the birth of Christ."

I waited for some acknowledgement from Antaeus, but got only a blank stare in return.

"Sorry, old boy, I still need more."

"*Jesus*, you know—the Son of God?"

"Oh, is *He* having children now? Apparently it's proper for *Him*, but not his angels."

The fourth giant spoke in another ancient language. I could only guess its origins to be Africa since this last giant looked to have *that* heritage.

"Shut up!" Antaeus yelled. "Shut up, you bloody imbecile. Nobody understands you!"

Antaeus looked back at me and smiled.

Calleus, once again, blew his horn, and I was reminded of Harpo Marx. "What are you guys? The Marx Brothers of the underworld?" I said.

"*We*, old chap, are the offspring of the angels and mortals."

"Come again?"

"You see, heaven had a war, too," he winked. "The angels, who had fallen for a time, consorted with humans and gave birth to a new race— yours truly."

"A new race of four—and I use the term loosely—*people?*"

"Well, there are many more of us," he said, rolling his eyes. "This region of Hell is scattered with us. If it hadn't been for *him*, we wouldn't be in this mess," he said, pointing to the fourth giant.

The fourth giant shouted again in his obscure language. I didn't know what he said, but from his tone, I didn't exactly need a translation.

"Yes, of course, same to you, old boy" Antaeus responded.

Calleus blew his horn again.

"I didn't want to do it," Antaeus said angrily, "but no, everyone wanted a vote, and thus, the Tower of Babel was born. Up until then, everyone spoke one language. Everyone understood each other. Until *Nimrod* here said, *hey, let's build a tower to God. It will be fun,*" he said. "Not so much fun *now,* is it?" he screamed at the fourth giant.

"So, his name is *Nimrod?*" I said. In my time, accusing someone of being a *Nimrod* was the same as calling them a moron—now I knew why.

"Nimrod, ha. *Numb-rod* should be more like it," Antaeus said.

"Well, Antaeus, it's been a pleasure," I said, ready to leave.

"Wait. Come closer."

I swayed a little closer. His arms were buried at the elbows and pinned to his side, but I still avoided getting too close.

"What's your hurry, old boy?" he said.

"I've been on a long journey," I said sadly, "on a road with no turns. I have to find my brother. I need to talk to him."

"You must love your brother very much."

"I *did* love him, at least in life, but I see now that he was just my brother of the flesh, not of the spirit. Argenti...he was my brother of the spirit. It's funny that the man I loved in life is the one I now hate, and the one I hated in life is the one I needed in death. It's strange, don't you think?"

"Closer," he said sympathetically.

"I can't understand why people do the evil things they do, but maybe we all have it inside us, like a cancer just waiting to take root and flourish."

"Yes, I understand," he said softly.

"You know what else is funny, Antaeus?" I stepped closer.

"What's that, mate?"

"Well, you see..." I stopped short with a realization.

"Yes," he said.

"You speak English very well."

"Why, thank you, my friend."

"You never heard of Jesus and the last man you spoke with was from the Trojan War."

"Yes."

"I'm no Einstein, but I do remember my ancient history. The English language wasn't around back then. Why would you lie about that, Antaeus?"

Without warning, Antaeus yanked his hand out of the ground and reached for me. I dove out of the way, rolling beyond his reach.

"Wait, don't go!" he yelled. "Tell me more about this war, and your new country!"

"Some other time!" I shouted as I hot-footed it in the opposite direction.

"Wait! Come back. Say something—anything! I just want someone to talk to me!"

I tried to find the symbolism in this ring of Hell, but found none. In order to find the symbolism, I needed to be able to define the sin. This had been the first and only time I'd seen someone punished in this place, not for a particular sin, but because of their simple nature. I mean, who gets to pick their parents?

CHAPTER 50
Thoughts of Home – Argenti

❧❧

I put the gun to Argenti's head and pulled back the hammer. "Say it. Say you killed them," I yelled.

"Screw you, Dante!" Argenti yelled back.

I pulled the trigger. Argenti closed his eyes as the gun clicked.

"Since you were in the war, you must have gone through boot camp," I said. "I remember my drill instructor telling us that the loudest sound in the world is when your rifle misfires with a *click* when you're expecting a round to go off."

I leaned in closer to Argenti. "I guess this is kind of loud too, huh?" I said tauntingly. I pulled back the hammer a second time. The son of a bitch would admit that he'd killed my family or die.

"No more lies, Argenti. It's time for the truth."

"You can't do this! I want my lawyer!"

"Say it!"

"No!"

I pulled the trigger a second time. Again, it clicked.

Argenti screamed.

"Everyone who has sinned, goes directly to Hell. You know who you are." I smiled as I cocked the gun a third time.

"I killed them, okay?" he yelled, finally admitting the truth. "Now, please, stop."

I released him to reload my .38. "You really are a piece of filth, aren't you, Argenti?"

I didn't expect him to reply, but he did just the same. Unfortunately, it wasn't with words. He picked up the case full of cocaine and swung it

339

wildly, hitting the side of my head. White powder flew every which way, along with my .38.

Argenti went for my gun, but I grabbed it first. He had to take second prize, which was turning tail and running away.

I ran out of the small private airport and down the block, certain Argenti was still nearby somewhere.

I spotted a subway entrance. Argenti would try to blend into a crowd. I ran down into the belly of the Boston subway system and looked around. It may have been Good Friday, but there were still enough people around to make me stay careful.

Then, all at once, I saw him. Jittery but keeping it under wraps, he waited for his salvation to arrive in the form of a subway train.

I slowly walked up behind him, but he looked over his shoulder and saw me. With no other option for escape, he jumped into the subway pit and ran. I had no other choice. I followed him into the pit.

Growing up, we'd always been told never to go into the subway pit and *never* to touch the third rail. Since we never went into the subway pit, however, we'd always wondered exactly *which* rail was the third one? I stood like a statue in the pit, between the rails. I knew which direction Argenti had chosen to run but I couldn't see him through the darkness. I couldn't see any movement but knew he had to be squeezed down under the platform somewhere.

Poised with my pistol drawn, I gave the commuters quite a show. Out of the blue, I heard a subway car coming toward me. I didn't know exactly where Argenti was, and I didn't know if he was waiting for me to pass him so he could sneak up behind me and snap my neck. All I knew was that *he* was the one who would have to move first. At least, that's what I thought until I heard a second subway car coming at me from behind.

I could have hopped over to the next track, but why bother? So I could be squashed by the subway coming toward my *face* rather than the one racing toward my *back*? Instead, I stood my ground. I vowed not to budge until Argenti showed himself. The subway train behind me honked its horn. It was such a strange sound. We heard it so rarely because there was never a need to use it. The subway pit was a no-man's land and not even the certifiable would venture into it. "Come on. Come on," I muttered. "Where the devil are you?"

One of the crowd finally yelled down to me. "Move!" she shouted.

When I instinctively turned to look, the man behind her grabbed my attention.

It was *him,* the stranger from the warehouse Argenti had ordered me to set on fire, the same man I'd later seen in front of the courthouse.

Again, he wore the clothes of a half dressed soldier.

Both subway trains drew closer, but all I could do was stare at him. At the warehouse so many months ago, he'd been both fearless and silent when he faced imminent death.

Who is this guy, Joe? Why is he tailing you?

He slowly smiled at me, like a friend who knew a secret I had yet to discover. Time seemed to slow down.

Suddenly, out of the corner of my eye, I saw movement. Argenti crawled out of his little crevice, like a sewer rat. I pointed my gun, but it was too late.

He hopped across the tracks, vaulting onto the opposite platform. I didn't have time to follow him, so I jumped for the nearest platform. Several in the crowd helped me up as the subway train thundered by me, the same way the other train must have barely missed Argenti.

I looked around, but the soldier guy was gone.

I didn't have time to look for him or to find out who he was. Both subway trains sped by, and when gone, I spotted Argenti still on the opposite platform.

He was on his rear, probably shook up from his second near-death experience today, with several people clustered around him, checking to see if he was okay. I quickly aimed my gun as I called out a warning to them.

"Stay away from him!"

Argenti saw me and leapt to his feet. Picking her up, he hid behind a little girl. "No!" her mother screamed, but Argenti shoved her aside.

"What are you?" Argenti yelled. "A damned bulldog?"

"Give it up, Argenti!"

"Toss the gun to me, or I swear to Christ, I'll snap this kid's neck like a toothpick."

"You swear to Christ, huh?"

"Yeah."

I surprised myself when I didn't put the gun down. Argenti must have seen the resolve in my eyes, because he made a move for the stairway.

"Don't do it!" I yelled.

I was a good shot. In fact, I was an expert in small arms, but I didn't know if I could take the shot with him behind the kid. However, he gave me little time to consider my next move.

I shot the trashcan that sat between him and his stairway to freedom.

"I said *don't*!" I yelled. Argenti froze in his tracks.

The little girl's mother screamed, as did the people on both platforms. They scrambled for cover.

"Throw me the piece, Dante!"

"I thought you weren't a killer."

"I'm cozying up to it!"

I looked at the little girl in Argenti's arms. About six years old and, needless to say, she looked petrified.

"Please do what he says!" the mother shouted to me.

I wasn't paying attention to her, but her daughter. If I took the shot, even if I took him down, that kid would have to live with the memory of watching a man die for the rest of her life. If Argenti killed her, her parents would be forced to live with *that*. I knew that pain, and I refused to burden another with it.

"Okay," I called out to Argenti as I lowered my piece.

"Throw it over here."

I threw my gun, but purposely missed the platform. Instead, I tossed it into the rails. "Whoops," I said sarcastically.

Argenti gave me a *screw you* look as he dropped the kid. She ran for her mother, and he ran for the stairs. As quickly as I could, I pulled out my backup piece, which was strapped to my ankle, but he'd gone.

I ran up the platform's stairway, determined to get Argenti on the street.

I burst out of the subway exit and into the street just as Argenti ran out of the subway entrance across the street.

"Everyone down, down, down!" I yelled and aimed my snub-nose.

People ran, ducking for cover. I took a shot at a fleeing Argenti. He dove into an alley when my second shot ran out.

I moved cautiously into the alley. I knew he wasn't armed, but instinct took over. Scenarios spun in my head of Argenti finding a steak knife in the trash or jumping out at me with a baseball bat abandoned by some kids who'd decided to play stickball instead. At the far end of the deserted building, I saw an open door.

❧❧

I threw caution to the wind and ran through the entrance of the old brick building. Argenti *wasn't* waiting for me behind the doorway. Instead, I heard his footsteps as he ran up the stairs to the roof. I chased him, but this guy just refused to let it end. He crossed the roof, but didn't stop. The dung pile was as strong as he was fast. He bounced to the next roof, so I followed.

"Damn!" I said, about as amazed that I made it as Argenti must have been.

We must have been about eight or nine floors above the street. Argenti jumped to the next roof, so I followed again.

I had to hand it to the guy; he wanted to live. The third time, however, was the charm… At least, for me.

He jumped for the third roof and barely made it, or barely missed, depending on how you look at it. He clung onto the edge of the roof as I looked at the gap between my building and his. I could see why he hadn't made it. It was a long jump, but a damn sight shorter than the fall if he couldn't hang on.

I backed up and sprinted for the other roof. I also jumped, and landed with inches to spare. I rolled across the gravel half proud of my accomplishment and relishing the prospect of what was to come.

Argenti hung on as best he could as I stood over him. That's when the SOB surprised me yet again. "Help me," he said.

CHAPTER 51
Canto XXXII – Circle IX – Round I – Caina – Traitors to Family

❧❧

The cold wind tore through me like a blind man's carving knife on Thanksgiving Day. I still had the metal spear with me, but I would have gladly traded it for a warm blanket or even a fisherman sweater. I found myself wishing that I'd died wearing my winter coat, and fondly remembering the ocean of boiling blood.

According to the angel, this circle was a frozen wasteland split into three bands—traitors to kin, to homeland, and to guests. It was the first circle, Caina, treacherous to kin that interested me. My brother had betrayed his family, his own brother, and I intended to find out why.

When I'd spoken with the angel so long ago, he'd told me that this circle was named after Cain, of Cain and Abel fame. Abel had been betrayed by his brother and over something as goofy as jealousy over who God loved most.

Another cold blast of wind slapped me out of the darkness, reminding me of the bitter chill of a Boston winter night, too cold to even snow and with a wind chill factor of what felt like below absolute zero. Some winter nights, the life expectancy in the elements was under ten minutes. Here, there was no life expectancy, only temperatures that could make blood freeze solid.

As I walked, the frozen dirt became sheets of ice. The farther I traveled, the thicker the ice became, until there was no dirt, only ice. I found myself wondering where all the sinners were located when the answer finally presented itself. The traitors were all around me. Frozen solid into the ice, only their shivering heads and bluish faces protruded out of the ice-covered ground. They gazed up at me. I'd imagine a wandering traveler must have been a rarity here.

"Anybody here speak English?" My breath billowed out a frozen mist, and I hugged myself for warmth.

"Yo, I speak English," a black man answered. I instantly placed his accent for Chicago. "I'm Jamiel Washington and you must have thumbed for the wrong ride to end up here, nigga."

"I didn't end up here. I'm just passing through," I answered.

"Yeah, so am I." He laughed as best he could through pale lips.

The other heads joined in.

"I'm looking for my brother. His name is Michael Dante."

"So?"

"So, do you know where he is?"

"Oh yeah, sure," he said, mocking me. "Just walk five and a half miles in the direction of my nose, and he'll be the third head on the left. Do I look like a God damned tour guide to you, mofo?"

"Right, thanks for your help and that incredible wit." I turned to leave.

"Wait!" he said.

"What?"

"You bail me out and I'll bloodhound for you to your bro's crib," he said through his shivers.

"I thought you didn't know where he was."

"Yeah, but I have blood in this crib. Someone's bound to be down with it. So, put that ice pick you're carrying to good use and let's get crackin'."

I held the metal spear over my head and then plunged it down into the ice. Instead of poking a hole, the freezing metal vibrated a painful jolt back to my already icy hands. "Damn it!" I screamed in pain.

Instead of being disappointed, this Washington character actually laughed. The other heads joined in.

"I love that schtick," the head next to him bellowed.

"You knew that was going to happen?"

"If you didn't, you be trippin' foo," Washington said.

"So, what are you in here for? Bad jokes?"

"Never you mind, dawg."

When he called me *dog*, it reminded me of another black man I'd met and then everything clicked.

345

"Wait. You have a brother named *Bugsy Siegel*, don't you?"

"What the hell? You the all powerful Oz?"

"You're here because you betrayed him."

"You lyin' fool!" he said. Suddenly, he was very uncomfortable.

"Your very own brother," I said. "You should be ashamed of yourself."

"What book are you readin' from, dawg? He didn't put blood first. Son of a bitch capped my ass."

"Really?" I said. "Well, your brother asked me to deliver a message if I ever came across you."

"Yeah, what's that?"

"He said..." I leaned in and whispered. "...*Go to Hell.*"

"Screw you! Screw you!" he screamed, jerking his head to try to get out of his encasement. "I'll kill you, nigga! I'll kill you!"

"See you around," I said as I left. "You too... Shecky." I grinned at the head next to him.

♨

And so it went. I walked the frozen paths, using the metal spear as a cane to keep myself from slipping on my keister.

I'd come to a group of heads, stop for a while, and move on when Mickey was nowhere to be found.

I both hoped and feared that, each time I stopped, I would find him. Each time I paused for a rest, I feared that I would be frozen solid into an iced statue... A statue that symbolized hatred and anger.

Then, at long last, both my dream and nightmare came to be.

♨

I looked down at Mickey from the frosty darkness.

Supposedly, he'd died in his nineties, but to me, he still appeared young and strong. He looked the same as the day I'd died, except for one distinct difference. He no longer had the crescent scar under his eye.

"Why?" I asked.

"Holy shit," Mickey said. "Joey? Is that you?"

"I asked you a question, Michael. Why? Why the drugs? The lies? All the people who suffered because of you. Why?"

"Have you been looking for me since you bought the farm?"

I didn't answer.

"What do you want me to say, Joe?" he said. "That I did it for the dough? The bread was good, but that wasn't why. Truth is, I did it because I could, because I liked it, and, what the hell, because of the loot, too."

"You betrayed me and anyone who ever trusted you, and that's all you have to say?"

"What do you want from me? You want me to say *I'm sorry*? Well, when *Hell* freezes over!" he shouted. The son of a bitch laughed at his own bad joke. "Here's something you probably didn't know... I framed you for everything. With you dead, Internal Affairs had a feast on your remains. I never got caught. When historians look you up, all they'll find is a murdering drug smuggler, that is, if they even think to look you up at all. I was brilliant! Brilliant!"

"Michael?" I said amazed at his callousness. "How could you..."

"Who do you think shot you on that roof the day you died?"

"You?"

I couldn't believe it. All this time, I'd only thought that Mickey had *had* me killed. I never once even considered that he was the one who'd actually pulled the trigger.

"Now Joey, don't cry," he said smugly. "The tears will freeze and shatter your eyes, and that is *not* a pretty sight. Trust me on that one. Now, is there anything else? If so, make it fast, because I have a tennis lesson at 9:00."

"You son of a bitch!" I raised the spear over my head to give Mickey an answer he'd never forget.

"Come on!" he yelled, changing his tone from arrogance to anger. "Give me your best shot! What do you think you can do to me?"

All the shivering heads that were planted around him started to cheer me on.

Frozen mist streamed from my lips as I screamed like a Roman gladiator about to decapitate his fallen rival. Instead, I held my pose.

I wanted to jam that spear through Mickey's eye like a fork through an olive, but for some reason, I heard Virgil in my head. And the angel, as well. Both sides of my conscience were in a spiritual tug of war. I heard the angel tell me to do what *must* be done, as well as Virgil coldly saying that Mickey wasn't *ready* yet, and just leave him be.

There had to be something beneath Mickey's hate, something that made me love him as a brother.

"You just don't get it, do you?" Mickey yelled. "Hate, anger, revenge—none of it matters here! If you can't *kill* me, what good is it?"

I didn't answer him, because I realized that it wasn't only my brother's hate I had to look beyond, but *my own.*

"There's nothing you can do to me that hasn't been done before," Mickey added, "so just get it over with."

I looked around to see all the traitorous heads looking in our direction. Some cheered for me to give Mickey what he had coming to him.

I looked back at Mickey and into his eyes. Beyond the anger, there was something else.

What's that look, Joe? Self-pity? Guilt? Shame? Do what must be done, Joe. Do what must be done.

I slowly put down the spear.

"What the hell are you doing?" he yelled.

"You went before Minos, didn't you?" I asked softly.

"What?"

"When he asked you what your sin was, what did you say?"

"*Kiss my ass*, that's what I said," Mickey callously responded.

"He asked you what sin kept you awake at night. The one sin above all others and you told him. Didn't you? You told him. You betrayed your brother. That's how you ended up here. This sin is killing you inside."

"You don't know what you're talking about!" he yelled.

I finally knew what to do to him. It was something that *hadn't* ever been done to him before… At least not here.

"I forgive you, Mickey," I said. I was as surprised to say the words as he was to hear them.

"No, no! You *can't* do that—not *here!*" he yelled.

"I forgive you, brother. Once you forgive yourself, the ice will melt around you and you'll be able to walk out of here on your own."

As I left, Mickey taunted me, but it didn't bother me because I now knew it was coming from a shameful heart.

"I'll tell you something else," he yelled, "I lived a long and happy life! I saw a man walk on the moon, the millennium bug squashed like a fly under a frying pan, and the Red Sox win the World Series!"

That last one stopped me dead in my slippery tracks.

"When?" I said.

"When what?"

"When did the Red Sox win the World Series?" I asked.

"In 2004, and I was there to see it! We partied in the streets for a week!"

"Now you're just making stuff up." I grinned and walked away.

"I had more than any man could ever dream," he screamed as I left. "Thousands wept at my funeral. Thousands! I had it all, Joe. Everything. Everything!"

CHAPTER 52
Canto XXXIV – Circle IX – Round III – Judecca – Traitors to Lords

੭৶৶

I t was easy to figure out where the center of Hell was, because the ground sloped downward, slowly and gently. The darkness of the ice plains became a dim memory as daylight and the typical stretches of sand lay before me. It was neither hot nor cold, and I felt no winds and sniffed no scents. This place seemed devoid of anything that would make a human body feel.

I followed the slope and beheld a sight that I had never once seen before in Hell. I saw where a downward slope met an upward slope, and knew that I had hit stone rock bottom.

I put down my metal spear, rested my keister atop one of the many boulders and looked around.

For the first time in my journey, I had neither purpose nor goal. It occurred to me that my only intention in Hell had been one of anger and hatred. I realized it was worse than wasted time. It was *nothing*.

I was nothing.

I palmed my eyes and lowered my head, saddened by the realization that I'd perpetuated evil by *being* evil.

"Please don't leave me here," I whispered, hoping God would hear.

I lowered my hands, opened my eyes, and saw something that reminded me of so long ago that it could have only happened at the beginning of my journey—footprints.

As before, they were baked into the hard dirt of the dead infertile plains that stretched endlessly before me.

I followed the phantom prints around some high-walled slick rocks to find the angel soldier. He stared into a deep dark pit, but took notice when he saw me.

"Hey Joe, how you doin'?" the angel asked with a warm smile.

I gawked from both joy and shame. He was still dressed as a soldier but no longer armed to the teeth with weapons. Instead, he simply wore a small backpack.

He was surely a sight for a tired traveler.

"You waited," I said as excited to see him as I would an old friend.

"Well, I *am* an angel after all." He winked.

"I believe you," I said.

"Come here, I want to show you something." He pointed into the pit.

I looked down to see a dark void with such a small pin-point of light at the bottom, it might as well not have been there at all. It reminded me of lying in a field in the pitch of a New Hampshire night, and staring up to see only one lone star.

"You see here?" He pointed into the ditch beneath us. "This is the exact heart of Hell. This is where Satan was buried long ago, but he escaped and has been a nomad ever since."

"How could the devil escape God's punishment?"

"A great quake shook the foundations of Hell itself. It shattered the bridge over the sixth bolgia and crumbled the cliff to the seventh circle."

"Why?" I asked as I peered deep into the pit, skittishly so as not to fall in.

"Depends on who you talk to. Some say that Satan escaping caused the quake."

"What do others say?"

"Others say that Satan was able to escape *because* of the quake...and the reason?"

"What?"

The angel just smiled.

"You found your brother, didn't you Joe?" he said, replacing my question with his.

"Yeah, sure did."

"Did you do it... What needed to be done?"

"No... I forgave him, instead."

I was surprised to see the angel respond with a smile.

"You don't get it, do you Joe? *That's* what was needed to be done."

"What? But—" I stopped short. All this time, I'd thought the angel was egging me on, supporting me in my quest for revenge. I felt like a fool. "So, is this it?" I said, relieved. "Are you taking me to heaven?"

"Yep, straight away, but there is, however, one small question I'm required to ask—for the paperwork, you see."

"Sure, shoot."

"Who are you?" he asked.

"What?"

"Who are you, Joe?" he repeated.

"Who am I?"

"For the paperwork."

Didn't Virgil want to know this, Joe? Answer the angel...you're a good and fair man!

I hesitated for the longest time. I didn't know how to answer him.

"I don't know," I said.

The angel sighed and shook his head.

"Is there a problem?" I said.

"It just makes things a bit *sticky*, that's all."

"Why?"

"You see, Joe, my job is to help lost souls find their proper place."

"You mean like Minos?"

"Bite your tongue," he said, insulted. "I'm nothing like that gorilla. Minos judges those who deep down inside, already know their sin. I, on the other hand, help those who *don't* know their sin."

Out of nowhere, the angel grabbed my throat and squeezed it like an orange.

"What are you doing?" I coughed out as I struggled.

"Interesting feeling, isn't it? Not being able to breathe, I mean. Just when you think you're about to pass out, you continue on. The pressure builds up until you feel your head about to explode, but still you continue on."

"I don't understand," I gurgled.

"Who are *you*, Joe?" He lifted me until my feet no longer touched the ground and threw me against some boulders with the ease of a well-oiled pitching machine. "You didn't think you could take a stroll through Hell and leave unscathed, did you?" he asked as he approached my prone body.

352

I gasped for air and knew that, just from the one encounter, he was stronger than Geryon could ever be.

"You call what I've been through *unscathed?*" I said.

"Well, everything is relative, after all."

"I don't understand," I choked out as I sat up. "You're an angel, aren't you?"

"Yes, I am." He reached down and yanked me to my feet. "Did you think that God simply made a mistake and put you here by accident?"

"God didn't put me anywhere," I said defiantly. "I put myself here."

The angel's response was very simple—a backhand, sailing me across the sand, closer to the rock where I'd been sitting—and my spear!

Without a second thought, I crawled to the spear, jumped to my feet, and pointed it at him as if I was holding a rifle when the only ammo left was my bayonet.

The angel didn't even acknowledge that I now held a weapon. He strolled around me as he spoke.

"What did you think would happen if you could actually leave this place? Did you think that the gates of heaven would just open up for only you and a chorus of angels would sing your name? Did you think that the Almighty would throw His arms around you and say, all is forgiven?"

With speeds that would have made Superman proud, he was suddenly next to me and floored me with one punch.

I held onto the spear and tried to drag myself away, but he jerked me to my feet.

"Do you think you're better than everyone else here?"

"No! I don't. Not anymore."

"Yet you think you've earned a seat with the Most High, don't you?"

"I'm not sure anyone could earn *that*," I said.

"Then tell me—*who are you?*"

"I don't know!" I yelled.

"There's no one here to help you, Joe. *This* is the end of your journey."

I backed up and pointed the spear at him.

"You haven't the faintest idea of what faith is," the angel said. "Not once did you walk with God, not truly."

When did you know for sure that God was with you, Joe? Didn't Virgil ask you that once?

"Anna was born on the fifth of April," I responded.

"What?"

Confused, the angel moved toward me. I backed up and kept the spear pointed at him.

"Kathleen was born on August fifth," I choked out through my pain. "Bea and I were married on the third of September. It was a beautiful autumn day. God was with me all those times." A realization swelled in my chest, forcing a saddened grin. "God was with me *all* the time." I said.

"Very touching, Joe, but if you don't mind, it's time to take you to your proper place."

This is it, Joe! The moment Virgil spoke of when you abandoned him on the seventh circle. This is the moment when you have to decide between who you are and who you want to be. Who are you, Joe? Who do you want to be?

I looked at the spear that I'd tried to use as my defense against all the evils of Hell and I finally realized that no *weapon* could save me. There wasn't a weapon forged that could protect my soul.

I smirked to myself when I realized the puniness of it all. I was trying to stop a locomotive by blocking its path with a sheet of paper.

I tossed the spear to the angel and put my arms out in defiance, like Virgil did when we were cornered by Geryon's ships in the seventh circle.

"I'm not afraid," I said, and I meant it.

The angel didn't need it, but he held up the spear, and I knew he intended to impale me.

I closed my eyes, waiting for the inevitable.

I called out the words I'd often used in life. Words I'd said a thousand times over, but never once meant. Words I'd said the day Anna slipped from my hands, but until that moment, I hadn't really known their meaning.

"God, help me!" I yelled.

I waited for the spear to pierce my chest, but it never came. I felt no pain or fear. I slowly opened my eyes to see Virgil.

This being who was truly Satan was defending *me*.

He held back the spear and kept it from hurting me.

"No one is alone when they walk in the light." Virgil punctuated his words with a backhand, sending the angel across the sand.

"Virgil!" I shouted as I ran to him.

"Enter the pit and don't be afraid. In it, you will find your escape. Go now," he said as he handed me something.

I was too preoccupied to notice what it was. "The angel…" I started.

"Leave him to me," Virgil said. "Go, and go quickly."

I lowered myself into the pit where Satan had been buried untold centuries ago. I fully intended to leave and would have, too, if I hadn't heard the angel's next words to Virgil.

"Hello, *brother*," he said to Satan.

I looked to see what it was that Virgil had shoved into my hand. I didn't know what to think when I saw the bracelet Anna had given me, my badge, and the crucifix I dropped over Bea's grave. All of them symbols of my life—my family, the law, and God. These were symbols of things I held so dear, but had never truly respected.

Was Virgil following you the whole time? What are you waiting for, Joe? It's time to high tail it out of Dodge, and I mean pronto. You can't do it, can you? The devil or not, how can you leave him now?

From the mouth of the pit, I watched the angel stroll around Virgil, as if to inspect him.

"Do you believe, even for a second, that you can be forgiven?" the angel asked Virgil.

"If this is the question you ask, you know nothing of free will," Virgil said.

"What do *you* know, other than your own sin?"

"If it's me you hate, brother, then that's a sin *you* must face."

"It's *you* who betrayed those who loved you most," the angel said.

"Yes, and for that sin, I must forfeit all until the end of time."

"Oh, but there *will* be an end to time itself, brother. What will you do then?"

"Only what the great Father wishes," Virgil said.

With a flash, the angel stood next to Virgil. With a right cross, he sent Virgil soaring across the sand. Before Virgil hit the ground, the angel sprinted with a burst of energy to be there next to Virgil when he landed.

The angel pinned Virgil against some rocks.

"Still want to be like God?" the angel said. He lifted his angelic mitt and the metal spear hopped from the desert floor into his grasp. He plunged the spear into Virgil's side—the same side I imagine the Roman soldier pierced on Jesus. For the first time since I'd met him, Virgil *screamed* in pain.

What are you thinking, Joe? He betrayed TT and Hector. Didn't he? If they made it to the virtuous, they may never have left, and in the end, maybe never have found their faith. If Virgil is really Satan, why would he help you? Why would he fight the angel? Was it that Virgil wanted forgiveness too? Could Virgil actually be trying to help?

I'd been taught that Hell was Satan's domain and that the demons tortured sinners for their own personal pleasure, but that's not what I saw here.

Demons were tortured here, as well. Maybe not *tortured*. When Virgil was challenged in the circle of hoarders and wasters of money, what had he said? Maybe the better word is *tormented*. Their beautiful angelic bodies forced into that of giant grotesque insects and ugly monstrous machines, and handicapped to only seeing body heat or movement.

Demons didn't run this place, and Satan wasn't the king of some dark empire. They didn't want to be here anymore than we did.

Hell, from what I could see, the demons didn't even *like* Virgil. Why would they? He'd betrayed them all.

Where we had nine circles, demons had nine species—reptile, mechanical and insect, each of which could travel the air, land, or sea—three sets of three.

Instead of escaping into the pit, I stared at the things Virgil had given to me—the badge, the bracelet, and the crucifix. They were trinkets to me now. What they represented, however, meant everything. I no longer needed them so I tossed them into the pit.

I stepped out from the rocks in full view of the angel and Virgil.

"Angel!" I yelled. "Leave him alone!"

The angel let go of Virgil and moved toward me.

"My name is *Virgil*," he said calmly.

"I know what you want, *Virgil*," I said.

"Joe, you don't have the first damn clue as to what I want," the angel said.

"So tell me, what do you want?"

The angel pulled out a bugle from his backpack. He smiled at me warmly and blew the horn, which resulted in an ear-splitting shriek that could have shattered time itself. I fell to my knees and desperately covered my ears, as did Virgil.

The angel finally removed the horn from his lips and I stood on wobbly knees.

"What did you do?" I asked.

"You're about to find out," the angel smiled.

Suddenly, from the pit, a tower of light blasted upward. It shot up as far as the eye could see and maybe scraped the top of Hell's ceiling.

Winds blew hard and the ground shook violently. From the cracks, angelic hands reached up and seized Virgil.

I hung onto a boulder for some false sense of stability as the angel came closer.

From the light, angels flew out of the pit, and I didn't know whether to cheer or hide. They were stunning beings with wings of light, but I just didn't know if they were here to help me by taking me to my *proper place* or to damn me by taking me to my *proper place*.

They surrounded me. As I turned away from one, I backed into another.

"Who are you?" one of them asked.

Surprised to hear the same question that both Virgil and the angel had asked, I turned away from one, only to have another angel of light confront me.

"Who are you?" another asked.

No matter where I turned, I came to face another and each one asked the same question of me.

"Who are you?"

With the ground shaking and splitting everywhere, I struggled to stay on my feet.

"Who are you?" another demanded.

I couldn't answer. What did they want to hear? I just couldn't take anymore.

I covered my ears and closed my eyes.

"Stop it! Stop it! Stop!" I screamed. If I screamed any louder, Geryon would have heard me from the bottom of the pit where I'd left him.

Suddenly, the ground stopped shaking, and everything grew quiet. I opened my eyes, coming face to face with Virgil. We stood alone now. Even the angel soldier had gone. The ground had stopped shaking, and the tower of light was no more.

"Who are you?" Virgil repeated.

CHAPTER 53
Thoughts of Home – Joe

❧❧

Argenti hung on to the roof's edge as best he could and I stood over him. That's when the SOB surprised me yet again.

"Help me," he said.

I didn't know whether to shoot him or laugh at him. I squatted down and studied him.

"How does it feel?" I asked.

"Dante, please…"

"It's not a rhetorical question, Argenti," I said. "How does it feel to look death in the face? How does it feel to know that the only person who can help you…*won't?*"

Argenti squirmed to try and maintain some kind of balance, but he took the time to answer me just the same. "It feels pretty bad."

"It should," I agreed.

I no longer felt pleasure in his anguish. I no longer felt my own pain. I felt what a Vegas gambler must feel the split second the roulette ball landed on his number. The second before the realization of his prize hit him, but right after it happened.

All that remained in me was the resolve to get this thing done.

"Dante, please…I know things…I can tell you. We can strike a deal," he said as if there was anything this scum could say to persuade me to help him.

"I don't deal with the devil," I said.

"Please, don't let me die!"

"You killed my family. Do you really think there's anything you can say that will make me help you?"

"You don't know everything," Argenti pleaded. "I can tell you things. Please!"

I stood and coldly glared down at him, as he desperately clung onto the roof's edge. Slowly and unhesitatingly, I placed my foot on his fingers.

"Dante! Please!" Argenti pleaded.

I ignored him, crushing his knuckles under my heel. Argenti screamed as if he was calling for his mommy, but I washed the screech from my mind and pressed even harder.

Finally, Argenti let go and fell to the cement below.

"Go to Hell, Dante!" he yelled on his way down to his final demise.

I looked down to the street below. "Lead the way," I whispered to the dead man face down on the pavement. From above, as though in a heavenly seat, I watched as a crowd gathered around his body.

CHAPTER 54
Canto XXXIV – Circle IX – Round III – Revelation
❧

I'm a murderer," I said. "Oh God!" I yelled through my tears. "I killed Filippo Argenti. How could I do that? I'm a blasphemer and a bully. I would have committed suicide, too. You could put me in any circle in this place, and I'd have done something to deserve it. I'm not a good man at all. My heart is as dark as any. I'm—"

"Forgiven," Virgil said.

I wiped the tears from my eyes.

"In that pit awaits your escape from this place," Virgil said. "You are now *ready* to leave, Joseph Dante."

"What about Argenti, and Mary… And Mickey… They…"

"They are on their own journeys Joseph, of which you were merely a part. In the end, all journeys become one." He smiled, and this time, it was a warm smile. He turned to leave.

I just couldn't let it end, not like that. "Wait!" I said. "You're going to go, just like that?"

"What else is there?"

"Come with me."

"I cannot," he said. "But thank you, Joseph. You're the first to ask."

"The first?" I thought for a moment and, finally, it hit me. "I understand now."

In life, we defined ourselves by the things we'd done or who we think we are, be it a cop or father or husband. Not so in death. Especially in Hell, we are defined undeniably by one thing and one thing only—our sins. And the one sin above all others that Minos sees when he looks into the eyes of each sinner.

I watched in silence as Virgil walked away.

Never in my wildest dreams had I thought that Satan would be the defender of my soul, but I'd never really known him. All I'd ever heard or seen of the devil had been from Catholic school and horror movies.

Satan had separated from The Almighty because he'd wanted to be more like God. In this place, that was *exactly* what he'd become, ironically, in spite of himself.

As Jesus did on Earth, Satan walked through Hell, trying to save souls. He would choose each soul, one by one, and protect their paths with all that he had until they were ready to leave. I guess, sooner or later, we all become *ready*.

Maybe Satan would leave Hell one day… After all who entered after him left. Maybe that would be the *end* of time.

I entered the pit to find a small bubble of a cave and a spring.

It had been so long since I'd taken a drink, yet I instinctively stuck my cupped hand into the water and sipped. I wasn't afraid that this water had been electrified, made acidic, or was some putrid sludge. I just knew it was fresh and clean—as water should be.

It was incredible. I took another drink and drenched my face and head with it. It felt so good… I couldn't hold it in, so I laughed out of pure joy. I never knew how thirsty I'd been until that very moment. I could feel myself being renewed, even reborn.

"So, you ready or what?"

I turned to see the angel soldier grinning at me.

"You?" I said stunned.

Moments ago, he tried to damn me for all eternity, but now?

"Time's a wastin', pal. We got to start climbing," he said. "The only way out is up." He pointed down into the pit.

"Up?" I said, confused.

"Sure, you'll see. Come on."

"You're coming with me?" I asked.

"With what lies ahead, you're going to need an angel by your side." He winked.

"Are you?"

"What… An angel? You bet your sweet bippy."

"On *my* side?"

The angel smiled. "Still want to know what caused the great quake that shook the very existence of Hell?"

"Yeah, I do." I had to admit, I was curious.

"The answer's up there," he said, again pointing *down* into the pit. "So, let's get crackin'. After you."

"Uh uh… You first," I said.

"Why, Joey, you don't trust me."

"It doesn't matter. I trust God."

The angel smiled as he lowered himself into the infinite ditch.

I squatted down to lower myself into the pit, too, but the weirdest thing happened.

I was now looking *up* to the pin-point of light. It felt as if gravity had shifted. Instead of descending *down* into the pit, I was climbing *up* the side of a mountain.

"You ready?" he said. "It's going to be quite a climb, and man oh man—it's going to be long."

"You just lead the way. I'll keep up."

So, I followed the angel I only half trusted—this new *Virgil*.

What awaited me? Bea? My girls? God?

Whatever it was, I knew that I would never again be alone.

I had my faith, and I'd been forgiven.

CHAPTER 55
Thoughts of Home – The Light
❦

I looked down to the street below. "Lead the way," I whispered to the dead man face down on the pavement. From above, as though in a heavenly seat, I watched as a crowd gathered around his body.

I looked for the roof's exit but suddenly, out of nowhere, a shot rang out. I quickly squatted down, running for cover as I tried to make sense of things. I heard another gunshot from one of the other rooftops. I looked around, but I couldn't see anything.

It must have been one of Argenti's men. As I hunted down Argenti, this new mystery guest must have been chasing after me.

Well, I wasn't going to give him the satisfaction. I was about to run for the roof's exit when I realized I'd done what rookies are trained exactly *not* to do—I'd dropped my pistol.

A cop dropping his piece is about as much a subject for humiliation as being caught naked in church. I saw my backup piece across the roof and crawled for it. I heard another shot. The slug struck the roof between me and my revolver.

"Screw it!" I said as I got up and sprinted for the door, silently praying that it wasn't locked.

I got to the door just as I heard another shot and I took each flight of stairs in nearly a single hop.

I ran out of the building to the street to discover the growing crowd had vanished. They'd obviously fled when they'd heard the gunshots.

I needed to find a phone to call for backup. One of Argenti's men had to be nearby, and I didn't want him taking pot-shots at me or anyone else.

363

What the devil are you doing, Joe? Looking for an open store in Boston on Good Friday? Good luck!

As I looked for a safely positioned phone booth, I saw the impossible. Argenti was alive!

He stood up and stretched, as if shaking off a bad night in the red light district.

"You son of a bitch!" I yelled. "Will you ever die?"

"Screw you, Dante!"

If I'd still had my gun, I'd have emptied it into his skull. Instead, all I could do was tackle him.

We rolled across the cobblestone street, choking and punching each other. It was obvious to me that he no longer cared to make a deal. He didn't care if he lived or died. He wanted me as dead as I wanted him.

Just when I thought nothing could stop our struggle or release my death grip from his throat, the weirdest thing happened.

A bright light appeared from above. It pierced the sky like a spotlight through the darkness, except it wasn't dark. It was mid-day, and I saw no source from which the light came.

Argenti and I let go of each other, both gasping for breath. A second light appeared from across the street.

"What the devil?" Argenti said.

The first light moved toward us. Argenti ran, but the beam of light was too fast. It enveloped Argenti as the second beam of light came for me.

I refused to let Argenti get away.

There must be some explanation, Joe! You just don't have the time to figure it out. Run! But where? Follow the prize, Joe. Follow the prize.

I ran after Argenti and into the first tunnel of light.

The light was bright, but not blinding. I was enveloped in the same light as Argenti, but he'd disappeared.

"I'm going to kill you, Argenti!" I screamed.

Suddenly, both lights were gone. I stood alone, but I was no longer in the cobblestone streets of Boston.

EPILOGUE

All my life, I've needed something to hate. But in death, I was able to give hate the slip. I'd made my peace with Dante long before he'd found me in that God-awful cage. Ironically, it was *his* hate that handed me a clean slate.

After Dante and I were separated, I walked for I don't know how long. Well, I walked as best I could with one leg in a splint.

The man hated me. What the heck… I had it coming. In life, I'd been a Jack-boot bully, and he'd blamed me for fitting his family with wings.

I found an empty place in Hell, and rested my rump on a rock.

It was daylight here in the eighth circle, at least in this pit. The desert stretched in every direction for as far as I could see.

I considered myself a tough guy, but everyone has his bottom line. I'd been alone for so long, I put my head in my hands and cried.

Come on, Filippo, hold it together. Be a man, you son of a bitch!

"Please, don't leave me here alone," I said to a God that could hopefully hear me from so far away. Then I said something I'd said a thousand times in life, but had never once meant. This time, however… This time, I meant it as if my soul depended on it.

"Sweet Jesus, please help me."

Suddenly, I felt someone staring at me.

I looked up to see Virgil.

The last I'd seen of him, he'd told Dante that he was Satan—the Evil Spirit himself.

Was he?

I didn't even care anymore. All I knew was that I was no longer alone.

"I don't know if I'm *ready*, Virg," I said. "But, I want to know what happened to my wife and daughter."

Virgil reached for me and I took his mitt without hesitation.

He pulled me to my feet, and slowly smiled.

We walked toward the infinite dead horizon that lay ahead.

My name is *Filippo Argenti*. This is my journey.

Breinigsville, PA USA
12 May 2010
237887BV00001B/10/P